The Last Maúl

The Chronicles of the King
Book Two

KIM KOUSKI

The Last Maúl | The Chronicles of the King
Book Two

FIRST EDITION
V04092022

ISBN: 979-8-9852994-3-4
Little Roni Publishers | Clanton, AL
littleronipublishers.com
@LittleRoniPublishers
facebook.com/LittleRoniPublishers/

PUBLISHED IN THE UNITED STATES OF AMERICA

The Last Maúl

The Chronicles of the King

Book Two

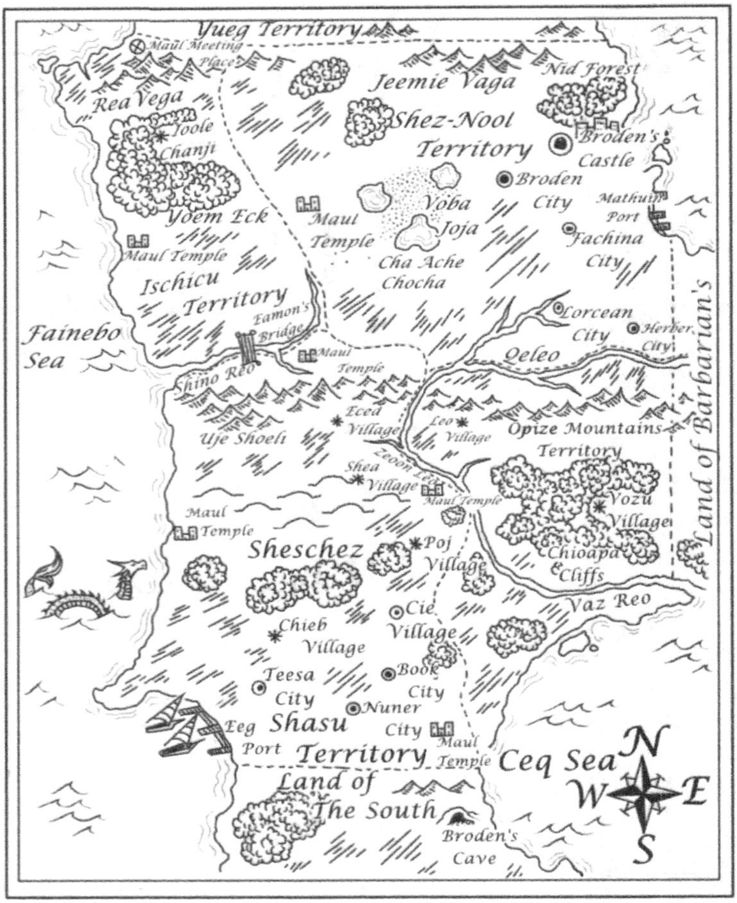
Yueg Territory
Maul Meeting Place
Rea Vega
Toole
Chanji
Jeemie Vaga
Nid Forest
Shez-Nool
Territory
Broden's Castle
Broden City
Voba Joja
Mathuin Port
Fachina City
Maul Temple
Yoem Eck
Maul Temple
Cha Ache Chocha
Ischicu Territory
Eamon's Bridge
Lorcean City
Herber City
Fainebo Sea
Maul Temple
Qeleo
Shino Reo
Eced Village
Leo Village
Opize Mountains
Territory
Uje Shoeli
Shea Village
Zeoon Leo
Maul Temple
Vozu Village
Land of Barbarian's
Maul Temple
Sheschez
Poj Village
Chioapa Cliffs
Vaz Reo
Cie Village
Chieb Village
Teesa City
Book City
Nuner City
Eeg Port
Shasu
Territory
Maul Temple
Ceq Sea
Land of The South
Broden's Cave
N
W
E
S

Cast of Characters

Attiyq – *Att-eek* – Creator God, *"The Attiyq"*

The Prince's Party
Moji Conell De Caprise - Prince *Coo-nell*, next in the line of the throne
Lord Émer Muiris Amgets- *Ee-mer* - Conell's best friend and guard
Frigg – *Fr-ig* – Conell's friend and advisor
Imogene (*Chuoha*)- Imogene, a woman from Peoria, Illinois (*Chew-o-ha* meaning princess.)

The Great Beasts of the Attiyq (also known as angels)
Áepoo – *Awe-poo* – the man/horse
Asechi – *As-e-chi* – the eagle/horse
Etta – *E-ta* – The lion/horse
Oota - *Oo-ta* – the bull/horse

Additional Characters/Names
Jezebel – regent-queen of Ezasu
Argus – *Ar-gus* – a demon, consort to Jezebel
Brón – *Brr-on* – Demon daughter of Argus
Amhras – *Am-ras* – Demon son of Argus
Ruárc – *Ru-ark* - a guard
Toál – *Too-al* - Ruárc's younger brother
Anu – *An-ou* – The (deceased) leader of Émer's people
Clemwyn – *Clem-win* – Conell's teacher when he was a child
Aho Cian – *Awe-ho* – Priest, *Ky-an* – priest of a small village
Upeshi – *Up-e-she* - Barbarians
Nute – *New-t* – king of the barbarians
Voobo - Maúl – *Voo-bo - Mah-uel* - Émer's people
Laoise – *Lay-oh-ees* – Émēr's mother
Aine – *Ay-N* – Émēr's sister

Maul Creed

To Fear the Attiyq,
Father of all those who follow Him,
who gave His life to rescue His people,
who rose from the dead and rules over all.
To maintain His word among your tribe.
To serve the descendants of King BrodÈn.
To protect the sick, innocent, and defenseless.
To give support and protection to widows and orphans.
To never commit a crime or offense against an innocent.
To refrain from harming an innocent.
To live for honor and glory.
To despise monetary reward.
To fight for the welfare of all.
To only obey the authority of the Attiyq.
To fight for the honor of all Ma'l.
To avoid all unfairness, cruelty, and deceit.
To keep the faith of the Attiyq.
To speak the truth always.
To respect the honor of all women.
To never refuse the challenge from an equal.
To refuse to turn your back on an enemy.
To die with your sword in your hand.

A Maúl must be like the wind and sea. Soft but powerful, gentle but frightening. His roar must be as a whisper and his whisper as butterfly wings.

- Anú, leader and founder
of the Maúl warriors.

1

You never heard them coming. Lord Émēr Muiris Amgets, the last of the Voobo Maúl warriors and Captain of His Majesty's royal army had failed his prince and family.

Émēr steadied his nerves and shoved the thought from his mind. The Upeshi, the barbarian from the East, sneered at Émēr as if he heard the taunts. The cries and screams of the dying villagers, Émēr's people, echoed in his ears. *Maúl never fail*, rang the chant in his head.

The Upeshi lunged and swung his massive sword. The blade arched downward towards Émēr's legs. He raised his father's war hammer, and the weapons clashed.

You never heard the enemy approaching, just as you never heard them years ago in the castle. He blinked twice and calmed his breathing.

Hate flowed into his hands and feet. *Protect the village. Focus.*

A small child bumped into his leg, making Émēr stagger. The enemy lunged. Émēr shoved the child behind him and stepped to his right. The Upeshi charged, and the sharp tip of Émēr's hammer sank into one of the blue swirls painted on the man's stomach. The Upeshi dropped to his knees. His dark eyes rose to Émēr's as the life fled from his face. Émēr swung the hammer down onto the barbarian's head. The enemy dropped to the ground. Émēr scooped the child into his arms. The boy buried his face in Émēr's shoulder and wept.

Caven, a fellow villager, held out his arms to the boy. "Grady, come, I will take you to your mother."

Émēr handed the trembling boy to Caven and nodded towards the village. "How many warriors have we lost?"

"Most are dead, My Lord," Caven replied as Grady wrapped his arms around his neck. "How did they find us? Barbarians never cross the mountains for fear of what lies beyond them."

"I do not know what drives them. They swarmed so quickly as if the witch drove them." Émēr shook his head. "Take the women and children into the woods and hide them in the caves. If the Upeshi find you, they will take you as slaves. My prince and I will hold them off as long as we can."

A pained look creased the young man's smooth face. "Lord Émēr, let me fight."

"No, someone must lead the others. Go!"

Caven reluctantly nodded and herded the women and children into the woods.

A war cry erupted, and a barbarian charged at the retreating villagers. Émēr stepped into the Upeshi's path. The man wore only a loin cloth and the blue swirls that covered his torso. His white hair stood straight up from the top of his head. He brought his weapon down on Émēr, but Émēr raised Father's war hammer and blocked the attack. The barbarian snarled as Émēr stepped to his right. The Upeshi stumbled forward but regained his balance. When Émēr rushed him, the barbarian kicked at his legs, and he tumbled onto his back. The hammer slipped from his sweaty palm.

The man sprang onto Émēr's chest and wrapped his dirty fingers around his neck. As the pressure increased, his ears rang, and his vision began to darken. The man leaned forward and grinned. Émēr struggled against the stench that emanated from the man's body.

The Attiyq fights for you, young warrior…

The soft words of Effin, Émēr's former mentor, settled over his mind.

The old teacher's scarred face peeked out from a bush of gray hair. The elder cocked his head at young Émēr. "Trust in the Attiyq. He gives victory to those who wait upon him." The old man chuckled and leaned on his wooden cane, his dark eyes gleaming with delight. "Do you trust in Him or in your own strength?"

Attiyq, help me! Strength rushed into Émēr's arms and legs, and he jerked his torso upwards. The man toppled. Émēr rolled away, gasping as his fingers searched for Father's hammer. Weapon in hand, Émēr jumped to his feet.

Émēr's opponent rose and paced before him, anticipating the next move in his dance with the Maúl.

The Upeshi growled. The Maúl grinned.

This was to be the Upeshi's honor kill, and Émēr was about to steal it from him. For the Upeshi, the slaying of a Maúl meant his people would esteem him high above the other warriors, but now the dance belonged to the Maúl.

The man's anger surged as he rushed at the Maúl. Émēr extracted his sword and the blade sliced across the man's stomach. The Upeshi collapsed onto the ground.

Émēr caught his breath and wiped his dry lips with his shaking hand. Memories sprang up before him and wrenched the breath from his lungs. Maúl blood saturated the grass as blood had soaked the floor of Brodén's castle years ago. Villagers with whom he had grown up lay dead or dying in the small settlement just as Father and the Voobo Maúl clan lay dead or dying in Brodén's Citadel. Even the wind echoed the same mournful cries. And as before, he never heard the footsteps coming.

Resting his palms on his knees, Émēr surveyed the attack. Why did he hear only the wind? Barbarians feared the Maúl and rarely attacked the village, so why attack now? He closed his eyes and took deep breaths, his stomach churning at the sound of vultures piercing the sky. Forcing the questions from his mind, Émēr searched for his prince.

Conell DeCapris, the banished prince of Ézású, swung his sword at his opponent and shoved him back with his shoulder. As Conell battered the weakened foe, Émēr wrestled with the despair creeping up his spine. Despite his skill and ferocity, despite the skill and ferocity of his prince, the enemy still flooded the village and overpowered them.

A familiar war cry pierced the compound. Émēr turned. His mother stood in the doorway of her house and slammed a shovel over her attacker's head. The barbarian staggered back but regained his footing. A snarl fell from his chapped lips as he lifted his sword.

Émēr yanked a knife from his boot and hurled it at the man. The blade buried deep into his back, and he dropped to the ground.

Émēr rushed to his mother. "Mother, stay in the house!"

His mother looked past him, and her eyes grew wide. "Niall!" she screamed as she hurried to her brother who lay on the ground.

Émēr turned. "Mother, stop!"

A barbarian used his wrist to block Niall's arm as the valiant Maúl swung his weapon at the enemy. The Upeshi plunged his weapon into Niall's chest. With blank eyes, Niall stared at the enemy. The barbarian sneered and yanked his sword from Niall's chest. The old man dropped onto his back and lifted his shaking hand as the barbarian raised his weapon to deliver the last blow.

Laoise Amgets threw herself over her brother and wrapped her arms around him. Unaffected by Laoise's screams, the Upeshi planted his feet, pleased and ready to kill them both.

Émēr sprang towards the enemy, hoping to drive him away from his family. "Barbarian!"

The Upeshi faced him and twirled his weapon in his hand. When the barbarian jumped at him, Émēr swung his hammer onto the creature's head and cracked his skull. He folded to the ground.

Émēr rushed to his uncle and gently pulled Laoise away from

him. "The barbarian is dead, Mother, you and Uncle are safe." He knelt next to Niall and brushed away the older man's graying hair from his sweaty brow. "Uncle, I am here."

Blood soaked Niall's gray tunic. Laoise ripped open Niall's shirt and examined the wounds. "We must get him into the house. Quickly!"

Niall searched Émēr's face. His breath came in deep wheezes. "Émēr … my son. Find them."

Émēr gently lifted his uncle in his arms and carried him into the house as Frigg guarded the way. Laoise led them into a small bedroom. Émēr's younger sister, Aine, pulled down the blankets as he laid Niall on the bed.

Imogene Reazly, the supposed Seer of the Attiyq, pressed her fingers on his wrist. She opened his eyelids and peered at his pupils. "His eyes are dilated, and his heartbeat is fast and weak. He's going into shock." She slipped a pillow under his feet and held out a fistful of rags to Émēr. "Help me to close off this wound. We have to increase his blood pressure, or his organs will fail."

Laoise grabbed Imogene's wrist. "Child, it is too late."

Imogene jerked her hand from Laoise's grip and shook her head. She pressed the rags over the wound. Niall's blood saturated the sheets, and his face turned ghostly white. Imogene peered at Niall's back. "He's bleeding from the back and the front. We must stop it. We need to control the bleeding."

Émēr took his uncle's hand. "Uncle, do not leave me."

Heavy footsteps echoed from the living area. Émēr drew his sword and stood in the doorway. Frigg stepped beside him.

A pale-faced young man stood in the room. Blood covered his hands and face. "Émēr, where is my father?"

Émēr let out a breath of relief and lowered his weapon, gesturing for Frigg to do the same. "This way, Erák."

As Erák charged past the dining table, he accidentally knocked over Mother's favorite vase, the one Father bought for her on their wedding day. It shattered against the wooden floor. No one seemed to notice.

The dark-haired young man took his father's hand and choked back his tears.

Niall gave his son a weak grin. "I love you." A cough erupted from his chest, and his breathing became labored. Blood dripped from the corner of his mouth, and his color turned to a dark blackish blue.

'I know, I know, Father. Save your strength."

Laoise leaned into Émēr. "Erák will need to take the responsibilities of his clan soon. He will need your help and guidance."

"Mother, he is only nineteen years of age. He is too young." Émēr shook his head. "Why did this happen?"

"Do not question the ways of God."

Imogene slipped a rag into Erák's palm and slid his hand under Niall's back. "I need you to press up into the wound to stop the bleeding. That's why his color is turning blue. He's losing too much blood."

He stared at her then back at his father.

"Please do this." She placed the other rags on Niall's chest. "Stay with me, Niall."

Another dirty but wise face appeared in the doorway. His messy gray hair stuck against his damp head. Meallan, Uncle's childhood friend.

Émēr wished them all away, but everyone remained as they had at Father's funeral, each one repeating the same dry words as Mother struggled to stay upright. "I am so sorry for your husband's death. May he always rest in peace in the Attiyq's arms."

But where was the Attiyq today and yesterday?

Meallan roughly scrubbed away his tears. Men of Vuzo do not cry. "*Serqar Tumsiad*."

Niall gave his old friend a weak grin. "You know I hate that name."

Meallan stood next to the bed and chuckled. "You will rise from this, *Serqar*, as you always did."

Niall's smile faded. "Cadi."

"Mother is safe," Erák said. "She is in the woods with the others."

He nodded. "Tell her I love her. You are *Acajo* now, Erák."

"No, Father, you will still lead this clan, not me."

Niall tried to raise his hand, but it dropped by his side. "*Acajo.* Be blessed."

Erák reluctantly nodded. "*Acajo.*"

"Do not fear, *Serquar*," Meallan said. "I will look after them. If you sleep with your elders tonight, then I will take Cadi for my second wife and your children will take my name. She will live in my house and eat at my clan's table. If she finds another man, I will release her to do as she pleases. She will always be protected."

Niall nodded. "Thank you, *Ssikbrak Rucdk*."

Meallan chuckled and shook his finger at his old friend. "Now you sound like *Serquar*." He kissed Niall's forehead and pushed back his hair. "All will be fine, *Serquar*, I promise. Rest." Meallan slipped from the room and stood at the window.

"Émēr," Imogene said. "I need you to get these people out of here."

Émēr fought back his own tears. He did not cry and betray his weakness at his father's funeral, and he would not betray his weakness here before his mother. Men never recovered from such wounds. Niall would not rise again.

With a trembling hand, Niall reached for Émēr's wrist. "Find weapons. Kill her."

Émēr shook his head and slipped his fingers into his uncle's palm. "No, I will not leave you."

Niall winced. "Please." The old man's light purple eyes focused on his. "Find…" He moaned and scrunched his face as pain wracked his body.

Blood bubbles popped up from Niall's wound.

Imogene placed another rag over Niall's open chest wound. "I'm thinking the sword may have punctured his lung. Ok, I need to keep the air from escaping his lungs. Erák, you hold that rag against his back. Laoise, I need a tube of some sort so I can inflate his lung."

Laoise pulled Imogene's hands away. "You have done enough."

"I can save him. Get me a tube, a hollow reed, or something."

"Reeds do not grow in this area, child."

Aine led Imogene into the small sitting area. "Let them have some time."

Tears welled up in Imogene's eyes as she looked back at him. "I can save him. I know I can, I just need a hollow reed."

Laoise tugged her brother's hand from Émēr's fingers and dabbed a cool, wet towel across Niall's forehead. "Hush, brother, all will be well."

Erák sat next to his father and held his hand. "It will be well, Father. Mother is safe, and so I am. I will be the leader now. No harm will befall us. It is alright if you decide to rest in the Attiyq."

Niall smiled. "I am proud of you."

Émēr placed his hand on his mother's shoulder. "I will not leave you, Mother."

Conell barreled into the room. "Frigg, watch the door."

The young man nodded and made his way to the front area. His glances jumped from the dying man in the other room to the battle outdoors. He looked down, then up at Conell, before stepping out of the house.

"I am sorry, Émēr," Conell said. "I tried to get to your uncle in time, but I could not. Aine said Imogene tried to use her healing on him but has failed. I am so sorry."

Émēr gave his Mojí a nod. "Thank you, My Mojí. How is Imogene?"

"She is very upset, but she will survive."

Niall raised his trembling arm to Conell, only to drop it on the bed. "My Mojí, find… weapons."

"Yes, Niall, we will once the village is protected."

"No, Mojí … Now. Find." Niall arched his back and moaned.

Conell's lips pursed and shot a look to his Captain.

Émēr shook his head. "Mojí, no."

Niall's pleading eyes bore into Conell's.

The Mojí lowered his head. "Yes, of course, Niall, we will go

now." He severed a lock of his hair and placed it
"I give you my word, I will find them, and I will
family is now my family, and they are under the Kin

Niall gave him a weak smile and kissed the g
take."

Erák wrapped his fingers around his father's closed fist. "We take."

His father smiled.

Conell let out a deep sigh then turned to Émēr. "My Captain, we must leave now."

Émēr shivered, even in the warmth of the morning. "I cannot leave them. Erák is only nineteen years of age, too young to lead his clan. Aine is unmarried and needs me to find her a husband. If one can be found. Mother needs me to lead them and protect them. No one is left. All who would protect them are dead. We must find a safe place … No, I will not leave my family."

Erák lifted his chin. "I am not too young. I will carry on my clan's name. Go, as my father asked."

Laoise kissed Émēr's cheek. "My precious son, follow your Mojí's orders and my brother's request. Go. We hide under the Attiyq's shadow. No harm will befall us."

Niall lifted his bloodied hand to Émēr's cheek. His cold fingers brushed the few markings of the Maúl that covered Émēr's face.

"You … Maúl. Always. Strong," Niall said. "Never …. Forget."

Cian's shuffling footsteps sounded on the wooden floor. Émēr and Laoise allowed the priest to step between them. Erák rose from his father's side.

The Áho placed his hand on Niall's forehead. "You are blessed, Niall Amgets, son of Kama. It is time to rest and go Home. You will find peace in the arms of the Attiyq."

The sides of Niall's lips turned upward, and his gaze lifted to the ceiling. "Look at the angels…" he whispered as the breath left his body.

Cian closed Niall's dead eyes. "Rest."

Erák lowered his head and bit his lip. "All be will be well, Father.

ıise."

An oppressive silence hung over the room. Shouts and the clang of weapons drifted in like distant bells. Émēr shivered as a thought stabbed his heart.

Where was the Attiyq?

He jumped when a rough hand fell on his shoulder.

Conell whispered in his ear, "We must leave."

Émēr turned to his Mojí. "Do not ask me to abandon my family. I cannot leave ones so fragile. There is no one here to protect them!"

Laoise tightened her shawl around her and rubbed her arms. A chill settled upon them, and the room dimmed as when a cloud covers the sun. "Death has touched us all." She shook her head as if to push away the vile thought and tugged her son to the front doorway. "You have no choice but to honor the request of my brother. You will leave now and find the weapons of which he spoke."

He stared into Mother's green eyes that reflected the leaves in the trees. Father had said it was Mother's eyes that held him captive—a Maúl enslaved by a loving woman, a man who refused to escape this prison. Émēr swallowed the lump in his throat. Mother's strength filled the room as it did the day she stood next to Father's grave.

Aine rose from her chair and wept in Mother's arms. Mother cried, but silently as Maúl women do. Although she did not use the sword, Mother was Maúl.

Erák wrapped his arms around the two women but held back his tears. "I must find Mother. I must tell her."

Laoise patted his cheek. "Yes, take her deeper into the woods. We will try to join you."

"And tell her of my oath," Meallan said.

Erák smiled, then exited the small house.

Émēr kissed Mother's bloodied hands. "Mother, please do not make me go. Father would insist I stay."

Mother forced a smile across her wet face and touched his cheek. "Your father's last words were to guard and serve the prince. That is what you will do now. Do not dishonor your father's name."

Meallan squeezed between Mother and son. "Émēr, she is now my sister, and you and your sister are my children. My sword now belongs to the Amgets clan. Go, Émēr, son of Cadoc Ailill Amgets. No harm will befall your family. I will lead them to safety and guard them with my life."

Before Émēr could respond, Imogene jumped and slapped at her neck as if a bug had bitten her. She shivered. "I feel like a goose walked over my grave." Seeing no bug, she rubbed the back of her neck and looked at Émēr. "Can't we take them with us?"

Aine slipped past Émēr, led Imogene to the door, and kissed her forehead. "No, the beasts cannot take us all," she declared. "You will move faster without us. I will remember you always, Imie, daughter of Frank Reazly."

Imogene glanced at Conell and Émēr. "We can't just leave them."

Conell placed his fingers under Imogene's elbow. "We have no choice."

"But—"

Meallan dropped to his knee before Conell and balanced his blade on his fingers. "My King, my sword is now yours. We will hold back the enemy while you escape."

A pained look gripped Conell's face. Émēr moaned and looked down. A *quv,* a vow made before the King. Only death would release the giver.

Conell released Imogene's arm and touched Meallan's weapon. "I accept your sword, Meallan, son of Llew."

The man grinned as he stood and gave Conell a quick nod. He ran out of the house, and moments later Émēr heard him explaining the Mojí's plans to their fellow warriors. The men shouted and plunged into the battle with renewed vigor.

Conell slipped his head out the door. "Áepoo, we need you."

A draft of air caressed Conell's silver hair as the sound of thumping horse hooves drifted through the doorway. Four beasts with two arms and four sets of wings appeared in the field: Áepoo, half man and half horse; Asechi, a horse with an eagle's head; Etta, a horse with a lion's head; and Oota, a horse with a bull's head.

Conell drew Imogene out the door and lifted her onto Áepoo's back.

"Wait," Imogene said. "Why can't Áepoo just kill these guys?"

"I am not permitted to kill, Dear One," Áepoo said.

Conell gave Imogene a reassuring pat on the knee as Aine and Laoise escorted Émēr out the door. Cian followed, and Frigg guarded the small group as they mounted the beasts.

Émēr clung to his mother and sister. His voice cracked. "Please, do not make me go. I can protect you. Let me lead you into the woods."

Laoise slid her hands from his shoulders down to his hands and grasped his fingers. "Not as well as the Attiyq," she replied with a motherly smile, the same one she used when he was a child and feared the creatures of the woods. "We will be fine. Go." She squeezed his hands one last time and released him.

Aine wrapped her arms around her brother's waist and laid her head on his chest. "Find us," she whispered as she withdrew from him and slipped into Mother's embrace.

Laoise kissed her fingertips and waved her farewell to Émēr.

Émēr nodded and blinked back his tears. Cian led Émēr to Etta, the lion-beast. Émēr leapt onto Etta's back as his eyes locked on his small family. Every muscle in his body ached to dismount and return to them, but his mother's stern look held him in place.

Cian's sharp gaze caught Émēr's. "If you disobey now, you will dishonor both your mother and father. Do not break your oaths."

Émēr nodded as Cian climbed onto Oota's back.

The Enemy's voice rings louder than a large bell. The Attiyq's voice is as a whisper. Who will you hear?

~ Anú

2

Emēr glanced over his shoulder as the angels ascended. Mother and Aine grew smaller until Mother slipped her hand into Aine's, and the two women entered the house. If he jumped from the lion's back, he could still save them. As if reading his mind, the beasts rose higher into the air. Soon, the small house disappeared as treetops rushed under them.

Anger burned in Émēr's heart. It bolted through his chest, tightened his throat, and wriggled through his brain like a mad worm. His head ached with the pounding of his heart which birthed a haunting question.

How could the Attiyq be so cruel as to kill his uncle and destroy the village? How could He make Émēr leave behind a young man, a young T'Tisho and his mother? Destroy what was left of his family?

He closed his eyes and shoved the heretical words down into his belly. Such thoughts would mean death to a Maúl. No one ever questioned God or His ways. Sacrilege. But now the planted choruses mocked him. The beating of wings followed the rhythm of his heart and added fuel to the pagan thoughts.

Why?

Cian's voice carried over the sound of the roaring wind. "We must stay behind the mountains."

Émēr's jaw tightened. While Mother and Aine fell into the hands of the barbarians, Cian wanted them to hide behind mountains.

Argus stretched his large white wings and cracked his neck. He tied his long white hair back into a ponytail, then crossed his large arms over his chest as he glared into the mirror that hung in Jezebel's private chambers. The cloudy vision in the mirror wavered before the colors became clear.

Argus's son, Amhras, lay his head on Argus's shoulders. His gray, chiseled face framed his dark eyes. "Father, why do you allow them to torment you?"

"One day, they will all be destroyed." Argus stroked Amhras' long sliver hair as he gazed at the scene displayed in the mirror. His enemies, Conell and his worthless group, stood around a dying Niall. The corners of Argus's mouth twisted upward into a grin. "Niall, The Worthless, is dying! Another pathetic Attiyq warrior is now gone from our sight. Even now, we win! The Attiyq allowed him to die." Argus leaned into the mirror and whispered at Niall's image, "Tell me, Worthless One, where was your God?"

Angels floated down through the ceiling of the Amgets hovel and surrounded Niall. A blinding light filled the room, making Amhras shield his eyes. Their hair floated as if in water and blended into their clothes. Their large white wings pumped slowly up and down as they surrounded the dying man.

Argus narrowed his eyes. "Amhras, do you remember when they loved me? All of them told me how beautiful I was. I wore the jewels of the Attiyq. I sang the songs that made them all smile. It was me. Me! Friends and comrades who claimed to love *me*. But they all betrayed the greatness of me." He stomped his foot. "As long as I sang the songs they wanted to hear and did what they demanded, they loved me. But once I began to question why the Attiyq was greater than any of us and received all the worship, they deserted me. No one stood by my side. I was to have that throne. But the Attiyq was always jealous of my greatness."

"I know, Father. He was wrong to cast you away."

"He trembled at the competition. That is why He sent me away. He is as a child. He gave my beautiful jewels to His pathetic humans!"

Amhras snuggled his father's neck. "Do not think of it, Father."

"How could He leave me to rot in that small cell? How could He do that to me, the one He said He loved? He never cared. God of Love. He is an insult, a pox, a blemish to the world." Argus crossed his arms over his chest and glared at the angelic host.

Japik, an angelic female with long blond hair, stood next to Niall. Her long curling locks fluttered, stirred by the Breath of the Attiyq, which drifted around and through His angelic beings. Japik smiled at Niall as his spirit rose from his dead body. She slipped her hand into his then turned to Argus as he watched in the mirror. She shook her finger at him, scolding him as if he were a child.

Amhras fell to the ground, trembling. "Do not look at her, Father!"

Argus growled and slammed his fist against the side of the mirror. Japik laughed as she led Niall to the Attiyq's throne room.

"Why do they do this to me? First the Attiyq sent Áepoo, now Japik. Who will be next?" Argus asked as he watched the angel soar. "I wanted her to join me. I would have given her greatness. I know she cared for me. And yet, even now she betrays me."

As men gathered around Niall's body, Argus searched for his seer. She sat in another room and wept with Émēr's sister, Aine. Argus lifted an eyebrow and yanked Amhras to his feet.

"Look, my son! The Attiyq no longer watches over them!" Argus said. "Look at the Maúl's sister. She is no longer a child. Eighteen years of age. Look at how lovely she is." He shrugged. "A little old, but I can tame her."

Imogene's insecurities flared like flames from her body. Argus leaned into the mirror and took in the sweet, burning stench that smelled like putrid roses.

"Smell her fears, my son. She is alone with no one to watch her. She still misses me. I know she does. Soon she will be mine again."

Amhras nudged Argus's elbow. "Father, look, the one called Frigg."

Frigg stood outside the house but kept far from the battle. An attacker approached him, but the boy scurried back into the doorway. The barbarian laughed and turned back into the battle. The red-haired boy peeked back inside the house, only to turn away and kick the ground. Argus leaned forward and stared at the lonely young man.

"Amhras, there is a sadness upon this one. He needs a friend. He is forgotten," Argus said. His lips curled. "I will be his friend."

"Do you think he has forgotten your kindness to him?"

Argus lifted his eyebrow. "I hope not. I can use this abandoned creature just as I use all forsaken children."

Cian shuffled into the room and stood next to Niall.

Argus gritted his teeth and let out a roar. "Cian! Curse him! The fly that is always buzzing in my face!"

Amhras screamed and dropped to the ground. "Father! Do not look at him!"

Argus jerked Amhras to his feet and slammed his face into the mirror. "Kill him, Amhras! I command you!"

"Father! Please no!" Amhras wiggled from his father's clutches and huddled in the corner.

The air became still and quiet. The old man's lips moved. The scourged words streamed from the priest's mouth and lingered in the air like drops of ice. Then as wasps, they swarmed through the mirror and covered Argus's face. Their deep stingers penetrated his soft skin, climbed into his eyes, and swirled down his throat. He screamed as he danced around the room, trying to swat them away. Large red-and-black welts broke out across his skin. Tears sprang to his eyes. His stomach flopped, and he vomited into a washing bowl. Argus struggled to catch his breath as he leaned against the washstand.

Amhras rocked in the corner and wept.

When Cian finished, the foul creeds settled into the floors and ceilings. Argus wiped his mouth and glared at the defiled monster.

Brón, his favorite daughter-demon, floated up from the floor and slipped her soft arms around Argus's waist. Her long black hair was teased down one side of her gray face, giving her a crazed look while the other side descended straight to her shoulders. A bird's skull pinned back her tangled bangs. She snuggled her thin face against Argus's back. "Father, let me comfort you."

He shoved his cherished child. "Not now!"

Brón whimpered and cowered against the wall. "Father, do not look at him! He will destroy you."

Argus flung his arm in her direction and a Shadowy Mist encased his darling creature like a spider hunting prey. Brón screamed as the mist locked her in its jaws and dragged her down through the floor.

Amhras hid his sobbing face in his arms. His long white hair trailed over his bent knees.

The last of the Anú's children stood beside Niall's body. Rage covered Émēr's face. Argus furrowed his brow. Where did the rage come from? Bright red flares shot out from Émēr's body. Questions boiled in the Maúl's mind. *Why? Why has this happened? Where is the Attiyq? Why was the village not protected?*

Argus looked over his shoulder. "Amhras."

The young demon slowly came to his feet and stumbled to his father. "What is your will, My Father?" His voice trembled, and he wiped away his tears.

"What do you see?" Argus motioned to the mirror.

Amhras took a deep breath and steadied his trembling. He peered into the mirror. "He is … questioning the Attiyq!"

He nodded. "Yes, he is. Amhras, I need you now." Argus looked down at his son and stroked Amhras' cheek "Do this and I will reward you."

"What is your bidding, Father?" Amhras whispered. He glanced at Cian, then back to his father.

"The Maúl is now yours."

Amhras licked his lips until he spotted Cian.

Argus moved Amhras' chin to face him. "Do not fear the priest, my son. All I want you to do is focus on the Maúl. I will deal with Cian." He brushed Amhras' hair from his face, making the young demon smile.

"I will not let you down, Father."

"Be careful, my son. Japik is with the young man, but you are stronger than she. Do not fail me."

Amhras nodded and stepped into the mirror. The demon's murky eyes absorbed the light. The small bedroom dimmed, and the air chilled. The mother shivered and drew her shawl around her. Shadows slithered across the room and wrapped the demon in a warm embrace. Amhras snuggled his face against the Darkness. And it returned his love.

Amhras studied Cian before slipping behind him. Cian slowly turned his head to Amhras. Amhras paused and watched his father through the mirror.

Argus swallowed. If Cian felt his son's presence, he would chase the young demon from the room. Argus gritted his teeth until Cian turned away from Amhras' direction and closed Niall's dead eyes.

Amhras stepped behind Émēr and hugged him. "You are mine now, my Love," he whispered in Émēr's ear. Shadows peeked from under the bed and jabbed at Émēr's feet. They raced away when he shifted his legs. Amhras stepped away from Émēr, and a shadow ball formed in Amhras' hands. He molded it until it grew into a larger black orb. Then, holding it in his palms, he blew the sphere into

Émēr's body. The Dark melted into him.

Argus held his breath. If Japik returned, she would banish his son and his spell. Amhras was strong but not enough to defeat one of God's elite. The Maúl could still defeat Amhras' attack as Cian had done. "Let it stay, Émēr, let it stay."

Émēr winced and rubbed his forehead. He shook his head and focused on his uncle. The Dark squeezed Émēr's waist like a snake suffocating its pray and anchored its tail to his heart. It peeked out of Émēr's eyes, then settled back into his skull. But a tinge of gray lurked behind the purple hue of his eyes. The lovely mother dragged her son to the doorway and kissed his forehead.

Argus scrunched up his face. "Revolting."

Amhras stepped behind Imogene, the weak Oracle, and kissed her neck. She jumped and slapped at him as if he were a bug. Amhras gave his father a sly glance.

Argus chuckled. "Yes, my boy, you may have her once I am done." He extended his hand and helped his son through the mirror, back into Jezebel's room. "You have pleased me."

Amhras grinned. "Father, you are most kind to me. Thank you."

Conell's voice drifted through the mirror.

Amhras' face fell. "Father, the prince means to destroy you."

Argus shrugged. "It will be well, my son. Remember your pet, The Dark, now sits upon the Maúl. Anú will pay for his cruelty."

"And the priest?"

He sighed. "Yes, the priest. He must die. His words are poison. Beware of him, my boy."

Conell leaned out the doorway and summoned Áepoo.

Amhras hissed and buried his face in his father's arm.

Argus stroked his son's head. "Do not fear, my little one. Áepoo will not harm you. But where are you going, son of Brodén?" He cocked his head. "The Queen comes. Amhras, leave me now. I will join you later. I promise."

The demon grinned and kissed his father. "I will wait for you."

Amhras disappeared into the floor seconds before the door to the Queen's quarters swung open. Argus waved his hand over the mirror, and the images disappeared.

The lovely and foul Jezebel stood in the doorway with her hands planted on her thin hips. "What are you doing in my quarters?"

"Waiting for you, my love." Argus marched across the floor, the floorboards creaking under his weight. The light from the windows peeked in, but the dimness of the room chased it away. Keeping his gaze locked on her eyes, he kissed her hand.

Jezebel yanked her hand away. "Now that you've lost your tiny seer, you come running back to me? Be careful, my love, that you do not tread on my courtesies. I am still Queen."

Argus swallowed his laughter. What a fool. "My Queen, you are right. I have overstepped my bounds, and I beg for forgiveness. But it is you who holds my heart, not the child. Remember, she is my seer, the creature who will lead us to the weapons strong enough to destroy God." He bowed. "My winged men just informed me that Ruárc succeeded in taking the village, but my seer and her cursed companions escaped on the winged beasts of the Attiyq."

She brushed past him and stopped before the full-length mirror. "You told me this would work."

No matter how many times she waved her small hand over the glass, no picture appeared. Argus suppressed a snicker.

The Queen plopped into her dressing chair and moaned. "What curse is on me that prevents me from seeing what lies beyond those mountains?"

Argus shrugged and strutted to her side. His long fingers massaged her shoulders. She leaned back, and he whispered in her ear. "Perhaps the Attiyq is stopping you."

She flicked her hand and pulled away from him. "I hate the Attiyq. And I hate that mirror. It never works for me." Her thin fingers fluffed her hair.

He rubbed her shoulders again, and his fingers felt the tiny bones in her neck. How easy to snap such fragile cartilage? His gripped tightened, only to pull back. "Do you doubt me now?" His deep voice echoed off the walls.

Her glazed eyes stared at her reflection in the mirror. "No, of course not."

"Then I promise, I will find them for you, my love." He kissed her neck.

As the Great Beasts soared near the Opez Mountains and circled south, Émēr scouted the land and spotted *Zeoon Leo's* blue river cutting the borders between Opize and Shasu Territory. Nestled in the crook of the two lands was a small clearing. Émēr reluctantly recanted his anger. Cian was wise. The small group would be safe for the time being.

"Mojí!" Émēr shouted over the rushing wind and pointed to the spot. "There is a place near *Zeoon Leo* that will hide us."

Conell nodded.

Émēr glanced over his shoulder. Mother and Aine were now a day's march from the river. Captives or worse… He rubbed away the burning tears. Once the Upeshi captured Aine, they would rip away her innocence in one horrid scene. They would sell Mother to the highest bidder. Healers were rare in the Eastern lands, and travelers paid high prices for such people. Émēr shivered and raked his hand across his face.

Uncle Niall…

Émēr clutched the white stone hanging around his neck. Niall had slipped it over Émēr's head at Father's funeral. *"This represents the Attiyq who is always with you. Pure as innocence but strong to withstand wind and rain. A pure foundation." Niall nodded towards the castle. "Go, young one, and protect your prince according to your father's last wishes. Your mother and sister are now under my care, you are released from this responsibility until my death. Then their lives will be in your hands."*

Tears again sprang up in Émēr's eyes. His responsibility, and he had abandoned his post. Émēr shook his head. "Attiyq, why?" He bunched his hands into fists. "No! I will not give into these blasphemous thoughts! It is against the elders' teachings!"

Stop the witch.

His mother, sister in the hands of the enemy. Destroyed. Cursed.

Guard your prince.

You shall respect all weakness and establish yourself the defender of them.

"Why am I following these orders?" he whispered. "Everyone is dead. Their blood flows through my fingers. I could not save my uncle, my sister, my mother. Anú, forgive me!"

The beasts circled the clearing and gently landed. While his companions dismounted, Émēr sat on Etta and stared at his prince, the one he had sworn to protect and follow. "They might still be alive. Will you make me stay?"

Conell pursed his lips, and his pain-filled, lime-green eyes captured Émēr's. It was the same face that looked upon his own parents' graves years ago. "Émēr, I love your mother and sister as if they were my own. But I promised Niall I would fulfill his last wish. All will die if you return. I need you here. I give you my word on my father's heart I will not forget them but will hunt with you to find them."

A chill swept over Émēr, making his body feel like flimsy weeds. His flat voice startled him. "And if I choose not to stay?"

"Please do not do this," Conell said. "You are my captain, and I need your sword at my side. Meallan may be dead now, also. Will you turn away his loyalty?"

Cian looked over his shoulder as he led Oota the Bull Beast to the water. "You are Maúl, follow your Mojí's orders."

Émēr gritted his teeth but slid off his mount. The Lion-horse danced away from him. Émēr snatched at Etta's mane. The beast jerked away and trotted to the river. He looked back at Émēr and roared before drinking from the river.

A firm hand dropped on Émēr's shoulder and made him jump.

"Captain, do not fret, the Attiyq's strong hand rests upon your loved ones," Áepoo said.

Émēr shrugged off Áepoo's hand. "Áepoo, I gave my sword to those who are weak, to protect the widows and the fatherless, including my mother and sister. Now I am forced to break that oath."

Émēr picked his way over the sandy beach to Etta. The animal darted away from him.

He raised his hands. "Please, Etta, I only wish to help you. Please allow me that honor."

Etta snarled at him and shook his mane.

Cian's brow furrowed. "Something has made the beast skittish of you." The old man placed his hands on Émēr's shoulders. "Something is different about your eyes."

Émēr turned from the old man. "There is nothing wrong with my eyes. Etta, please, let me help you." He cupped water in his hands and poured it over Etta's back. The lion-horse purred and shook off the excess water, giving in to the calming effect as Émēr gently rubbed his hands over his torso.

Áepoo stepped into the river and splashed water across his chest and head. Émēr trudged through the waist-high water and poured water over Áepoo's body.

Áepoo shook away the excess and grinned. "Thank you, Maúl, that feels good against my aching bones."

Émēr smiled. "I thought angels felt no pain."

Áepoo brushed the water from his arms and chuckled. "Sometimes we do. It is good that you take care of Etta. He loves to be indulged."

"Angels who enjoy a human's care. It seems quite odd."

"Cian is right, Maúl. Etta senses something is wrong and now flinches from you," Áepoo said.

Émēr shrugged. "What is wrong? Perhaps it is because I have abandoned my family to the enemy's sword?"

Cian led Oota into the water, while Asechi watched from the shore. The Áho washed Oota and nodded towards Asechi. "It seems the eagle-beast does not like the water."

Áepoo glanced over his shoulder. "No, he does not like to be wet."

Cian chuckled and wiped down Oota.

Émēr cupped water in his hands and approached the eagle-horse. "Please, Asechi, I mean you no harm."

Imogene walked to the river, while Frigg gathered wood for a fire. She washed away Niall's blood as she bit her lip. Tears simmered in her soft orbs and her lower lip quivered.

Conell watched her from the corner of his eye. "Are you alright?"

She shook her head. "I could have saved him. I've seen that procedure done millions of times. I've never done it, but I could have tried. I needed a tube. A stupid, dumb five-dollar tube. But no one would let me try."

Áepoo wrapped his large arm over her shoulder. "Child, there was little you could do. Yes, you do know how to do it, but have you done it before?"

She laid her head on his chest. "No."

"Then how do you know he would have lived? He is happy now, safe in God's arms. Why blame others or yourself?"

She wiped away her tears. "You make it sound so black and white."

Conell motioned with his hand. "Come, *Chuōbá.* It is time we find some food and get some rest."

She nodded and followed him to the beach.

Émēr tried to pour the water over Asechi, but he only nipped in response.

"Áepoo," Imogene asked. "Would Asechi really bite Émēr?"

Áepoo chuckled. "No, child, he is gentle. Asechi, he is our friend, he will not harm you." He called out to Asechi and spoke strange words to the animal.

Asechi squawked and flapped his wings but nodded his head. When Émēr poured the water over him, Asechi fluffed his feathers like a sparrow in a puddle.

Émēr grinned. "See, I am not your enemy. Now this is a sight. Angels who feel pain and fear water. At least the Attiyq laughs."

Áepoo shook the water from his back. "He does more than laugh. Trust me, Captain, He is more aware of your problems and cares more for your tears, then us who serve Him."

Émēr studied Áepoo as Cian poured the water over the animal's back. "Perhaps. If the Attiyq cares so much, then why did my uncle die?"

"What happened between Niall and the Attiyq is between them, not you." Áepoo brushed the water from his hands. "Émēr, Argus is weaving a spell over you. If you do not fight it, you and your family will die."

Émēr scoffed. "What does Argus have to do with me? He longs for the girl and my prince, not an untrained Maúl. I am nothing to the demon." He joined Conell and Imogene as they arranged the wood for the fire.

Cian sighed and sat on a log that extended into the river. He dangled his withered hands between his legs and glanced at Áepoo. "My old friend, I fear for the captain. I felt something in the room where Niall died, something evil. Nevertheless, I ignored it and focused on Niall. I could have saved the captain from heartache, but I failed. Argus is not finished."

Áepoo walked from the river. "I too fear for the captain. But the Attiyq's hands are on him. Argus is as a child. The Attiyq gives you His powers."

The old man nodded. "If Émēr does not realize what the Attiyq has given him, Argus will win. I pray Émēr discovers this soon."

The man-horse placed his hand on Cian's shoulder. "As do I or all will be lost."

The sun slowly made its way to sleep in the east, sending her blush and orange fingers over the horizon, and the large milky-white moon rose proudly in the west to take her place. The sound of the river flowing along the riverbed added to the rhythm of the chirping crickets. The cold wind whipped at the flames of the small campfire.

Émēr tossed more logs onto the fire and turned the skewered fish that Frigg had caught.

Imogene held out her hands over the warmth of the fire. The flame's light bounced off the bruises from her face. Émēr looked away. Each day, he was forced to see the black-and-blue marks covering her child-like face. *Protect the innocent.* He had failed. The Maúl never fails.

But was she innocent?

He paused.

The Dark crinkled its brow. *What did your eyes see in the prison, Maúl? A Zuuho. A woman steeped in sin and covered with filth. Her arms exposed as only a Zuuho can expose herself. Her eyes blinded to the ways of TTishos Honor. Look at her, Maúl. The Zuuho now sits covered in borrowed honor. Whose clothes does she wear? What now covers the Zuuho's disgrace? Aine's honor now covers the Zuuho. Yet Aine's own honor could be torn apart this very night. Aine the Zuuho.*

A chill scraped its sharp finger down his back, making him shiver.

"Not to mention," came a whispered voice from the dark, *"she took your sister's place."*

Émēr jumped from his seat, and his purple eyes scanned the woods behind them. Yet, the darkness offered only shadows that embraced the tree branches. He closed his eyes, slowed his breathing, and allowed the sounds to drift over him. They were distant, far, as if hiding on the other side of the world. Undetectable.

Conell followed his gaze. "Is someone out there?"

The captain caught his Mojí's stern face peering at him from the other side of the campfire. "No, I thought I had heard something, but . . . it was nothing."

His Mojí narrowed his eyes and cocked his head.

Émēr understood that expression. Émēr Muiris Amgets did not hear something yet claim it was nothing. He gave Conell a brief smile. "It has been a long day. I fear for my family."

The sternness escaped Conell's face. "Yes, of course."

Imogene handed a cooked fish to Émēr. "Eat something. It will make you feel better."

He nodded and offered her a small smile. The Attiyq gave this girl to him to protect and become his responsibility. *Yes, innocent.*

The Dark growled at him and retreated as Émēr took his seat across from Imogene, Conell, and Frigg.

Conell handed Imogene a piece of fish. When her swollen eyes met his, he shoved the meat to her face. She gave him a sour look, and he placed the fish in her lap. She picked off a few bits and chewed slowly. Her lost gaze was fixed on the fire.

"*Interesting,*" whispered The Dark. *"All the Zuuho does is stare into something. Shake her, Maúl! Make her speak to you! The seer is now silent. Perhaps she is not a seer, but a complaining child?"*

A grin formed on Émēr's lips. *She had said that hearing from the Attiyq is like finding shoes that she loved.*

The Dark thoughts stabbed his heart. "*Yet when has she babbled of finding shoes? Listen to her useless words. She now fears Argus. She weeps over a beating. Yet look at you, Great Maúl. How many times have you endured a horrible beating, and yet here you sit, a strong man, while she is useless? Why do you endure her weakness, Great Maúl? What of Aine and Mother? What has become of them? Does the Great Seer care for your loved ones, or does she care only for shoes?"*

No. Émēr wrestled the conflicting thoughts. *An illness held her mind, making her unable to grasp reality. That was why she spoke of strange things. It is wrong to beat a woman! Any woman!*

The Dark cocked its head. *"Maybe your Mojí was right, maybe you should have left her back in the prison."*

Émēr rubbed his forehead. The thoughts that seemed to stab his heart and linger in his head seemed to be beside him now. He glanced around him and saw no one. Yet, something was there, something he could not see. *How can I fight this?*

"Is it an illness?" The Dark asked. *"To retreat from the enemy is cowardice. Better to die by your enemy's sword, than to run to your mother's arms. Look at her, Maúl. What does the Great Seer do now? She sits and eats and stares into a fire, while your sister lies pinned beneath a barbarian."*

Anxiety twisted around Émēr's heart as the scene played out in his mind. A wave of panic overtook him. A twig snapped. He jumped to his feet and grabbed Father's *Atobo.* Again, his ears had grown deaf.

Cian's old frame entered the camp light. He waved down Émēr's war hammer. "Forgive me, captain, I did not mean to frighten you.'

Émēr sat down on his log. "You did not frighten me, Áho."

Cian sat next to Imogene and patted her leg. "How are you feeling, dear?"

"I'm tired." She laid her head on his shoulder.

"I know, child. I will find a place for you to rest soon."

Émēr struggled not to roll his eyes, but they rolled on their own accord.

"She is so weak," the Dark whispered. *"Would a Maúl woman act so pitifully? Did your mother weep at your father's funeral? Did not your mother take you and your sister to your home and tend to you, putting her own pain aside? And yet, this insignificant creature moans of being faint and tired. A 'perfect' seer."*

A fount of anger spewed from the pit of Émēr's stomach. Rage slithered up to his chest and clenched his heart. *Sister! Mother! Why is this weak doe so tired?*

"Imogene, what does the Attiyq say about my mother and sister?" he blurted.

The fragile rabbit who hides in borrows lifted her head. The firelight bounced off her watery eyes. "I don't know," came her useless words.

Words emerged from the roiling pit and wriggled from his mouth like worms. "How can we defeat the witch if you refuse to help us?" The callousness of his voice shook him.

Her mouth dropped open and her eyes blinked. "It's not like I'm not trying."

Émēr quickly rose and bowed. "Forgive me, My Lady. I will take first watch, My Mojí."

Cian leaned back on the log and crossed his arms over his chest. "That, Captain, is an excellent idea."

Conell glared at him. "Make it a long watch, Captain."

Émēr stumbled from the warmth of the campfire and into the cold, dark forest. His friends' confused soft voices wandered across the warm forest: Imogene stifling a sob, Conell growling a curse, and Cian explaining that the Maúl had spoken out of his suffering not his true heart.

"The girl has done nothing wrong." Émēr's body trembled. "Argus tried to hurt her. She has the right to weep. Forgive me, Attiyq, for such cruel words."

Émēr leaned against a tree and stared at the stars twinkling in the skies. Anú, the first of the Maúl and the greatest of his kind, often wrote of the stars. Émēr's mind searched for Anú's words.

> When I stare at the stars thrown against the black skies,
> When I see the brilliance of the heavens,
> I must ask, who am I that Your eyes lock on me?
> Am I greater than the stars that fill the sky?
> Yet You, oh Attiyq, see me greater than the majesty
> stretched across the night skies.

A smile lingered on Émēr's face. "Father, I miss you. I miss watching the stars with you."

"The Attiyq sees us as greater than His own creation." Young Émēr smiled at his father.

The words soothed his broken soul. "Oh, Attiyq, help Imogene to hear from You. Protect what is left of my family. I miss Father and now I miss my uncle. Do not take what is left from me. Attiyq, You took my place and became the sacrifice so I could live. Do not leave me alone." He rubbed the stone that hung around his neck, finding comfort in the strength and smoothness of it.

"Forgive my cruel words. The girl is not Maúl. She is not a *Natu* Warrior. She is not as a woman who holds a sword and spreads fear across the lands. Father refused to spar with the *Natu* because of their fierceness, so why do I now expect this ill woman to be as a woman warrior who fights stronger than a man? A female who wears the flesh of their dead around their necks?" A shiver slipped down his back.

He walked down to the river and kicked a stone into the water. A loud splash broke the silence. The crickets stilled, then continued their chatter. He sat on a log and rubbed his face.

"Yet what good is she to you?" the Dark questioned. *"Think of it, she is to hear from the Great One, yet she hears nothing. As you hear nothing."*

He winced at the words as he dangled his hands between his legs and rubbed his palms. Aine's words echoed in his mind. "*They sell the women to the Slave Runners. I do not wish to disappear."* He shivered.

"Please Attiyq, do not let Aine be sold to men who have no respect for her honor. Protect her. Do not let her disappear." His stomach flopped. "Please do not let the cursed ones beat Mother until she heals their sick. Protect her and do not let them toss her aside once they are done. Help me to help them."

For the first time in his life, his hands shook. He took deep breaths to push aside the fear. *Focus.*

Father's words drifted forth from his memories. *"Put your fear aside, my son. Focus on the present. The future belongs to the Attiyq."*

He took deep breaths. The anxiety slowly released its grip on his chest, but the thoughts persisted.

The Dark continued. *"It is a full circle, Maúl. She is useless to you. She is nothing. She was ill when Toál threw her into your cell, and now her mind is beyond repair. Argus broke her and now you depend upon her to find your loved ones. What if you fail? What if the Attiyq fails you? How will you ever fulfill your vows, Maúl? You should not have come here. You should have stayed with your loved ones. Now all is lost."*

You shall follow the Orders of your Leader without question.

Émēr shook his head. *I will not listen to such blasphemous thoughts.*

"Why did this happen?" The Dark asked. *"Why does the Great Attiyq, Creator of the Universe, allow all this pain and suffering? The One who promised to never leave your side. Where is He now?"*

Émēr stared into the gloom. "Attiyq, why have You abandoned me?"

"Why do you think He has abandoned you, Émēr?" a voice asked.

He jumped off the log and searched the blackness.

Cian's shuffling footsteps cracked the twigs. The Áho smiled at Émēr as he eased onto the log. "You are as a mouse, young Maúl. This is not like you."

Émēr lowered himself next to the priest and dragged his hand through his hair. "Forgive me, Áho. Thoughts seem to have taken life in my mind. Thoughts I have never allowed to venture through me. Thoughts of…"

"Fear?" asked Cian.

Émēr nodded. "Even when the witch threw us into that hell prison, I did not fear, but I trusted the Attiyq. I gave courage to My Mojí and Frigg. I strengthened them. I cared for them. A Maúl never shows his fear to the enemy. Now my strength has betrayed me. My thoughts are my enemy."

Cian looked at him with eyes full of compassion and warning. "You have allowed these evil thoughts access. A man is as he thinks. You think of fear so your hands tremble and your face drops. You listen to lies from the enemy about your mother and sister, yet you have not trusted the Attiyq to care for them. The Attiyq Himself made us His own by His sacrifice. No one can take you from His hand. You are His. Yet now you follow dark whispers and shadows instead of the Light of the Attiyq. Allow His light to penetrate this darkness that surrounds you. Your family will live and prosper for they are in His hands."

"But how do you know this?"

Cian chuckled. "My young one, you are as a babe. I remember the promises He gave me years ago."

"And if He changes his mind?"

The swish of an arrow broke Émēr's words. The shaft slammed into Cian's chest, and he fell back onto the ground.

"Áho!" Émēr dropped to his priest's side.

The old man gurgled as blood trailed from his mouth. Another arrow flew over his head. More arrows struck the surrounding trees. Émēr dragged the old man behind some bushes. The thick bolt protruded from the *Áho's* chest. Émēr moaned and pressed his hand around the wound as blood saturated Cian's shirt.

Cian grabbed Émēr's shirt and pulled the young man to his face. The old man placed his hand on Émēr's head. "I bless you . . . in the name . . . of the Attiyq."

"Do not speak, my Áho."

Cian waved away Émēr's words. "You are now . . .His. You are the priest. Guard them. Guard . . . her. Serve Him and King." Cian's hand slipped from Émēr's head.

Another man killed by the enemy.

And Émēr never heard it coming.

He closed Cian's eyes. "How can I be priest, my Áho, when my faith is failing?"

More arrows landed around his feet and into the trees near him. He raced for camp.

"Mojí! Argus is here!"

Conell and Frigg jumped from the log and grabbed their swords. Imogene's pale face stared up at Émēr. He yanked her to his side. Anger burned within him and conflicting words fought for their hold on his mind.

This was her fault.

Guard her.

A useless seer.

You shall respect all weakness and establish yourself the defender of them.

You are now Priest.

"Where is Argus, Captain?"

His Mojí's words broke through the battle in Émēr's mind. He looked into Imogene's frightened eyes. An ill child lost in a strange world, and she was depending upon him, the last of the Maúl, to protect her. He squeezed her hand, and she wrapped her trembling palm under his arm.

"He is coming behind me. Cian is dead."

Imogene tugged at his sleeve. "He's what?"

"My Mojí, call upon Áepoo!" Émēr yelled as he searched the dark skies for Argus.

The flying demon landed behind Émēr. Imogene whirled and

screamed. Émēr pushed her behind him and draped his arm across her body. Conell and Frigg joined him, swords drawn.

Argus folded his wings behind his back as his winged men landed behind him. The moon hid behind the clouds and the nocturnal insects raced to safety. A chill encased the beach. The Dark caressed Argus's feathers and sneered at Émēr.

Émēr's breath caught in his lungs, and his hands shook. Imogene's fingers dug into his arm.

Argus performed a sweeping bow. "We meet again. I apologize for the inconvenience and of course, the death of that pest of a priest. But now that he is gone, we can … talk." A grin covered his dark face.

Conell slipped beside Émēr. "Do not look into his eyes, look at his forehead."

Émēr nodded and forced his eyes on the demon's brow.

Argus laughed. "Yes, I do have that way of casting spells." His eyes fell on the girl. "My dear seer, how I have missed you. Perhaps now you could share my wine with me? Or is this too fast for you?" He spread his arms.

A small whimper escaped her lips as she dropped to the sand and struggled to catch her breath.

Keeping his eyes on the demon, Émēr hauled Imogene to her feet. She wrapped her trembling arms around his chest and buried her tear-streaked face in his shoulder.

Argus offered her a sympathetic grin. "Is it something I said, child? How I have missed you." He held out his hand.

Conell raised his sword. "Enough!"

Argus lifted a finger. "Before you call upon that meddlesome Áepoo, maybe you should tell the dear captain what happened that night. What really happened."

Conell licked his lips. "Now is not the time."

Frigg glanced at his Mojí. "What night?"

"Come now, Prince Conell." Argus slipped his hands behind his back and paced the beach. "Please do not tell me you have forgotten the night Émēr's clan died? Or Frigg's father. Or your own parents?

The attack on the castle that brought us to this place?" Birds dashed across the dark sky to safety. The stars hid behind the clouds.

Émēr shivered. Imogene's breaths came in quick gasps. The captain's eyes turned to his Mojí. The words floated over his tongue. Words that made no sense. Forbidden.

"What does he mean, Mojí?"

Argus extended his hand to Conell. "Yes, Great Mojí, the last of Brodén. Tell the child of Anú the truth of that night. How you are to blame for his father's death."

"Áepoo!" Conell shouted.

The Horse Angels appeared between the demon and his prey. Frigg jumped on Asechi's back. Conell lifted Imogene onto Áepoo, then he hopped up behind her.

Otto, the bull-horse whom the priest rode, did not appear.

Etta roared at Émēr and pawed the ground. Émēr stared at his Mojí. "What does he mean, Mojí?"

Áepoo's gentle voice floated across the beach. "Come, Captain. We must leave now."

Émēr blindly hauled himself onto the beast's back. As the creatures charged over the field before gaining flight, Argus's laughter turned Émēr's blood to ice.

Forgiveness is soothing to the soul.
It keeps the Devil at bay.

-Saying from Brok,
Seer of The Maúl.

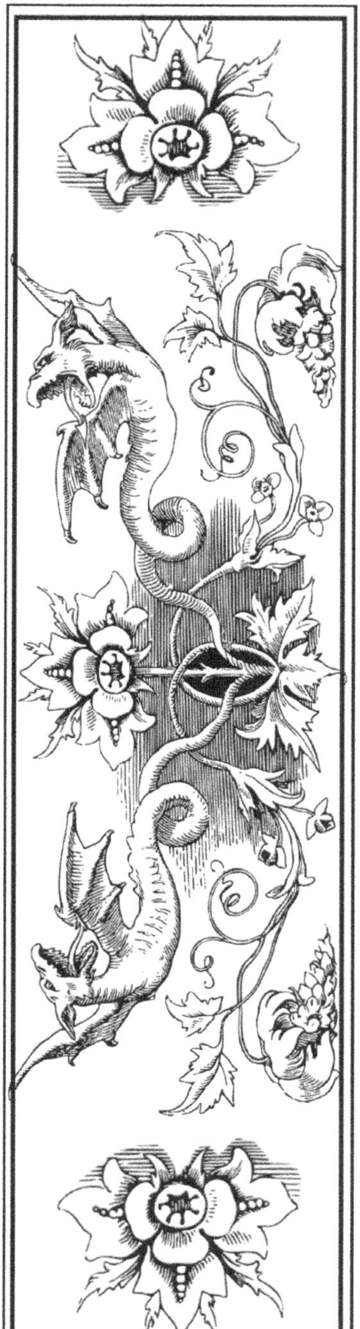

3

The wind whipped through Etta's mane as his great four wings beat a soft rhythm. The gentle cadence cocooned Émēr. The turmoil of the last few days wafted past his mind and a peace settled on his weary soul.

Émēr stared at his Mojí's back. What did Argus mean when he said it was his Mojí's fault? Surely this was the demon's trick to dissolve the group.

They were heading North into Ézású Territory and kept the Ceq Star to their backs.

"Émēr," came Conell's voice ahead of him. "We must land."

His Mojí's words broke through his questions. Yes, land, find answers. "Opize Temple is near the Opize

Mountains. Father trained me there for many years. It is hidden in the forest. No one will find us there."

His Mojí nodded. "Áepoo, take us to the Maúl Temple."

The group veered to the east and the dark blue, snow-laden peaks of Opize reflected in the moonlight. The large stone Opize Temple sat nestled against the mountain base. A lump formed in Émēr's throat, and he bit back the tears. The wind fingered his hair. "Oh God, give me grace. Help me to walk where Father walked. Help me enter those gates with honor."

The angels circled the area above the temple, then landed in the nearby field. Their hooves clomped on the dry ground until they came to a stop. Émēr sat on Etta and strained to listen. Again, his ears grew deaf to the distant sounds. His eyes scanned the black skies as he slid off his animal. "I do not see Argus."

Áepoo stretched his arms and cracked his neck. "No, Argus is a coward; he will not follow us."

Conell jumped from Áepoo's back and helped Imogene down. She lay her arm on Áepoo's back and nestled her face in the crook of her arm as tears slid down her face. "How can Cian be dead? Why is death so easy here?"

Áepoo placed his hand on her shoulder. "Do not grieve, child. The priest is happy now in the arms of the Attiyq. I myself carried him to the Great One."

She gave him a tiny smile, and Conell led her towards the temple.

Émēr blocked his Mojí's path. "Tell me Argus's words speak lies. Tell me they are not true."

Conell licked his lips. "Émēr, it was years ago…"

Émēr stepped back as if someone had thrown cold water in his face. "What did you do?"

Frigg wedged between them, facing Émēr. "Captain, it is late. Please, let us speak of this in the morning. I do not wish to meet the demon again tonight."

Émēr roughly shoved Frigg aside.

Conell placed his hand on Imogene's back and steered her into the temple.

Émēr took long steps to his Mojí. "Do not enter my temple! Turn your face to me now."

Conell stopped.

Fire burned in Émēr's belly. "Do not be a coward. Face me."

His Mojí faced him. The shadows hid Conell's features, but his frame looked like that of the King. Émēr looked away.

You will serve your King and Lord in valor and faith.

Conell paused as if picking his words with great care. "Émēr, I was only a child. Only seven years of age. I … made a mistake that haunts my dreams and my mind every day. I have not been able to escape its grip. Please, let us speak of this in the morning. Weariness is heavy upon us all. Thank you, Áepoo."

"We will need to leave later tonight," Áepoo said.

Conell reluctantly nodded.

Frigg took two flint stones and sparked a flame on an old torch hanging outside the temple doors.

With a seething glare, Émēr brushed past his Mojí and shoved open the massive wooden door. The creaking door slowly opened. The *Moodark Raan*, the Meeting Room.

Dust and spiderwebs covered the spacious *Moodark Raan*. The moonlight shone through the broken glass windows and danced with the floating dirt. A large black chandelier drooped like a spider from the rafters, its barren arms draped in cobwebs. Ghosts from Émēr's past emerged from the wood floor. His schoolmates raced past him and quickly found their seats on the long wooden benches that faced a mural of Anú bowing to a Bright Light—the Attiyq.

"And yet your faith is fading. How can you ever be like Anú?" The Dark asked.

His mind wandered to the past and a smile rested on his lips as happy memories washed over him. The first day of a new year. The soft chatter of the fathers and mothers who stood against the walls and gossiped over who would teach which classes and the students who failed the Elder's tests.

Émēr's gaze settled on the first bench to the right. His favorite seat. His young friends would turn and wave to him. Boys who were to grow into Maúl. Émēr lifted his hand to wave back, but then he saw his father. Father. Always keeping a watchful eye on his only son. Now gone. His smile disappeared, and his hand lowered. They were now specters who ruled the temple.

Frigg shined the torch light around the room. "Are there sleeping quarters here?"

Émēr nodded as the visions scampered away from him. "Yes, but not here. In the other building." Frigg turned to leave, but Émēr caught his arm. "What do you know of the Mojí's words?"

Frigg shrugged away from Émēr. "You forget, my father also died in the raid. I do not have the answers you seek. You and the Mojí are closer than I could ever be to either one of you. So why do you ask me? You are his confidant, not I."

Émēr stared at him. "What do you mean?"

He shrugged. "What does it matter? You saved him, not I."

Conell led Imogene into the chamber. The girl plopped into the sacred *Erkol's Chual*, the chair reserved for the eldest of the Elders, the bravest of men, and slung her weak arm over the back of the seat, burying her red, splotchy face in her elbow, still unable—or unwilling—to control her tears.

"Look how pathetic she is," whispered The Dark. *"The seat reserved for the brave has become a foxhole for the timid."*

"Captain," Conell said, unwittingly interrupting Émēr's conversation with the Dark. "Are there blankets here? It will be cold soon." He glanced at Émēr with compassionate and pleading eyes. "I promise, I will explain everything tomorrow."

Let it go, Émēr. He closed his eyes, but his anger gripped his throat. His head throbbed with each heartbeat.

"Do you really want to let it go?" The Dark asked from behind him. *"What about Maúl honor?"*

Émēr shivered as rage hurled the heretical words from his mouth. "No. We will speak of it now, My Mojí."

Conell raised his hands. "If you insist, but please, we must find blankets first."

With a curt nod, Émēr snatched Frigg's torch, using it to light a lantern hanging on the wall, then exited the meeting hall. A long, open, dirt pathway led to the dormitory located across from the *Moodavk Raan*. Émēr paused. The *Maúl Druk,* the great Maúl banner, had once hung in the open courtyard. Every child understood the flag of the Maúl, and every enemy quivered when the Maúl warriors raised the great banner in battle. Only the barren pole remained.

"Remember the Maúl Druk," came Father's voice from his memory.

Émēr smiled. "The blue background on the flag represents the Maúl heart, loyal and faithful to his God and his King. The Green thin strip means the Maúl despises monetary rewards. The red thin strip means we never refuse a challenge from a foe, and the yellow strip means the Maúl must care for widows, children, the ill, and the honor of all women." His grin grew larger. Even stinky girls.

A lump formed in Émēr's throat. "It includes all women, including an ill seer who is far from home." He closed his eyes and took a deep breath. "Jezebel may have destroyed all the Maúl flags, but I still have one in my heart." *The Maúl must be loyal to his God and his King.* "But does that include a traitorous King?"

Émēr stared up at the three-story eating and sleeping quarters. He smiled. He and his childhood friends, Dia, Grwn, Mostyn and Pari, all ten years of age, slept on the third floor. "Pari, you said we guarded the world from that third-floor window." Tears came to his eyes. "I am sorry I was not with you to hold off the enemy the night of the attack. Even in death, you still held your sword."

Sawyl, his cousin, slept on the second floor along with Father and the more advanced students. Émēr blinked away the image of Sawyl's headless body lying next to Father's corpse.

He entered the dark doorway to the sleeping quarters. He could still smell the scents of meat, breads, and vegetables cooking from the first-floor kitchen and the sounds of the children's utensils clicking on their plates. Once they finished their meals, the children would scamper to the training buildings.

Émēr placed his foot on the bottom step and looked up the dark stairway leading to their quarters. Ghosts of Dia, Grwy, Mostyn and Pari waved him up the stairs.

"Come on, Émēr!" said Dia. "We played a trick on Efan! Eggs in his shoes! He's been cruel to the younger children."

Pari stood tall. "Maúl protect the weak!"

"We will get in trouble," Émēr said.

"We take punishment with gladness!" Dia said.

The vision disappeared, and Émēr found himself standing in the dark, the torch light bouncing up the empty staircase.

He ran up the steps to the third level, quickly found blankets in a cupboard and shook out the bugs. Aine hated bugs, but she was not here to hate the crawling insects. He made his way back to the Meeting Hall.

Conell gave him a brief smile of gratitude and handed the blanket to the girl.

Imogene wrapped it around her shoulders. "I can't believe Cian is dead. I hate Argus! I wish he was the one who was dead!"

Conell sat next to her. "As do I, *Chuōbá*. But we must keep moving until the appointed time."

"But why did Cian die? Why couldn't he stay here with us? We need him."

He shook his head. "I do not have the answers you seek."

The Dark stared at Émēr. *"Why did he die? Is the Attiyq so weak He is unable to protect even His servants?"*

He swallowed. *I do not know.*

Frigg glanced at Émēr. "You were with him, what happened? Why did you not hear Argus's arrow?"

Émēr shrugged, struggling to repel the stab of guilt. "I do not know happened. We spoke, and then an arrow pierced his chest."

"But you are able to hear these silent things. How could you not hear?" Frigg faced the young captain.

Émēr crossed his arms over his chest. "Say what you mean, Frigg."

Frigg took a step to Émēr, but the captain stood his ground. "I mean that you were the last one to see the priest alive."

Émēr gestured with his hands. "So now it is my fault the priest is dead?" His gaze fell upon Imogene. "What of the girl? She no longer speaks for the Attiyq. And you, Mojí, what did Argus mean when he said you were responsible for my father's death?"

Imogene rose from her seat as the blanket drifted to the ground. "What do you mean I no longer speak for the Attiyq?"

Émēr turned to the girl. The fire burning inside him made his head feel numb. "You grow silent now. Before you babbled of your mother in New York and your friends and other nonsense. Now you grow quiet." He turned to his prince. "I demand answers from you."

Rage shrouded Conell's face. "All right, I will give you answers. I was only seven years old." As quickly as it surfaced, Conell's rage fell away. "I overheard two guards speaking of an ambush against my father. I was angry with him, and I did not share these words with him."

Frigg stared at him. "You refused to speak to the King about an attack? Why?"

"I was young and naïve. I thought my father could fight off an attack. And I was angry at him about something, I do not remember what."

The words hit Émēr like a fist to his stomach. "My clan and father are dead because you were angry with the King?"

Conell lifted his hands as if to beg for forgiveness. "Émēr, I did not tell you because I feared losing you. You are as a brother to me. I have carried this secret with me for ten years and it has tormented me."

Wrath gurgled in Émēr's chest, and his heart pounded. "Tormented you? My father, my friends, my family, dead. And you are the tormented one?"

"My Captain," Conell said. "I have kept myself alive to one day escape with you and Frigg, to give you my last gift."

"Gift?" Émēr's eyebrows rose. *Walk away, Émēr. Conell was only a frightened child who knew no better.* But a burning force spurred him on.

"*I* kept you alive. What other secrets have you kept from my eyes? What other shadows do you possess?"

Conell shook his head. "I have no other shadows."

The captain stared at his Mojí. His prince had betrayed him. He blinked several times. "You betrayed me."

A deep pain lay in his Mojí's green eyes, and his voice was soft and broken. "I did not betray you, Captain."

"What word would you give it?"

Imogene cocked her pretty blond head. Her hair had grown out to her shoulders, framing her angry, bruised face. "How about a mistake?"

"No one has asked you, Seer."

Imogene scoffed. "Oh, you are such a piece of work, Émēr. Mr. High and Mighty who does no wrong."

"Maybe you should speak the words of the Attiyq, or have you forgotten Him already? Is it Argus you now see?"

Imogene's eyes grew wide. "What?"

"Enough, captain," Conell growled.

"What other secrets do you keep from me, Mojí?" Émēr asked.

"I have no other secrets." Conell led Imogene to a nearby bench.

She marched back to Émēr. "What. Did. You. Mean."

Émēr raised his eyebrows. The meek rabbit was turning into a fierce tiger. "I mean that you are now silent after your meeting with Argus. Do you now long for his embrace?"

Her shocked face turned red. She slapped his cheek. He tottered and his hand dropped to his war hammer hanging from his belt. Father's *Atobod*, designed to destroy the enemies of God, not ill women.

Rage shone in Imogene's eyes. "You Monster! How dare you! He almost raped me, and you accuse me of wanting it?" Tears sparkled on her eyelashes. "Every night I hear his voice, every time a twig snaps, I think it's him." Her lips trembled. "I see him everywhere I go. I can still *smell* him."

Émēr's hand caressed the wooden shaft of the Atobo. "Drop all of this feigned innocence. Hear from the Attiyq!"

You shall respect all weakness and establish yourself the defender of them.

A useless seer!

The yellow line represents the Maúl's duty to protect the weak and the ill.

Imogene raised her palms and her voice cracked. "You don't think I've tried? I can't get him out of my head."

The pain in the girl's soft brown eyes burned Émēr's heart, but anger gobbled up his budding compassion and left him cold inside.

Conell stepped between them. "Get some air, Captain. That is an order!"

Émēr's breath came in deep gasps. "Do not fight me, Mojí, you will not win."

Conell pointed to the door. "Go outside, now."

"You side with a seer with a sick mind, and you abandon my sister and mother."

Frigg tugged on Émēr's arm. "Come, Captain, you need to calm yourself. I do not think this is how you should act."

"I will help you find the weapons and find my family, but that is the extent of my loyalty to you." Émēr stormed out of the temple.

The cold night air did little to calm Émēr's ravaged heart. A voice inside him asked, *Why do you speak this way? The girl is ill. Your Mojí was a child. Why do you grow angry over such innocence?*

Áepoo stomped on the packed soil, and his strong voice sliced the night air. "Captain, have you believed the lies of the enemy? The Attiyq has not abandoned you nor can He. His covenant with you is strong, and He is faithful to follow it. If you do not fulfill your purpose, then evil will prevail in this land. Others are depending upon you to take your place in the Attiyq."

Émēr kicked a small stone. "Angel, you do not understand. All these years, I have blamed the Upeshi for Father's death. Revenge kept me warm each night. And now I discover the one whom I was to protect is now the betrayer." He glared at Áepoo. "One word.

That is all it took was one word from the Mojí and my father and clan and friends would be alive." He spread his arms. "Look around you, Angel. What do you see? Death! That is what you see. How can you say the Attiyq is for me when I find out *My Mojí* betrayed *me*? Where was God to intervene on that night? Where were *you*?" Émēr rubbed the stone around his neck. "How am I to become Maúl? What is to happen to the remnant of my family? You claim to have power over Argus, yet here we stand, running from him in fear."

Áepoo remained silent as he stared at Émēr before he galloped, spread his wings, and soared into the sky. The other beasts met him, and they flew V-shaped into the moonlight.

Émēr watched them sail into the night sky. He lowered his gaze as shame and loneliness shrouded his heart.

You are priest now.

"What if I do not wish to be priest? All I have now is a traitorous prince, an ill girl, and a weak Frigg who cares more for riches than honor. What if I want nothing more of this?" The words shocked Émēr as they rolled off his tongue.

His feet led him around the grounds of the temple. Memories of clinking weapons and laughing voices lingered in the empty compound. Visions of Dia, Grwy, Mostyn and Pari raced past him.

"Come, Émēr," Pari waved at him. "We learn more of swords today!" Émēr ran with the boys to the combat building, only to watch them fade into the darkness moments later.

On the cold morning of the Maúl funerals, young Émēr dammed his tears inside of him as the boys' widowed mothers tossed flowers into their sons' tiny coffins, their soft weeping drifting across the fields.

Grandfather stood beside him as he, too, tossed flowers on the small wooden boxes. "Maúl keep their tears within them. Anú never wept, so we must never weep."

His friends would laugh if they saw Émēr weeping. To honor them, he took deep breaths and focused on the daisies and wildflowers scattered over their small caskets.

Now the silent compound crushed his eardrums, and Émēr covered his face with his hand as the tears ran down his face. *The*

Maúl-child hid with a traitorous prince while his brothers-in-
dropped to the ground and pounded on the packed

"Why?" he whispered. "Why did I survive to l
The tears escaped the locked box that he had created yea
flowed freely down his cheeks. Giving in to his emotions for only a moment, he took three deep breaths and wiped his face with his sleeve. Father would rather see him strong and Maúl than weeping as a child.

He strode to the entrance of the temple. A large wooden frame covered the walkway leading from the road to the compound. Beams crisscrossed the top of the boardwalk. The older students claimed ghosts lived in the crossbeams.

He grinned. "Do you remember, Father? I was only five years of age when you and I crossed this bridge for the first time." He trailed his fingers over the wooden railing and glanced up at the "ghosts" playing on the rafters above. "The boys would drop eggs from up there." His voice cracked. "I dodged the eggs then begged you to let me do it again." He paused, recalling the pleasure he had seen in Father's eyes. A tear slid down his cheek. "It was the first time you said you were proud of me." He leaned back against the rail and ran his hand through his hair. "Father, I have no idea what to do now. "I do not know if I believe in all of this anymore."

Émēr strolled to The Great Yuey Tower, the massive five story wooden pylon that loomed above the compound. A doorway opened to a winding, stone stairwell. He followed the stairs up and around. The children would scramble up the stairs, racing each other to the top. He paused, struggling to remember the prize for winning. "Honor. We won honor." His fingertips lingered on the plank walls adorned with tiny, dirty fingerprints.

The top floor opened into the battle room where the Maúl kept their battle plans and lessons for the children. He stepped into the large chamber. The ten long benches that crossed in front of him faced a large desk for the warrior-teacher. A cold, moaning draft squeezed through the cracks in the windowpane. He shivered. It always sounded like the spirits of the dead pleading to come in for a last dinner or a smile or just to sit by the fire and chat. They would tap at the glass plane until the sun rose and chased them back to their graves.

A large wooden cabinet stood next to the teaching desk. He chuckled. "Fancy items weigh down a man's soul."

He opened the cabinet doors. Of course, the shelves were empty.

Eleven-year-old Émēr had stood beside the Witch-Queen as she tossed the sacred scrolls out the window.

"I hope you remember, young man, that the Maúl are evil, cursed by God. He never intended any of this to be. Your father and his fathers were sinners, doomed to hell."

"I will not abandon the Attiyq or the ways of the Maúl," young Émēr had said, staring straight ahead, his back tall and straight.

"Guards, teach him a lesson."

Émēr stared at the empty shelves. "The Attiyq gave Anú the very words to save our souls." He shut the doors. "That was so long ago." He leaned his back against the cabinet and rubbed his face.

The guards broke Émēr's ribs and his arm and still he was defiant. He gazed at the ceiling. "Why is it so hard now? Why do I question the one for whom I fought?"

He sat at the old desk and traced the grooves in the wood. He moved his hands apart as if unrolling Father's scrolls. Father's deep voice would boom across the room as he described each move. Émēr moved his fingers across the imaginary scroll as he followed each illustration. Father always said, "Practice will make your feet fast and your hands fly. The Attiyq blesses those who seek His face day and night. He perfects those who pursue Him."

Outside, the floorboards would creak, and child-like whispers slipped through the door cracks. Father glanced at the door and would raise his voice so the children in the hall would hear him. Fathers gave special lessons to their children, but Émēr's father believed that all children deserved to learn.

A smile broke out across Émēr's face. Father would place a finger over his lips. Another secret between them. The other Maúl warriors would frown upon such actions.

Émēr massaged his temples to sooth his headache. Imogene was ill and deserved his respect, not his insults. He rubbed his stinging cheek. At least she had a mighty arm.

A deep yawn escaped him, and he laid his head in the crook of his elbow. The distant sound of clinking weapons and father's deep voice filled his memories. They comforted him like mother's songs. His eyes grew heavy and soon sleep overcame him.

A sharp object poked at Émēr's throat. He moaned and shifted his weight. His back hurt, and his face throbbed. Again, the object poked at his neck. He opened his eyes.

A thin man with long shaggy hair stood over him. His sword point pressed against Émēr's throat. The man grinned.

Deception can sometimes stand in front of us. Will you not see it?

- Anú

9

Emēr raised his hand against the sunlight streaming through the window and stared at the dirty man. Again, he had heard nothing. He cursed himself as he slowly raised his head. The man pulled the *Atobo* from Émēr's belt.

"I mean no harm," Émēr said.

The man gestured with his sword for Émēr to rise.

Émēr stood up and raised his hands.

"Who are you, and why have you invaded my temple?" the man asked.

My temple? This man could not possibly be Maúl. His face showed no markings, at least from what Émēr could see of it under the shaggy brown hair that fell to his dark eyes. Nor did he carry and clothe himself as a Maúl. His light brown shirt hung loosely on his lanky frame, and his brown trousers were stained and full of holes. Surely the man must be a highwayman.

The vagabond slipped his sword under Émēr's chin. "I would hate to spill your blood here."

"I am," Émēr began, pausing to consider whether or not to give the man his name or simply state what the man should already know if he was a real Maúl. Émēr would never be mistaken for a robber. "I am Maúl. This is the temple I was raised in as a child."

The thin, dirty man laughed. "A Maúl warrior? Now you jest. I know my Maúl brothers, and you are not one of them," he smirked as he pushed the tip of his sword against Émēr's throat.

Émēr narrowed his eyes. Killing the stranger would be easy. But what of Imogene, Frigg and his Mojí? He blinked. Maúl Brothers? How could this dirty beast claim to be Maúl?

The strange man stepped aside and waved his sword towards the door. "Let's go."

Émēr eased past him and made his way down the staircase and out the door. He shielded his eyes as the sunshine revealed the decay of the once Great Temple. Some of the tiles had fallen from the rooftop, and weeds covered the once pristine courtyard. The old well that had been their water supply now sat dry, and rust covered the bucket wheel. Pain stabbed Émēr's heart. Time had not been kind to his old home.

The man chuckled and used his sword hilt to shove Émēr forward. "Is this place new to you, 'Maúl'? I thought you were raised here," he taunted.

Émēr traipsed across the empty compound to the Meeting Room. The instant he opened the door, Émēr's heart jumped into his throat. A fat brigand with an ugly face stood over Imogene, his sword pressing against her pale throat. His large belly stretched out his filthy shirt and spilled over his dirty, brown pants.

Imogene's words tumbled from her trembling lips. "I don't know!"

The filthy creature traced his chubby finger along her jaw. "Now, you are a pretty girl. I would hate to mar that lovely face. Tell me what I want to know. Who paid you to invade this temple?"

"No one!" She jerked away from him, but he yanked her back.

Émēr quickly made his way to the man. "Let her be!"

The rogue stood and lifted his sword.

Émēr stared at the weapon then shifted his gaze to Imogene. She tried to stand, but the man forced her down.

Émēr brushed past the man unhindered and knelt beside Imogene, his eyes scanning her face and arms. "Have they harmed you?"

"No." The hurt from the last words Émēr had spoken to her still darkened her brown eyes. "Where have you been?"

"I am sorry I was not here. Where are the others?"

"Outside." She bit her lip and glanced up at the smirking guard.

"It will be all right." Émēr forced a smile. "The words I spoke last night did not come from my heart. Please, forgive me."

Her face softened. "I'm sorry I hit you."

He grinned and rubbed his jaw. "You have a strong arm, My Lady."

She smiled.

Evidently tiring of the scene, the thin man who had escorted Émēr to the Meeting Room yanked Émēr to his feet and slammed his fist into his stomach. Émēr dropped to the ground, gasping for breath.

Imogene wrapped her arms around him. "Émēr, are you alright?"

When she tried to stand, Émēr pulled her down as he pushed the words from his throat. "Stay down."

"Take deep breaths. In and out. That's good," Imogene replied, her nurturing side coming to life in the midst of violence.

Émēr breathed deeply until his stomach calmed, then he faced the thin stranger.

The slender man grinned. "I do not give you permission to speak, *Cho*. Fergus, this intruder claims to be Maúl."

"A Maúl?" Fergus raised his double chin and extended his

flabby arms. "I am Maúl and this is my temple."

Émēr stretched to his full height. "The real Maúl are dead. As you both look to be around my age, if you have any Maúl blood at all, you must have been a child who survived the massacre. Or a *zuesoque*." The Maúl word surprised Émēr. He had not used the Warrior Tongue for ten years, yet the words came quickly to him.

The Dark clicked his tongue. *"But are you still Maúl?"*

He forced the thought aside. The Dark chuckled.

"What?" Fergus' black eyes bore into Émēr's.

Émēr glanced at Imogene's pale face staring up at him. He lifted his gaze to Fergus. "If you are Maúl, then why do you not know the Maúl language? I said you are either a child who survived the massacre or a child who plays pretend."

Fergus swung his large fist.

Émēr blocked the punch with his forearm, twisted his arm over Fergus' bicep, ramming his face into the ground. Émēr pressed his hand against the guard's neck and raised his locked arm. "I will break your neck with great joy."

Fergus clenched his teeth and moaned.

"Let him go, or I will spill her blood." The thin, dirty man pressed his sword to Imogene's neck.

She whimpered and Émēr released him. "Ah, is that Maúl honor? Threatening an innocent girl because you are too afraid to fight me?"

Fergus climbed to his feet. "You will not call me false again or Llyr will kill the girl."

Émēr snickered. "A man who pretends to be Maúl yet sheds innocent blood. I am sure Anú is quite pleased."

"Enough, Fergus!" said a voice behind them.

Émēr turned to see a fit dark-haired man standing in the doorway. This one too was around his age. He frowned. Were these truly the surviving children of the Maúl? The man's chiseled face bore none of Anú's markings. All Maúl had their victories laid out in the patterns. To live without them showed a coward who hid under the beds.

The young man waved down Llyr's sword. "Let the girl go."

Llyr stepped away from Imogene and the man entered the room. *"Eeshooby jovue eesoxt qaeque ottght teashght."*

Émēr again raised his eyebrows. *May your sword find its mark*. The traditional Maúl greeting given to equals. "*Eeshooby a Attiyq ochochuque jext ilstrsh*." May the Attiyq's angels guard you. He bowed. How was it that this false Maúl knew the ancient words? He helped Imogene to her feet and gave her an encouraging smile before placing himself between the men and her. "I thought the Maúl were gone forever."

The man gave Émēr a cold smile. "I am called Māhōn, the leader of this tribe. The markings on your face show you are Maúl of the Old Order. We have heard rumors that one survived the attack but was later killed by the Queen."

"I am Émēr Amgets, son of Cadoc Ailill Amgets. I am the one of whom you speak. I escaped the Queen's clutches, but the Queen does not abandon her pursuit. We seek sanctuary in Anú's temple."

"Those with you, who are they?"

"They are my cousins."

Māhōn extended his hand towards the door. "Please, I wish for you to join them." His smile advanced no further than his lips.

Émēr glanced over his shoulder to Imogene who stood trembling with her arms wrapped around her small chest. He looked back at Māhōn. "Let her go, her mind is ill," he said in the Maúl language.

Again, Māhōn gestured to the door.

Émēr hesitated only a moment before he led Imogene outside.

She tucked her fingers under his arm. "What's happening?"

"You are safe, my sister," Émēr whispered.

She gave him her funny look. "What?"

He winked at her.

"Oh." She nodded and winked back.

Mojí and Frigg sat under a tree guarded by five more men. That brought the number of supposed Maúl warriors to eight, none of whom had the markings of Anú on their faces. Yet, these five were different. Unlike Llyr and Fergus, these warriors had trim, muscular bodies and carried swords and mallets. Émēr frowned. Surely Llyr and Fergus could not be Maúl. But these men?

Conell helped Imogene sit. His sharp eyes searched her face. "Are you alright?"

She nodded. "They just asked me questions."

Conell glared at Émēr. "I am pleased you decided to join us."

Émēr avoided his friend's gaze and sat next to him. "I am sorry. I needed time to think."

"Forgive us, my brother," Māhōn said to Émēr. "Are these your cousins?"

He nodded. "Yes, this is," he paused. "Cahal."

Conell caught his gaze and nodded.

"The other man is Pol," Émēr said. "And the young lady is Aiden."

Māhōn bowed. "Forgive me, friends, I did not know you were friends of the Maúl."

Conell stood and bowed. "There is nothing to forgive. Our actions would have been the same."

Frigg helped Imogene to her feet.

Māhōn eyes roamed over the girl and he smiled. "You are very lovely, Aiden. But the bruises on your face…"

She looked to Émēr and Conell for an answer. "Well, um, I …"

Émēr slipped his arm in front of her. "She is also my sister. If you wish to speak to her, then you must address me first."

The young man's eyebrows slowly rose. "Your sister? Forgive me, brother." A strange grin lingered on Māhōn's thin lips. "Then you are now my sister as well. You will be safe here."

A shiver raced down Émēr's spine and he stepped in front of Imogene.

Ignoring Émēr's defensive posture, Māhōn motioned to the kitchen. "Come inside and enjoy a meal with us, brother."

Émēr gave a quick nod to his Mojí and darted his gaze to the girl. Conell pulled her back as Émēr led the group to the kitchen hall.

Émēr kept pace with Māhōn. "There are no markings on your face."

Māhōn nodded. "We try to blend in with others. The markings give us away. We have abandoned many of the old Maúl ways in order to survive."

"But Anú's words state that a man puts his faith in the Attiyq in the face of danger. That is why the elders ordered us to wear them. One must die in the Faith and for the Faith."

"But will you die for the Faith?" The Dark asked.

They entered the old dining hall. The long tables and benches that the children occupied years ago still stood vertically across the room. The group sat at one of the tables and Fergus slammed plates in front of them. He plopped a basket of bread, cheese and hard-boiled eggs, and a bowl of dark yellow sauce in the center of the table. Before walking away, he glared at Émēr. Émēr nodded to him. Fergus growled and stomped from the room.

Māhōn sat at the head of the table, the place reserved for the senior elder even if the elder was not present. Émēr suppressed a disgusted sigh and took some bread, overlooking Māhōn's obvious insult.

Māhōn watched Fergus stomp from the dining hall then turned to his guests. "Excuse me, my friends."

As Māhōn rushed after the large man, Émēr leaned towards Conell. "Mojí, I am not sure these men are Maúl. I believe they could be bandits or rebels. They do not speak or act like Maúl, but like regular men. Maúl are taught not to pound the grass and rocks as they walk. We are taught to be ghosts. This man's hand never rests upon his sword; his eyes do not search for the enemy. He stomps on the ground like a lord in the castle. They are sloppy. Do not trust them until I know for sure."

Conell nodded. "But as he said, they must blend in."

"Maúl do blend in, yet we are always separate from others. It is a rule, a trait. Māhōn does not follow Anú's teachings," Émēr said.

Māhōn returned and took his seat. "Please forgive Fergus' rude behavior. I have spoken to him about it; he will not trouble you again."

Émēr glanced at the empty doorway. "Thank you, my brother, I am grateful to you. I ask that he and your men respect my sister's honor."

"Of course." Māhōn gave him a cool grin. "We will not speak to her unless we have your permission."

A slight chill slithered down Émēr's back and he held Māhōn's gaze for a second, before Māhōn looked away to the courtyard.

Émēr pulled a hunk of bread, an egg, and some cheese from the basket and gave them to the girl. Her lips pursed, and a frown covered her small face. She snatched the food and shot him a glare from the corner of her eye. He suppressed his grin. His words of permission did not sit well on her heart. He would pay for this later.

As the ranking Maúl elder at the table, Émēr assumed the honor of being the first to dip the bread into the sauce, but Māhōn slipped his bread into the sauce before Émēr.

Émēr raised an eyebrow. Māhōn's cold eyes stared into Émēr's as Māhōn's bread plunged into the dip.

"I did not think we were prisoners, brother. Is it necessary to keep us under guard? We only seek sanctuary." Émēr dipped the bread into the sauce.

Māhōn popped the bread into his mouth. "You are not prisoners; you are free to go anywhere in the temple. I have not yet decided where you stand—by the witch's side or the side of the Maúl."

Émēr frowned. "We do not stand by the witch's side, but by King Brodén. I want the witch and her demon lover dead. She held me in her prison, but I escaped. Now I wish to take my sister and my cousins to the coast and across the seas. As far from the witch's presence as possible."

Māhōn leaned back in his chair and rubbed his chin. His dark eyes narrowed. "How do I know you will not bring the witch here? She has already destroyed the scrolls and the Maúl weapons."

Growing weary of the pretender, Émēr asked in the Maúl language, "Who was your *Gaevee*?"

Māhōn only stared at Émēr.

Émēr kept his eyes locked on Māhōn. "Mine was my father.

Yours must have been your grandmother. You are slow and inept. A fool," he said in the Maúl tongue. He shoved a piece of bread into his mouth.

Conell coughed, muffling a snicker.

Émēr cocked his head at Māhōn. "You do not understand what I said, do you?"

The corner of Māhōn's mouth twitched. "You asked who my *Gaevee* was. Then you accused my grandmother of teaching me."

Émēr's smirk slowly faded. "Forgive me. You know my language."

"I am not the fool you take me for."

Émēr leaned his elbows on the table and placed his fists under his chin. "How did you survive the attack? And how did you outmaneuver the Queen's hunting parties?"

"We blended in with the people of other small villages, kept away from the temples. How did you survive?"

Émēr gave a sharp look to his Mojí. It never occurred to him that anyone would ask how he survived. "I was to protect the prince. I followed my father's orders. We parted ways some time ago after we escaped the Queen's hand. I longed to protect what was left of my clan as I am now head of my family. Pol, Cahal, and Aiden are all that is left of them. I only seek to protect them. The prince has gone across the seas."

Frigg took a sip from his water glass. "Yes. My cousin traveled far in order to save us from the Queen's hunting parties."

Māhōn slowly chewed his bread as his dark eyes studied them. "Ah."

"So, Māhōn," Conell said, "How long have you and your clan lived in the temple?"

Māhōn shrugged and picked up his water goblet. "A few years. We found it on a hunting excursion. My clan and I decided to reclaim it."

"Where are the women and children?" Imogene asked.

Émēr gave her a long look, indicating that she needed to keep quiet.

Conell placed his hand on her arm and gave her a similar look before he addressed Māhōn. "What she means is, if this is a clan shouldn't there be women and children in the temple?"

"We left them behind in our village, to protect them. It is interesting that your sister speaks while you demand that none speak to her." Māhōn stared at her over the rim of his glass. "Why is that?"

Imogene squirmed in her seat.

"My sister is not well," Émēr said. "Her mind is ill and weak. She forgets things at times."

Māhōn stabbed at a piece of cheese with his knife and brought the food to his mouth. "Ah. That is a shame."

Conell brushed the crumbs from his hands. "We have taken enough of your hospitality; we must be moving on."

Māhōn dabbed his mouth with a napkin. "Moving on? I insist you stay. Our brother has come home, and we must celebrate." He leaned towards Émēr and smiled. "Brother, we have scrolls. We wish for you to examine them."

Émēr glanced at Conell, then back to Māhōn. "Scrolls?"

Māhōn grinned. "Yes, brother, scrolls the queen did not know of. We have kept them hidden for these long years. Come and see." When Émēr balked, Māhōn raised his hands in acquiescence. "I see you are conflicted. I will give you time to decide. If you choose to stay and become my true brother, then we will rejoice and read the scrolls together. If you choose to go, then go." He stood, bowed, and left the room.

Émēr watched him disappear through the door. His eyes turned to his Mojí. "What do you wish to do?"

Conell leaned back in his chair and shrugged. "I do not trust these men."

Émēr stared at the empty doorway. "I agree. It is as if I see a shadow of a man, but once the lights appear, it is only a rack. But still…" He turned back to Conell. "If some of my clan did survive, then I must find out."

Frigg covered the leftover food with his napkin. "We could use their help. More Maúl could help us defeat the witch."

Imogene brushed the crumbs from her dress. "Not to mention they could help us find your mom and sister. But on the other hand, they might not be your people. I hope they are though. But, man, Māhōn is creepy. And what was the bread thing about?"

"The elder at the table takes the first dip of the sauce," Émēr said. "Māhōn made it clear he does not see me as the elder."

Conell nodded. "Imogene's words ring true. They might not be your people."

Émēr turned to Imogene, "What have you heard from the Attiyq?"

She shrugged. "I don't know. I had a dream about Cian last night if that helps. He was happy." A smile remained on her lips.

Émēr swallowed his impatience. How could a dead, smiling priest give him any wisdom? But the feel of his hand lingering on his war axe still sat in his mind. She was ill, and he swore to protect her. "Yes, that is nice."

Frigg nodded towards her. "The girl needs time to heal. Let us stay for a while and rest."

Conell looked to Émēr. "I will leave it to you."

Émēr nodded. "I wish to stay."

Imogene dropped her fists on the table. "Great! That's settled. But I have a question. Émēr, I need *your* permission to talk to anyone *here*?" She made a circling gesture over the table with her finger. "Really?" She cocked her pretty head.

Conell chuckled. "Now she has you in a net, My Captain. How does it feel?"

He gave his Mojí an annoyed look.

Frigg snorted.

Émēr picked his words carefully. "Well, Aiden?"

Imogene placed her chin on the back of her fingers and lifted her eyebrows.

"I am the head of my clan," he continued.

She pursed her lips and nodded.

"And I do have the right to tell those whom I think will harm you to stay away from you …"

Conell snickered.

Frigg laughed and shook his head.

"Yes. Go on." Imogene fluttered her eye lashes.

Conell laughed. "*Chuōhá*, do not torture my captain. Please for your own safety, do as he says."

Émēr touched her bruised cheek. "I do not wish to see more of these on such a lovely face. Please, until I know if these men are of my clan, please, stay away from them."

She dropped her arm and rolled her eyes. "Fine whatever. I will. It's not like I even want to talk to those creeps anyway. Still, it's the principle of the thing."

Émēr and Conell exchanged an amused look. A pain stabbed Émēr's heart. Was it worth tossing aside Mojí's hands because of one mistake? The black words crept again into his heart. *Your Mojí betrayed you.* He took a deep breath and shoved the words aside.

Māhōn returned to the dining hall and handed Émēr a scroll. "You question my Maúl blood. Perhaps this will prove my heritage."

Émēr spread the scroll on the table. Frigg moved the basket, and Imogene held down the scroll's corners.

Written on the thick paper were pictures of men holding swords. Maúl words were scribbled under the pictures. Émēr gasped. A Maúl teaching scroll. He dragged his gaze to Māhōn. "How?"

Māhōn grinned. "I hid this from the Queen. It is what I use to teach my Maúl warriors. I have a few others if you wish to see them."

Émēr's face broke into a wide smile. "I would love to see them."

Conell gave his captain a long look that said be careful.

Émēr nodded and rose from the table.

Imogene grabbed his arm. "Where are you going?"

"I need to see these scrolls." He touched her face. "I will return. Stay with Cahal."

Conell tapped her arm, and she released him.

Émēr followed Māhōn into the training center. Five old scrolls sat on the table. He gently unrolled the nearest one, his gaze absorbed in the hand-drawn figures. As with the previous scroll, drawings of offensive and defensive maneuvers covered the old paper.

"You saved all of these?"

Māhōn grinned and nodded. "Yes. These belonged to my father. I could not leave them in the hands of the witch."

Émēr's calloused finger passed over each figure, and he read every word several times. He frowned. Something was missing. He read the scroll again, word by word. Still, something was wrong. "Wait." He tapped the paper. "These scrolls. Something is missing."

Māhōn raised his eyebrows. "These are the scrolls my father used."

"I do not see Anú's fingers on them."

"His fingers?"

Émēr's sharp eyes bore into Māhōn. "Every Maúl knows of Anú's fingers. It is where the author incorporates the Attiyq's words, comparing the move to the Great One."

Māhōn nodded. "Yes, Anú's fingers. My father survived the massacre at the castle. He was the only one, besides you. He wrote these after the attack. He saw no need to add 'Anú's fingers' to his scrolls. He was wounded and near unto death. He quickly wrote these for me."

Émēr studied Māhōn's face. He could be lying, yet he could be telling the truth. No one was sure if any Maúl survived that evening. Émēr ran his gaze over the scroll. They seemed to be recent—maybe ten years old. And if the man was wounded, then he would not have time to compare the moves to the Attiyq. What if Māhōn and his men were the last of the Maúl? What if he could show Émēr the teachings he needed to move to the next level? "I understand," he finally replied and Māhōn's returning smile gave him no assurance.

Girl twisted her fingers as she stood in her lord's chambers, her heart beating as a rabbit caught in a trap. Lord Argus knew of her treachery. She saw it in the way his feather's tightened when she entered a room. When he coolly brushed past her in the halls. And he no longer summoned her to his chambers in the evening. The silence grew heavier by the day and surpassed his fists in driving fear into her heart. She bit her lips to stop the tears. Her master's fists taught her years ago to never display her weeping.

Lord Argus studied himself in the full-length mirror. His gaze switched to her reflection. She swallowed. He looked over his shoulder at her, but his reflection remained the same, facing him, facing her. Her stomach lurched.

A young man with long silver hair stepped into the image and nuzzled her master's neck. The image of Lord Argus reflected in the mirror leaned his head to the left and caressed the young man's face while the material form of Lord Argus stared at her over his shoulder.

His reflection and the strange man watched her. Her gaze searched the room, but only Lord Argus and she remained in the chamber. The images smirked at her.

The dread in her stomach swarmed over her and washed away her courage. Her chest rose and fell in deep gasps. The young man took long steps to stand behind her reflection in the mirror. She whirled, but no one stood there. She turned back to the image. The man slipped his hands around her image's throat.

Girl screamed and lunged for the open door to the chamber. The door slammed. Girl pounded on the wood and struggled to turn the doorknob. A chair slid past her and wedged itself against the handle, and the shutters banged over the windows.

Shutting out the light.

Locking her in.

She whirled back to the mirror. Lord Argus studied his reflection; the young man had disappeared. Girl's stomach flip-flopped and she collapsed to the floor. Her eyes locked on the mirror as she struggled to breathe.

Lord Argus turned to her. "Is something wrong?"

The cold air that oppressed the room wrapped around her throat like icy, gnarled fingers. She squealed, racing her hands over her neck and torso to dislodge the invisible foe. All the candle wicks in the room burst into small flames. Soft light nipping at the darkness. And the darkness fought back.

The rats!

Girl bit her quivering lip. Her gaze dropped to the floor, and a sob escaped.

Her trembling hand searched for the letter she had written to Father, tucked away safely in her pocket. A letter he would never read. But it was there, with her. Hidden. Maybe Father would find it one day and know she loved him. And forgave him.

She crawled to the wall and pressed her back against it. If only it would whisk her away to the Attiyq. Forever free.

The Attiyq. Girl forced herself to breathe in spite of the scene before her. While the Attiyq's presence filled her heart, soul, and mind, it was Lord Argus's large frame that dominated the room. A foul chill penetrated Girl's bones and made her shiver. Darkness hovered in the corners. Light peeked through the shutters, then scurried away, leaving waltzing shadows to frolick on the walls.

Lord Argus turned back to the mirror, and the reflection wavered into a young man with designs on his face studying scrolls. Girl looked away. The Maúl who had sneaked into the castle and freed Imogene.

"Do you recognize him, Girl?" Lord Argus growled.

Girl closed her eyes and nodded.

Lord Argus sneered. "Poor Girl. If only you had cried out to him. You do know he would have saved you. This one is noble. The last of Anú." He shook his head and clicked his tongue. "Oh well."

The young man who stood behind her reflection stepped beside the Maúl. Lord Argus's fingers traced the silver-haired man's face in the mirror. "Girl, this is Amhras, my son. Is he not handsome?"

When she did not answer, he turned to her and narrowed his eyes.

She nodded quickly.

Lord Argus grinned. "He is not for you, though. Amhras, make me proud."

Amhras smiled at his father and smirked at Girl. A black image extended its hand from the Maúl's chest and held Amhras' fingers.

Amhras kissed The Dark's hand. The Dark stepped from the Maúl and whispered in his ear, *"You are abandoned. Stay with Māhōn. Learn from him. He is your only hope. You cannot be Maúl without these scrolls."* The heaviness in Girl's heart lightened when the Maúl turned away as if he would reject the lies, but The Dark recaptured his attention. *"Your Mojí betrayed you."*

The Maúl's face tightened as the words slipped into his ears and through his body. Lord Argus traced his finger over the Maúl's body. The young man shivered, and the blackness increased.

A female angel with long blond hair stepped behind the Maúl and stood on her toes to whisper her own words into the Maúl's ear. Amhras screamed and dove into the ground. The Dark scurried back into the Maúl. The blackness in the Maúl's eyes turned back to gray. Lord Argus recoiled his finger as Girl raised her head and gasped.

The angel cocooned the Maúl with her long white wings. She raised her blue eyes to Argus. The same eyes that held the wrath of the Attiyq, now bore down on him. Argus snarled. The woman sneered at him and slowly pointed her finger at him. He cursed her; she laughed at him. Argus slammed his fist into the wooden frame.

"An angel," Girl whispered.

Argus's eyes slowly turned to Girl. His footsteps thundered on the wooden floor. Dark red eyes glared from his pale, revolting face.

The stones from the wall pricked her back. Her heart beat faster. Focus on the floor, not at him. She should have gone with the Maúl.

He yanked her to her feet and slapped her. Her body crashed to the floor, and white spots danced before her.

The Dark that spoke to the Maúl was now in the room. The black blob lay beside her. A toothy grin covered its skinless face and its orbless eye sockets stared at her. Its cold, spindly finger raked her cheek. She squeezed her eyes closed.

Argus grabbed her by the front of her dress and jerked her face close to his. "Where is your angel, Girl?"

His foul, hot breath pricked her eyes. Finally, her tears betrayed her.

Argus dragged her to the mirror and slammed her face into the

Maúl's reflection. "Look at him! The one you tried to help now belongs to me. Just as you belong to me."

Girl kept her eyes closed. Her wet cheek crushed against the glass. A sob escaped her. Argus cast her away. She landed on the stone floor, her breath ripped from her lungs. Pain sparked in her head and raced down her back.

The Dark leaned over her and cocked its skull head.

Argus's footsteps stormed towards her huddled form.

She scooted back against the stone wall.

The angel in the mirror cocooned the Maúl. Her eyes locked on Girl and gave her a soft, reassuring smile. The angel's gentle words drifted across the room. *It will be alright. The Attiyq is here. Let Him fight for you.*

Argus stepped in front of Girl who cowered but raised her eyes. His black-red orbs glowed. The light from the shutters fled from the room. The candles flickered and extinguished.

The Dark enveloped Argus and sang softly, *"Where would I be without you? How would I survive? Lost am I in a world askew. A world that says good-bye."*

Girl clenched her eyes shut and screamed.

Argus knelt before her. "Why did you do this to me? Look at me!" He grabbed the back of her hair.

Her neck popped and her eyes burst open.

Argus waved a paper in front of her face. "Is this what you want, Girl? A letter to your father?" He ripped it up and tossed the remnants behind him.

The Dark spun under the falling pieces and raised its hands like a child enjoying the snow.

Her hand dove into her pocket. The letter was gone. The pieces scattered across the room. *Father!*

"Trust me, he is happy you are gone. You are a shame in his eyes. And it is your fault your father now hates you. He does not even remember your name."

She gritted her teeth. "You lie!"

"After all I have done for you. I gave you a home. I gave you all of this." He spread his arms wide. The Dark caressed him. "And you betray me!" He slammed his arms on either side of her head, his lower teeth slipping above his bottom lip like fangs. A mad wolf.

By now, her sobs flowed freely and Argus stroked her hair away from her face. She cringed, and her stomach heaved.

"Tell me, Girl, where is your precious Attiyq now? I am all you have. He has abandoned you, but I am still here. I will never leave you." He kissed her temple and slid his lips down her neck.

She froze. *Stay still, do not fight. Please, Attiyq, let this end. Let me come Home. I want to be with Mother. I want to be with You.*

"Remember when you first came to me?" he whispered in her ear. "You were only eleven, a child given promises of greatness. And remember the night I gave you great honor in my bed? You were thirteen. I made you into a woman."

Girl bit her lip. All Argus ever gave anyone was pain and humiliation. Shame clung like a heavy garment for five long years. Argus had reduced her to a thing. No longer human. Perhaps Argus was right: Father would not want her back.

Argus's gaze bore into her gushing eyes. "Why do you weep? After all I have done for you? Do you even remember what day it is? This is the day I brought you here. The day of your new birth with me. We can celebrate, you and me," he placed his lips against her temple, "together."

She fought down her vomit and raised her knees to her chest. The tears dammed and hidden for five years streamed down her face. Her brothers would no longer claim her. No man would take her hand in marriage. *Just kill me.*

Argus wiped at her tears and licked the salty dew from his fingers. "Why would you betray me for *him*?" He pointed at the Maúl in the mirror. "Do you think any man would want you now? Do you dream of this Maúl when you are with me? Do you think he will rescue you? Will any man or thing rescue *you*? You are used. Soiled. Tainted. A joiner. Even God turns His eyes from your stained body." He grabbed the front of her dress and slammed her back against the wall. "Stop crying!"

Her head bounced against the stones. Lights blinked before her eyes. Pain exploded in her head. A warm, wet substance flowed down the back of her neck. *It must end soon. Soon. Yes, soon. A little while longer. Mother, wait for me!*

He kissed her and pressed his forehead against hers. "I have plans for you, Girl, plans that will bring you joy. This is your Celebration Day. You see, I also give futures just as the Attiyq promised futures for those who follow Him." He focused her face on the mirror. "Your Attiyq guards him, but who guards you?"

The angel's eyes locked on hers. Warm comfort filled her soul.

Does it hurt to die? her mind asked.

Argus whispered in her ear, "I give you one last gift for your special Birth Day. The Slave Runners." He removed the wooden slave bracelet from her wrist. It dropped to the ground with a dull thunk.

His words struck her harder than his fists. She blinked away her tears, struggling to see his face through the blurriness. "Please, no. Please kill me."

He kissed her neck. "No, my love. I cannot do that to such a trained joiner. Others long for you. Why would I deny them? See? I kept my promise. I did teach you a trade that you can use for all your life. It is time to go." He dragged her to the door.

Will you always be led by your fears?

-Anú

5

The ancient and strong Maúl village now lay smoldering like an old woman's nightly fire. Vultures drifted in the sky and observed the last of the Maúl scattered across the green grass.

Ruárc walked beside Nute, leader of the Barbarian tribe, as the Upeshi herded the Maúl women and children to the Barbarian Lands. The Opez Mountains rose majestically beside the forest trail as if to wave goodbye to the last of the Anú. Nature reclaimed her spender after the slaughter of so many people as if it never happened.

A captured child dropped her doll and a few pieces of clothing and almost tripped over them. Her mother quickly gathered up the belongings, then shooed her child along behind the row of captured slaves.

Sadness struck Ruárc. The Kalk, as the Upeshi called themselves, forced the prisoners to carry their own possessions, treasures that now belonged to the Barbarians. Soon the straggling line of survivors would be property of the Slave Runners. Foul men with a filthy trade.

He glanced over his shoulder. The path was clear of any pursuing enemies. Still his skin twitched.

"I smell fear on you, Lessrama," Nute said.

"Why must you call me Lessrama? You know I hate it."

Nute laughed. "The Small One hates his name. When you become strong, then I will call you by your given name. Tell me, Lessrama, what do you fear?"

"The last of the Maúl Warriors still lives. Émēr will hunt us down until we all die. I fear his sword."

Nute nodded. "Yes, I too understand that fear. Yet the Maúl and the Kalk have been at war for thousands of generations, and my people wish to follow in the steps of their forefathers. It will be good to revive that hatred. His tribe now lies within my hands, and the war begins. You hold Amget's *Haorar* mother and her lovely daughter. The Maúl warrior will pay to get back his *Haorar*—forgive me, I mean Healer mother—and his young sister. The younger Maúl women and children will bring us great profits."

"I thank you, Nute, for giving them to me. I now owe you a life debt. The Maúl will not abandon his sister and his *Haorar* mother. Soon I will deliver to the Queen what is hers, then the witch will no longer pursue me. I fear her wrath as well as the Maúl. There is no escape from her hand."

Nute laughed. "You speak of the *Wescr*, the Witch Jezebel? Now you see why I call you Small One. The Kalk does not fear the *Wescr's* hand, yet fear seeps from your veins. Jezebel cannot come to this land, for she fears the Kalk."

"She has the demon, Argus, who flies as a great bird. He will find us."

Nute shook his head. "Now you fear the *Eger Aro*, the Evil One? Do you also fear rabbits and small birds? *Eger Aro* will not venture here. As for the Maúl, Lessrama, you hold the *Haorar* and her child in your village, do you not? Let the last of the Maúl come to you. Let him seek your face."

Ruárc stared at the dirt road winding ahead of him as it cut through the trees. If only he could disappear in that green tangle. "Nute, you do not understand Argus's strength. He flies on wings as a bird, he eats man-flesh, he is a demon."

"The *Eger Aro* is a demon, but he only brings dishonor to the lands. It was by his hand that the war between Kalk and the Maúl ended. His hand that shed their blood. It was to be the Kalk who were to destroy Anú's children." He paused and stared at the trees around them. "It is odd, Lessrama. The Maúl were to capture the *Eger Aro,* and yet, it was the *Eger Aro* who destroyed them. The captured bird became the hunter, and the hunter became the captured bird. My hatred for the Maúl and Anú runs through my blood and warms me at night. Yet, I honored them. They were *Humurad,* Honored Ones, respected by my people. Now only one remains. And soon Argus will eat his flesh. Then my people will have no reason to stay in these lands we have held for thousands of years." He turned brilliant blue eyes to Ruárc. "Soon you too will have to leave. No one will remain."

"My seers have warned me," Nute continued, "that the *Eger Aro* will conquer not only this world, but the worlds beyond. It is good that we leave."

"I will take my clan to other lands, serve other kings. Perhaps we will meet again?" Ruárc said.

Nute nodded. "Perhaps. Have you heard a new tribe has risen from the dust and dares to call itself Maúl? They are not of Anú's hand and have little *humurad.* We will not fight such insects. They only shame us in the eyes of our ancestors and do not bring honor. We will find a new people to destroy, people who bring *humurad.* You may accompany us, Lessrama."

Ruárc grinned. "I am *humurad,* Great Nute, as are my sons. But I cannot. I must keep my word, my *prukeka,* and bring the Prince and the Queen's trinket to her."

Nute placed his fist against his chest and gave a small bow to Ruárc. "Lessrama, do not allow your fear to blind your eyes. The *Eger Aro* is only as strong as you allow him to be. *Guudbaea*, my friend."

Ruárc gave a low bow. "Nute, you are a friend of my father and my sons, and you are mine. I pray Oozeka leads you to your new future. When will you leave?"

"Next spring. The winters are coming soon. The little ones cannot travel in the snow." Nute gave him a final wave, then slipped into the woods.

A bird caught Ruárc's attention. When he turned back to Nute, the entire procession had disappeared into the woods. A shiver spread down Ruárc's back. As foul as the Upeshi—he paused and smiled, the Kalk—were, they still amazed him. He turned and followed the path to his small village.

Remember your honor always. Never kill an unarmed man. That is not the Maúl way. Only cowards kill a man with no weapon.

-Anú

6

They were wasting time. Émēr leaned against the doorframe and stared out over the compound. *But to become a true Maúl. To advance from the child's level. To become a greater warrior who could free Mother and Aine.*

Conell rested against the other side of the frame. "It has been two weeks since you started your training, captain. I know how important this is to you, but I think we should be moving on soon."

Émēr nodded. "I agree, but I am learning so much, and I feel strength growing within me each day. Soon I can move to an adult level and leave the child behind. The seer is growing stronger also. Soon she will be able to hear from Him." He turned to his Mojí. "Mojí, I believe these men might be of my clan. That somehow children did survive. If they survived, then should I move on?"

Conell's lime green eyes studied Émēr. "You will not come with us?"

He shrugged. "I am not sure. I feel I must stay with Māhōn, to learn all that I must." He paused. "I know I must move on to find Mother and Aine, but maybe I will return once they are safe."

"And not come with us to find the weapons? We must defeat the witch." Conell kicked at the dirt. "I know you are still angry. I understand that, but I need your sword. Frigg is still inexperienced, and Imogene cannot even hold a sword in her hand. I cannot fight alone."

Émēr crossed his arms over his chest and pursed his lips. "And what if these are all that remain of *my* people?" He winced at his words.

Pain crossed Conell's face. "You will never forgive me, will you?" His sad face gazed over the compound before returning to his old friend. "Perhaps you should stay here. I can take Imogene and Frigg with me." His gaze studied the ground.

Émēr watched his prince's face. Conell made plans to fight without him.

Obey those placed in Authority, for they are placed there by the Attiyq's hand.

Émēr groaned inwardly.

Stay and guard your prince, Émēr. Father's last order.

Your father's last words were to guard and serve the prince. That is what you will do now. Do not dishonor your father's name.

"Mojí, I will stay with you, but you must understand. Everywhere I look, I see the ghosts of my friends. I survived; they did not."

"This is why I never told you."

Māhōn trotted over to them as he strapped his sword to his side. "My men have spotted Slave Runners along the main highway. They might know of your family."

Conell caught Émēr's eye. Émēr knew what he was thinking. If these slaves were his family, Émēr would stay with Māhōn. But could he truly abandon his Mojí? Mother would insist he stay with the King's son.

Émēr gave his Mojí a tight smile and extended his hand towards the courtyard. "My cousin, I will follow you."

Conell returned his smile in kind and gave a short nod of thanks. "I will ask Pol to stay with Aiden."

Māhōn frowned as his fingers fumbled with the sword's buckle. "There is no need for that. My men can stay with her."

"I think she would be more comfortable with Pol," Conell replied as he walked away.

Émēr placed his hand on Māhōn's shoulder. "Forgive him, my brother, he does not yet trust you." He tightened Māhōn's sword belt.

Māhōn shooed away Émēr's hands. "I have it. Thank you. And I am sure any of us would do the same."

"What have your men discovered about the Slave Camp?"

Māhōn shrugged. "Not much. Only two slaves. A man and woman. I hope, my brother, that she is of your clan. I do not want to see you suffer anymore. I know how hard this has been for you."

Émēr nodded. "It has been hard, my brother."

Māhōn grinned. "Stay with me, and I will be your *Gaevee*."

Émēr returned the smile.

Stay with Māhōn.

The march to the slave camp was slow and calculated. Émēr's legs longed to race along the dirt road. Māhōn insisted they keep to the woods but follow the road.

Émēr glanced behind him. Māhōn and his men crunched the leaves and twigs below them, while Émēr traveled softly. He stopped and crouched behind a tree.

Conell slipped beside him. "For Maúl, they are as noisy as maids at a tea party."

Émēr nodded and motioned to the others. "I know, My Mojí. My mind is confused."

Māhōn joined them and raised his fist, stopping his men. "The camp is beyond these trees. Émēr, go and scout."

Conell patted Émēr's shoulder and nodded towards the camp.

Émēr traveled softly over the twigs and dried leaves. A rabbit raised its head from the foliage and wiggled its nose then returned to eating. The birds' chirping gossip filled the air around him.

The colorful tents appeared through the trees. Émēr crawled across the forest floor to a small bush and pushed back the branches. Four large red-and-blue-striped tents sat snuggly in a clearing. The Queen's flags flew on poles attached to the small pavilions. A small animal carcass burned over a fire in the center of the small commune. A corral made of rope confined the horses and pack mules.

Finally, Émēr caught a glimpse of four traders who were sitting on folding chairs that surrounded a large campfire. His eyebrows rose at the unexpected elegance of the troupe. These men behaved and appeared as lords of the King's court not slave traders. They were said to be cousins of Barbarians, ungodly men whom the Attiyq crushed under His mighty fist. They were to have scared faces and live in filth.

Instead, fine, silk doublets enveloped their well-fed frames. Dark, cotton trousers were tucked into shiny, black, leather boots. Hats with large colorful feathers sat firmly on their heads. Grease-slicked hair framed their clean-shaven faces.

Each man had a sword strapped to their sides, but they brushed their swords aside, one even unstrapping his weapon and laying it on the ground. Émēr frowned. This could only mean that these men were unable to maneuver their weapons. They were for show. Émēr studied a large man with blue tattoos who stood at the edge of the camp. An Upeshi guard. Another man, dressed in servant's brown clothing, served the out-of-place aristocrats.

Two slaves sat beyond the camp, a man younger than Émēr and a girl around Imogene's age. A grin washed over Émēr's face. Erák. So, the young man survived. His face and arms showed bruises, and Émēr raised his eyebrows in pleasant surprise. Erák was a silversmith. He knew little of the sword, yet with such bruises, Erák must have fought hard against the Barbarians.

Erák's gaze darted around the camp, and he would often whisper to the girl. She only shook her head and kept her gaze fastened to the ground. Émēr bit his lip. Aine had black hair as rich as midnight. This girl's hair was soft brown like a doe's coat. Émēr stiffened when he saw that the sleeves of her dress were torn away. A *Zuuho*. A joiner. Nevertheless, he could not free Erák and leave the girl behind. Maúl stood against slavery. The Attiyq demanded all men and women be free.

Émēr returned to the others. "Māhōn, there are four traders, one servant, one barbarian guard, and two slaves. One of the slaves is my cousin; I am unsure about the woman."

The leader of Māhōn's scouting party nodded. "We will surround the camp in pairs. Two will kill the guard, and the rest of us will kill any who give us resistance."

Émēr and Conell darted behind the trees as they made their way to the camp. The rest of Māhōn's men, including Māhōn, did the same until all surrounded the small encampment.

The two assigned to the guard crept up behind him. A twig snapped. Émēr winced. The barbarian whirled around, but before he drew his weapon, Māhōn's men found their mark. The guard crumpled to the ground. The Slavers jumped to their feet and fumbled for their weapons.

Māhōn pointed his weapon at the men. "I suggest you drop your weapons, gentlemen."

The men dropped their steels and raised their hands.

Erák's face beamed as he held out his arms to his cousin. "Émēr! You are alive!"

Émēr knelt before him and examined his wounds. "Yes, my cousin, we survived. Mother, Aine?"

Erák shook his head. "I am sorry, my cousin. I do not know of their fate. They were not with us when the barbarians sold us a few weeks ago."

Émēr nodded and pursed his lips. His eyes flickered to the girl. She had not moved and focused her gaze on her bloody hands. He tried to push aside her hair, but she jerked away from him.

He turned to Conell. "I need keys."

Māhōn raised his weapon to the nearest Runner. "Keys, if you please."

A short, plump man tossed the keys to Émēr who caught them and gave the man a sarcastic nod of thanks.

He unlocked the restraints and the chains fell from Erák's wrists. Erák stood and stretched his arms and legs.

The girl remained still, as if her mind clung to another time and place. He unlocked her chains, and her hands dropped onto her lap.

The short, pudgy man raised his finger, but kept his eyes on Māhōn's weapon. "Please, you may have the man, but leave us that woman. She is a joiner, a *Zuuho,* and will fetch us a handsome profit."

Émēr lifted the girl's head. A large bruise covered the side of her face, and her eye was blood red. Another bruise lay under her other eye, and a cut dug into her lower lip. She kept her gaze focused on a bug crawling across her leg. Lifelessness hung over the girl as if she already lay in her grave.

Émēr faced the Slaver. "You did this to her?"

The man shook his head. "No, no, her former master beat her. He said she had betrayed him, that he no longer wished for his eyes to fall upon her. Yes, she is bruised but is quite . . . talented, from what he has said."

Erák grabbed Émēr's arm. "She belonged to the Queen's angel guard."

"Argus?"

His cousin nodded. "She has not eaten for a few days. Whenever the Runners force food down her throat, she vomits it up once they are gone. She is very weak."

Émēr knelt for a closer look, wondering if this girl could be the friend of whom Imogene had spoken. "Girl?"

Her gaze rose to meet his. As she studied his face, her small hand traced the sacred markings on his jaw.

He pulled her sinful hand from his holy symbols, but she seemed oblivious to the offense he took at her touch. She threw her arms around his neck and sobbed into his shoulder.

Indecision pricked Émēr's heart. She was clearly a *Zuuho*. Such women were prideful and mocked those who walked in Righteousness, yet this one acted innocent. Frightened. Alone.

Still, he untangled her foul arms and held her at a distance. "My . . . lady. . . I do not know you." His skin crawled at her defiled touch.

"I saw you outside the castle walls. Is my friend, Imogene, alive?" Her swollen lips muffled her words.

Conell narrowed his eyes as he stood over her. "So, you were the one who betrayed us to Argus."

Her face grew white, and she crawled away from Émēr.

His Mojí nudged Émēr's arm and gestured his head to the Slavers. Leave the girl here, it said.

Aine's words raced through Émēr's mind. *Young, poor women go into the castle with promises to become handmaidens and store owners but never return home.*

This defiled creature may have been one of those girls. He knelt beside her and lifted her beaten face. "Argus did this to you?"

She nodded. "You are Maúl. You are noble and trustworthy. I beg of you, My Lord, send me home to the Attiyq. That is all I want. Please."

A wave of repulsion skipped across his stomach. How could such a foul creature speak of God and Home? This vulgar animal should have called out to him when they rescued Imogene, but she stayed with the demon. She had made her choice.

"Woman," Émēr said, "I will return you to your village."

Tears dripped from her bloody eyes. "My only home is with the Attiyq. I beg of you, send me there."

A smirk crossed his lips. "You ask to be with Attiyq?"

She nodded. "Yes, please."

He shook his head. "I cannot do that. My vows forbid me."

She sat back on her haunches and sobbed. "Then I will hate you forever."

Émēr blinked at the audacity of her, a *Zuuho,* hating him, a Maúl, for refusing to put her out of her misery. Perhaps he should consider leaving her to the Slavers. Then Imogene's face invaded his mind. Her wrath would be like waves on the ocean if he left Girl behind. "You spoke of Imogene. Do you wish to see her? She has spoken of you often. I know she would want to see you."

She shook her head and wiped the tears from her face. "I cannot face her."

"Imogene would never forgive me if I left you here to die. Do you now wish for me to face such wrath?" He raised his eyebrows. "Come." He gingerly placed his hand on her arm and helped her to stand.

The leader of the Slavers lifted his hand. "Please, My Lord, leave the woman with us."

"It is for the best, Émēr," Connell concurred.

Girl's legs buckled.

Émēr picked her up in his arms and shot a determined look to his Mojí. "She comes with me. Aiden's wrath will be unbearable if we do not take her."

Conell rolled his eyes and nodded.

Another trader with a large hat perched on his head like a bird cleared his throat and straightened his tunic. "Please, have mercy on us. You have your kin. If you take the girl, what will we have?"

Conell placed his sword at the peacock's throat. "You have your life. That is more than most men would give you."

Peacock's eyes grew wide, and he nodded. "Take our slaves, but leave us."

An unpleasant grin crossed Māhōn's lips, and his eyes possessed a frightening glare. "I will be happy to give you a reward for the girl."

The leader grinned. "That I will accept."

Émēr shook his head. "Māhōn, I said no. I will not be disgraced."

Māhōn's crazed eyes turned to Émēr. He drove his sword into the trader's stomach until the point of the blade protruded from the man's back. Smiling at his victim's gargled scream, Māhōn yanked his weapon free, and the carcass dropped to the ground.

Girl cried out and hid her face in Émēr's chest.

Māhōn turned to his men, blood dripping from his blade. "Kill them all."

The remaining traders and the servant fled into the forest. Māhōn's men hurried after them. Screams echoed from the woods. Birds flew from the trees. Then all was silent. Émēr shuddered. Māhōn's men returned and wiped the blood from their steels.

Girl's breath came in deep gasps, and her large eyes locked on Māhōn. "Please let me die now."

He cocked his head and grinned. "I would never let a beautiful creature such as you perish."

Girl tightened her trembling arms around Émēr's neck and buried her face in his chest.

Conell glared at Māhōn. "Why did you kill them?"

Māhōn shrugged. "And let them escape to tell the Queen? I am to protect my clan." He waved his hand around the camp. "Take everything including the animals. And especially take the girl."

Émēr held Girl on his lap as he rode one of the Runner's horses back to Anú's Temple. His Mojí, riding next to him, sat tall in the saddle, his sharp glances sending Émēr silent messages. They were to leave soon.

Girl rested her head on his shoulder. Her body lay tense in his arms, but her trembling had stopped. Her blank eyes stared off into the distance.

Émēr glanced down at her several times. She acted and looked like Imogene after Argus's attack. Frightened and lost. Maybe he had judged her too harshly? Maybe Girl was as lost as Imogene. She had said she had seen him at the castle walls. Erák said she had betrayed Argus. He closed his eyes as his stomach dropped. She had not betrayed him but suffered for him. But still she had decided to stay with the demon, when she could have cried out to him. He would have taken her with him.

She was tainted, impure. No man would take her hand in marriage. Maybe death was her only option. If she asked again, he would give her this one gift; he owed her his life. Cian, being the priest, would have words of wisdom and comfort for her. Now Émēr was the priest. A priest who questioned his God. He winced. His words of comfort included the blunt end of his war hammer.

He led his horse next to Erák. "Cousin, how many survived the attack?"

Erák gave him a mournful gaze. "Not many, Émēr. Most of the women and all the children were captured by the Upeshi. Most of the men died. Meallan, he is gone too." His eyes misted over. "My father. They took my mother. We parted a few days ago. She would not stop crying."

Émēr grasped the stone around his neck. "I am sorry, Erák. I should have stayed."

Erák smiled and placed a firm hand on Émēr's shoulder. "It is not your fault. What have you found of the Attiyq's great weapons?"

"I ask that you not speak of it again. I do not want Māhōn and his men to know of them."

Erák nodded. "I will follow you. You are now the leader of the Amgets clan."

Émēr gave him a quick look. Leader and a priest. He was failing at both tasks.

His Mojí slowed his horse to keep pace with Émēr's beast. "I did not think the Maúl killed the unarmed."

Émēr watched Māhōn as he led the group up the trail. "It is something they do not do. I do not understand."

"We need to leave these people."

"Perhaps. Anú always ordered us to only fight those who were our equal. Any man who holds a weapon is an equal. A man without one, only cowards fight. I do not understand Māhōn's ways."

"Be careful, My Captain. My heart tells me Māhōn is not of the Maúl but is something different. I understand your reasoning, but I do not think you are following your heart, only your fears."

"What do you know of my heart?"

Conell's face grew tight. "I spent five years with you in that hell hole. I know you better than you believe." He glared at Émēr.

Émēr looked away. "It seems Māhōn and his men veer far from Anú's orders. We were taught to allow an unarmed man to go free. Mercy for the unarmed and the weak."

"You saw the blood lust in Māhōn's eyes. You have told me stories of Anú. Would he also have such blood lust?"

Émēr locked his gaze on Māhōn. "Things have changed, Mojí." He looked at Conell. "They have had to adapt."

Conell snorted. "Adapt. Is that the word Anú would use?"

"No, he would not."

"We leave tomorrow morning."

Émēr nodded.

Doing the right thing can sometimes be next to impossible, but it can be done.

- Cadoc Ailill Amgets

7

It took a half an hour to reach the Temple. Two men left as sentries opened the gate doors. Māhōn led his men into the courtyard and spread his arms wide. "Gifts from the Traders!"

The men laughed and pulled the items from the horses.

Frigg and Imogene walked up to Conell and Émēr as they led their animals into the compound and away from Māhōn.

Imogene spied the new supplies as the men shuffled through them. "Looks like you had some fun."

Conell slipped from the horse. "Fun is not what we had." He handed the horse to a sentry, who led the animal away. "Imogene, you will do as Émēr said. You will not talk to these men, nor are you allowed to be alone with them."

"Why, what happened?" she asked.

Māhōn strolled over to them and laughed. "We have had a wonderful haul, my brothers." He shook out a long light blue gown and handed it to Imogene. "This is what a lovely woman should wear."

Conell snatched it from his hands. "Thank you, I am sure she will appreciate it."

Imogene gaze darted from man to man.

"Thank you for your kindness, my brother," Émēr said.

Māhōn tipped his head to Imogene then returned to unpacking the stolen merchandise.

Conell glared up at Émēr. "So, do the Maúl also rejoice after such slaughter and distribute the possessions of the dead as if they were bandits?" He handed the dress to Imogene who gave him a small smile. He grinned softly, then looked away.

She held it against her body. "It is pretty."

He glanced at her, but Frigg pulled away his attention. "My Lord, what happened? And who is the girl?"

"A woman who seeks our help," Conell said. "She was Argus's slave. A joiner."

Frigg's eyes grew wide. "A real joiner?"

"No," Émēr answered. "I would not call her a real one."

Conell reached up to take Girl from Émēr. She gasped and wrapped her arms around his neck.

Imogene cocked her head. "Is that who I think it is?"

Girl gave Imogene a weak smile. "I am happy to see you are well." Her head dropped, and she whimpered.

Imogene motioned to Émēr to lower Girl into Conell's waiting arms. Conell laid her on the ground as Émēr jumped from the horse and pushed the animal away.

Imogene placed her fingers on the inside of Girl's wrist. "Her pulse is very fast." She pinched Girl's skin. The skin puckered. She lifted Girl's arm and ran her hand over her underarm. "She's not sweating, and her eyes are glazed over. I think she's dehydrated."

Émēr squatted beside Imogene. "She has not eaten for many days, and she has vomited what the Runner's forced her to eat."

Imogene stroked Girl's cheek. "Oh, hon, we should have gone back for you. I'll get her some broth and vegetables to eat. We must get food and water down her or her organs will shut down. Bring her into the meeting area."

Émēr lifted Girl in his arms and made his way into the meeting room. He placed her on the pew and stared into her eyes. He blinked. They were a beautiful deep blue with darker blue specks. Like sapphires sitting on cotton. How could Argus beat one with such gorgeous eyes?

Imogene returned with a tray loaded with a bowl of soup, a plate of green vegetables, and a decanter of water. "Alright, hon, I need you to sit up."

Girl gasped and waved Imogene away. Her eyes barely opened, and her breathing became labored. "Father, I am sorry."

Émēr frowned. "She wishes to die. She may get her wish."

"Émēr," Imogene said. "Get behind her, and sit her up."

"Imogene," Émēr said, "she does not wish to live."

She snapped her fingers and pointed to Girl's head. "I don't care what she wants. Get behind her … Now!"

Émēr glanced at Conell who raised his hands in defeat.

Frigg chuckled. "Better do as she says, Captain."

Émēr scowled but slid behind Girl. Her tainted body rested against his chest. He glowered at Conell.

Imogene placed the bowl against Girl's lips. "Here, hon, drink."

Girl turned her head away.

"Would God want you to take your own life?" Imogene asked. "In my…village, it's a sin." Imogene caught her gaze and placed the bowl against Girl's lips. She sipped the liquid and ate some of the vegetables. Imogene placed the near empty bowl on the tray. "Good girl." She picked up the decanter and held it to Girl's lips. "It's going to taste a little salty and sugary but drink it anyway. You need the sugar and salt to fight the dehydration. I'm going to need you to drink all of it."

Girl cocked her head in confusion. At Imogene's urging, she drank the liquid. She coughed and swallowed it then collapsed on Émēr's chest.

Māhōn entered the meeting area and nodded. "Good, Aiden, keep the girl alive. We need her talents for the temple."

Imogene furrowed her brow. "Talents?"

"She was Argus's joiner," Émēr said.

Imogene dabbed the liquid from Girl's chin. "Joiner?"

Conell shrugged. "Yes, Aiden, she will be used to join with other men who will pay her handler for her … services."

Imogene slowly rose and faced Māhōn.

Émēr shot an alarmed look at Conell, who stepped beside her.

"Let me get this straight." She took a step to Māhōn. Conell slipped his arm between them; she slapped it away. "Are you telling me that you are planning on using this girl," she pointed to Girl, "as a prostitute because Argus raped her?" She placed her hands on her small hips. "Are you out of your freaking mind?"

Māhōn narrowed his eyes. "For one who is to be silent, you do not obey well."

She stood on her toes and glared into his eyes. "Let's just say I'm sick in my head."

Māhōn's eyebrows rose. A red hue crept up his face and his eyes became slits. "It seems, my brother, that your sister knows no manners. Perhaps you should teach her."

Conell pulled Imogene away. Their arguing words slipped past Émēr as he stared down at the defiled woman lying in his arms. Her face shimmered and changed to Aine, lying alone in a strange warrior's embrace. Men ready to sell her to the highest bidder. Men holding back Mother, who wept over the stolen innocence of her daughter, both women calling out his name but hearing only the wind. Aine raped by strange men and eventually dying alone before her twenty-fifth birthing day. Her used body tossed into a ditch where animals gnawed on her soft flesh.

He swallowed the lump in his throat.

Pari's image appeared on the front pew. The young boy placed his small arm on the back of the seat and stared at him. "What are you going to do, Émēr? What would Anú do?" He pointed a pudgy finger to the painting of the first leader of the Voobo Maúl, whose tunic was painted in the Maúl Blue with strips of yellow, red, and green.

The yellow represents care for the widows, children, the ill, and the honor of all women.

All women. Including *Zuubos.* Girl's sobs became soft whimpers. Her life was draining from her.

Émēr shook his head. "I do not know what to do."

Pari grinned at him. "Yes, you do, Émēr. You always did know the most perfect thing to do."

The thought came like a lightning bolt and drove to the front of his mind.

Émēr closed his eyes. "Oh Attiyq, please no."

Aine's soft face rose before him. The Elders often spoke of deeds being seeds of sacrifice to the Attiyq. This would be his seed for Aine. Maybe the Attiyq would have mercy on his sister if he gave mercy to this soiled creature?

He whispered in Girl's ear. "My Lady, I have a solution that will not involve your death, nor will I be held responsible for destroying your life. But you must agree, or I cannot save you."

She looked up at him and shook her head.

"Become my wife and I will protect you,"

She closed her eyes. "I cannot. Please send me home to my God."

"Anú has ordered me not to fight those unarmed, and that includes you." He raised his eyes to the others. "I have a solution. I will take this girl to be my wife."

Conell's mouth dropped open. "What? Captain, think of what you are doing!"

"What I am doing? You have said you would take Aiden's hand if the demon defiled her. Now you wish for me to turn from protecting my sister?"

Conell shook his head. "No, of course not. I can take her hand if you wish."

"No, I must do this," Émēr said.

Māhōn growled. "I will not allow it. She belongs to ..."

Imogene punched Émēr in the shoulder. "Way to go, cowboy."

Émēr flashed his gaze to Imogene. *Cowboy?* He shook away the thought. "I do this in honor of my other sister who is held in bondage. A seed to the Attiyq. I take … Girl to be my … wife. As my wife and under my clan whom I now lead, she will be protected as the Slave rules become invalid once a freeman marries a slave. She belongs only to me, and I decide her fate. I claim she will not fall under the rules of *Zuuho.*" His stomach soured. But Father always said doing the right thing was next to impossible, yet it could be done. And sometimes it had to be done.

Māhōn dark, savage eyes ground into Émēr. "You steal from this temple? That thing," he pointed to Girl, "will save this temple and rebuild the Maúl way. I know men who will pay plenty for one night with her. And yet you take her talents for yourself?"

Pari cocked his head and stared at him. Émēr flicked his eyes from person to person, finally landing on Anú. Émēr motioned to Imogene to take his place. He rose, and she shimmied behind Girl.

Émēr planted his feet. "Brother, I am giving a seed to the Attiyq. It is called *ashayu,* a word every Maúl knows, but it seems to have escaped you. It is the most respected of all vows, and every Maúl honors it."

Māhōn's eyes grew into thin lines. "She has not yet accepted your vows, *Brother.* If she does not take them," Māhōn leaned into Émēr and whispered, "She will be my bride."

Émēr took a step back.

Imogene grabbed his sleeve, and her eyes grew wide. "Oh, God, Émēr, please don't let him do that, please?"

Her pleading words dug deep into his heart. Who would plead for Aine? He dropped to his knee and took Girl's hand into his own. "Death will not visit you, My Lady. Please, take my vows."

Girl moaned and turned her face from him.

Imogene whispered in Girl's ear, "Tell me what's going on,

on?"

Girl said soft words to Imogene.

Imogene nodded. "Oh, you mean you can't … *be* with him. Yeah, I never thought of your trauma and what Argus did to you. It's going to take a while to get through all of this."

Girl stared at Imogene. "You are not to know what happens between a husband and his wife."

Imogene chuckled. "Girlfriend, you'd be surprised as to what I know."

Her eyes grew wide.

Imogene looked up at him. "Here's the score, Émēr. She's basically pretty traumatized, and she can't *be* with you in the sense of *being*."

He cocked his head. "I do not understand."

"You know, being. She can't sleep with you."

"She is unable to sleep?"

"Aiden, speak your mind," Conell urged.

She clicked her tongue and rolled her eyes. "Oh, you guys, seriously. She can't join with you, Émēr."

Heat rose in Émēr's face, and he looked away. Conell groaned and rubbed his forehead. Frigg and Erák exchanged shocked glances.

Māhōn laughed. "What does it matter?"

"It matters to her," Imogene declared.

Yes, it did matter. It would matter to Aine. Émēr took her hand in his. "My Lady, I give you my word I will not make you do something you cannot do. If I must, I will take another woman to be my second wife. She will bare my children, but you will live in safety under the Amgets clan name. Will you agree?"

Girl winced.

"Girl, please, do this," Imogene said. "Don't let these guys win. Don't let Argus win."

Girl raised her eyes to Imogene, then turned her stunning sapphire eyes to Émēr. A shiver wiggled down his back. She was so beautiful despite the bruising. But she was impure, tainted, spoiled. He desired a pure woman picked by his uncle and mother. The two clans would become one, his mother pleased with her selection, his village celebrating. Pure children coming from a pure womb. His children from Girl would be impure, tainted. Rejects to society.

There was no celebration with this wedding. His mother would be displeased. What would Father's words be? What would Aine's words be? Aine. No, he did this for Aine's honor and only her honor, if the Attiyq accepted this sacrifice. "Will you take my vows, My Lady?"

Girl nodded. "Yes, I take your vows."

Émēr took a deep breath. "In front of all these men and my clan, I take you as my wife. I will protect you, guard you day and night, provide for you and hopefully one day, you will bare my children. I will love you and only you. I will be faithful to you until my dying days. Will you take me as your husband?"

Girl let out a deep sigh, and her voice was without emotion as if she already lay in her grave. "Yes, My Lord, I take you as my husband. I give you my respect, and I will obey you always. Will you take me as your bride?" Her eyes welled with tears, and her lips trembled.

He stared into her sapphire orbs. Horrible pain lay behind the stunning blue. He swallowed. What did Argus do to her? Maybe he judged her harshly? She was like a wounded bird, seeking refuge. Was it too hard to give it to her?

"I take you as my bride." He leaned down to kiss her, but she backed away from him. A woman who tossed away the Attiyq's words would enjoy a man's kiss. Yet she refused. Maybe her heart was pure despite what the demon did to her body? He raised her hand and kissed the back of her fingers.

Erák spread his hands over the couple. "I, a member of the Amgets clan, who has witnessed this marriage, claim it to be valid. Together you are both One, husband and wife. May the Attiyq's eyes always be on you and bless you forever."

The group mumbled, "So be it."

Émēr took both of Girl's hands in his. "You are no longer a *Zuuho*, but *TTisho*. You will wear the clothes of the proper Lady." He faced Māhōn. His Mojí, Erák, and Frigg joined him. "I ask that you and your men stay clear of my wife and my sister as they heal from their wounds. Please ask me before speaking to them. And you will refer to my wife as Lady Amgets, not 'Thing'." Émēr raised his chin. "If you wish for us to leave, then we will leave."

Māhōn raised an eyebrow and sneered. "I am your *Gaevee*. You do not have to leave. But if you insist upon taking money from this temple and turning your back on your brothers-in-arms for a worthless creature," he paused and raised his hands, "forgive me, Lady Amgets, then you will pay us by chopping wood for all of us. It is the least you can do for your brothers. Or will you turn from this vow?"

Émēr glanced at his Mojí who nodded. He resisted a deep moan. To chop wood again. Father made him chop wood for the first ten years of his life. He reluctantly nodded. "I will chop wood for you."

Māhōn gave a small bow. "You will start today." His eyes lingered on Girl.

Émēr stepped in front of him and blocked his view. Māhōn slowly raised his eyes to Émēr and bowed his head, then he and his men exited the room.

Émēr let out a sigh of relief.

Conell leaned over Imogene. "*Chuōhá*, see to Girl's recovery. We must leave as soon as she is able to walk." He turned to Émēr. "Captain, we are leaving this place once Girl is capable of traveling. I will not stay here any longer. What I have seen…We must leave this place soon."

Imogene grabbed his arm. "Wait, I have a question."

"Émēr." Conell paused as if choosing his words. "I know you long to stay to learn the ways of Maúl, but are the ways of these men what you really wish to learn? I understand them wanting to use the girl, but to forget the sacred vows? And to treat with disdain an important decision? I am sorry, My Captain, but I cannot leave Imogene here. We must leave."

Imogene again tugged at Conell's arm. "I have a question."

Émēr lifted Girl into his arms. "I must agree, My Mojí."

Girl laid her head on his shoulder and closed her eyes.

Imogene slipped in front of the men. "You can't just say you're married and *be* married. You have to have a ceremony and cake and stuff. Stand before a priest and make vows. There has to be flowers and flower girls and guys in tuxes. Girl, you have to try on like a hundred dresses and say Yes to The Dress."

Girl stared at Imogene. "What does she mean, husband? I am to speak to clothing?"

Émēr smiled at his bride. "She came to us like this. I am unsure of many of her words." He made his way to the door. "I do not know your true name, My Lady."

She rested her head on his shoulder. "I am Ūmá."

Émēr maneuvered through the doorway. "Daughter of?"

"I have no father," she whispered.

Imogene jogged in front of them and held out her hands. "Oh no you don't. You guys can't take this from me. I want to be a bridesmaid!"

Conell placed his hand under her elbow and gave Émēr an amused grin. "Come along, *Chuōhá*."

"You guys are killing me," Imogene said as Conell tugged her away. "And what did you mean by saying you'd marry Ūmá? Not that I care. You can marry anyone you want."

Conell raised his eyebrows.

"Do what you want," she said as she walked beside Ūmá.

Émēr chuckled. Now Conell sat in Imogene's net.

Do not judge those whose hearts are hidden from you.

-The Attiyq.

8

Émēr wiped the sweat from his brow and pulled his shirt over his head. He stretched his arms and winced. His muscles ached, and his hands throbbed from chopping wood. He had chopped wood from the time he sat Ūmá in her bed and left her with Imogene until the sun began to set. Six straight hours of splitting timber. And still there were many rooms that needed wood. He would be here for a while.

Mojí, Frigg, and Erák offered their help, but he refused. This was for Aine. He would pay Māhōn's price for taking Ūmá's hand. Each chop of the axe echoed Father's words. Doing what was right was difficult yet could be mastered.

He slowly climbed the stairs to his sleeping quarters that he shared with his Mojí. He stopped at Imogene's door.

Manners demanded that he say goodnight to his bride. He lifted his hand to knock. The sound of weeping came from the room. He cracked opened the door to see Imogene spooned against Ūmá, her head on Ūmá's shoulder. Both women wept.

He closed the door and frowned. His women shed tears. Did mother and Aine also weep when darkness fell? What had happened to demand such strong emotions? He shook his head and made his way to the bathing room. Women were far beyond his understanding.

He woke the next morning with his arms and body stiff and sore. He cracked his neck and dangled his feet over the side of the bed. Another day of chopping wood. Imogene said it might take two weeks before Ūmá was ready to travel. Two weeks of performing a child's chore in order to keep a tainted wife whom he despised. He ran his hand over his face.

He made his way to the dressing table. Pouring water into a basin, he washed his face and torso. He frowned. "Please, Attiyq, see my sacrifice and protect my sister and my mother." He stared at his reflection in the mirror. "And help me to love my wife."

He stared at the ceiling then closed his eyes. "Father, this was not supposed to happen. I was to be a full Maúl and lead the King's army by your side. My pure wife and I were to live in the castle, Mother and Aine in the village. I would raise my pure children in the ways of the Maúl and the Attiyq. And yet, here I stand, a disgrace to you and Anú. I am a priest who questions his God. I run from an insane witch, serve a betraying prince, and chop wood for a *Zuuho*." He tossed the towel onto the floor.

He put on clean clothes and anchored his Atobo to his side then made his way to the dining area.

His Mojí grinned and broke off a piece of bread. "How do you feel today?"

Émēr yawned. "Horrible. I long to sleep for days. But I must chop the wood."

Conell grinned and peeled a hardboiled egg. "We can help you."

He glared at his Mojí. "You are enjoying this too much, my prince."

Conell chuckled. "It is good to see you squirm."

Imogene stepped into the room; her eyes were red and puffy. Her green cotton gown with a laced front and long sleeves gave her a *TTisho* appearance. She plopped next to Conell and buried her face in the crook of her elbow. "Hey, guys. What? No rabbit? Did you kill all of them?" came her muffled voice.

Émēr had to chuckle. Would his sister ever become *TTisho?*

Conell raised his eyebrows at Émēr. "Did you not sleep well last night, *Chuōhá*?"

She snatched Conell's plate. "No, I did not sleep well. I would give anything for a drop of Mountain Dew and an Egg McMuffin. That's what's wrong with this world, no caffeine or fast food." She shoved the cheese in her mouth. "All you have is stupid cheese, rabbit, and boiled eggs." She peeled the shell from the egg.

"Where is Ūmá?" Émēr asked.

She yawned and stretched her neck. "Sleeping. She's exhausted. She needs to rest."

Conell rose and filled his plate with more cheese and bread. "That is a lovely gown, *Chuōhá*. Where did you find it?"

"From that dead Slave guy's stuff. He had a ton of women's dresses. Creepy." She stared at the plate, then pushed it away and massaged her temples. "He's coming, isn't he? I don't know how to fight this anymore."

Conell cracked open his hardboiled egg. "Fight what, *Chuōhá*?"

Her trembling hand rolled her egg around her plate. "You didn't hear what she told me last night. What he did," her voice cracked. "What he did to her. He's coming, isn't he?"

Émēr caught Conell's gaze. "Who do you speak of, Imogene?"

She sighed and straightened. "I don't think I want to do this anymore. I want to go home."

Conell began to place his hand over hers but pulled it away. "Tell me, *Chuōhá*, what do your words mean?"

"Argus! He's coming, isn't he? I am tired of crying and tired of running." She pushed back her hair. "You didn't hear what she said."

"You speak of Ūmá, last night, yes?" Émēr asked. "I heard weeping coming from your room."

Her blank eyes focused on his. "She said she stayed in the castle because Argus uses three strikes and you're out of the game."

"Three strikes?" Conell asked.

"First time you try to escape, he locks you in the dungeon. My first strike. I got the dungeon. Second strike, he puts you in the dungeon but also surrounds you with meat. The rats come. She got the second strike. Third strike." She rested her head into the palm of her hand. "He ties meat on you. Oh God, I have two strikes left. I can't do this anymore."

Conell let out a deep breath. "You mean if a prisoner tries to escape Argus the third time, he . . . "

She crossed her arms over her stomach and leaned over the table. "Yeah. She said, um, Ūmá said Argus put her in the cell when she tried to escape the second time. She said rats crawled over her legs." She pressed her fingers against her lips. "She said there was a girl-servant who tried to escape three times. She said the girl screamed all night until … she stopped."

Émēr stared at Imogene's pale face. That was why his women wept. And that is why Ūmá stayed in the castle. Argus would have captured her and locked her in a dungeon with rats who would eat her while she still lived. He closed his eyes. *Oh Attiyq, forgive me!*

Émēr squeezed her hand. "I will not let that happen to you, my sister. You will not meet the same fate; I give you my word."

Conell placed his hand on her back. "You are safe, *Chuōhá*."

She gave him a sad smile. "Yeah."

Imogene's tearing eyes locked on Émēr. "He raped her every night for five years. Every. Night." She swiped her fingertips under her eyelids. "That's what's going to happen to me, isn't it? I just never thought this could happen to me."

"No, *Chuōhá*, it will not happen to you. I will see to it," Conell said.

Émēr looked away. How could the Attiyq allow such a horrible thing to happen?

A deep sigh escaped Imogene. "She hates who she is, what she is now. He promised the same stupid things to her that he promises everyone: Love, a place, nonsense junk. And everyone runs after him like the Pied Piper of Hamelin. And then he destroys them. Her daddy handed her over to him when she was only eleven.

"Émēr, she said she didn't call out to you because for some reason the Attiyq told her to stay put. She was obeying Him. That's why she stayed."

Shame rushed across his mind and travelled to his hands and feet. He judged her wrongly, found her guilty without knowing the facts. She was braver than he could ever be, a greater Maúl than Anú. And her hands were empty of weapons. He had to see her; tell her he was wrong. He would be a faithful husband, true to her only. He owed it to her.

Imogene messed with her hair. "She told me of her last day with him. She stood in his chambers. She thought of escaping, but he locked her in. He locked the doors and windows. She couldn't get out." She shivered. "She said Argus was looking at you, Émēr, in a mirror."

Conell caught Émēr's gaze. "The captain?"

She nodded. "He was saying something about you had to stay with Māhōn. And that you weren't a Maúl."

Émēr straightened. "Why must I stay with him?"

She shrugged. "I'm just the messenger." Her eyes turned to Conell. "I don't want to do this anymore."

"You have to do nothing, Imogene," Émēr said. "Conell and I will protect you."

She offered him a small smile. Disbelief hung in her brown eyes. "I had another dream . . . from Him." She looked up at the ceiling. "It wasn't about your sister and mom. I'm so sorry, I'm trying." Her eyes held an apology she did not owe.

She was pushing herself for him. And the stress was destroying her. It was selfish to push one so broken. Émēr patted her hand. "It is alright, we will find them."

"It was about Māhōn," she said.

"What is about Māhōn?" asked a voice behind her.

Émēr looked over Imogene's head.

Māhōn leaned against the doorframe.

Imogene whirled and her pale face turned to Conell.

He helped her to stand and rushed her through the door. "It is nothing. She dreamt you stood in a park."

Māhōn watched them cross the compound. "A what?"

Émēr leaned back in his seat and cursed his hearing. Māhōn's loud footsteps were silent to him. He rose from the chair. "Excuse me. I have wood to chop."

Imogene made her way across the field with a tray balanced in her hands. Émēr dropped the axe onto the tree stump.

She grinned. "I thought you might like some lunch." She placed the tray of food and drink on the ground next to him.

"Thank you, my sister." He poured the water from the decanter into a metal mug.

"I wanted to tell you more of what Ūmá said. She said that there was an angel who, I guess, follows you."

"An angel?" He sat on the ground and extended his hand.

She sat next to him and handed him the plate filled with bread, cheese, and cooked meats.

"Yeah, Ūmá said she saw the angel in the mirror, and she has long blond hair. Argus freaked when he saw her. She wraps her wings around you whenever Argus talks to you through the mirror." She paused and looked back at the meeting hall. "We can't stay, Émēr. Māhōn's bad news."

He slowly chewed his food. "Bad news?"

"He's not a good guy. I had a horrible dream about him last night." She took a deep breath as if she intended to tell him of the dream, but she shook her head and expelled the breath with a slight shiver. "I can't talk about it."

Émēr briefly placed a comforting hand on her shoulder. "When will Ūmá be ready to travel?"

"Well, my guess is we need to stay at least two weeks, but I think we can leave in a week. Maybe."

Émēr responded with a decisive nod. "You will stay with one of us at all times," he ordered. "I will not permit you to be alone with him." He caught himself and adjusted his tone. "Imogene, my dear sister, I ask that you stay with one of us at all times. Please do not be alone with Māhōn."

She giggled. "Émēr, you're such a trip."

He joined her laughter. "I hope that is a good thing." He stood and extended his hand to Imogene. "I will walk you back to the meeting area."

When she accepted his assistance, a deep shame stabbed at his heart. "Imogene, I was cruel to my wife. I judged her wrongly."

She offered him a soft smile. "Yeah, you did." She stared over the green and flowering field. "It's so pretty here, as if bad things can never happen." She turned her sad gaze back to him. "He tortured her, Émēr. The day she left, she had given up hope, prepared to die. He beat her as bad as he beat me. He showed himself as a demon. Scared the dickens out of her. She had nightmares all last night. I don't know if she'll ever come back from this. She might never be the wife you want or need her to be. But what you did was amazing and incredibly brave. I'm proud of you."

The smile he flashed her was small and sad. "I will only take what she gives to me."

"When you're done here, come up and see her. I think she'd like that. But bathe first, cause you kinda stink." She wrinkled her nose.

He laughed. "I will."

After escorting Imogene to her quarters, Émēr finished chopping wood for five more rooms before Māhōn appeared for their mock combat session that ended with an intense study of the scrolls that had purportedly belonged to Māhōn's father.

Stay with Māhōn. You cannot become a Maúl without his teachings. The thought whipped across his mind like twigs tumbling over the waterfall.

She said that there was an angel who I guess follows you.

Protect the Weak and the Defenseless.

The lines in the flag represent the Code of the Maúl.

You have failed at being a priest, and now you stand between failing at Maúl and succeeding. Which shall you choose?

Émēr shook off the conflicting dialogue in his head and focused on Māhōn's teachings.

The sun began to set when Māhōn finally rolled up the scrolls. "You have done well, Émēr. But you must understand we have to reinvent the Voboo Maúl. I know you wish to return to the old ways, but the old ways no longer exist. If we follow the ways set down by Anú, then all of us will die. The Queen now rules these lands."

Émēr nodded. Perhaps Māhōn was right. But perhaps he was wrong.

After taking a quick bath in the river that flowed near the temple, he made his way up to his bride's chambers. Wild blue flowers grew along the path leading to the sleeping quarters. He grinned and used his knife to cut them; they would be his peace offering. Plus, they were the colors of Ūmá's eyes. After grabbing a flask from the kitchen, he filled it with water and placed the flowers in it. They flopped over the sides.

Butterflies attacked the inside of Émēr's stomach as he climbed the steps to Ūmá's room. "Stop being a child and go to your bride. You spent five years fighting the Queen, and now you wiggle over the smile of a woman. My woman. My tainted woman."

He paused at her door and pushed back his hair. Before knocking, he sniffed under his armpits to make sure that he was presentable.

Imogene opened the door with a large grin and a wink. "Ūmá, look who's here…" She stepped aside to let him in. "I'll be outside," she whispered with a punch to his arm as she scooted out the door.

Horror rushed over him as the door closed. He gathered his courage and turned to see Ūmá pushing herself up in her bed. Paleness still covered her black and blue face, and her lower lip was swollen. But it was her blue eyes that commanded his gaze. Beautiful, stunning. She wore a lovely beige silk nightgown with long sleeves that covered her arms, ending at her fingertips. A true *TTisho*. Imogene must have found it in the clothes Māhōn pillaged from the Slavers. Ūmá's recently washed, doe-colored hair framed her elfin face.

Ūmá kept her gaze downward, only occasionally looking up at him through her lashes.

Émēr walked to her bed side and presented the flopping blue flowers.

Her head rose and a small smile grew across her swollen lips. "Are these for me?" Her bright eyes jumped from the flowers to him.

He nodded. "Yes, My Lady. Ūmá. My Bride."

She sniffed the flowers and her smile grew. She fingered each one and placed them on the table next to her bed. "They are lovely, thank you, My Lord."

He grabbed a chair and shuffled towards the bed. So many words tumbled in his mind, but what to say? "How are you feeling?"

"I am so tired. I am sorry I am not serving you."

He shook his head. "Oh, My Lady, I do not need serving. Being my servant is not what I want from you. You are free from Argus's ways and being a slave. You are now my wife." He paused. "I heard you weeping last night."

Her face fell. "Forgive me, My Lord, it will not happen again."

He leaned forward. "No, Ūmá. That is not the meaning of my words. I do not wish for you to weep in another's arms, but in mine."

He placed his hand on hers; she pulled it under the blanket like a rabbit disappearing into a hole. Pain stabbed at his heart, but he shoved it aside. "I am your husband; I want to share these difficult times with you. Do you understand?"

Her watering blue eyes rose to his and a shiver raced down his back. It was like looking into twilight.

"I do not understand," she muttered.

"I want to share these pains with you, Ūmá. You do not have to carry this burden alone."

"As you wish, My Lord. But I do not think it is proper for you to know … what Lord Argus did to me." She blinked back her tears. "He …" She wiped them away. "As I said, it is not proper."

He smiled. "You are a *TTisho*, a true one, My Lady. Please, do not think it is improper. Allow me to decide what is improper. I want to know one day. But if you wish, later."

She nodded and stared at his flowers. "Where did you find them?"

"Along the path."

"My mother loved these flowers." She returned her gaze back to him. "I miss my father."

"You said you did not have one."

Her fingers played with the blanket edging. "I do. He would not accept me as I am. I am no longer his. I do not even know where he is." She swallowed the lump in her throat.

Sadness enveloped him. "As you are? Ūmá." He leaned towards her. "I have not been honest with you. We—Imogene, Pol, Cahal, and I—are running from the Queen. Cahal is Mojí Conell, prince and future King of Ézású. I am his captain of the guards and his protector. I once held the High Title of Lord Amgets of Opize and other silly titles. My Mojí ordered that I keep silent regarding his identity. That is why he wears the bandage around his arm. It hides the mark of the King."

She blinked several times.

"If—when—we defeat the Queen, My Mojí will take the throne, and I will present you as a member of His Majesty's Court, a Lady of

High Standing, *TTisho-ge.* Instead of being a servant, you will have servants. We will live in an apartment in the castle. I will see to it that you wear silk gowns and jewels every day. That is what your father will know. I will not mention your painful history—that is in your hands—and I will honor whatever decision you make. But know this: your former life is now erased. We will find your father. I promise."

Her eyes glimmered, and a smile raced across her lips. She winced and placed her fingers on her wounded mouth.

He sat on the edge of the bed. She tensed.

"Ūmá, forgive me." He tried to touch her hair.

She moved away.

He dropped his hand. "I judged you harshly. I was wrong."

Her fingers gingerly lowered onto his hand. "I judged myself, and I too am sorry. I am sorry I cannot give you what you want." She began to tremble. "I want to, but I cannot."

"No, Ūmá, it is not your fault. I do not blame you. I am sorry the Attiyq has put you through all of this."

Her head straightened as if she was offended for the Attiyq's sake. "It was the Attiyq who gave me strength to go on in spite of Argus ... so there is no need for sorrow. I am not angry at Him. I .... hate Lord Argus. The Attiyq comforted me when Lord Argus ... finished. The Attiyq led you to me, and you rescued me from horrible men. I do not know why He chose me to suffer for His sake, but I take the suffering with joy, and my faith in Him has grown. Do not blame the Attiyq. I endured for Him."

Her words sunk beyond the questions and the nagging sorrow. She was a *TTisho-ge,* a beautiful one with sapphire eyes. "You are a woman with much wisdom," he whispered as he moved the pillows down onto the mattress. "You need to sleep. And do not speak to Māhōn on the words I have spoken to you. I will worry about him; you rest."

She snuggled into the blankets.

"Sleep, now, my love." He kissed her forehead.

She looked up at him and smiled. Her fingertips brushed the markings on his face, sending goosebumps up and down his arms.

"I knew you would come for me." Her eyes closed.

Émēr stepped into the hallway and closed the door behind him. He let out a sigh of relief. He survived. A grin crossed his lips. He had fought countless battles, survived prisoners who sought to kill him, knew the mysteries of the Maúl, and a simple woman made him tremble. He shook his head.

He had been wrong about her tainted life. She was pure *TTisho.* A true Lady of the King's court. Her eyes were bewitching, soft as moonlight. Perhaps Mother would approve of her. He frowned. But her past—No. The past was gone now. He erased it—No. The Attiyq erased it as He erases the past of all who trust in Him. Mother would understand.

"Émēr, I spoke to Imogene," came a voice near his side.

The voice sounded like the voice of his Mojí, but Émēr only heard the words of Ūmá. *"You rescued me,"* she had said, her blue orbs brimming with compassion for him. Yes, rescued. He had never been a hero to anyone. A smile played on his lips. A hero. Father would approve. Pari would be pleased. They had always spoken of saving young women from the dragons. Somewhere, Pari was smiling.

"Émēr?"

Again, Émēr's ears told him he heard his Mojí's voice, but his feet took him down the hallway. His new bride would wear fine clothes and jewels, that is, if they survived the witch. All would be blue to match her Sapphire eyes. Sapphire, that would be her name from now on. He chuckled. Mother would be angry when men cast eyes of envy on his new bride. She always scolded the men who stepped out of line. Mother would have to understand why he took the once tainted woman as his wife. But would she understand? If they told no one, then who would know? Others would know and could use it against them. "I hope I did the right thing."

A hand turned him. "Captain!"

His Mojí stood beside him.

Imogene giggled and shook her finger at him. "Oh, Émēr, I know what you were thinking! You bad boy!" She opened the door and peeked on Ūmá before shutting it quietly. "Bad boy."

A grin played on Conell's face, but he kept his voice stern. "Did you hear my words?"

"Words, My Mojí?"

"I wish to speak to my Maúl Captain of the Guards, not the love-struck husband." He let his grin show. "Although my eyes are pleased to see such happiness."

Émēr nodded. "Yes, of course, My Mojí." He grinned. "She said I was her hero."

"Good." Conell opened the door to their quarters. "Now, may we discuss battle plans?"

Émēr rushed into the room. "Yes, Mojí."

Imogene followed him and took a seat at a small table.

Conell closed the door behind him and sat in one of the chairs next to Imogene.

Émēr stood beside the meeting table and stared into space. *Yes, I did the right thing. I* know *I did the right thing.*

Are you sure?

Émēr winced.

Conell cleared his throat. "Captain, would you like to take a seat, or would you prefer daydreaming of your bride?" He motioned to the seat next to him.

Émēr blinked at the faces looking up at him. Imogene grinned and pointed to the chair across from Conell. Frigg and Erák chuckled. He quickly plopped into the chair. "Frigg, Erák, when did you arrive?" The two men exchanged grins.

"Cousin, has your bride bewitched you?" Erák asked.

Imogene nudged him with her elbow. "She's done more than bewitch him."

Conell chuckled. "Keep your mind focused, Captain."

Émēr nodded.

"I have spoken to Imogene about her dream." Conell nodded to her. "She said she and Ūmá were back in the Queen's dungeon, while we, meaning Émēr, Frigg, Erák and myself were dead. Māhōn had left them with Argus. I fear Argus may have found us. Imogene says moving Ūmá might be too risky, and she needs rest. We will always have to be on alert until we can escape.

"Émēr, what have you discovered about Māhōn? Imogene believes he might not be whom he claims to be."

Émēr shrugged. "I am still uncertain, My Mojí. He claims they have had to rewrite the ways of Anú in order to survive." He placed his elbow on the table and rubbed his chin with the back of his fingers. "I understand his fears, but—"

"It doesn't jive," Imogene said.

"Jive?" Erák asked.

"Make sense," she said. "I mean, I've seen Émēr, and he breaks out Ninja stuff all over people. He's not afraid of anything. These guys, they don't jive."

Conell looked at her from the corner of his eye. "I think what she means is Māhōn's men do not act as Maúl."

She pointed her finger at him. "Bingo, right."

Émēr nodded. But still the words bit at his mind. How could he become Maúl without teachings? "But also, he has scrolls that Jezebel has not seen. He knows the Maúl language. He speaks it when we are together. He—" Émēr stopped and flicked his fingers. "I do not know the words I speak."

Imogene laid her hand on his arm. "That's because you really do believe you have to go school to learn to be Maúl. You don't get it, do you? You don't need his scrolls." She spread her arms across the table. "Who here married a girl that no one wanted, and everyone wanted to pimp her out? Who here has fought everything and everyone? You." She pointed to Émēr. "Why do you think you need scrolls to be Maúl? Émēr, you are the shining example of Maúl. Look up Maúl in the dictionary, and your picture will be there."

Her words drilled past the questions. Maybe she was right? "Dictionary?" He furrowed his brow.

She waved her hands and shook her head. "Never mind. Just trust me, you're there. You're it. You're the Maúl."

"So, when do we leave?" Frigg asked. "And where will we go?"

"I found a map in the items Māhōn took from the slavers." Conell pulled a map from a bureau drawer and laid it out on the table.

"We are here, in the temple." He pointed to the picture of a crudely drawn fortress. "We need to stay away from villages as the Queen will be watching them. We need a place that will give us refuge and will allow Ūmá to heal and Imogene to hear from the Attiyq. I have spoken to Erák. Before the attack on the village, he spoke to traders who said the Queen has been watching for escaped prisoners in all Ézású, including the ports. We need to leave Ézású to regroup. So…" He trailed his finger down the map and tapped at a picture of a cave, "Brodén's cave."

Frigg's eyes grew wide. "Brodén's cave? That is in the Southern Lands! We cannot go there."

"What's wrong with the Southern Lands?" Imogene asked.

"Ézású," Conell said, "has been at war with the Southern Lands for centuries. But if we stay in the cave and away from the traders, we might be safe."

"Might be?" Imogene raised her eyebrows. "If we get caught, will we be prisoners of war?"

Erák frowned and shrugged a shoulder. "Yes, we would become prisoners and possibly executed."

"As opposed to being caught by Argus and executed?" she asked. "Boy, talk about picking your poison."

Conell nodded. "Aye, and poison it is. But if we go to the cave, we can hide and regroup."

Frigg tapped the picture of Brodén's Cave. "I see no choice. We go to the cave. The harvest time is near, and the roads will have more travelers. Then the snows will come. Staying in the cave will keep us hidden and safe from the elements."

The men and Imogene nodded, but Émēr stared at the map. To leave his temple and his home, to desert a possible brotherhood and the only scrolls left to him. To leave Father's memories. Ūmá's blue orbs floated into his mind's eye. The woman he swore to protect. The vows he made to the elders and to her. He nodded. "Yes, the cave." He turned to Imogene. "When will my wife be ready to move?"

"I'm going to squeeze in a good week, maybe less."

Émēr crinkled his brow.

She hid her grin. "In a week or maybe less."

"We will need supplies," Erák said. "If we are to hide in a cave and avoid hunting parties, we will need food and water. But how we will we get there?"

"We have the most fabby transportation." Imogene gestured with her hands. "Trust me when I say, they will knock your socks off."

Erák gave her a confused look and opened his mouth but turned to Conell.

Conell gave Imogene an amused glance. "We have the Attiyq's angels who serve us."

His mouth opened again, and again he clamped it shut.

Imogene pinched her thumbs and forefingers together and drew them apart in a line. "Awesome!" she said in a singing voice.

"Frigg, you and Erák start to gather dried meats and fruits from the kitchens," Conell said. "But do not allow Māhōn to see you. I do not, under any circumstances, want him to know our plans. We will store the food in bags here in our quarters. Imogene, work with Ūmá, have her ready by next week. Captain, keep Māhōn distracted as much as you can. I am sorry, but I cannot trust him. I fear he is as Imogene said, not what he appears to be. I will keep an eye on his men; make sure they keep away from Ūmá, Imogene, and our food supply. Imogene, I do not want you to leave my side. We leave in a week, at the midnight bell."

The Attiyq has weapons not made of human hands.

- Japik.

9

After dinner, Émēr slipped away from the group. His heart ached at the thought of leaving his family temple. His childhood remained planted in these crumbling walls. Departing this place was like abandoning his clan.

He strolled across the compound along the moonlit path. Maybe one day his new bride would walk with him on such a path. A stab of guilt bit at his heart. What would Mother say? What would others say? "I did the right thing. I know I did the right thing."

His feet led him through the gates and out into the forest. He extracted his war hammer and closed his eyes. Letting his senses reign, he practiced moves Father had taught him long ago. He stopped and allowed the hammer to dangle at his side. "But how can I leave? Without the training, how can I move from child warrior to an adult warrior? I do not want to stay as I am. Attiyq, give me wisdom. How can I turn my wife and Imogene over to the demon? Why do You allow such horrors to happen to those who are good? What kind of God turns His own children over to His enemies to consume them?"

Ūmá's words rang louder than Brodén's battle horn. *So why would my anger be against Him?*

Émēr plopped onto a log. "Why is my anger against You, Attiyq? What has happened to me?" Cian's words also bounced in his head. *Argus is after you.* "Attiyq, show me."

A woman dressed in white silk trousers and a long white tunic sat on the log beside him. He blinked several times. Moonlight danced across her long blond hair.

She said that there was an angel who I guess follows you.

"It is very difficult, is it not, captain?" A light shone from her bright, gray eyes.

"I am sorry, My Lady?" he asked.

"Trying to decide to follow the Great One or Logic."

He shrugged. "I feel I will never become Maúl, never learn the ways of my ancestors. I have failed at being the priest, and now I fail at being Maúl. Why does the Attiyq punish me?"

"Punish. That is what you feel is happening?"

"Well, yes. Why else am I denied Maúl training? Why else has my mother and sister been handed over to the enemy? Why else has my uncle taken his last breath? Why else was I made the priest in Cian's stead?"

"Many questions for such a brave soldier."

"And yet I do not have answers, only questions."

She nodded and sucked on her lower lip. "You believe that these are punishments? Could this instead be a great path that He has chosen for you? A path that has already been laid with riches? Do you not believe that your sister and mother are safe, and your uncle is cradled in the Attiyq's bosom? The Attiyq has promised to destroy your enemies, Maúl. They will attack you from one direction, but He will cause them to scatter from you in seven directions. His Name is mighty to save. He is Fire who consumes His enemies. Listen to His still, small voice, and He will give you all this land. Argus knows this, and he trembles. Fear draws Argus and his children. It is a curse. Argus can only ride on Attiyq's Glory in order to steal from you. Your faith in God is real and destroys the demon."

He stared at her soft, gentle face.

She looked past the trees as if something stood before her that only she could observe. "There is freedom on this path, freedom for all, and yet you have called it punishment." She turned her shining face to him. Authority covered her countenance, a soldier who knew her orders. "Do you truly think you can defeat Argus with swords and arrows? Do you truly believe that this is how Anú learned? By scrolls and teachings? Or by the hand of the Attiyq? When will you see this battle in the light of the Attiyq's Holy Word? You asked a question, what if the Attiyq changes His mind? Will a God who has given you so much, including His life, change His mind? Will one who makes the mark of the covenant change His mind?"

"Argus is using me."

She nodded.

"How do I stop him?"

She cocked her head. "What did Cian do?"

Cian's strong voice echoed in his ears. The invisible hands in the Queen's forest that grabbed at Émēr and his companions. It was Cian's words that broke the spell.

Émēr raised his hands to his chest. "Forgive me, Attiyq, and have mercy on me and my doubts. Argus, you no longer have control over me. I stand under the Attiyq's wings."

Something snapped in his mind like a twig broken under the weight of man's foot. The Dark that had invaded him screamed as a Power ripped it from Émēr's shoulders like an old, torn shirt. He breathed a sigh of relief as he felt the evil snatched away and tossed aside. His hurt and anger were washed away in a clear, spring river, and he felt clean inside as when Mother washed the bed linens in their home. His evil thoughts disappeared and in their place were the

Words from the Attiyq's books. He straightened and smiled. He did not need Māhōn's scrolls. Sounds from a distance filled his ears as did the whispered words of those back in the camp. His hearing returned. He turned to the woman. "Thank y—"

She was gone.

Under the wings of the Attiyq is where the enemy has no power.

-Anú.

Argus sipped at the wine and glanced over the glass rim at the eleven-year-old girl who stood before him. Her dark, curly hair framed her small face. A beauty who had not yet matured and who showed off the fruit he desired. He would wait for this tasty blossom to ripen before he plucked it. His New Girl. Beside her sat her father. The peasant of all peasants twisted his worn hat in his hands as he studied the statues scattered around Argus's den.

A servant placed a wine glass in the father's hand. He sniffed the red liquid and drank, lifting his brow. "Thank you, Lord Argus. It is a good wine. We do not have such luxury in Cie Village."

Argus made sure his smile reached his eyes. "I am pleased you find it pleasant. I obtain my wines from the Southern Lands."

The man nodded. "Such expensive tastes. It is an honor."

"I serve the Queen. She demands such things."

The New Girl's gaze fell on the tapestries of children playing by creeks and the colorful flowers in vases that sat on the small tables. Argus grinned as he watched her. Her fool father was ready to hand over his virgin daughter to him. Humans are very stupid. Girl's dark brown gaze landed on Argus as if to challenge him. He raised an eyebrow. She had a great will like his seer. It would be enjoyable to break this small one. A challenge, but he enjoyed challenges.

Argus placed the glass on the table. "So, child. Do you enjoy reading? Riding horses, playing instruments?"

Girl nodded. Her thick, black hair bounced around her face. "I want to study the great philosophers. Father has already taught me a lot about them."

A drop of fear slipped from her frail body, making the room smell like exotic flowers and Argus's toes tingled. He sat back and interlaced his fingers. "If you leave her with me, she may become an Ambassador of the Queen or a Lady in Waiting. She will be given an education, learn to read, write, learn science, botany, music, astronomy and yes, philosophy. She will learn about the great writers of Ézású." Argus sipped his wine and held the man's eye. "Will you agree to hand her over to me?"

The man licked his lips, then turned to Girl. "It is up to you, Alia. What do you want to do?"

"I want to be a philosopher, Father."

The father grinned. "My smart girl. She gets her intelligence from her mother."

So, the father asks Girl what is her choice? Interesting. Argus smacked his lips. Girl and her sweet, tasty will. A treasure he will hold each night until she bores him.

A small tinge trickled across his brain like a cat digging claws into flesh. It was small, an annoyance. He shrugged it off as he studied Girl's face, body, hands. She was perfect. His bed longed for new, innocent blood. He was lonely now that he had lost his last Girl. But the old Girl was tainted, worn, and useless. Broken. And it was her own fault. *These Girls...* It was always their fault. He offered them a new world and they defied him. He laid out the promise of a new life and what did they do? Fight, bite, and scratch. Always weeping and begging for mercy. Trying to escape. It was their fault his fists found their small round faces. Their fault he dragged them to the dungeons. Their fault until they learned the sweetness of submission. All they had to do was obey. *Worthless. All of them.* But this one would be different. *Yes, very different.* An intelligent fighter with a will. Argus's blood pumped in his ears.

The irritating "claws" slipped farther into his head. He winced as a shudder skipped down his back. He placed the glass on the table and focused on the father and Girl. The room began to weave before him. White spots flashed before his eyes. The claws dug and ripped into his brain. Argus jumped from his seat and clenched his head in his hands. The hot, stabbing claws spread along his temples and down the back of his skull. Deep, red welts appeared on his arms and chest. His skin turned black like soot. Claws swelled from his fingertips. Fangs stretched from his mouth. He dropped to his knees and threw back his head. A deep howl erupted from his chapped lips.

The father's mouth dropped open, and he reached out with a trembling, uncertain hand. "Lord Argus, are you alright?"

Argus raised his swollen head. "Do not touch me!" he screamed, his voice harsh and gargling.

The father backed away. Girl clung to his leg. He scooped up Girl and bolted for the door. Argus's bloodied eyes grew wide. *My Girl!* Argus grabbed the man's leg but the father kicked and yelled. Girl screamed as Argus's clawed hand clenched the pant leg. Then someone heaved Argus back, away from father and daughter. He lost his grip, and the man stumbled further away. Argus glared over his shoulder. *Japik!*

The angel's small hands were wrapped around his leg. She released a single hand to wag her finger. "Ah, Ah, Ah!"

Argus kicked at her and looked at the father. "Help me!"

The father had backed to the door and his voice trembled. "No one is there."

Japik shouted in the man's mind, *"Run!"* With Girl in his arms, the father raced from the room, the door slamming in their wake.

Argus smashed his fists into the floor and cursed the Attiyq.

Having released Argus, Japik hovered in the corner. "What is wrong, demon? Have you lost something?" She laughed. "The Maúl has found his voice which rings with the authority of the Attiyq!"

Argus howled and lunged at her. "You stole my Girl!"

"I am not the one who steals, demon. It is the Attiyq's servants who take back what you have stolen." Japik crossed her arms over her chest, her long blond hair hanging about her glowing face. "Poor baby. Do you need a bottle?"

Argus regained his feet and hurled everything within reach at the imp of Attiyq. Candles, furniture, tapestries that he ripped from the walls; he even pitched the wine bottle, his hatred spewing all over the room as the red liquid ran down the walls.

Japik dodged it all with ease. "You are growing old, demon. You have lost your aim. But you were never good at anything." Then she was gone, her snorts and chortles echoing off the walls.

Argus breathed heavily. The raging claws subsided from his head and his body morphed into his former handsome self. It was over.

A small hand slipped onto his shoulder. Brón's small face leaned around his shoulder. "Father, I heard your screams."

Argus dropped into a chair. "Émēr has found his strength. Tell your siblings to beware of him. Bring me Amhras, he must know of this development."

Brón knelt beside him and pushed away his damp hair. "Father, my heart breaks for you. Let me comfort you. Do not allow this one human to destroy you."

Argus kissed her hand. "My dear daughter, he is like Anú." Brón swallowed hard. "I know, I know. Go, tell your brother the attacks must be stronger, fiercer, and you come to me tonight."

Brón smiled and melted into the floor.

Argus dropped his face into his hands. "So, Anú, you return for your revenge."

A cough came from the doorway. Five of the Queen's guards

Daughter! Leave me now! I asked you to put fear into the heart of the prince, and instead, you long for my attention."

"Father, it is not my fault! The Attiyq healed his heart of my wounds. I cannot be blamed for this! Give me another chance!"

"A chance to do what?" Argus waved his hand over the mirror.

Japik appeared next to the Maúl, and her steps matched his. She laughed at the demons watching through the mirror.

Eagla screamed and covered her face.

Argus shook Eagla. "You are fear! You are not to fear another!"

"Father, I am sorry, but she is so strong. I cannot fight her. Give me the seer. Who watches over her? No one. I can defeat those who do not call upon the Great One. Give me the weak one. Father, let me make you proud of me."

He nodded. "She is yours."

Eagla gave a smug grin at her sister and disappeared into the ceiling.

Brón pouted and dropped into the floor.

Argus rubbed his forehead. There was still one person whom he could trust to destroy the Maúl and retrieve his possessions. He jumped through the window and spread his wings.

Hear another's words before you declare him guilty.

-Anú

10

Argus climbed through the open window of his beloved disciple, the only one who saw Argus's greatness and loved him, obeying his every wish. Argus's gaze roamed over his follower's muscular back as he washed at a basin. He was a true beauty.

Māhōn's head rose, his senses strong. "I am glad you are here, Master. I have missed you," he said with sincerity and knelt before his master.

Argus extended his hand, and his loved one kissed each finger. "As I have missed you." He caressed Māhōn's cheek. "My disciple, my heart is broken, and I need you to mend it."

Māhōn snuggled his face against Argus's hand. "What can I do for you, my love?"

"The people who have taken refuge here wish to destroy me. They have something that belonged to me, my medallion which I need to reclaim my throne. Kill Émēr and the others but bring the one called Aiden to me."

Māhōn nodded as he stared up at his master. "I ask one thing, My Lord, give me the woman Ūmá. I understand you have trained her well, and she could bring in much money to the temple. Émēr stole her from me and made her his own. He cares nothing for the Ways of the New Maúl. Your Maúl. Please, Master, may I have her?"

A smile slowly crossed Argus's face. Girl would get what she deserved. "Of course, she is yours."

Māhōn bowed before Argus. "Thank you, Master." He sat on his heels. "I also noticed your seer is rebellious. I could tame her for you."

Argus laughed. "You are ambitious, my son. A child of my loins." He caressed Māhōn's face. "Yes, my child, tame my seer. Help her to see things our way."

"The New Maúl thanks you, My Lord."

Argus leaned down over his disciple and whispered, "There is another, my love. Amgets has a sister, hair as black as midnight, young, fresh, untouched. I also give her to you as your wife."

A large grin crossed Māhōn's face. "My Lord, you have blessed me with so much. Leader of your Maúl, taming a seer, a woman who will bring us great profit and now a wife. Oh, Master. You are my true god." Māhōn bowed, then rose and took Argus's hand. "Stay with me."

Argus chuckled. "I will need you to become my enemy, my love. Stay with the one called Cahal, be his confidant. Convince him that you are on his side."

Pain crossed Māhōn's handsome face. "How can you become my enemy, my love?"

"You can do it; I know you can. Try for me."

"And my men?" Māhōn asked.

Argus stroked his face. "Sacrifices must be made, my child. I will give you a better Maúl. General Bode will be with you. He will help you."

Māhōn lowered his gaze.

Argus snaked his finger under Māhōn's chin and raised his face. "Will you do this for me? For the New Maúl? For your place by my side?"

He nodded. "Yes, Master."

"Oh, and I will need you to do something else for me once Amgets is dead. A girl with dark hair and brilliant dark eyes. Her father took her from me. She longed to be with me, be mine forever, but her father disapproved of us. Once Amgets and Cahal are dead, I will need you to find her for me and bring the poor, frightened child home . . . to me. She is in Cie Village. Kill the villagers including her cruel father and family. Will you do that for me?"

Māhōn nodded. "I will for you, Master." He kissed Argus's hand. "Stay."

Argus made his way to the window. "I cannot. Remember my words. Be my enemy. I will return to you, I promise."

Māhōn smiled as his Master flew away.

Émēr stopped in the temple compound and listened to the voices drifting in the air. He smiled.

"Émēr is amazing! He is a true Maúl and so handsome," said his Sapphire. "I had dreamed of him coming over the walls for me."

Imogene giggled. "Yeah, these guys are something else. Conell has been kind to me lately, and he prayed for me when I was sick. I don't really remember much, but it seemed…well, nice."

Sapphire laughed.

Émēr shook his head. It was wrong to eavesdrop on the *TTishos'* conversation. He blocked out their voices.

Other voices drifted across in the air: Conell speaking to Frigg and Erák as they dropped off food bags, Māhōn giving his men the next day's orders, the flapping of wings.

He cocked his head.

No, it was many birds as in a flock.

He furrowed his brow. What would have such large wings?

Men's screams ripped across the courtyard, followed by the dull sound of bodies dropping to the ground. Émēr slowed his breathing and strained to hear.

Argus!

Émēr froze. Argus brought his army. He sprang from his spot and raced across the yard; his heart stuck in his throat. He grabbed his Atabo from his belt. Ūmá! His Sapphire. If Argus touched her, he would forget his vows he made before the elders and would skin the demon.

His feet pounded on the wooden floors as he passed Mojí's quarters. "Mojí! Argus is here!" He swung open Ūmá's door. It banged against the wall.

Imogene stood before a mirror as she admired her pale purple gown. She jumped and squealed. "Émēr! What the— "

Ūmá bolted up in bed.

Émēr rushed to Ūmá and grabbed her arms. "Ūmá! Tell me you are fine!"

Her blue eyes grew wide with fear. "Have I done something wrong?"

Imogene pried his grip from Ūmá's biceps. "Émēr, what is wrong with you?"

He pulled back her covers and lifted Ūmá from the bed. "Argus is here, we must leave."

Imogene brought her hand to her mouth. "Oh God. Wait, put a blanket around her first." She draped a blanket over Ūmá.

Conell appeared at the doorway. "Émēr, what has happened?"

"Argus." Imogene pulled out two overnight bags from the closet.

Émēr carried his wife to the hallway. Conell grabbed Imogene's hand and her bag and towed her from the room.

Frigg and Erák stomped up the stairs, both carrying bags of food.

"My Mojí, what has happened?" Erák asked.

Conell passed them as he tugged Imogene behind him. "Argus has found us. Grab all that you can, we are going to the cave."

Frigg glanced at Erák, and both men scrambled for their room and grabbed the few bags of food they had already saved.

"Mojí, call for Áepoo!" Émēr called as he maneuvered down the stairs.

Ūmá's trembling arms tightened around his neck.

He lowered Ūmá onto the bottom stair and wrapped the blanket around her shoulders. "My Sapphire, stay here, while I check the compound." Her frightened eyes stared up at him. He touched her cheek and kissed her forehead. "Stay with the others."

He stepped into the yard. Mojí and the others joined Ūmá. Émēr held out his hand to stop them. Conell slipped through the doorway, but Imogene pulled him back and shook her head. He tapped her hand. No, she mouthed. He pulled her hand away.

He slowly made his way to his captain. "What do you hear?"

"Māhōn is coming. I do not hear-," Émēr whirled, his stance lowered and his Atabo raised.

Argus descended in front of them. Ūmá gasped and cried out. Conell raised his blade.

Māhōn appeared from around the corner of the building and placed himself between Argus and the two men. "You are not welcomed here, demon. Brother, take your clan and go. I will hold him off."

Argus tucked his wings behind him and laughed. Leather-winged men surrounded Émēr and Conell, forcing the two men to stand back-to-back. The demons' charred, skeleton faces twisted and hissed at the pair. Fangs protruded from their mouths and long claws from their fingers. The air smelled of decaying bodies. Émēr gagged.

Émēr looked back at Ūmá's pale face. Blue jewel orbs stared at him from the shadows. He motioned his hand to Frigg to stay. Ūmá shook her head and tried to break free of Erák's hold. He drew her back. Imogene rushed into the compound. Her small hands gathered up the skirt of her pale purple gown.

"Imogene!" Ūmá's small hands reached out for her.

Erák held her tight. Ūmá clung to his arms wrapped around her waist. Her face crunched in fear.

Imogene stood in front of Māhōn. Her tiny body trembled as she faced the demon.

Argus's eyebrows rose, and a laugh escaped him. "The tiny mouse now faces me? Am I to be insulted?"

Conell's eyes grew wide. "Woman, have you lost your mind?"

She straightened, but her voice trembled. "If you want to kill me, do it now. But you need me. I'm the seer, remember? You're *nothing* without me!" She glanced over her shoulder. "Call them, Conell, do it now!"

Argus slapped his sword against his leg. "I will enjoy breaking you, woman."

Imogene's eyes narrowed. "Bite me!"

"Áepoo!" Conell's strong voice rang across the yard. He hauled Imogene behind him. "You are a foolish woman."

"Yeah, I know," she said.

The four angelic beasts dove from the sky and settled between Conell and Argus's band. A tall, skeleton demon with long gray hair that covered his shoulders, slashed the air with his long, shining sword. Sharp teeth jutted from his mouth, and his tongue slipped in and out like a snake's. His leather wings were torn and hung like ripped drapes. He wore a red robe, and a large gold crown sat on his head. Battle metals covered his boney chest and his eyes glowed dark turquoise from his skull face. He stepped towards Imogene who screamed as Conell darted in front of her.

Áepoo's sword blocked the creature's blow. "So, General Bode raises his ugly head from the sand. It has been some time since I last saw you."

Bode paced in front of Áepoo, his skinless feet leaving imprints of his long toes in the sand. "The Great Áepoo. Still sniffing at God's feet? Join us, and you will become greater than He."

Áepoo laughed and twirled his sword over his wrist. "Now why would I join one so foolish as to throw away the Anointing of the Living God? You are only a third of heaven and yet you still think you can win against the Great One?"

Bode took a step back and lifted his chin. "Of course, we can win. Our King Argus leads us."

Áepoo laughed and kicked him back. "It is time we leave these children to play with their toys, Prince Conell."

Conell nodded. "Agreed!"

The angels shoved the demons back. Erák tugged Ūmá into the courtyard. Émēr placed her on Etta's back and jumped up behind her. Erák and Frigg climbed on Asechi, the eagle beast.

Conell lifted Imogene onto Áepoo's back then mounted.

"Never in my life have I seen a woman do something so…so, unbelievably senseless," Conell said.

"It worked. Let's just say, I have the heart of Éowyn."

Conell pulled her close. "Do not do that again."

Émēr's arms tightened around Ūmá's waist as he clung to Etta's mane. "Hang on, my Sapphire. Soon we will be far from him."

Māhōn grabbed for Oota, but the bull nudged him away. Argus's men separated him from the others. He withdrew and unsheathed his sword. "Go, brother!"

Émēr watched what was left of his clan face certain death. Maybe Māhōn was a traitor. Maybe he was true. But either way… *The Maúl guards the honor of his fellow brothers and sisters.*

He jumped from Etta's back. Ūmá screamed and tried to scramble from the animal but Áepoo held her back.

Émēr joined his brother-in-arms. "We will fight together."

"Captain, get back on the beast!" Conell said, snarling. "That is an order!"

"I cannot leave my brother." Émēr turned to the demon.

Argus lifted his chin and sucked in his breath. "Really? A cockroach shall fight me?"

Áepoo pawed at the ground with impatience.

"Áepoo," Conell said, "we must take Māhōn."

Áepoo nodded towards Māhōn. "Oota will take him."

Conell waved Émēr back. "Captain! Bring him! Bring Māhōn!"

Émēr drew Māhōn to the beasts. Māhōn jumped onto Oota, and Émēr climbed behind his Sapphire. He wiped the sweat from his brow and thanked the Attiyq. A small sound escaped Ūmá's throat and Émēr rested his chin on her head and Etta soared above the darkening lands.

"I am sorry, my Sapphire, but I thought I had lost you. I felt as if my world had crumbled. I did not mean to frighten you." He nuzzled her neck, but she lifted shoulder in avoidance.

"I am sorry, My Lord, I do not mean to do this."

His arms tightened around her. "Do not be sorry, My Lady."

"Seeing him back there," her voice cracked. "I am sorry." Her body shuddered as her tears streamed down her cheeks, and she wrapped her arms around his waist. "I hate Argus with my soul. What he did to me, what he did to others in the castle." Between gulps Ūma recounted the entire tale.

Émēr closed his eyes. He had judged her as a *Zuuho*, a creature cursed by God. No one should be judged this way. Her strength surpassed Anú and the elders of his tribe. No human was as strong as her. *I renew my vows before You, Attiyq, to cherish and protect the one whom You have given to me. I will forever keep her safe for Your name's sake. Help me, Attiyq, give me grace to make her my wife forever.*

He kissed the top of her head. "My Sapphire, I swear to you. You will never go back there again. I will see to it. Do not punish yourself, My Lady. We will be fine, I promise."

He cradled her in his arms while the warm breezes caressed them. If only Etta would fly to the ends of the earth, away from Argus, the Queen, the weapons, and all of mankind. He would find a secret place where this amazing creature could heal.

Mojí's firm voice pierced the calm night air. "Áepoo, take us to Brodén's Cave."

His Sapphire eventually fell asleep in his arms. The blue-white mountains of Opize came into view. His eyes scanned for any sign of his home. The wooden domains that once spotted the fields were now charred skeletons. Silence enveloped the once busy village. He swallowed the lump in his throat. Mother. Aine. The sacrifice he had made before the Attiyq became his biggest blessing. Hopefully Mother and Aine still lived. The angel seemed to believe so.

The beasts landed close to the cave entrance. Ūmá stirred in his arms. He climbed from Etta's back and helped Ūmá from the beast. She tugged the sleeves of her nightgown till it reached her fingertips and wrapped the blanket around her shoulders.

Émēr grinned. A true *TTisho.* It was time he made future provisions for his wife and surviving family.

Erák and Frigg slipped from Asechi. Erák leaned against the animal's back and laid his head on his wrist. "Please tell me that did not happen. Never in my life have I seen such horrible creatures."

Frigg patted him on his shoulder. "You will see more, I am sure." He pulled the bag of food from Asechi's back.

Māhōn jumped from Oota and helped Frigg with the provisions. "It is good you stole my food."

Frigg shrugged. "I suppose it is. I do not understand how a creature so beautiful can be so evil."

Māhōn looked at Frigg from the corner of his eye. "You believe Argus is beautiful?"

He hauled a bag over his shoulder. "He healed my wounds. How can he be so evil?"

Māhōn tossed a piece of rotting fruit from his sack. "Perhaps he is only misunderstood. Evil is never fixed in time but is only defined by the one who sees it. What if Argus is good and the Attiyq is evil? Would a good God allow you to suffer as you have? Or would He rescue you? If Argus healed you, then perhaps he is the one who is good? But I too have many questions."

Frigg nodded. "It seems the questions grow larger in my mind."

Émēr led Erák away from the others. "I have something important to ask of you. As you are my only surviving male relative, I ask that you become Ūmá's *Radaakar*. If something happens to me, I want you to become my family's redeemer, to take my wife as your bride, and you will care for her all your days till your death. Any of my surviving children will become yours. My mother and Aine and Imogene will become your mother and sisters and live in your house. Ūmá will remain *TTisho* as will my sisters. Will you please accept this arrangement? I have no one else to guard what is left of my family."

Erák gave a small bow. "I am honored. Yes, I will be their *Radaakar*."

Émēr placed his hand on his cousin's shoulder. "I knew you would do this for me. Your father smiles from heaven."

Erák grasped Émēr's shoulder. "Thank you, my cousin. You have brought joy and honor back to my family. Yes, my father is smiling, but because you are still alive, and you have put our clan first. You have honored me and my family." He picked up a bag and made his way into the cave.

Émēr took Ūmá's hand. "Everyone, please listen. In the event of my death, Erák will become my family's *Radaakar*. My family will become his family."

She squeezed his hand. "My Lord, please I do not wish to go with another man."

Émēr kissed the back of her fingers. "I cannot die knowing my wife will become *Zuuho*."

Māhōn placed a bag over his shoulder and ignored the announcement.

"Please, Ūmá, if I die, I must know you and my family are safe," Émēr said. "Agree to take Erák's hand if I am killed. Please, my wife, do not put this burden on me that you will suffer after I am gone."

She offered him a small smile. "Yes, my husband. Thank you."

He kissed her forehead then nodded to Conell and Frigg. "Cahal and Pol are witnesses to this agreement."

Conell helped Imogene from Áepoo's back. "I accept this arrangement and will see it is done."

"What's a *Radaakar?*" Imogene asked.

"It means if something happens to Émēr, then Erák will take Ūmá's hand in marriage and will give her a home. It means a redeemer," Conell said.

Frigg nodded. "It is as you have spoken. I am witness."

Etta poked his soft nose against Émēr's back. He laughed and buried his fingers in Etta's long mane. "I am back, my friend. If I join the Attiyq, then I ask that you hide my wife and Erák. Will do this for me?"

The lion nuzzled his hand.

He stroked the lion's face. "I take that as a yes."

Áepoo trotted to Ūmá's side. She took a step back, but he smiled. "Do not fear, My Lady."

Émēr slipped his arm around her waist. "He is called Áepoo, an angel of the Attiyq. You do not need to fear him."

"I know, Ūmá, daughter of Fillian," Áepoo said, "that you have many questions as to why you suffered. Argus never had power over you, as you were always in the Attiyq's hands. Know also that the One we serve has seen your tears, and He says, I have wept with you each night as you endured pain and humiliation. Do not question why these things have happened to you; just know that all will work out for your good.

"Now He has rescued you from your pain and has broken into these worries that haunt you day and night. He came to you on your worst day, the day your father handed you over to the demon. But know now, My Lady, that you can face anything with the Great One at your side. He longs to help you and prove to you that He will walk each day with you through all these heartaches until He walks with you into His kingdom.

"Every angel in heaven knows your name, Lady Amgets, and how you did not turn from the Great One as the rats watched you in the dungeon and as Argus tormented you day and night. The Great One sent us to shut the rats' mouths that night and protect you from those who would wish to destroy you. We guided this strong Maúl warrior," he nodded to Émēr. "To your side, whispered the words of marriage and freedom to him and have brought you here. This brave and powerful Maúl warrior will guard you well, as we will also. Fear not, My Lady. Now you are safe."

Tears welled up in Ūmá's eyes, and she nodded her thanks.

Émēr grasped the angel's forearm. "Thank you, my friend."

Áepoo took Émēr's elbow. "It is an honor to serve such a strong Maúl warrior as yourself. You are the greatest, second to Anú himself." The beasts galloped into the darkness before rising into the sky.

Māhōn hauled a bag over his shoulder. "Not all of us have had the Attiyq's blessings on them. I have lost my men and my temple this evening. I wish to build a fire and sleep, that is if you do not mind, Prince Conell."

Conell squared his shoulders, ready for a fight.

Māhōn shrugged. "I heard what the horse-man called you. There was never a need to hide your identity from me, Prince. But I understand the need for caution during these times." Māhōn lit a torch and peered into the cave. "It seems I now owe you a debt, my brother. Thank you for not leaving me in the enemy's hands."

"It is my honor," Émēr replied as he watched Māhōn step into the cave. Once Māhōn disappeared into the darkness of the cave, Émēr placed both hands on Ūmá's shoulders. "My Sapphire, I am not certain Māhōn is who he claims to be. I question my own thoughts. Please, my wife, stay close to me for your own safety."

She gave him a shy smile and nodded. "Yes, My Lord."

He slipped his arm around her waist and led her into the cave.

Not all enemies are enemies.

-Anú

11

Ruárc bowed as Ookeza, his sun god, slipped under the earth to sleep. Dark shadows advanced over the huts of his small village. Without Ookeza's warm embrace, a chill settled into the commune. He bowed again. "Bless my night travels, Ookeza."

Chara, his wife, slipped a heavy pack onto his shoulders. He smiled as she slid her robust arms around his waist. A smile lingered on his face. Chara's large stomach pressed against his back. "Husband, watch your steps. I do not want you to become food for the demon."

He took her into his arms and played with her curly, red hair framing her chubby face. Hair kissed by Ookeza and a smile brighter than his god that broke through the darkest hour. "I will be careful, Chara, do not fear." He tightened the sword belt. "Remember, keep guard against the demon."

She nodded. "May Ookeza protect you, My Lord."

He kissed her. "As with you."

She brushed away a strand of his hair from his eyes. "Toál would be pleased to see his brother being so strong, as would your mother."

He grinned. "Father would say I am a fool as I survived and his favorite Toál died."

"Your father is dead, so his words lie with him in his grave. Let them lie there."

"If I do not return, then take the children and hide in the mountains. If I survive, then I will meet you at the base of Ur Mountains, east of us. Stay within the barbarian's territory; the witch will not venture here. If I do not return in a year, then it means the Mojí or the demon's sword has found me. Watch Amgets' mother and sister at all times as we will need them to bargain with Émēr for the girl and her medallion."

Chara flashed her charming smile. "You will find them. You are the best tracker in the land."

"How did you get so smart?"

She kissed him. "I married you."

He pulled her into his arms. "I am as a lost man in a desert when you are not at my side. I promise we will leave this place once I return. I will not go back to the Queen."

He picked his way down the darkening path that led away from Chara's beauty. A grin covered his face as the sound of four children followed him.

Aurc, his eldest son, grabbed his hand. "Father, I am ten years old now and almost a man. Allow me to come with you and fight the enemy."

Ruárc ruffled the boy's dark hair. "And who will be here to guard the prisoners and protect your mother and siblings? You are the eldest and that burden falls upon you, my brave one."

Aurc wrinkled his small nose. "But surely Muarc can watch them."

Ruárc knelt. "He is only seven years of age, a child. Your sisters are only six and nine years of age. Who will protect them?"

Muarc crossed his pudgy arms and pouted. "I am not a child. I am a man."

Ruárc fought the grin threatening his lips. "I need a man to protect your mother and your sisters." He bore a serious gaze into Aurc's black eyes.

Aurc twisted his small lips and gave a sharp nod. "Yes, father, I will guard the village and destroy any enemies who come near us."

Ruárc laughed. "Now you are a man."

Chia, his youngest daughter, climbed on his back and wrapped her small arms around his neck. "Father, give us a ride." Her curly, red hair tickled his back.

Nika, his eldest daughter, took his hand and rocked back on her heels. "Yes, father, give us rides before you kill the enemies of Ookeza!"

He laughed and disengaged his children. "There will be time for rides when I return."

Chia placed a necklace made of beans into his hand. "Here, father. To bring you luck. Mamma and Nika helped me make it."

He grinned and slipped it over his neck. "I am most honored for your great gift." He fingered the treasured necklace and tugged his youngest into his arms. She was the image of her mother and her hair was kissed by his god. He held his children tightly and prayed for safety.

He released them and they gathered around him. "You all obey Aurc and your mother, understand? I will return, I promise."

The young ones nodded, and Aurc's chest rose. "I will make you proud, father." Ruárc ruffled his son's hair. "May Ookeza's hand be on all of you."

Aurc bowed. "As with you, father."

Aurc held back his siblings as he stood tall in the path. "We will make you proud, father. Destroy the enemies of Ookeza!"

Ruárc waved before continuing down the path. A deep sigh escaped him. Leaving his family was like leaving his soul behind. First Toál died, then his mother and thankfully, his cruel father. Now he must walk away from his wife and children again. He readjusted his backpack. They were safe in the Barbarian's country. He chuckled. "I know, Toál, you do not agree with me. If you were here, you would insist I take my sons with me and allow our enemies' blood to flow over their hands. Not this time, my brother. If I fail, the witch will kill them all. And now they are all I have. At least now, Chara and my little ones will be safe." A shiver slipped down his back. "Argus would feast on my little ones. Not even you could stand such horror. If I cannot find DeCapris, then I must run, my brother. I know your eyes shame from me, but to see my daughters in the demon's bed. To use them as he did the others, to us. Please, Toál, understand, I cannot fight anymore. My little ones need me."

He pulled a map from his pocket. The last time he saw Conell DeCapris and his followers they were on flying horses and heading north. Why north? He lowered the map. Flying horses. Where did the prince find flying horses? The faces of his little ones rose in his mind. He closed his eyes. "Turn around now. Take Chara and the children and run. Fast. Toál, is this the price of honor? Fighting flying horses?" He studied his map. "I cannot win this, even if I hold Amgets' family. But how far can we run where the witch's eyes do not search? How far east can we go?"

The map depicted a small Maúl Temple within the safety of the Opize Mountains. "Amgets would take the prince to a place of safety."

Ookeza's star children sparkled against the dark sky, and the lovely face of Ookeza's sister, the moon goddess Keza, lit the path.

"Ookeza, forgive me for traveling while you sleep, and I pray that you ask your sister to guard me as I travel and guard my family. I give you my word, if you assist me in finding DeCapris, the girl, and the medallion, then we will leave this place and never travel while you sleep."

He finally stopped for the night and prepared the fire to cook his game. The Star Children played in the night sky as he used the fire's light to read his map. Rumors flew among the Barbarians of a new Maúl tribe rising from the ashes. A tribe that abandoned the Old Ways and followed new paths. Paths that brought dishonor even to the Barbarians. But Amgets' obsession with the Maúl would lead the young man to the New Maúl temple. He shrugged. Perhaps the new tribe would have information about Amgets? DeCapris would never trade the girl for Amget's family, but would Amgets trade his family for the girl?

Ruárc slipped the pack under his head and watched the Star Children play. "Please, Ookeza, help me to find Amgets and the girl. Please protect my Chara and my little ones." He yawned. "And please do not let Chara know that I long to be with the girl for one night. Not even you could protect me from my wife's wrath."

Hide under your enemy's feet, where he never looks. Then attack him when he is not aware.

-Anú

12

Mojí held Imogene back as he peered into the cave. Māhōn, Frigg, and Erák gathered around him.

"Captain," Conell called.

Émēr pulled candles from the bag of supplies and used Māhōn's torch to light them. He peered into the cave. "Aiden, stay with my wife."

"Pol, Erák, stay with the girls, Māhōn, come with me," Conell said.

Imogene rubbed her arms and pulled her cloak from her bag. "It's freezing in here."

Ūmá's teeth chattered, and she pulled the blanket tighter around her shoulders. "I agree; it is cold." She weaved against the wall.

Imogene wrapped her cloak around Ūmá as she maneuvered her to the cave's entrance. "Émēr, get back here. We need to make a fire. Ūmá's freezing."

Émēr quickly turned back. Ūmá's lips were turning blue, and she was shivering. He cleared away the sticks and made a small fire.

"Her body heat is getting lower. We have to do something before hypothermia sets in." Imogene gently laid Ūmá on the ground and wrapped her head in the hood of the cloak.

Erák gave her a funny look. "What?"

"She's cold. Erák, put some of those rocks into the fire, but only for a second, just to get them warm. We'll put the rocks under her arms and on her sides."

Émēr placed a few stones around the fire. He dumped the food from one of the bags, then placed the hot rocks into it. "How will this help her?"

"It will warm her up slowly. If we move too quickly, her heart will stop. She'll die. We're going to go slow."

"Should I rub her arms?"

Imogene shook her head. "No, if we warm her too quickly, it might damage her heart. We need to go slow. I need you guys to go find her a warm place to sleep, not out here in the cold. Frigg and Erák can stay with us. Erák, you and I are going to lie next to her under the blankets until she gets warm."

Erák slowly gave Émēr a confused look. "I do not know if this is proper to do."

She lifted Ūmá's blanket. "Get down here. I'll be on the other side. There isn't time for formalities."

Émēr nodded. "Do as she asks. My wife must be kept warm."

Erák gingerly slipped under the cover as Émēr covered him and Ūmá.

Conell lifted his candle and peered into the cavern. "It is said that Brodén's Cave was a place of safety for the King's men. There may be blankets somewhere. Of course, it has been a very long time. Frigg, you stay with the women. If you see danger, put out the fire and bring the women deeper into the cave. Māhōn, I ask that you accompany us."

When Māhōn balked, Imogene pointed into the cave. "What are you waiting for? Go see what you can find."

Émēr kissed Ūmá's forehead. "My Sapphire, I will return soon."

Conell gave a candle to Māhōn. Émēr took the lead while Conell made sure Māhōn walked between them.

Their footsteps echoed down the chamber. Émēr glanced over his shoulder. The fire glowed around the small group. Alone and unprotected.

Like your mother whom you left behind?

Émēr cringed at the familiar voice. "She is protected by the Attiyq. I will not listen. You are defeated," he whispered.

The words soothed his soul, and he let out a sigh of relief. He lifted his light to the walls. Strange letterings covered them. He traced the letters with his finger. "Mojí, these words are of the old Maúl tongue. Why would King Brodén use them?"

Conell shrugged. "Brodén and Anú shared a deep respect for each other as warriors. Perhaps the Maúl guarded this place?"

"What was the purpose of this cave?" Māhōn asked.

"My father told me once that Brodén used this cave as a defense against his enemies. But it was abandoned centuries ago. No one knows why," Conell said.

Émēr extended his candle closer to the walls. "I can understand some of the writings, but some do not make sense."

Māhōn gasped and grabbed Émēr's shoulder. "I thought I saw a man's face! There!"

Conell lightly touched the stone. "It is nothing but ridges and water. Brodén was wise. When the light reflects off the stone, it looks like a man's face." He moved the candle around the stone. "See? It looks like a man."

Émēr chuckled at Māhōn's expression. "Maybe we should have left you with the women."

Māhōn gave a small growl. "It looked like a man."

The cave ended at a stone wall. Émēr placed his hand over the cold stones. "There is a draft." The flickering light revealed more Maúl writings. "Mojí, there are more writings here."

Conell leaned over Émēr's shoulder. "What do they say?"

Émēr drew his fingers across the carvings. "'The Great Anú, the first of the Maúl, the greatest of all warriors, the first before time, rules from his fortress where no man can find him or those who pursue him. He stays hidden like the *jado*, safe in his hole yet attacks like the wolf that appears from the midst. No one can stand before him, and no one is his equal. He is as the fog rolling in from the sea then is gone as the sun breaks through the clouds. He is a ghost that haunts his enemy's dreams. He is the great Anú. Follow the path to Anú's treasures. Track the footsteps of those who lay their swords at his feet. Pursue the ghosts of Anú.'"

Émēr paused to read further. "There are other writings, but it is mostly of Anú's battles alongside King Brodén." He straightened and rubbed his chin. "Mojí, these symbols claim Anú had a castle, yet the elders' tales say he lived in the woods. So, which is correct?"

Māhōn shrugged. "I knew little of Anú. Father only taught me from his scrolls."

The light from Conell's candle revealed holes the size of platters drilled into the ceiling. "Look here," he said.

Émēr nodded. "Arrow holes. This was used as a fortress at one time. The archer would shoot arrows through the holes to the enemy above." The torch flame fluttered. Émēr held out his hand. "The draft is stronger here." He took a step towards the wall. "Follow the path to Anú's treasures."

He shined the light on the wall. More words covered the damp rocks. "'Only the brave Maúl can follow Anú. Only those with pure hearts may read his words. Only those who seek the Great Attiyq may follow.'"

Māhōn peered over Émēr's shoulder. "What does it mean?"

Émēr stared at the flicking light. "It means that the tunnel continues."

"A secret passage?" Māhōn asked.

Émēr nodded. "A message from Anú. 'Place your hands in Anú's palms. Follow his steps to his secrets.' This was a game we played when we were children and living at the temple." He handed his candle to Conell, then pressed his palms into the openings in the stone. He pulled them back and tapped his fingers five times into the fingertip impressions then pressed his palms tightly into the small cavity. The rock wall swung open, and a whish of wind played with his hair.

Mojí and Māhōn gasped.

Émēr grinned. "Anú had many tricks."

The candlelight revealed a steep stone staircase leading down. Spiderwebs crisscrossed the ceiling down to the steps. "Imogene will be upset over the spiders." He chipped away the webs with his hammer. "Stay here until I reach the bottom."

"What about traps?" Māhōn asked.

"I doubt Anú would place traps in his home." Émēr paused, his foot dangling above the first step. He glanced at Conell. "I hope this was his home." He proceeded, testing the first step before descending. When he reached the bottom, he called out, "Come down, but with care."

Conell and Māhōn joined him at the bottom of the stairwell.

Émēr stepped through the arched doorway and lit the candelabras that stood on either side. Light filled the landing. "Mojí," he whispered. He turned and the light revealed two large angelic statues guarding the doorway.

Conell stepped through the door and onto a large balcony. The two men crowded around him.

"I do not think this is Anú's castle," Māhōn whispered.

A large wooden stairwell with black, iron balusters in the shape of thin tree limbs curved down to a large courtyard from the veranda. Two other balconies with the same balusters veered off in opposite directions and curved around the courtyard. Émēr lit the candelabras that stood around the terrace, then shone his candle over the side. Several stone pillars stood on the courtyard below. He followed the light up to the arched ceiling, observing the swirl designs.

Aside from the spiderwebs that adorned the candle stands in the courtyard and the stair railing, the ornateness of the fortress gave all indication of Brodén's abode as opposed to the humble dwellings of the Maúl. A large statue of King Brodén stood in the center of the courtyard. Two more curved, wooden stairwells were located off the left and right balconies. "Mojí, what is this place?"

Conell shook his head. "My father never said that Brodén had an underground castle."

"There is your answer, Émēr." Māhōn pointed to a large, tattered banner that hung over the arched doorway. "It is Anú's flag. This was Anú's fortress." He smirked at Émēr. "It seems that Anú enjoyed the finer things in life after all. Perhaps Anú was not as pious as you thought."

Émēr suppressed his growl. "I must find a warm place for my wife to rest. If I remember correctly, the sleeping quarters were always kept to the right." He made his way down a hallway with arched ceilings. Large murals covered the walls. One depicted King Brodén slaying his enemies. Another portrayed Anú bowing down to the Attiyq. He paused. *Oh Attiyq, give me your wisdom and your strength. I do not wish to lose my way again.*

Émēr stepped inside the sleeping quarters and lit a lamp hanging on the wall. The light revealed a large room with bunk beds lined along a wall. A few chairs sat scattered around the room. Large built-in closets stood opposite the beds.

Conell shook out a blanket. "I know this is not the proper place for the women, according to the ways of the Maúl—and you are correct, Imogene will most certainly be upset about the spiders—but it will have to do until we can find better accommodations."

"Mojí, could this have been the first Maúl castle?" Émēr asked. "Could Anú have slept in this place? His footsteps on the stairs?"

His Mojí smiled. "I would hope he did. Come, let us get the women."

"You have got to be freaking kidding me!" Imogene stared down the web-laced stairwell. "Do you think for just one time you can find us a non-terrifying place to sleep? Dracula would love this place."

Émēr smothered his grin.

"Who?" Conell asked.

"A monster who sucks human blood. Don't ask."

Émēr chuckled and made his way down the stairway with Ūmá in his arms. Conell took Imogene's hand. "Come, *Chuōhá*."

Imogene held up her candle and gingerly stepped onto the stairwell. "You owe me so big, Émēr!" She squealed as the spiderwebs brushed against her arms. "I swear, if anything big and crawly jumps on me, I will hunt you down like a dog."

He laughed. "And I will fear you."

"Yeah, you'll fear me alright." A palm-sized spider scurried across the stones. "Oh God, that's moving!" She tromped down the stairs, passing Conell.

Imogene brushed the webs from her clothes and checked for spiders.

Émēr led the way through the grand doorway.

"Are those angel statues?" Imogene ran her fingers over the cold stone wings. "So pretty." She stepped out onto the balcony and peered down the stairs.

Conell leaned against the doorway and watched her.

Her eyes took in the high ceiling, the large staircase, and the Brodén statue in the center of the room. The bottom of her light purple dress rustled along the floor and the sleeves of her dress covered her fingers.

Émēr had to smile when he saw Conell watching her. "Imogene would fit in well with the castle," Émēr said in his native language.

Conell grunted and studied a pillar. Frigg and Erák gathered around him.

"Mojí, what is this place?" Frigg asked.

Conell glanced down at him. "I am not sure. Émēr thinks it could be Anú's first castle."

"But was not Anú to have lived in the woods? And such luxury. It is better than Brodén's castle."

"Amazing!" Imogene whispered. "How did this place survive after all these years?"

Émēr hurried to the sleeping quarters. "Imogene, come. My wife must rest."

Conell took her by the elbow and led her down the hallway.

She stopped at the murals. "Is that?"

"Yes," he said. "I promise we will explore later."

Émēr entered the sleeping quarters and laid Ūmá on the bed, then covered her with the blankets. "I am sorry this place is not as clean as it should be, but it will keep you warm." He piled more blankets over her as she snuggled down into the mattress.

Imogene paused at the doorway. "This is really creepy, like the folks just hopped up and ran out." She pointed to a chair scooted out from the table. "Like some guy sat there and then ran off two seconds ago."

Émēr motioned to her. "Please Imogene, my wife."

She made her way to the bed and felt Ūmá's forehand. "She still has a bit of a fever."

Émēr handed her a handful of green weeds. "Here, mother brewed these into a tea when I was young and made us drink it when we were sick. It broke our fevers."

She sniffed them then made a face and pulled away. "Ugh! That is horrible."

"It smells bad, but it will work."

She took the herbs. "I guess we can find a way to cook them over our fire."

Conell nodded. "There should be a kitchen on the bottom floor. We can find a pot and boil the herbs at the cave entrance. I will accompany you." He led her out the door.

Māhōn shook out a blanket and lay on the bed. He folded his hands under his head and stared at the ceiling. "Now this is a castle I would live in."

Erák and Frigg exchanged glances.

"Perhaps we should sleep elsewhere," Frigg said. "I do not think it is proper for us to sleep with the women."

Erák nodded. "I agree. We need to find new sleeping arrangements."

Māhōn lifted his head and frowned. "And where would you suggest we sleep?"

Émēr shook out a blanket. "There is an eating hall next to this room. We will take our mattresses and sleep there. As Frigg said, it is improper for us to sleep with the *TTishos*."

Māhōn snorted. "Those women should sleep in the eating hall and we should sleep in this room."

Erák gave Māhōn a sour look and pulled a mattress from the bed. Frigg followed Erák's lead, and the two young men dragged their beds down the hall.

Émēr gave Māhōn a long stare. "I would hope you follow the men down the hall. I will not permit you to shame my clan."

Māhōn rolled his eyes. He pulled his pad from the frame, gave Émēr a smart salute, and strutted out of the room.

Émēr shook his head. "Attiyq, I ask for Your strength." He dragged the pad from the room. The soft voices of the men echoed down the hall. His fingers gently touched the walls. "Anú, you walked these halls. But why?" The desire to explore the castle consumed him.

Frigg lit the candles in the eating hall while Erák pushed the tables to the sides of the room and laid out the mattresses.

"It will be wonderful to explore this old place," Erák said. His eyes shone and a grin covered his face. "Father would have loved it. The legends said that Anú lived in the woods, but the Elders said Anú had a secret place. This must be it."

Émēr smiled. "Many would have loved this place." He secured his bed near the doorway. "I will speak to Mojí about guarding the entrance."

Imogene peeked into the room. "We're back. Oh, you made yourself comfy here."

Frigg raised his eyebrows. "Comfy?"

She giggled. "Comfortable."

"Ah, comfy."

She raised the cup. "I have your stinky mixture. Should she drink it all?"

Émēr nodded and took it from her. "I will accompany you."

Conell met them in the hall and steered Émēr away from the others. "I will have you, me, Frigg and Erik as guards tonight. We each take a watch. Māhōn is to stay in the room."

Émēr nodded. "I am sorry I brought him, My Mojí." He paused. "And I am sorry I said such words." Guilt twisted in his stomach like a knife. "I should have known better. I do not know my own mind."

Imogene matched their stride. "We're all very stressed. We just have to make sure we don't eat each other. It's easy to tear each other apart, but harder to put us back together."

Conell grinned. "You are wise, *Chuōhá*."

When they entered the room, Ūmá was dozing on the mattress.

Imogene felt Ūmá's forehead then gently shook her awake. "I'm sorry to wake you, but you have to drink this."

Ūmá winced as she drank the green tea. She made a face, then dropped her head onto the pillow.

"I'll stay with her tonight," Imogene said.

Émēr hesitated.

"I'll call you if I need you," Imogene reassured him.

Émēr kissed Ūmá's forehead. "I will be near, my Sapphire."

A wise man knows his enemies are as close to a man as his shadow.

-Anú

13

Emēr's eyes fluttered. He stretched. Sleep was a good companion last night, and she wooed him into her embrace. Not even the sound of the mice and snakes in the castle woke him. Without the sunlight filtering through a window, he was unsure if it was morning or afternoon. After lighting a candle, he crept into the sleeping quarters. As Ūmá and Imogene slept, he touched Ūmá's forehead. The fever was gone. He sighed with relief and tucked the covers around her body.

After rummaging for a quick breakfast, he made his way to the cave entrance. Frigg snoozed against the rock wall. Émēr couldn't hold back a grin. Frigg looked like a sleeping child, not a guard. "Frigg," he whispered.

Frigg slowly opened his eyes and yawned. "Captain, are the guards in the cell?"

"No, but come, you need to be with the others." He gently lifted Frigg to his feet and led him back to the sleeping quarters. Émēr winced. The last time he had led the boy in such a manner, he had led him from a bloody castle. Émēr banished the memory and steered Frigg to his bed. As he laid the boy onto the mattress, Māhōn's words drifted across his mind. *What if Argus is good and the Attiyq is evil?* Émēr frowned. Māhōn had already planted seeds of doubt and discord. He would need to watch over the boy more closely to protect his impressionable mind from the crafty wolf.

Émēr made his way into the hallway and raised his light to the large murals. Legends said that Anú refused to allow anyone to paint his image, claiming such a deed allowed a man to become prideful. Yet, a man with shoulder-length black hair tied back from his face led an army of men carrying long bows and sharp swords into the woods. Others were on horseback and carried the Maúl flags. The enemy ran from the army and over a hill. And still the Maúl pursued them. Émēr stared at the leader. He resembled Émēr's father and his father's father. He shook his head. It must be his mind longing for his family.

He crossed the large balcony and lit the candelabras at the top and bottom of the stairs. Light flooded the courtyard. From the dim light, he could see other rooms branching off from the enclosure. The itch to explore tingled in his mind. At first he thought to explore with Conell, pleased with the idea of descendants of Anú and Brodén walking the ancient dwelling together. But there was one room he wished to discover by himself. He made his way back up the stairwell and crossed to the other side. The first room revealed the weapons. He peeked inside. Shields, swords, lances, and other weapons of war lined the walls. He grinned like a child with toys. He bowed and stepped from the room. It would be rude to discover the great room without his prince by his side.

The scent of old papers and books from the next room wrapped around him. A lump rose in his throat, and he breathed in the old smell.

The boy Émēr sat in his old pew in temple school. Father smiled down at him and placed his large hand on young Émēr's shoulder. Warmth raced down his back and into his toes. His friends chuckled in the corner and hid the eggs from the teacher. Émēr bit away his grin. Another trick on the cruel older boys. All was right in the world. Mother would be waiting at home with Aine who played games with Erák. The witch and her demon lay tucked away in the future, Father ruled the clan, and God delighted in the boy Émēr. He was innocent again. Pure.

The light from the candle presented an assortment of dusty books and cracked scrolls crammed into a large yawning bookcase. He blinked several times. This was real and not a dream. His fingers lightly touched the crinkly scrolls. They crackled at his intrusion. He pulled a scroll from the bookcase and gently placed it on the table in the center of the room.

Anú touched these scrolls. Émēr slowly unrolled the parchment. A large man's fingerprint marked a corner. Émēr placed his finger over it. Anú. He lifted his face to the ceiling. "Thank You, Attiyq for what You have done. Forgive my cruel heart, forgive my brash words. Help me to do whatever You wish."

He pulled up a chair and sat down to read the words of Anú.

A wise man knows his enemies are as close to a man as his shadow.

Why do you refuse to see such sin?

Why do you mock such wisdom?

Why do you call those who befriend you the enemy?

Émēr paused. What if his enemy was as close as his shadow? What if all their enemies were as close as a shadow?

To see your shadow, you must light a candle. Only then will all be exposed.

He rubbed his stubbled chin. Maybe it was time to light candles.

A whispering sound came from behind him. He looked over his shoulder and slowly rose from his chair. The hair on his arm stood, and his skin prickled. The whispers stopped as if insulted by his attention. He slowed his breathing and listened. The soft wind blew from the cave and into the corridors. It did not sound like wind. Something was watching. Something was present.

General Bode resisted the urge to slam Amhras into the castle wall. The arrogant demon prince strutted around the Maúl sitting at the table as if the human were a statue erected for Amhras' greatness. If they weren't careful, his crowing would alert the Maúl to their presence in the room.

"Oh, it has been so long!" Amhras said as he wrinkled his nose at Anu's scrolls. "Father must know of this place and destroy it!"

Brón wept fake tears. "Poor Father. He will be heartbroken to see the Maúl has found this horrid, diseased castle. We must protect poor Father!"

Bode rolled his eyes. The children of the King of Demons were fools. "I am sure my king will want this information."

Amhras flicked his fingers at Bode. The General's hand twitched with the longing to destroy the galling ant.

"I will tell My Father," Amhras said. "I am the one who comforts him."

Brón stomped her foot. "Why must you always comfort Father?"

Émēr rose slowly, and his eyes scanned the walls.

Bode slammed his sword against his leg. "Quiet! He hears us."

Amhras held his breath, and Brón slapped her hands over her mouth.

"What if he uses the Attiyq's words?" Brón whispered.

Amhras motioned with his hand for her to be quiet.

Laughter came from the hallway. Émēr chuckled then left the room.

Brón let out a sigh of relief. "How can he hear us? Only the humans we entice can hear us!"

Bode made his way to the hallway and watched Émēr climb the stairs to the upper hallways. "This one is strong. Not as strong as the pest Cian, but he is growing stronger each day." He returned to the study and closed the door. "My troops!"

Four demons appeared in the room. Their skeleton faces shone from under their black armor. Their ripped, leather wings filled the room. One stepped forward and knelt before Bode.

"We are here, Captain. What is your bidding?"

"You are to guard this room. Do everything in your power to distract the Maúl."

The demon licked his lips and kept his gaze locked on the floor. "My General, it is said this Maúl is strong."

Bode kicked the demon in the face, sending it crashing into the wall. Bode placed his sword under its throat. "I gave a command. Do you wish for me to speak to King Argus of your fears?"

The demon shook its head. "No, my General! We will distract the Maúl as you have asked."

The demons stood before the bookcase and drew their swords.

Bode nodded then left the room. "Come, children. Let us see what else this Maúl can discover."

Brón and Amhras raced for the door and fought over who would leave first. Bode gave a long sigh and followed Émēr up the stairs.

A woman's soft laughter echoed down the hallway. Imogene was up. Dismissing the whispers as his imagination, Émēr carefully placed the scroll back into its home. He bowed and exited into the hallway. "I am sure you are laughing somewhere, Pari, my friend."

Émēr found Imogene and the men standing on the main balcony. "Ah, you are up. Mojí, I have found the main Library. I would like you to see it."

Conell grinned. "I would be honored to see it."

"Imogene," Émēr said. "How is my wife?

"I think she's okay. Her fever has broken. I was going to find food, but I'm not sure what's here." She pulled her blanket over her shoulders.

"Not to worry, My Lady, Erák and I will find food for you." Émēr glanced at Māhōn who was studying a mural. "Brother…"

Māhōn turned and raised his eyebrows. "Yes, my brother?"

"Perhaps you, too, could help us find food?"

His dark eyes flickered to each man. "Well, normally my men find food while I perform the more difficult duties of the home."

Imogene rolled her eyes. "I think there's still food in the bags. Why don't I get them? Erák, will you help me set up the kitchen?"

Māhōn laughed. "I see your sister is well-trained."

Imogene glared at him. "What?"

Émēr turned her by her shoulders and led her down the stairwell. "I think the kitchen is this way. Erák, will you find us some game?"

He led her past the massive statue of King Brodén and lit the candles on the web-draped candleholders scattered around the room.

Imogene shrugged him off. "One of these days, I'll punch that Māhōn right in the face."

Émēr chuckled. "I am sure you will."

She wrapped her cover tighter around her shoulders as her gaze roamed the room. "It's still so cramped in here, almost like being in a tomb."

Émēr blew the dust off a candle and lit it. He dipped his hand in a shallow pool that butted up against the wall. Water slowly trickled from a hole near the ceiling. He examined it with the light of his candle. "It seems the water is coming from an aqueduct in the wall." He cupped the water in his hand and brought it to his mouth.

Imogene slapped his hands. "Don't drink it! Do you not realize how dirty that water probably is? Why would you drink dirty water?"

He grinned at her and brought his cupped hand to his mouth. "It tastes quite fresh."

"You can't taste the microorganisms. We'll have to boil it unless you want to get typhoid fever." She pulled him from the pool. "No drinking dirty pool water."

"I doubt Anú was ill from his water."

"And I doubt that Anú drank water from a dirty aqueduct."

He opened his mouth then closed it. "I think that is the kitchen area." As he led her to a room opposite the pool, he paused to listen. Whispers, again? Pushing the thought from his mind, he continued on his way to the kitchen.

A gaping fireplace sat across the room, its large mouth now dark and ominous. Pots, pans, and ladles hung from the ceiling, and plates and cups lined the walls. Long tables were arranged in the center of the room, and a box held cutlery of all kinds. Imogene pulled down a pan and blew out the dust. "I guess this is where the magic happens."

"Magic?"

"Food making stuff."

Émēr nodded. His fingers glided across the wooden table. *A wise man knows his enemies as a man knows his shadow.* "Imie, what do you think of Māhōn?"

She smiled at his use of her nickname, a name he realized he had not used since his former frustration with her inability to hear from The Attiyq.

"My honest opinion?" she asked as she arranged the pans in a row and pulled a cloth from a drawer that hung from under a tabletop. "Your honest opinion."

"He's insulting, creepy, strange, bad…" Her voice trailed off. "I keep having dreams of saving kittens in a pool while he stands on the side, watching me. I know I must get them out of there, or he'll kill them. I don't like him." She shook the dirt from the rag. "We need to clean this stuff before we can use it. Any chance of making a fire?" She nodded to the fireplace.

He scrunched his face. "I do not think it is wise to use the fireplace. The chimney might be blocked."

She nodded. "Well, hopefully, Erák has returned with food. Let's go see what he's found."

What was to be a simple task of carrying the pots to the entrance of the cave proved to be a huge chore. Émēr bit the inside of his cheek as Imogene filled two large pots with water and asked him to carry them. She followed with a box filled with knives and utensils.

They reached the mouth of the cave and found Erák building a fire. "I found a few rabbits and some apples," he said. After tying three large sticks together with some rope, he made a tripod and hung the pot over the fire. "Why do we need to boil the water?"

"Because it's full of germs," Imogene said. "We can't drink it."

Erák glanced at Émēr who shook his head.

"It is times like this that I remember my training of restraint," Émēr said.

Erák chuckled.

"Cousin, tell me your opinion of Māhōn," Émēr said.

Erák cut the meat into smaller pieces. "I feel that I cannot give my opinion of him. I do not know him as well as you do."

"Then tell me what you do know."

"I am torn. Māhōn is crafty but tries to fit in. It could be said that some of his words and actions more closely resemble those of an enemy not a friend, but he did save our lives." Erák shrugged. "I have known men who were cold to others but stood strong in battle. Perhaps he is one?" He packed mud around the fruit.

Imogene raised her eyebrows. "What are you doing?"

"Mud apples. I wrap mud around them and cook them," Erák said.

Okay, that's germs."

"It will be fine, my sister." Émēr laughed as he placed the apples into the fire. "I found some of Anú's scrolls."

Erák's muddy hands grew still. "Did you say scrolls?"

Émēr nodded. "Anú's scrolls. This was Anú's castle."

"Do you know what was in the mud?" Imogene asked.

"But Anú was said to live in the woods. Why an underground castle? Mud is mud, My Lady."

Imogene sighed and let the mud issue pass. "I question an underground castle, too." She slid the meat into the pot, added some potatoes, and slowly stirred it. "I mean, why was he living underground?"

Émēr shrugged. "I do not have the answers that you seek. The Elders boasted of living in the woods and following Anú's footsteps.

Even my *Min Ehu* involved my living off the Northern Lands. I do not recall legends of caves." He tossed a branch into the fire. "I question so much now. All I have been taught is like clouds in the sky. They are—"

"Pretty but they don't last," Imogene concluded as she dumped small round onions into the pot.

Émēr nodded. "Yes, pretty but they have not lasted."

Frigg, Māhōn, and Mojí strolled from the cave.

Frigg raised his young face to the sunlight. "It is so good to be free."

Māhōn laughed and slapped Frigg's back. Both men chuckled and stepped from the cave.

"Young Frigg, perhaps I, a Maúl Master, could teach you the sword?" Māhōn gave a flourishing bow to Frigg.

Frigg nodded. "I do need a master to train me. I have had little training."

Émēr glanced up at him. His Mojí's foot tapped Émēr's shoe and nodded to the two men. *Watch them!*

He nodded and rolled the apples from the fire. "My Lady, I do believe your germ apples are done."

She gave him a sour look and Émēr expected nothing less.

Not everyone can be saved.

-Cledwyn

14

Ẻmēr fed Ūmá the last spoonful of Imogene's stew then patted her mouth with a towel. She gave him a weak smile as he kissed her forehead. "Rest, My Sapphire. I will return later." He rose from Ūmá's bed and handed the bowl to Imogene.

Ūmá's heavy eyelids slowly closed, and she nestled into the blankets.

Imogene felt Ūmá's face. "Her fever is broken, but I'd give it another three days; then, she should be fine to get out of bed. But we'll keep an eye on her. I really don't think we should leave here for maybe a month or so, just to be safe."

Émēr nodded. "I agree." He turned to his Mojí and grinned. "Mojí, please give me the honor of showing you the armory."

Conell smiled. "It would give me great honor."

Imogene nudged Conell in the ribs. "Do you think it's a great idea to share that with Māhōn?"

Émēr stared at the open door. Māhōn, Erák, and Frigg were eating Imogene's stew in the dining hall. "It would be impossible to hide Anú's weapons from Māhōn's prying eyes." He rubbed the back of his neck. "Yet, the thought of Māhōn carrying a sword..."

"I agree. We watch him. Also, My Captain, watch Frigg."

Émēr nodded. "Aye, My Mojí. I fear for our young one."

After meeting Māhōn, Erák, and Frigg in the dining hall, Émēr led his small party to one of Anú's great treasures. He slowly pushed open the wooden door and carried his lantern into the dark room.

Poles in both corners of the room displayed the large banners that Brodén and Anú would have carried into war. His Mojí stepped into the room. Émēr blinked at a sudden vision.

A large muscular man with short, dark hair sat across from a thinner man with shoulder-length, black-and-gray hair pulled back with a leather band, his shining eyes flashing with authority. Both men, looking to be around forty years of age, leaned over a table laden with scrolls. The candles burned low in the room, giving off a waxy scent.

The man with longer hair pressed his thumbprint onto the corner of a leather-bound book. "We must keep this secret. No one must know of this, for the demon's power is strong."

The other man nodded and picked up the manuscript. "I agree, my friend. We have little time."

Both men hurried from the room and disappeared down the hall.

Émēr shook his head. The men were gone, and the table sat empty in the middle of the room. *Was that King Brodén?*

Imogene touched his arm. "Are you okay?"

He rubbed his eyes. "Yes, I am only overwhelmed by all of this." He glanced down the hall, but it was empty.

Conell gently lifted Brodén's Flag and allowed the strong, flowing fabric to slide through his fingers. "Brodén's Banner," he whispered. "I have seen replicas, but never the original banner. Many of my great-grandfathers followed this banner into battle." He fingered the Maúl flag. "The colors are so bright even after all this time."

Émēr gave a short bow before the Maúl flag. "Anú carried this into battle as Brodén carried his. They rode together into war. I can only imagine how majestic the armies must have been."

He walked to the table and ran his fingers over the surface. *Who were those men? A vision of the past?* A line of swords hung in their sheaths along the wall. One weapon beckoned to him. The scabbard was of fine black leather. He pulled the sword from its sheath. He swung the blade, and it made a soft, swishing sound. Perfectly balanced.

He rested his thumb on a groove on the hilt and ran his fingers over the impression.

Imogene peered over his shoulder. "What a pretty sword!"

Émēr grinned. "Yes, it is pretty."

"I don't know much about swords, but why would anyone put a mark into a sword-handle-thingy?"

He looked over his shoulder. "Sword-handle-thingy?" He chuckled. "My Lady, this is a hilt. I can only think of one person who would put an impression like this on the hilt. It is Anú's thumbprint."

"So I guess the million-dollar question is, why did he put his thumbprint on the hilt?"

Émēr's gaze ran over the priceless weapon. *Anú took this into battle.* "It allowed him and his men to know Anú's weapon in the chaos of fighting. Look at these markings on the hilt and the blade. 'War is a force to rule the stars.' See these letters? He named his blade *Cukdilok Dulk* meaning Captured Stars."

She gave him a puzzled look. "Why did he name it Captured Stars?"

He shrugged. "I do not know."

"Well, I guess it's yours now. You are the last of the Maúl, so that leaves you the leader! Congratulations."

He shrugged. "Perhaps."

"Okay, so it's not a done deal, but until someone else shows up, you're the leader. So, keep it. I'm sure Anú would want you to have it."

Conell grinned. "Her words ring true. You are the leader of the Maúl."

But are you truly a Maúl?

Émēr nodded. "Yes, I am Maúl. I was born Maúl, and I will die Maúl." He took the scabbard from the wall and belted the weapon around his waist.

Erák ran his finger over the blade. "It needs sharpening. It will take me a while to make it battle-ready again, but I can if you want."

"Yes, please, later tonight?" Émēr asked.

Erák nodded. "By morning, I will have it sharp as in the days of Anú."

Māhōn leaned against the doorway and examined a sword he found on the wall. "So, the great Émēr, whose name is known by the All-Knowing Attiyq, now wears Anú's sword?" He straightened and harnessed his sword to his side. "Do you really think that your insane sister and a rusty weapon makes you the leader of *my* clan?" His steely gaze fell on Imogene.

Émēr stepped in front of her. "Of course not. It is only that I wish to follow in Anú's footprints. Come, there are other rooms to see."

He glanced at his Mojí, who took Imogene by her elbow and brushed past Māhōn.

"What did he mean by 'insane'?" she asked as Conell ushered her out of the room.

Māhōn planted his hand against Émēr's chest. "Do not think that because you have a sword that you will rule the New Maúl. I still have my temple. The New Maúl will rise to power."

Émēr's strong, purple gaze locked Māhōn in his trap. "You mistake my intentions. I do not wish to rule the New Maúl. I will rule the Old Maúl. If that is the Attiyq's wish."

Erák gently urged Émēr. "Come, Cousin, I wish to see more."

Frigg shook his head. "I am sorry, Māhōn, for the captain's rudeness. He is worried about his family."

Sneaking a triumphant glance at Émēr, Māhōn placed a strong hand on Frigg's shoulder. "It is all forgotten. These weapons will come in handy when the New Maúl rises. And I need strong men to fight by my side. Perhaps you could become a Maúl?"

Frigg's young eyes sparkled. "That would be wonderful."

Émēr turned and motioned to Frigg. "Frigg, come, we will venture into new rooms of Anú."

Māhōn nodded. "Go, we will train later."

Émēr slowed for Frigg to pace his steps, then he placed his hand on the back of Frigg's neck. "Be careful, young Frigg, I fear Māhōn might not be who he says he is."

Frigg shrugged him off. "You have the Mojí and a wife, I have no one." He waited for Māhōn and the two walked together.

Émēr frowned. *This is not going to end well.*

Imogene opened the door to the library and peeked inside. "Wow! This is some bookstore. Look at all these old papers. It's like Harry Potter's Library! A bit chilly though."

Erák furrowed his brow. "Who or what is the hairy potter? And what does a potter, hairy or otherwise, need with a library?"

She wiggled her fingers. "It's not the hairy potter. It's Harry Potter; he's a wizard"

Erák shook his head and entered the room. He gasped then leaned back into the hallway, his eyes wide. "Cousin, have you seen this room? Have you seen all of these scrolls?"

Émēr grinned. "Yes, Erák, I have. I already found the writings of Anú."

Imogene strolled along the built-in bookcase and then rubbed her forehead, leaning against the bookcase.

Erák placed his hand on her shoulder. "Are you all right?"

"Yeah, I'm just agitated for some reason." She shook her head. "Let's see what Professor Dumbledore wants us to read today." She drew out an old manuscript with a leather cover, the pages held in place with twine. "I wonder how old it is." She opened the cover, and the pages creaked in protest. She turned the book around. "I can't read any of this. It's Greek to me."

Erák grinned, mischief in his eyes. "It says 'Young women should do all the chores while the man relaxes under the trees.' "

Imogene clicked her tongue. "No, it doesn't." She held the book up to Émēr. "Does it?"

He laughed. "No, my sister, it does not."

She slapped Erák. "Jerk!"

He held his arm in his hand. "Aiden, you have broken my arm." She rolled her eyes.

Émēr chuckled as he took the book from her. His fingers gently touched the pages.

Poems from Anú, Leader of the Maúl.

His heart beat faster. "It says, Poems from Anú, Leader of the Maúl."

Imogene looked over his shoulder. "Poems?"

He nodded. "It says, *Men are blind fools, Following in dark footsteps. The Demon must be caged. Each seeking their own paths Lost in the forests owned by the King, The priest, The Seer. Lost are the morals. Lost are the hands and feet. Lost are the innocence of Children. When men stand and fight, When men stop the evil Then will the King Prevail. No one seeks wisdom. Never. Will the Attiyq Smile on men. All believe their words Are like sunlight to the dead used to Cage the Demon. Barbs of Anger Fly like arrows. Free the men.*"

"Interesting," Imogene said.

"It is probably how Anú felt when men acted as fools." Émēr tucked the book under his arm. "I found other scrolls over here." He led her to another shelf. "I was reading this one."

Conell leaned over Émēr's shoulder as his captain unrolled the ancient paper.

"It speaks of wisdom from Anú. These are the scrolls the witch did not destroy. The Attiyq has preserved them." Émēr laid the scroll on the table.

Conell ran his finger over the old words as the corners of his mouth turned upward. "We will be here for a long time. You might as well explore to your heart's content."

Erák sat on a chair next to Émēr and slowly read the scroll. "These are amazing. Father…" He paused and coughed. "Father would love these words. He would be pleased as I am pleased. Thank you, my cousin. You truly are the leader of the Maúl."

Émēr felt the warmth of a blush on his cheeks. "I am not truly the leader yet; although, I do appreciate your kindness."

Māhōn and Frigg entered the room. Émēr frowned. A smug grin covered young Frigg's face as he strolled across the room like the king. His innocent ways were fading.

Émēr motioned to the two men. "Come. Look at the words of Anú."

Frigg eagerly looked over Émēr's shoulder. His grin faded as he read the words. "These words seem so hard to understand. I will never become Maúl."

Māhōn placed his hand on the younger man's shoulder. "I will train you. I am the best teacher. And why look at all these dusty, ancient words? Surely these are not for today!"

"Frigg," Émēr said, "You have never mentioned this longing before. Do you want to become Maúl?"

He shrugged and stared at the floor. "Well, I did not long to venture down your path until I met Māhōn. He has made it easier for me to understand such mystic words."

Émēr frowned. "My young friend, becoming Maúl is hard and takes dedication. I will teach you if you wish."

Māhōn grinned. "I have told the strong Frigg I will train him. I was able to teach my other men in just a few short years. I say give this strong one a few years, and he will rise to the top of the New Maúl."

Frigg's freckled face lit up like a fire in the hearth. "That is what I want. Forgive me, Émēr, but Māhōn will become my new Master."

Conell stared hard at the two men. "Frigg, you can learn these new ways later. For now, we must arm ourselves against attack. I will need your arm and weapon in battle. Once the enemy is vanquished, then you may train."

A childish flash of anger crossed the boy's face, but Māhōn nudged him. "The *King* is right. It is best to wait. I will train you when all is done."

Erák pursed his lips and rose from the chair, but Émēr gently forced him to return to his seat. Conell narrowed his eye and shot a glance at Émēr who frowned but nodded. *Māhōn is drawing the boy away.*

Émēr forced a smile on his face. "I agree with Māhōn that it is best to wait. We will do these things later. Come, there is more to explore."

Émēr steered the two men to the door as Conell took Imogene's elbow and drew Erák closer. He whispered to them, and she shot a fearful glance at the men as they walked out the door. Erák shook his head and hissed angry words, but Conell motioned for him to remain calm.

Émēr led Frigg and Māhōn down the hallway, allowing them to walk in front of them. Māhōn held a deep conversation with Frigg about the ways of the New Maúl.

I should have left him behind, but if the Mojí can change perhaps I can save Māhōn. He is Maúl; I should give him a chance. Perhaps I can train him. 'Be the person you want others to be'. He grinned. *Cledwyn, you speak wise words even from the grave.*

"Māhōn, perhaps we could go over Anú's scrolls together with young Frigg, then all of us could learn the ways of the Maúl."

Frigg stared at him. "You have never offered this to me before, why now?"

Émēr looked away as guilt nipped at his heart. *I am not the priest.* "I know I have neglected you, and for that I am sorry. Please allow me to make this up to you. I am sure, as Māhōn has said, you would make a strong warrior."

A shy grin covered the boy's face as his innocence returned.

Émēr touched Frigg's shoulder. "Come, let us explore together."

Annoyance plastered Māhōn's face, but he nodded and extended his hand. "Yes, let us explore together. But remember, young Frigg, those scrolls are ancient. Times have changed. We do not need them anymore."

Émēr disguised his reactions and headed out.

History is a warning from the ghosts of the past.

-Anú

15

Imogene's eyes grew wide as she stared down the massive stairwell. "Oh my! Someone pinch me! Wake me up!"

Erák looked at her, shook his head, and stepped down the staircase.

She fluttered past him. "I feel like Scarlet O'Hara!" She leaned against the railing and smacked the back of her hand to her forehead. "Rhett, if you go, where shall I go, what shall I do?" When neither man commented, she finished in an undertone, "*Gone with the Wind.* And I nailed that accent…"

Erák slowly turned his head to Conell who chuckled and shrugged.

With great pomp, Imogene stepped onto the bottom stair and gazed at the end of the long room. Tattered, purple curtains hung behind a scalloped arch that opened onto a stage. In the center, sat a massive wooden throne. One of the arms of the throne was broken, and a rodent's nest sat on the seat. On each side of the great room were covered hallways, each one divided with arches that led into the throne room. A walkway covered the hallways and followed the perimeter of the chamber. Two large angel statues guarded the entrance to the throne room.

Émēr stepped beside her. "It is hard to believe this is Anú's throne room."

Imogene jumped then smacked him. "Don't scare me!"

Conell and the others crowded around them.

"Look at the floor," Imogene whispered.

Her gaze followed the dusty tiles. She stepped around them. "Émēr, there's some writing. What does it say?"

He brushed away the dirt. "It is a prayer to the Attiyq.

"May the Great One watch over King Brodén.

May the Great One's hand be upon Anú.

May His face shine upon Ézású.

May His path always lay before us."

Émēr stared at the throne. *Surely, Anú, this was not your throne room. What of being modest, humble?*

Erák stepped beside him. "Are you sure we are in Anú's castle?"

"I think, but my mind may be in another place." He took a deep breath and walked along the long walkway to the throne. His gaze took in the empty balcony surrounding the room.

Silent men with the marks of the Maúl on their faces leaned over the scalloped stone railing of the balcony. They wore black tunics and black pants. Swords hung at their sides. Two men walked in front of Émēr. He turned to see Argus behind him.

Émēr gasped and grabbed Erák's arm.

"What is it, Cousin?" Erák asked.

Émēr looked from Erák to... Nothing. Argus had disappeared. He shook his head. "It is nothing."

He blinked his eyes. His vision blurred, and two men appeared before him.

Again, the two thin men dressed in black cotton pants and black tops and leather wrapped around their arms and legs walked in front of Émēr. One man wore a red tunic over his black top. Émēr slowly glanced over his shoulder. Argus walked behind him with two other guards in the rear. This must be a dream. *They approached a man who sat on the solid wooden throne with a thick, purple fabric draped over it. Large purple and red pillows were scattered around the King's seat. A light from a window behind the King lit up the room and gleamed off the polished floor.*

Both men bowed before the King. Émēr studied the man. He looked more like Father than a great king. The man's lean frame sat back in the chair, and his sharp purple eyes observed the soldiers. His black-and-gray shaggy hair hung around his face that was covered in Maúl symbols. He wore the same black tunic and pants as his soldiers as well as a long blue robe. A simple crown sat on his head.

One of the men stepped forward. His body was thin but muscular. His hand gripped his sword, and his legs were planted on the stone floor. Maúl markings covered his entire face, each one telling of a battle. He lifted his shining eyes to the King and gave a short, quick nod.

King Anú smiled at him. "Augustine, you have proven yourself the Attiyq's champion, as have you, Dia. My champions of the Faith."

Augustine gave a small bow. "I am only your servant."

Dia, a stocky, shorter man with braided brown hair, grinned at Augustine then at the King. "We come to serve our King and our God." Dia stepped aside and presented Argus. "My King Anú, we bring you the demon caught by the hands of the Attiyq."

Argus strained against his bindings. "Do not think things have ended here, Anú. I will have justice. I will destroy you and all of your clan."

Anú grinned. "You cannot destroy me, demon, for I hide under the shadow of the Great Attiyq."

Argus's face crunched in pain, and he dropped to the ground. He cursed the Attiyq and struggled against the bindings.

Dia poked Argus with his sword. "Be silent, demon!"

Argus sneered at him. "You will die by my hands."

"Only if the Attiyq wills it."

"Émēr?"

He shook his head.

Imogene stood beside him with her hand on his arm. "Are you okay?"

The men, the King, and Argus were no longer in the room. The throne remained empty as did the walkways. "Yes, I am …*okay*."

A shadow shifted on the walkway. Émēr squinted, then it was gone. He lowered his head and squeezed his eyes shut. "I must be very tired."

She placed her fingers on the inside of his wrist and studied his pupils. "You looked like you were in La-la land."

"La-la land?" Émēr asked.

"In a different world. Did you see something?" she asked. "Do you feel nauseated or faint?"

"Yes, maybe. I am unsure." He rubbed his eyes.

"What did you see?" she asked.

Émēr weaved and she led him to the stairs, sitting him upon one of the risers. Conell and the others gathered around.

"Captain," Conell asked. "Do you need water?"

"No, I am fine."

Māhōn peered at Émēr.

Émēr's spine tingled with apprehension. He caught his Mojí's gaze and selected his words carefully. "I am unsure what I saw."

Mojí's eyebrow lifted, but he nodded. "You are tired, My Captain, and much has happened. Come, let us retire to our quarters."

Émēr nodded. "Yes, I wish to check on my wife." He gave Conell a brief stare as he rose from the step.

Those whom we leave behind will be picked up by the enemy and made into their ally.

-Augustine

16

Émēr sat at the long dining table and slowly chewed his food, his sense of danger growing with each bite as Māhōn sat at the table and picked at his food. Émēr gave a sharp glance at Conell before looking down at his plate. Imogene squirmed in her seat and used her fork to push her food on her plate.

She got up and took her dish with her. "I'm going to check on Ūmá."

Conell nodded to Erák. "Please escort her to her quarters."

Erák shoved his food in his mouth and rose from his chair.

Imogene shook her head. "I'm okay."

Émēr shook his head and pointed at Erák. "Go."

Erák opened the door for her, and she stepped into the hallway. Émēr listened to their footsteps as they walked along the hallway. Imogene murmured that Māhōn was creepy. Erák's pause forced Émēr to smother a grin.

"Creepy?" Erák asked.

"You know, makes your skin crawl and wonder who's behind you. I saw Argus in that room," she whispered. "I hate this place. I hate all of this place. Now I know why kids want a safe space."

"A safe space?"

"A place that makes you feel safe."

Erák paused. "We all wish for that, but such a place died long ago."

The door to the women's quarters creaked open, and Erák said his goodnights. The young man made his way to his quarters that he shared with Frigg, who had retired earlier.

Imogene tended to Ūmá, then the room was silent.

Émēr tapped his fork on his plate. *Did I make the right choice in coming here? She saw what I saw, and now she is filled with fear.*

Émēr yawned and stretched his arms over his head. "My Mojí, my heart was filled with joy when the son of Brodén and the son of Anú stood in the armory. One last time tonight?"

Conell grinned. "It would be my honor."

The two men rose from the table.

Māhōn watched them as he drank from his wine glass. "Would you like to have the leader of the New Maúl to escort you?"

The two men exchanged glances.

"This is in honor of our Fathers," Conell said. "We may all go there together later. All of us as one." He flashed Māhōn a grin.

Māhōn grunted and looked away.

Émēr entered the hallway and shut the door behind Conell. Émēr pointed down the hall. "I wish to check on my women."

Conell chuckled. "Please do not let Imogene hear you speak the words 'my women.'"

Émēr considered before nodding. "Perhaps you are right. Imie is…rebellious. My mother may not be pleased with such rebellion. But my mother is never pleased with the young women of today." He tapped on their door.

A sound of rustling blankets and Imogene's soft footsteps came from the room, then she opened the door. "What's up?"

Émēr bowed. "Please, may I check on my wife?"

She smiled. "Of course. She's asleep now."

He made his way to Ūmá's side. He placed his fingers next to her cheek then turned to Imogene. "Thank you, my sister."

Imogene gave him a smile and a wink.

He closed the door behind him and led her to a corner. "Imogene, forgive me, but I heard you speaking to Erák."

She cocked her head. "How did you hear me in the hallway?"

He pointed to his ears. "I heard you."

"Oh, that's right, X-men hearing."

He paused. "Anyway, I heard you speaking to Erák. You said you saw something in the throne room."

The silly smile that often covered her face fled, fear taking its place. "Yeah, I saw Argus and a bunch of guys that were like ghosts." She twisted her fingers. "I don't want to stay here. I don't care who Anú was; this place is creepy-city."

He placed his hands on her thin shoulders. "It is fine. I think it was only images from the past. They cannot hurt you nor would Anú harm one so innocent."

She licked her lips. "Yeah, I guess. What did you see?"

He took a deep breath. "Anú on the throne, two men escorting Argus to stand before Anú. They spoke of capturing Argus. One man was named Dia and the other Augustine. That is all I heard before the vision disappeared. And you?"

"I saw the same thing, only I couldn't hear what they said. Why are we whispering in my bedroom?"

Conell opened the door, peeked into the hallway, then closed it again. "We do not want Māhōn to hear us," he whispered.

She swallowed the lump in her throat. "I don't want to know why."

Conell patted her shoulder. "He will not harm you."

"Right."

"Get some sleep. Māhōn's eyes are not on you," Conell said.

She rubbed her forehead. "That makes me feel worse."

Conell chuckled. "Get some sleep, do not speak of this to Erák, Frigg, or Māhōn."

"About Frigg," she said. "You guys need to keep an eye on him. Māhōn is getting all bro-mance with him. Meaning, too friendly with him."

The two men exchanged glances.

"Yes," Conell said. "We have noticed."

Émēr nodded. "We have neglected Frigg. He was to be your advisor, and he has become—"

"A third wheel," Imogene said. "Meaning, he doesn't have a purpose. He's just tagging along."

"He wants to learn to be Maúl," Émēr said. "If that were even possible, it would take him years to learn to be as me."

She shrugged. "Why can't you teach him a few ninja moves, some cool stuff here and there, and then say, 'You're Maúl!' I know it takes from childhood to learn this stuff, but still, it's either you or Māhōn."

"Yes, and I would rather it be me," he replied with a deep sigh.

A yawn escaped her. "Well, you all need to leave now. We can discover more rooms tomorrow, and hopefully, no more ghosts."

After leaving Ūmá and Imogene's room, Émēr returned to the dining quarters with a pot of hot tea and a cup. He sat at the table and opened the poems of Anú. Most poems were written in the normal style of one line after another. But others were written in a staggered pattern.

Augustine and Dia
Augustine, the warrior, strong and brave,
Fought for his king and clan

And locked away the Darkness and his child.

Dia fought by his side
Power flowed through his arms,
And placed his enemies at the Attiyq's feet.

Both men fought
Back to back
Their ears closed to Darkness's ballad.

The enemy taunts
The swords slash
Against sinful words

Trapped forever Darkness remains.

Émēr sipped from his cup of tea and read the poem again. A shiver crept down his back. "The black shadow in the courtyard." He placed his cup on the table and quickly turned the page.

The sound of soft footsteps coming from the hall drew his attention. The door creaked open, and Ūmá peeked around the doorframe. "I hope I am not disturbing you, My Lord."

He stood and grinned. "No, My Lady, you are not disturbing me, but you must rest."

She shut the door behind her and pulled her blanket tighter around her shoulders. "Imogene is dear to my heart, but I do not wish to sleep anymore and she insists I must stay in bed."

He pulled out a seat for her. "Shall I get you a cup of tea?"

"No," she said. "I am fine." Her fingers touched the leather-bound book. "What is this?"

He sat beside her and moved the candle closer. "It is poems from Anú."

Her eyes grew wide. "Poems from Anú? Then this is …?"

"Yes, Anú's castle."

"Oh my!" A smile covered her face. "Oh please, we must see more!"

"I promise, I will show you tomorrow. That is, if Imogene gives us permission."

She giggled. "Read me some of the poems."

"If you wish. Anú was a creative man. It seems that he enjoyed poetry. Most of these are praises to the Attiyq, but then there are some as this one about Augustine and Dia."

"Who are they?"

He selected his words carefully. "Ūmá, I have seen things in the castle. So has Imogene."

"Seen things?" She looked at him from the corner of her eye.

"My bride," he said as he kissed her hand. "Do not think of me as mad. I feel as if the Attiyq wishes me to know things that I cannot know. I have never experienced these things before."

"What do you mean?"

He pointed to the page. "Augustine and Dia. Imogene and I both saw these men in the throne room of Anú. Argus was with them. They had captured him." His desire for answers opened a window in his mind for a thought to slip in. He shook his head at the suggestion. "I do not wish to consult a witch for answers nor will I. It is against the Attiyq. I must find answers from Him."

She read the poem, then sat back. "What does this mean?"

He shrugged and yawned. "I do not know, My Sapphire." He rubbed his eyes. "I am growing weary."

She placed her arm over his shoulder. "Now it is I who must help you to bed. Tomorrow you will show me the wonders of this place?"

He grinned. "It would be my honor, my bride."

Beware of Rumors of War.
Sometimes Rumors are mists that
disappear when the sun rises.

-Book of the Attiyq

17

Émēr stretched his arms over his head and glanced at the sleeping men. His Mojí's bed was empty. "The King is always awake," he whispered. He rose from the bed and poured water into the washing bowl. After a quick wash, he made his way along the halls and followed the sound of his Mojí's breathing. The young prince was in the library reading the old bound book. He looked up at Émēr and grinned.

"You are finally awake, My Captain."

Émēr bowed. "I am growing old and sleeping more."

Conell chuckled. "These books are amazing. They must be 1000 years old."

He nodded. "I agree, My Mojí. Did you see the poems of Anú? They speak of the two men I saw in my vision. I hope to find more of them."

His prince nodded. "These poems are interesting. Augustine and Dia. Those are the men, yes?"

Émēr nodded and looked over Conell's shoulder. Conell pointed to the page. "Here is a short history of them. It seems both were Maúl, born to different fathers, yet raised together. Both lost their parents in a battle with the barbarians. Both were raised here in the castle where they fought together. That is also where they seem to have disappeared. But maybe they left with Anú? I am not sure. I would like to find them. It seems Augustine was Anú's Captain of the Guards, as you are mine. He fought many barbarians and had a special task; although, I do not see it written on the pages."

Imogene poked her head into the room. "Who's up for breakfast? Guess what it is? Left over stew, yum, yum! And Ūmá and I found a bathing room near the water reserve. It wasn't the best of baths, but we feel better."

Ūmá looked over Imogene's shoulder and smiled sweetly.

A grin covered Émēr's face. "My Lady, you are up, how do you feel?"

"I am no longer feeling weak, My Lord. Imogene, please allow me to explore with the others."

"Don't push yourself," Imogene said as she turned away from the door. "Meaning, don't overexert yourself."

Émēr offered his arm to Ūmá, and she graciously allowed him to lead her down the hall.

Ūmá's yellow chiffon dress rustled against her legs. The sleeves of the gown covered her fingertips and the lace on her dress rose to her collar bone. She smelled of honeysuckle and her hair gleamed in the candlelight. He raised his chin. His bride was immaculate. Mother would be pleased.

Imogene was placing the plates on the table when they entered the dining hall. "I'm sorry it's left-over stew, but we need to eat it, so it won't go bad. I worry about our food. We'll have to find more if we stay here."

Conell's eyes roamed over her long dark blue gown. He grinned as she pushed up the sleeves. His grin disappeared when she struggled with the brown bracelet. Her lips pursed, and she gave a small, frightened shaking of her head.

He placed the metal mugs near the plates. "You look lovely today, *Chuōhá*."

She grinned at him. "It isn't easy wearing long dresses all the time. I thought it would be nice, but it's a bit of a pain."

He nodded. "I am sorry you still wear Argus's bracelet. I know it upsets you. I do not know how to remove it."

"Yeah, I know, I've tried hammering it off, cutting it off, everything. It just won't come off."

Frigg and Māhōn entered the room, and Māhōn slapped Frigg on the back. "Your father would be proud of you, Master Frigg. You did good in your lessons today."

A sloppy grin covered the boy's freckled face but quickly faded. "I miss my father."

Émēr frowned. "I thought we were going to wait to begin his teachings."

Māhōn shrugged a shoulder. "I thought I would start early."

Conell caught Émēr's gaze and gave him a long look. Émēr knew that look. It meant Conell foresaw danger.

Émēr sat Ūmá in the nearest chair and took the bowl of stew from Imogene. He placed a ladleful into each bowl.

Māhōn wrinkled his nose. "Surely the women can serve us. Maúl do not serve; we are served."

Imogene slowly turned her head to him. Conell took her elbow and led her to the seat near Ūmá. "Perhaps you should sit here."

She gave him a dirty look, and he suppressed his grin.

"The Book of the Attiyq says one must be a servant to enter His house. I do not mind serving others." Émēr put the empty bowl on the side table and sat next to Ūmá.

"I think there are only a few more rooms to explore," Imogene said as she blew on the hot stew. "What will we do after we're done?"

Conell shrugged. "We will need a plan. It seems odd that Argus has been silent these days." He gave a side glance to Émēr.

Erák nodded. "It is as if he lost our trail."

Māhōn shrugged. "We have passed into enemy territory. Entering this area would mean war for the Queen."

Conell nodded. "True. The Queen would not wish to war with the Southern Territories."

Imogene patted her lips with her napkin. "Who are the people who live in these lands? What would they do if they caught us?"

Erák furrowed his brow. "How can you ask such a question? Do you not know?"

Émēr raised his finger. "Forgive my sister. She has little learning of our history."

Imogene gave him a sour look.

"My Father tried to make peace with them," Conell said. "He proposed many treaties, but it seemed the people of the South wished for war. I have never seen them, but my father had many meetings with them as did Émēr's father. But they only wanted to battle."

Émēr shrugged. "My Father also claimed they wanted war, yet when I spoke to the merchants, they said the Southerners desired peace only. To be left alone to live in clouds, although I was not sure of their meaning. The merchants called the Southerners the Cloud People."

"Cloud People?" Ūmá asked. She gently dipped the spoon into the soup and lifted it slowly to her mouth.

Imogene followed Ūmá's example. "Did they live in clouds?"

Émēr lifted a shoulder. "The merchants said no one has entered their cities, so no one knew. The Southern traders met at the borders but kept their secrets. They said the Southerners wore clothes like ours, and they only spoke to the men of the tribes. Women mostly stayed in the villages; although, some merchants did speak of female traders."

Erák dabbed his stale bread into his bowl. "Are they violent? Surely someone has seen our fires. Yet we are still alone."

"This is Anú's castle, perhaps the Southern people fear this place," Ūmá said.

Émēr nodded. "Wise comment, my wife." He kissed her hand.

She smiled at him.

Imogene nodded. "If they think the place is like haunted or cursed, they would stay away. But why would Anú pick this place for his castle? Could the borders have moved so far North over the centuries?"

Conell placed his elbows on the table and rubbed his chin. Émēr stared at him. His Mojí was transforming into the King.

"If I remember correctly," Conell said, "My Father spoke of Anú at first not trusting Brodén, so Anú stayed to the South, across the borders. But then Anú was said to have joined Brodén because he was a great King and felt it worthy to serve him. Perhaps instead of fearing this place, the Southerners see it as a shrine and do not wish to disturb it. But we must be wary—they may wish to seek us out, and we do not know what they will bring. Friendship or spears. We will need to make sure we guard the entrance at all times."

Émēr and Erák helped Imogene carry the dishes to the kitchen where Ūmá filled a basin with warm water. Imogene handed her a bar of lye soap.

Ūmá raised her eyebrows. "My sister, soap for the dishes?"

Imogene dropped the soap in the water. "Kills germs."

Ūmá giggled. "You must hate these invisible germ creatures."

Imogene grunted. "They can kill you."

Émēr frowned as his wife plunged her hands into the water. "My wife, one day a servant will clean, and you will stroll under the trees with me."

She grinned at him. "Cleaning cleanses one's soul of evil."

He raised his eyebrows. "My Lady, how do you know the words of Anú?"

Her grin broadened. "My father taught me much before …" Her smile vanished, and she scrubbed harder at the plates.

He took the plate from her hands and rinsed it. "As you said, it cleanses our souls." He lifted her wrist. "You no longer wear Argus's bracelet."

She nodded. "He took it when he handed me over to the slavers. At least I no longer belong to him." Her smile returned, and she handed him a soapy plate.

After finishing the dishes, they lit all the candles in the main meeting courtyard and cleared the area of the cobwebs and dust. Imogene and Ūmá polished the large statue of Brodén in the center of the courtyard. Within an hour, the room began to look a little more like a castle and less like a cave.

Imogene wiped the sweat from her brow. "Now this looks better!" She tossed the rags onto the kitchen counter and jogged to the others. "So now where? We haven't seen that room." She pointed to the closed door across from the throne room.

"I would like to see Anú's throne room," Ūmá said. "I have learned much of him and now to see where he sat…"

Émēr grinned. "Of course, My Lady."

Imogene licked her lips. "I really don't want to go in there again. I'll wait out here."

Conell raised his candle and placed his hand on her back. "Come, we will go there together."

She gave a reluctant look yet allowed him to lead her into the room.

Erák opened the door with a flair of his arm and bowed before them. "My Lords and Ladies, come see the great Anú."

Imogene giggled, and Ūmá curtsied. Émēr gave him an annoyed look. He lit the candles on the staircase then escorted Ūmá to the lower floor. Māhōn stomped down the stairs and slipped past Émēr. He boldly strolled across Anú's floor to the throne.

Imogene turned to Émēr and whispered, "The rat goes to his home." She nodded to the nest on the seat.

Émēr bit his lip. "This is Anú's throne room."

Ūmá stretched to her toes to peer at the covered hallways. "This is beautiful! We must clean it in honor of Anú."

"You mean the next leader of the Maúl?" Māhōn kicked the nest from the throne and wrinkled his nose. "Someone needs to clean this."

Imogene opened her mouth, but Émēr raised his hand hoping to keep her quiet. "Yes, my brother, we will clean the room for the honor of Anú."

Imogene nodded. "Yes, for Anú and only Anú."

Māhōn fingered the torn curtains. "This fabric is of the Southern merchants. It seems your theory is correct. Anú did stay within the boundaries of the Southern Lands."

Ūmá tugged Émēr to the arched hallway and peeked around the massive column. The hallway ran along the perimeter of the room. Stone benches sat against the walls. Spying a leather book under one of the seats, Ūmá picked it up and sat on the bench. The light from her candle softened her face. Émēr smiled. She looked mysterious and enchanting in the dim light.

The light from Émēr's candle revealed a small room jutting off from the hallway. As he approached, he jumped when the female angel who had visited him in the woods suddenly appeared beside him.

"I want to show you something." She took his hand. "Come. You must see this. The Attiyq has brought you here."

He looked over his shoulder. The others were exploring the massive throne room, and Ūmá was engrossed in her book. A light glowed from the room, but the others seemed oblivious to its light.

The angel smiled. "The Attiyq has said this is for you only. Come."

After she guided him into the glowing room, he turned to her, but she was gone.

Three men leaned over a table and studied maps. Émēr recognized King Anú, Dia and Augustine. *King Brodén made his way into the room and dropped large keys on the table. "I would not ask this of you, King Anú, but we must bring our countries together."*

King Anú nodded. "I agree, King Brodén, it is the Attiyq's will that we do so."

Dia looked over his shoulder.

Émēr followed Dia's gaze as sunlight enveloped the massive throne room. "Where is the light coming from? I have seen it before, but now the room is darkened," Émēr whispered.

"I am happy we are not leaving this place," Dia said. He turned his sharp eyes back to the kings. "I have sworn to follow you, My King, and I will not leave you now. What are your orders?"

Augustine nodded. "I am also ready." He adjusted his red tunic, revealing the stitching of a large eagle with spread wings on the front of it.

King Brodén grinned. "It is as you have said. Your men are strong."

"I have faith in them. I will leave ten men here to guard the beast." Anú pressed on a stone, and the wall slid open. He used his candle and led the others down the stairwell. "Remember, my soldiers, do not give up your post."

"Are you sure, King Anú, that you wish to do this?" King Brodén asked as they descended the stairs. "You and your men serving me as warriors? To give up your lands and your castle?"

Anú nodded. "Yes, My King, the Attiyq has ordered it of us."

"You are brave, Anú, I will see that you and your descendants will always serve the king with great honor."

"My Lord, what have you found?" Ūmá stood beside him, shining her light into the dark room.

Émēr blinked. The rest of the room was dark again. The door in the wall was now solid, and the men were gone.

"It seems our great Maúl has found another room." Māhōn joined him.

"More secrets," Imogene said.

The others peered into the room. Émēr rubbed the back of his neck and looked for his Mojí as he stretched. He casually strolled from the room and took Conell's elbow. He kept his back to the others. "I have seen something," he whispered.

Conell nodded. "Not here. We will talk later."

They made their way back to the cramped room where Māhōn was studying yellow papers that were scattered on a small table in the center of the chamber. "This seems to be a meeting room. The language in these scrolls is odd. I cannot read it."

Émēr picked up one of the papers and scanned the writing. "It seems to be a list of supplies. These are mostly letters to the traders." He glanced at the wall that had slid back in the vision.

Conell picked up a paper, but his eyes followed Émēr's gaze. He dropped the paper and turned to Imogene. "Did you not say there was a room across from this one? Perhaps we should explore there next?" Before she could answer, he took her arm and led her from the room.

Sometimes one must step away from
his desires and follow
the Great One's paths.

-Anú

18

Émēr stood transfixed in the bed chamber. Imogene took in the massive wooden canopy bed that sat against the far wall.

"There is no way I would sleep under that thing," Imogene declared, eyeing the columns supporting a canopy that touched the ceiling. "I would be afraid it would fall on me."

Ūmá traced the dust on the doors of the large wardrobe cabinet, then she brushed the dirt from her fingers and readjusted her sleeves. "Is this Anú's chambers?"

Māhōn laughed. "Well, well, well, our *pious* leader." He glared at Émēr. "Perhaps he is less like you, Brother."

Émēr dismissed Māhōn's insult and gently pressed his fingers onto the mattress. "It is not as soft as I would have thought a king would have."

Imogene attempted to shake the large columns supporting the canopy. The bed remained secure. "Huh," she sniffed. "I still wouldn't sleep under it."

Ūmá took a seat at a nearby writing desk and opened a drawer. A small box and yellowed papers sat inside. She gingerly placed the box on the desk.

Émēr peeked over her shoulder. "Writing pens, only very old."

She picked up a paper covered in fluid letters. "Was Anú married? This is a note written to him, and I am thinking from a woman." She brought the paper close to her candle and chuckled. "It is a list of things for him to do."

"A Honey-Do list," Imogene said.

"What is a Honey-Do List?" Conell asked.

"Honey, can you do this. Honey, can you do that," Imogene said, smiling. "It's a to-do list."

Émēr dropped into a chair propped next to the desk. "Anú claimed a man did not need such luxuries. And yet, Anú lives as a king."

Erák brushed away spiderwebs from a large mirror. "I understand, but remember, Anú was King in this land. Perhaps this was before he came over the border?"

Frigg nodded. "Yes, perhaps the leader dropped such luxuries after he created the Maúl?"

Émēr shook his head. "No, he created the Maúl here, in this place. Wife, what book were you reading?"

She handed it to him. "I think it is a diary or a journal."

He thumbed through the pages, then stared at her. He leaned towards her. "You can read this?" he asked privately, and she gave a nod. "But this is the language of the Maúl…"

"My father taught me," Ūmá whispered, aware he remained close on purpose.

He placed his hand on hers and said low, "Please do not share this with the others, and do not tell Māhōn. I do not want him to know you can understand the Maúl language." Ūmá furrowed her brow and he added, "I do not want him to see you as useful."

Understanding dawned in her eyes and Émēr added, "I fear he will use you to translate the scrolls. I do not want him to know Maúl secrets."

She shot a glance at Māhōn and nodded. "Yes, my husband."

"Émēr, look at this." Imogene lifted her candle to a portrait hanging on the wall. "He looks like you in a way."

Ūmá rose and studied the picture. "He has your purple eyes. Who is this?"

Émēr took in the portrait of the long black-haired man who stood next to a brown-haired woman. A boy stood between them. Man and boy both had purple eyes that caught the attention of any beholder. He was the same man Émēr had seen in his visions. Anú. "I am not sure," he replied loud enough for Māhōn to hear. He glanced at his Mojí who nodded.

"Maybe it's Anú," Imogene suggested, oblivious to Conell's subtle gesture for her to keep quiet. "Ūmá's right—he has your eyes. Is he your relative?"

Émēr shrugged and took Ūmá's arm. "It is almost time for lunch. Perhaps we will explore more later."

After lunch, Frigg and Māhōn practiced fighting maneuvers in the main courtyard. Ūmá and Imogene folded clothes they had washed and dried. Conell and Erák sat next to them on a stone bench.

Émēr stood along the perimeter, engrossed in Māhōn's latest attempt to manipulate Frigg. He crossed his arms. "Frigg, do not look to the ground, but keep your eyes focused on your enemy."

Frigg quickly lifted his head and countered Māhōn's punch.

"Good!" Émēr said. "You are growing quicker."

Frigg grinned. "Thank you, Captain."

Émēr chuckled and made his way to his Mojí.

"What do you think?" Erák asked.

"He is quick, but it would take years of training for him to reach Maúl level," Émēr said, taking a seat next to his prince.

Conell nudged Erák and motioned to the sparring men. "Keep them busy."

Erák nodded and jumped from the stone seat. "Māhōn, that is very interesting, teach it to me."

Imogene gave Conell a side glance as she shook out a large sheet. "Ūmá, help me to fold this." She stood in front of Conell and handed the other end of the cloth to Ūmá. Then she opened the sheet and made a barrier between Māhōn and Conell. She gave him a wink, then babbled about her mother in New York.

"She is very wise," Émēr said, grinning to his prince.

"Yes, she is. What did you see?"

"Anú and Brodén along with Anú's two guards. They opened a secret door that was hidden in a small room I had found. The door opened to a staircase. I didn't see where the stairs ended, but something is down there that we need to see."

Imogene grinned at Émēr, then kicked his foot. "Hey, I'm going to be nice today. Ūmá and I are on a roll washing your things. Go into spooky throne room and grab those pieces of cloth. We can use them for blankets. I'm not going in there; it's too creepy." She winked.

Conell raised his eyebrows and grinned. "As you wish, My Lady."

He and Émēr made their way to the throne room. Māhōn watched them. Erák twisted Māhōn's arm, making him wince.

"I am so sorry," Erák said. "My father showed me that same move but a little different. Can you show me what you did?"

Émēr shook his head and chuckled as he and Conell made their way to the throne room. From there, he led Conell to the small room with the secret door and lit his candle. "In the vision, Anú pressed on this rock." Nothing happened. He pressed on other rocks and still nothing happened.

"Are you sure of what you saw?" Conell pressed on the rocks above Émēr.

"Yes, I am sure." He forced down his frustration and ran his fingers over the rocks. His thumb hit a small grove. He pressed on it and the wall swung open.

Conell glanced at the staircase then pressed the stone again to shut the wall. "Now is not the time to explore. I do not trust Māhōn being alone with the others. We will wait until everyone is asleep."

Conell snuck into Imogene's sleeping chamber and gently placed his hand over her mouth. Her eyes fluttered open, and she gave him a frustrated stare.

She pulled his hand from her mouth. "What are you doing in my room?" she whispered in the dark.

Émēr leaned over Conell's shoulder. "We need the help of the seer. Come."

"Now? We can't wait until the sun is up?"

Conell handed her a dressing robe. "No, *Chuōbá*, we need your assistance now. We are to explore the room."

She slipped into the robe and pulled on her shoes. "In the creepy throne room with the ghosts in a cave in the middle of the night. Oh, how lovely. A monster ball. You owe me."

They stepped into the hallway where Erák was watching the corridor.

Imogene pulled her robe around her shoulders as they quietly took the stairs to the lower level and slipped into the small room. "We really need to find some nicer places to stay."

Émēr pressed on the rock and the wall opened. Imogene and Erák gasped.

Imogene peeked into the dark stairwell. "You should be a ghost hunter, Émēr; you find the creepiest places."

Émēr held his candle over the stairs. "Mojí," he lamented as he pulled back and stared at him. "It is a spiral staircase."

Erák moaned and rubbed his face. "This is not good."

Okay," Imogene said. "We don't like spiral staircases?"

"Men used the spiral staircase to keep an enemy at bay. It is a line of defense." Émēr said. "It means someone dangerous was down there at one time."

"And you want me to go down there?" Imogene shook her head. "Nope, not going to happen."

"Erák, stay here and keep watch." Conell took Imogene's hand. "I will be with you."

Émēr led them down the staircase. The width was as large as his body, allowing guards to trap escaping prisoners. "I am thinking this is a dungeon."

"So Anú had a dungeon below the castle? Yeah, why not, add to the creepy-o-meter," Imogene said.

When they reached the bottom, an eerie darkness threatened to suffocate them. Imogene buried her face in Conell's arm.

He placed his hand on her head. "Do not be frightened."

Émēr lit the candles in the holders on the walls. The light revealed a large room. His eyes grew wide. "Mojí!"

Conell and Imogene crowded around him.

"Is that what I think it is?" Imogene asked.

Émēr nodded.

Always keep the enemy caged.

-Dia

19

The cage rose a story high and took up the length of the room. The bars were the size of an average man's biceps. The large door hung open like a monster's mouth, and the darkness gobbled up the feeble light from the candles. A shiver slithered down Émēr's back.

Two dirty skeletons lay like broken dolls behind the open door. Another four decomposed bodies lay near them. Six in number. Émēr knelt before them and bowed his head. "Dia and Augustine, and my brothers. You stayed at your posts and fought what was down here. May you find rest in the Attiyq." Émēr turned to Conell. "I am unsure about the other four. Anú had left ten men. Six are dead, four are elsewhere."

Imogene peered over his shoulder. "How do you know them? It's been like a thousand years."

Émēr picked up a piece of cloth. "Augustine wore the red tunic of his people. See the red cloth with the eagle stitching? I saw this same tunic in my vision. I will ask Erák to help me bury them tonight."

Imogene touched Émēr's arm. "We all will help. We'll tell Māhōn we found them in the throne room." She stepped over rocks and peaked into the cage. "Something big was in here. I think whatever it was, killed them. But the question is, do we want to know what it was?"

Conell and Émēr exchanged looks.

Conell shrugged. "Someone or something is speaking to us and wanted Émēr to find this, so I would say yes, we need to know."

Imogene opened the rusty cage door and peered into the darkness. She cocked her head and looked back at them. "Do you hear that?"

Conell shrugged. "I hear nothing."

"It sounds like babbling; I can't make it out." Her eyes grew wide, and she fell back with a scream. Conell caught her and helped her to her feet where she buried her face in his chest. "Something is in there!" she whispered.

Émēr held his Mojí back and he pulled out his sword. He crept to the doorway but saw nothing. Then he shoved open the door and stepped inside.

"Watch him, Augustine!"

Émēr spun on his heels.

Augustine and Dia stood outside the cage and held their drawn swords. Their fellow brothers stood behind them. A deep growl came from the back of the cage. Argus reared up on his back-hoofed legs and his head touched the ceiling. His back claws clicked on the stones and his clawed hand reached for him. Massive black wings sprung out from his back. Large fangs grew from his human mouth and his once black eyes were red against his skinless face.

Dia's face scrunched in horror as General Bode thrust his sword through his back.

"You have failed, Worthless One," Bode whispered as he yanked Dia's head back then jerked the sword from Dia's body and shoved him to the floor.

Augustine held his sword before Bode, his eyes wide. "You have no power here."

Bode winced.

The four Maúl warriors gathered around Augustine.

One soldier looked up the stairwell. "Brothers, the demons are here! Help us!"

The remaining Maúl stood on the top stair and gawked at the scene below. "I am sorry, my brothers! Demons never die!" cried one soldier. They turned and fled into the hallways. Their shouts of fear echoed along the cavern.

Augustine's face fell, and he planted his feet. His enduring brothers stood beside him.

"We die together, Augustine," one said.

Bode laughed and slapped his sword against his side. "More of God's Worthless Ones defy the great Argus. My Master said you will die here. Join us or taste my sword."

Augustine let out a deep breath. "The Great One stands with us."

Bode winced again.

Ambras dropped from the ceiling and sliced at the four remaining soldiers. His sword cut across their backs, and they dropped around Augustine. Augustine's wild eyes searched for Ambras, but the young demon had melted into the stone wall.

Bode sneered. "Where is your god, boy?"

Augustine turned back to Bode. His breath was labored and sweat ran down his face. "God, help me."

Ambras stepped from his hiding place and slashed his sword across Augustine's shoulder blades.

He moaned and fell to his knees. "Kill me now; I only go to my God. You have lost this war."

Bode leaned over him. "No, you have lost." He grabbed Augustine's hair and plunged his sword into his chest.

Émēr trembled as the vision faded. A growl echoed behind him. He turned.

Argus reared on his scorched back legs and lowered his snarling, skeleton face to Émēr. The demon's red eyes glowed in the darkness, and the candlelight revealed his long fangs.

Émēr rushed from the cage and struggled to lock the door. "Mojí, Argus is in the cage!"

Conell gave him an odd stare. "Émēr, there is nothing. What did you see?"

His wide eyes took in the empty cage and room. He peered into the pen and his shaking hands lifted his candle. "Argus! I saw Argus. He is not an angel; he is a demon. He killed the Maúl; he killed Augustine and Dia." He dropped to his knees. "The demons slaughtered them. All of them. Four escaped." Émēr shook his head.

Imogene peered up at Conell. "I saw it, too. I don't want to be the seer!"

Conell moved her behind him and examined the cage. "Do you know why Argus was in the cage or how they put him in there?"

Émēr looked up at him and shook his head. "I do not know, Moji. How can we fight against such evil power?"

Conell helped Émēr to his feet and led them both up the stairs. "Come Now we must sleep. We will find answers later."

Émēr's shaking legs climbed the steps. "I am sorry, Moji. I am sorry I showed fear."

Conell placed his hand on Émēr's shoulder. "I too would be afraid if I saw what you saw."

Émēr looked behind him and tears filled his eyes. "I must bury my brothers again. I have buried so many."

"I promise, Captain, we will bury your brothers tonight. Erák and I will help you," Conell said.

The whispers that Émēr heard in the library traveled up the staircase. A shiver swept over him, and he looked over his shoulder. The chanting sounds came from the black cage with the gaping door that lay open like a monster's mouth.

Imogene followed his gaze. "What is it?"

"Nothing." Émēr quickly escorted her up the stairs.

Amhras watched the group climb the stairwell and then turned back to the cell, tears on his cheeks. "Oh, My Father! How these humans have made you to suffer! Vengeance shall be swift!"

Brón stepped beside him and ran her small fingers over the bars. "Father has never spoken of these days. I believe it breaks what is left of his black heart. The Attiyq is cruel. Why must we be punished?"

Bode examined the cage. "I remember when my king was locked in this prison and we hid in the mountains. It was a horrible time." He kicked the skeletons. "Fools!" He glanced at Amhras who caught the demon's socket eyes.

"You, the great Bode, General of My Father's Armies," Amhras said. "These humans fought with their last breath against you, and yes, *WE* were able to destroy them, but still you were unable to free My Father from his prison! He suffered because of your weakness!"

Bode raised his sword to Amhras' throat.

"I am not the fool you think me to be, General," Amhras said. "Destroy me and My Father will destroy you!"

Bode turned to Brón. "Go and tell King Argus the child of Anú has found it, as well as the Maúl scrolls. I will join you soon."

She nodded and evaporated into the stone floor.

Bode stared at Amhras. "If this Maúl succeeds, then you will join your precious father in his cage."

Amhras swallowed and hurried up the stairs after the humans. Bode chuckled and followed.

Erák, Émēr, Conell, and Imogene brought the bodies of the Maúl into the woods and the men dug a grave. Conell and Émēr slowly lowered the skeletons into the hole and covered them with dirt. Émēr brought his hands down along his face and bowed his head.

"May you always lie in the arms of the Attiyq, my brave brothers. I will enjoy meeting you in paradise."

Imogene dropped flowers on the grave and Émēr looked away. He had dropped the same flowers on Father's grave years ago.

"Come," he said. "We need to return to my wife."

Émēr led the others to the cave and into the castle. Relief flooded his frame as he gazed upon Ūmá sleeping soundly and he kissed her forehead.

Imogene climbed onto her cot but left the candle burning. "I don't think I can sleep in the dark ever again."

Conell gave her a soft grin. "I… I mean, we… will be in the next room if you need us."

Imogene sniffed with wide eyes. "I saw him in a dream. He dragged me into hell." Tears sprung in her eyes. "I can't go back there."

Conell patted her arm. "He will not pull you into hell. We will watch over you."

Émēr rose from Ūmá's side and made his way to the door. The book she had been reading sat next to her bed. He picked it up and made his way to the hall. Leaning against a candle, its light showed the scribbled words. He slowly read each word, then read them again.

Conell exited the room and shut the door behind him. "She is asleep."

Émēr held up the book. "Imogene?"

Conell kept his eyes to the ground. "Well, yes, she was frightened. What do you have?"

Émēr studied the prince's red cheeks. "Ūmá said it was a diary by Augustine."

Conell shook his head. "This is what Imogene would say, creepy."

"Aye."

His Mojí lowered Émēr's hands as he held the book. "Let us read it tomorrow. Tonight, we need to rest. Tell Māhōn it is a list of chores for the servants."

"My heart is beating so fast; I do not think I can sleep."

Conell placed his hand on Émēr's shoulder and turned him down the hall. "Try."

The next morning, Émēr awoke early and crept from the room as Māhōn lay snoring on his cot. He shook his head. The man made a poor Maúl; the warriors were always alert to the slightest sounds.

He made his way along the halls and lit the candles. The vision from last night still hung in his mind, which kept sleep far from him. He yawned and stopped at the top of the stairs. The bottom floor was plunged in darkness. His heart rate increased and sweat dripped down his back. The once amazing castle seemed to press down on him and the urge to claw through the walls bit at his mind.

Émēr shook his head, saying inside, *"You are of the blood of Anú and you will not fear."* He forced his feet down the stairs and lit the candles on the risers and on the lower floor. *"I hide under the shadow of the Attiyq. Remember what the angel said. Argus has no control over me."*

Émēr ate a quick breakfast and afterwards made his way out of the cave and into the sunlight. The bright light bit at his eyes, but a sense of relief flowed over him as well. He followed the perimeter of what he thought was the second level of the castle. The sunlight shining in the throne room came from some source, perhaps another opening of the cave. "You are so full of secrets, Anú," he whispered to himself. Then prayed, "Attiyq, help me to find them."

Émēr followed the curve of the cave until the ground dropped into a deep gully. He knelt along the edge where rocks and dirt filled the channel. A path led from the rocks into the forest. He stood and listened. Only the sounds of the wind rustling the trees and woodland animals drifted to him. He picked his way down the ridge and stood on a large boulder.

"So Anú, did you and King Brodén fill in this gulley? Or did Argus. Or the escaping warriors?" Émēr's gaze followed the worn path through the woods. Jumping from the boulder, he knelt close to the ground. Next, he rose to walk alongside of the path, following it into the woods before kneeling again. The leaves were disturbed along parts of the trail. "Someone was here," he whispered.

Staying close to the path and not disturbing the leaves himself, Émēr followed the trail. It led deeper through the trees. He stopped and listened. Nothing beyond the natural noises of the forest.

"It is time to inform my Mojí," he told himself and quickly returned to the castle.

Prince Conell and Erák were found in the kitchen helping Imogene with breakfast.

Émēr stepped close and said low to the three of them, "I have found something outside that you need to see, but we must get past Māhōn."

"Well, personally, I'm tired of being a sitting duck," Imogene said, drying her hands on a towel. "I'd like to learn to fight. Conell, you had asked me if I knew how to use a sword and I said no. Now I want to know. I need to know. I won't sit here and wait for Argus."

Conell crossed his arms over his chest. "And how will that distract Māhōn?"

"When Māhōn and Frigg are training, we go outside. Émēr trains me for a while, and you look at whatever it is you are supposed to see."

"Perhaps. It could work," Conell said.

"I could help train her," Erák said. "That would give Émēr time to join you."

Conell caught Émēr's frown. "She is right. She does need to know something. Let her learn the staff."

Émēr clicked his tongue. "This is not a training temple."

Imogene nodded. "Maybe so, but you need a distraction, and I am tired of being a sitting duck."

"A sitting duck?" Conell asked.

"Yeah, just sitting around waiting to die," Imogene said.

Émēr rubbed the back of his neck and caught his Mojí's stare. "A staff would be a bit easier to learn..." He lifted his finger to her face. "But only for defense."

She grinned and bowed. "Yes, *Sensei.*"

He gave her an odd look, making her giggle. "We will start today. Mojí, I will show you the direction of the boulders and then join you."

"I know a bit of how to use the staff," Erák said. "And it would keep Frigg and Māhōn busy also."

Imogene frowned. "Māhōn and Frigg are becoming bros pretty fast. Bro means men who are close. I worry about Frigg. He is very impressionable, and you three treat him like he's an annoying little brother."

Émēr crossed his arms and leaned against the counter. "Yes, we have treated him horribly. We need to bring him back to us and away from Māhōn. We will start today."

After breakfast, Conell gathered the group into the main hall. "Émēr is going to teach Imogene, Erák, and Frigg—if you want to learn, Frigg—to use a staff for defense. We are still in enemy territory and we are unsure of who is still on our side. I want you all to be able to defend yourselves."

Ūmá tugged at Émēr's arm. "My husband, I also wish to learn the staff. Father and my brother had taught me to use the sword, and now I wish to learn the staff."

"My Lady, my sword will protect you."

"But my husband, please, let me learn."

Her bright blue eyes spun their deep spell over him, and he released a deep sigh. "Your eyes are enough to capture any man's heart, and I am glad they hold me as captive. Yes, my wife, I will teach you."

She grinned and leaned her head against his arm.

His heart drummed and he steadied his breath. Imogene grinned his way and heat rose in his cheeks. He coughed but slipped his arm around Ūmá's waist and led her to the stairs that lead out of the cave where the group squinted against the bright sun.

Imogene raised her hand to her forehead. "It seems like years since I've seen the sun. I don't know why Anú thought it was a great idea to build a castle underground."

Émēr chuckled and led the group away from the hidden pathway. He handed Imogene a staff and showed her how to place her feet and where to place her hands.

Māhōn leaned against a tree and watched them. He rolled his eyes and shook his head.

Émēr caught Māhōn's criticism and held out the staff. "Brother, please, show us what you have learned."

Māhōn pushed himself away from the tree and grasped the staff. "I will teach you the true way of the Maúl. Perhaps you could join our order?"

Imogene gave a nervous laugh. "I'm not really wishing to join any Maúl any time, but thanks for the offer."

He snorted and showed her how he placed his hands on the staff and planted his feet. Imogene nodded and hit him with a barrage of questions.

Émēr slowly walked back to his Mojí and whispered, "The path is to the right, around the cave entrance and down by the boulders. I am not sure where it leads."

Conell nodded and stretched his arms. He slipped his hands behind him and strolled around the cave.

Émēr kept Māhōn and Frigg's attention as he showed Imogene and the others how his techniques were like Māhōn's stance.

Māhōn looked over his shoulder, and Imogene gently tapped his stomach. "Oh, I'm so sorry," she said.

He shoved away her staff. "Please, watch what you are doing."

She grimaced. "I'm so sorry. I was just practicing. Is this how I need to do it?"

When Conell returned, he stepped past Imogene and spoke loudly enough for everyone to hear. "I see you are already trying to destroy us."

She made a face at Conell, and he chuckled. Émēr led Ūmá away and showed her how to hold the weapon. Conell followed them and positioned Ūmá's hands on the weapon. "I saw the path. What do you think?"

"I saw a light shining into the throne room as if there were a large opening in the wall. I am not sure who filled the hole, Argus or Anú," Émēr whispered.

Ūmá quickly looked up at him, but Émēr patted her arm. "It was a long time ago that Argus was here, Ūmá. Do not fear. But I did see tracks, so someone has been here recently."

"The Southern People?" Ūmá asked.

He shrugged. "Perhaps. But the tracks were fresh enough that they could have been from the previous night."

"The others need to know about the path, but do not speak of your vision," Conell said. "I have found something around the cave," he announced for everyone to hear. "Come, I will need all of you to see it."

He led the group to the ditch and the path leading into the woods. "See?" he pointed at the boulders and the path. "A trail that leads into the woods."

Émēr slid down the side and studied the path. "Māhōn, you can see where the leaves have been disturbed."

Māhōn examined the path. "Interesting that you found this so quickly."

Conell shrugged. "I noticed it when I stretched my legs. I leave the tracking to my captain."

"How long would you say they were here? Do you think they are dangerous?" Erák asked.

Émēr shook his head. "I do not think they are dangerous. They would have killed us by now. They are probably curious."

"So, do we not worry about this?" Imogene asked.

"They will come to us when they are ready," Émēr said and led the others back to the cave.

After dinner, Émēr slipped away from the others as they sat in the dining hall and made his way to the library. He shut the door and sat in a chair next to the burning candles. "Now my Maúl brothers, what do you want me to know?" He opened the diary.

Augustine had written his name on the inside of the journal. Below his name were written the words of the Attiyq.

"The Great One knows of His children's thirst and quenches it with His living waters. All who come to the Attiyq are found safe in Him."

Émēr smiled. "These are words I love, too. It seems you and I would have been good friends, Augustine." He flipped through the pages.

> *King Anú, the great King of the Southern Lands, the one true ruler and Priest of the Attiyq gave audience to the King of the North, King Brodén. My King, may he live forever, is the keeper of the demon, the one who watches over the Beast that betrayed the Attiyq who in His mercy gave the Beast lands to guard. The Beast failed in his task and instead sought to imprison those whom the Attiyq had cherished. The two great Kings and a seer came together and imprisoned the Beast.*

Émēr lowered the book and rubbed his chin. "They imprisoned Argus. But how did he escape, and how did three men imprison him?"

> *King Anú showed King Brodén the Beast. The demon ran against the cage and threatened revenge. King Brodén stood tall and refused to show fear. My King Anú was well pleased and the two Kings broke bread in the Great Hall. The sun shone through the Window of Angels and all were happy. King Anú showed King Brodén the sacred scrolls that only the Maúl can possess.*

Émēr studied the scrolls laying on the shelves. "Only the Maúl can possess. All of these are mine and for my clan."

Seek the words of King Anú: Each Maúl is the guardian of Life, each Maúl must take his stand and watch over the innocence that covers the lands. The Attiyq trusts us to bring each man, woman, and child into His strong and mighty hand. To spread His words across the lands. It is said that the man is the priest to his own temple. Each temple contains his clan and loved ones. If he does not become the priest, then he has failed the final test of the Maúl. – Words of King Anú.

Émēr released a deep sigh and rubbed the stone around his neck. "Oh, Augustine, I have failed at being the priest, and I have failed of becoming Maúl. I feel Maúl in my bones, yet my hands and my face markings are of a child. How can I become a priest and Maúl? Attiyq, give me wisdom. Cian, how I wish you were here to give me wisdom. It seems years since you have left us. I cannot be what you ask of me."

He flipped through the pages. Most of the diary was filled with Augustine's recording of the tasks the King asked him to do, information about the weather, and Maúl wisdom that he had learned. Émēr turned to the last few pages.

The Great King has given me, Dia, and other guards great honor. We are to guard the Beast. He has asked that we take wives from the villages and have families that will also guard the Beast. Anú wants no one to learn what is in the cage and will not be back again. He said, in his wisdom, we are the only ones who must know of the Beast. We are the guardians. May the Attiyq give us strength to do His will.

He turned to the last written page in the journal. The date was two years later.

I fear the Beast. I know my God is stronger, but the Beast is monstrous and consuming. His red eyes harbor evil that I have never seen. He locks me in a hold that I struggle to break. I have told Dia to beware of the Beast's eyes. I can see fear in even Great Dia's eyes, but he hides it from me. We all hide our fear, yet it screams from the darkness. I often regret staying behind.

I am hearing things also. I have told no one, including Dia. He is much braver than I. I hear whispers when no one is there. I hear these things in the hallways at night, I hear them in the throne room, in the scroll library, but mostly on the stairwell leading to the cage. The Beast talks to walls. I cannot see the creatures that he speaks with, and that is what I fear. What if I am going mad? What if being locked in this castle and the evil that comes off the Beast is pushing me to the brink of madness? How can I protect my people and my King if my mind is slipping away?

The other men fear the Beast also. I see it in their eyes and hear fear in their voices. I fear they will abandon the post. I will stay, as will a few others. I have told them they will have no honor if they run. They have told me honor does no one any good if they are dead. I fear it will be only us. How can we stop one so evil?

Émēr sat back and let out a deep sigh. "Oh, Augustine, my brother, you did not go mad, my friend. It was the demon who drew you into his madness. You stayed at your post; you are the bravest of all the Maúl. Rest in peace, my friend." He closed the journal and patted the cover as grief consumed him.

Émēr then rose and fingered the scrolls praying, "Show me, Attiyq, show me what You wish for me to see. Help me to continue Augustine's work."

Light footsteps in the hallway drew his attention. When the door opened, Ūmá's delightful face peered around the doorframe. Émēr's smile broadened and he pulled out a seat. "Please, My Lady, join me."

Ūmá slipped into the chair. "I thought you would be up, My Lord, so I thought I would come and see if I could give you some assistance."

"I am most pleased that you came, my wife." He paused. "I read parts of the journal. It seems Argus was imprisoned here and he killed Augustine and his men."

Her eyebrows rose. "I did not read of his imprisonment. What happened?"

"Augustine and his men died while trying to stop Argus from escaping. I do not know how he came to be free of the cage. But do not fear, my wife. I do not think he will return to this place." Émēr selected a scroll and unrolled it on the table. "Would you like to help me unlock the secrets of Anú? The Attiyq's hand will guide us."

A soft smile spread across her face. "Yes, indeed." She arranged the candles around the open parchment and she held up the light.

Anú's writing sprawled over the yellow parchment, curved letters forming words of life. Émēr traced the lettering. "Not even the elders of my clan or my father knew these existed." His gaze scanned the shelving stuffed with scrolls. "No one knows." He grinned at her and her eyes danced.

"Yes, my husband. My father spoke much of the Maúl. His brother, my uncle, was Maúl. He died before I met him."

"I did not know this. What was his name?"

"Diarmund. My father said he was a brave man."

"You do have Maúl blood, My Lady."

"That is why I remained silent in the castle. Maúl blood."

Émēr kissed her hand, making his heart race. He took a deep breath and studied the scroll. "These are new words to me, words the elders and my father never taught me. It seems Anú had a deeper vision of the Attiyq than any other Maúl."

As the light bounced off Ūmá's hair, her sapphire eyes glowed. She seemed small, fragile, like a blade of grass clinging to the side of a mountain, yet a godly strength lay in her eyes.

Émēr slowly read the words out loud:

"'Brok, son of Caradog, was the seer of the great Anú, a seer full of wisdom and favor from the Attiyq, his ear pinned to the mouth of the Attiyq, always listening for the Great One's whispered words. Anú saw the great wisdom of Brok and appointed him seer to the Great One. Brok served Anú with his right hand and in his left held his own staff of strength. Always Brok sat by Anú's side, giving him words of great insight. His words led to many victories for the Maúl. Anú treasured Brok.

"'On the day of his forty-fifth Day of Birth, Anú gave him a gift. It represented Brok's loyalty to the King and his God. A gift that was to be handed down to all in Brok's line. A chain made of gold and a treasured pendant. A large purple jewel sat in the center and the writing of Anú was embedded into the gold. Words that spoke of the greatness of Brok. Only Brok understood the words, for they were written only for him. Brok worked with Anú in a great task only known to Brok and Anú. Brok died the day Anú found victory over his enemy.'"

Émēr glanced up at Ūmá. She leaned over and reread the words. "My Lord, do you think this could be Imogene's medallion?"

"I do not know."

"'Brok left the world of Anú and entered the Attiyq's realm when he fought beside Anú in his special task of the Attiyq. King Anú rested with his fathers a year later. The country mourned the loss of the King.'"

Émēr glanced at Uma. "Special task? Augustine mentioned in the journal a seer who worked with Anú in capturing Argus. He must have died after they imprisoned Argus. And Anú died soon after Brok. No one knew Argus was here. They all died."

"'Brok died as his father had died, with his fingers clutching his sword. Anú wept over Brok, then took the treasured item from him. He returned home and placed it around the neck of Heffin son of Brok, son of Caradog. The Attiyq blessed Heffin with the gifting of the Seer. He was as strong as his father and served the Maúl well. After many years, Heffin rested with his father and his father's father. Many of Brok's line wore the treasured gift, each one trusting in the Attiyq and allowing the Great One to speak through them to the King.'"

"This is odd," Émēr said. "The medallion has been passed down from generation to generation. My question is how did it get to Imogene?" Ūmá shook her head in slow motion, deep in thought. "Does the medallion give the seer the ability to see?"

"Or…" Ūmá clicked her tongue. "Or does the Attiyq give sight to whom He pleases to see?"

They exchanged looks and a new chill swept from the top of Émēr's head to his toes. "Ūmá," he whispered, "if the Attiyq gives the ability to see to whomever He pleases…"

She nodded. "Then the medallion has no powers."

"Precisely," he replied and they fell silent.

Being a priest means one must protect the people whether one uses their sword or their words.

-Anú

20

Émēr forced the fear from his heart and stared into Ūmá's eyes. "You took a vow that you would obey me. Now I take up that vow. You must say nothing to Imogene, my clan, My Mojí, nor Māhōn regarding Anú's words. I fear for Imogene's life."

She licked her lips. "Argus is obsessed with finding her and will hunt her down to the end of the ages."

"If Argus should discover that the medallion has no powers, then there will be no reason to keep the seer alive." He rubbed the bridge of his nose as a heavy blanket covered his mind. It had seemed years since he had last slept. He rose and stared at the wall of scrolls. "My wife, even if I were to study every passage, every word, I fear that I would not understand Anú and his secrets. Attiyq, give me wisdom. I am Maúl, and yet, these words mean nothing to me."

Émēr's fingertips scanned the mountain of papers. Another scroll cried out to him. Its sound rose up from his chest and pounded in his head. A large scroll with ripped edges crackled as he unrolled the paper. Ūmá covered her mouth as she yawned.

"It is time for you to sleep, my love," Émēr said.

She shook her head. "Nay, My Lord. I will sleep when you sleep."

He smiled. "Then I must read quickly."

The scroll crinkled under his hands and threatened to crumble. Once unrolled, he read the words to Ūmá.

"'The Attiyq will have no others beside Him. He is the ruler of all creation. No one is His equal. Woe to you, oh Handsome One. For the Attiyq made you greater than His creation, giving you land to rule. But you allowed pride to become your throne and arrogance to be your scepter. Those whom He entrusted to you cried out to the Great One, for your hand was full of malice and hatred.

"'A war broke out between you and those who follow the Attiyq. The Attiyq gave great strength to those who followed Him, and they tossed you into a prison cell that was meant to hold you forever until the time of Judgment came and you would be destroyed by the Attiyq's great hand.'"

But are you Maúl?

Émēr shoved the thought away, but it persisted. He took a deep breath and leaned back his head. "My wife, do you truly see me as Maúl?"

She gave him a puzzled stare. "Of course, My Lord, you are Maúl."

"But I never finished my training. Imie says I am Maúl, but I question."

She chuckled. "You listen to the wrong thoughts, Émēr. You saved me, you saved Imie, and you saved your king. Now you seek Anú's footsteps. Yes, you are Maúl."

Émēr gave her a soft grin and squeezed her small fingers. "Thank you."

Ūmá tapped the scroll and peered over his shoulder. "Who is Anú speaking of?" Her long hair smelled like peaches picked from the tree.

"I do not know," Émēr replied and forced his eyes onto the paper.

"'"The Attiyq turned to Anú and gave him orders that only the Maúl can follow. Each generation is to guard the evil one. Each Maúl will hand to his son the commands to guard the one who tried to destroy the lands. Only the King and a priest can release the evil one, but who would try such a foolish thing?"'"

He paused and rubbed his eyes. "I wonder if Anú is speaking of Argus. The Maúl was to guard him, but if everyone is dead, who guards him? Argus escaped somehow."

Ūmá handed him the candle, then carefully rolled up the scroll. "Forgive me, My Lord, but you are weary and must find sleep. There is much to do if you are to teach me and Imogene to use the staff. Please, let us retire. You have cared for me, now it is my turn to care for you."

He opened his mouth to protest, but the stern look in her blue eyes extinguished his argument. He nodded as she helped him to his feet.

"I promise we will come here tomorrow to learn more of the secrets of the Maúl."

"Yes, my wife."

Ūmá giggled. "Imie often says the men of her world say, 'yes, dear.' "

Émēr chuckled. "Yes, dear." He returned the scroll to its place and ran his fingers along the edges of the other scrolls. "This castle has many mysteries. I want to know more of the Southern People. Perhaps we should have more training tomorrow? It will give me a chance to explore the paths around the open pit."

Uma laid her head on his arm. "Or perhaps all of us could hunt for berries or fruits? It would be a believable ruse since everyone knows we are low on food."

Émēr gave her a long, amused look. "My Lady, you are turning into a spy."

"I suppose I am, My Lord," his bride said with a grin and Émēr followed her from the library.

The squad of demons withered on the floor, their screams echoing off the walls. Bode stood over them and scowled. The blisters on his flesh had finally calmed. Amhras sobbed outside the castle, and Brón was far away. He shook his head as he yanked his screaming demons to their feet.

"Be strong!" Bode shoved a sword into a demon's trembling hands. "You are demons who fight against the Attiyq. We can still win this battle!" he thundered, even as doubts began to swarm in his own mind.

Morning arrived, and Ūmá led the way up the stairs and out of the cave. She stretched her arms in the warm sunlight and gave Émēr a grin and a wink.

He shook his head. "You are becoming Imogene."

"Nothing wrong with that!" Imogene said appearing right behind her sister. She slipped her arm under Ūmá's and tugged her down the road. "Let's find some berries. I wanna make a pie!"

Conell stepped beside Émēr who glanced at the empty cave and allowed a sigh of relief. "I am so grateful for my cousin. He will keep Frigg and Māhōn busy most of the day."

Conell matched Émēr's steps. "Yes, I noticed how quickly Erák begged Māhōn to help him with his 'Maúl' techniques."

Émēr grinned. "I talked to him this morning. He agreed." He slowed his steps. "Let us allow the women to move ahead so we may speak of Imogene's medallion."

"What of it?"

"My Mojí, one of the scrolls I read last night spoke of a medallion that King Anú gave to his seer. It has been passed down to generations until it somehow came to Imogene." He took a deep breath. "It has no powers."

Conell stopped walking and exhaled with force. "I was not expecting bad news. Who else knows of this?"

"My wife and no one else."

Conell paused in thought. "Imogene is of a place called New York, a distant unknown world. How could the medallion come to her?"

"My Mojí, that is a question I have pondered all night. I have no answer. Perhaps it has powers we do not understand."

Conell rubbed his forehead. "It seems this mystery becomes more tangled, like seaweed."

"I will check the scrolls tonight, My Mojí. Hopefully, the answer will be there."

Ūmá and Imogene veered off the trail and into the woods.

"Ūmá, Imogene, please stay on the road," Émēr called.

Imogene turned. "But there are berries this way!"

A twig cracked in the woods. Émēr held out his hand and stopped his Mojí. The sound of a foot cracking the leaves drifted into his ears. "My Ladies, come here!"

Imogene cocked her head in protest, but Ūmá tugged her to the men.

Conell scanned the woods. "What is it, My Captain?"

Émēr held up his hand. Another footstep.

He grabbed Ūmá and Imogene by their hands and pulled them back to the cave. "Someone is watching us in the woods."

A man dressed in a brown tunic and black pants stepped in front of them. His long black hair was tied back from his face, and he held his sword at his side. Maúl markings covered his face.

Conell and Émēr stood in front of the women, weapons drawn. Conell glanced at Émēr then at the stranger.

Émēr's breath caught in his lungs. His people! The Maúl lived!

The man studied Émēr's face. Shame crept over him. A child's story lay etched on his cheek and chin. The markings that covered the man's face told stories of victory in many battles.

"Please, we mean you no harm," Émēr said, using the Maúl words.

The man's eyes narrowed. "You have the markings of Anú, but you are not of the Southern Lands."

Émēr's heart pounded. "I am from the Northern Lands of King Brodén, but I come in peace."

Three men dressed in the same tunic and black pants stepped forward and blocked any attempt to escape.

"Please, we mean you no harm. I too am Maúl, a child of Anú," Émēr said.

"This man is Brodénian! Kill them all! He is not one of us," said one of the guards.

Émēr shoved his fear down to his toes. "Yes, I am a Brodénian, but I flee from the queen who rules the lands. Barbarians have slaughtered my people; I am all that is left. Please, I mean you no harm."

"This man is not Maúl! He is not one of us," said another guard.

Émēr shook his head. "Please, we seek sanctuary in Brodén's Cave. I have found Maúl writings! My name is Émēr. This is my wife, Ūmá, my sister, Imogene, and my … cousin Cahal."

"How did you find the scrolls?" the man asked. "That place is sacred to us. Anú ruled from his underground castle. The elders said he was sent by the Attiyq to guard against the evil that roamed the lands. His horns blew in the battle and the Evil Ones fled. The sounds broke their bodies and turned them to ash."

"We found the cave and needed a safe place for the women. I found the writings of Anú and we found his castle underground. I will show it to you."

The man shook his head. "No, we do not guard it. Only the children of the priests are allowed in the cave."

"Guard whom or what?" Conell asked.

"The One who holds evil in his hands. Anú imprisoned him, and Anú's children keep the evil in the cage."

"Do you mean the cage in the castle?" Émēr asked.

The man nodded. "Are you a priest?"

Émēr licked his lips. *Are you?* He took a deep breath. "Yes, I am a priest. I was made priest when our priest died. I serve the Attiyq."

Conell gave him a sharp, confused look. Imogene raised her eyebrows.

The man nodded. "Good, then you have come to guard against the evil. It has been centuries since anyone has entered or left Anú's castle."

"The Evil you speak of has a name," Émēr offered. "He is called Argus, a lord of darkness. He is no longer in the cage."

The Maúl's face fell. "What do you mean he is no longer in the cage?"

"He escaped many years ago and is ruling over Ézású."

The man raised his hand, and the three guards relaxed. "I am called Aabon. I am the leader of the Maúl of the Southern Lands. We have a small camp not too far from here. We have seen you at the cave's entrance. You have come to capture the Evil One?"

Émēr glanced at Conell, who gave a sharp shake of his head.

"The Attiyq has led me to this place, but I am unsure as to what we are to do yet. But if I can, I wish to follow in Anú's path."

Conell frowned, but Émēr ignored it.

Aabon gave him a small bow. "Then I am honored to be with you. Come, meet your fellow warriors, Priest. Give us a teaching."

Émēr licked his lips.

Aabon gestured with his arm. "Come, Priest, join us. Honor us."

He inwardly moaned but nodded. "Yes, but we cannot stay long, I must find the secrets of Anú."

A grin crossed Aabon's face, and he sheathed his weapon.

Conell matched Émēr's steps as the Maúl men proudly led the way to the small village. "Captain, do you believe it is wise to go with these people? And when were you going to tell me about being a priest?"

Émēr dismissed his question about being a priest. "If we do not, then we will create war. It is dishonorable to not go."

"It gives us great honor and pleasure to have a priest. I am called Felim," said one of the men. His youthful eyes betrayed his age. Émēr guessed him to be around fourteen years of age. A boy in the league of men. "My grandfather was the priest of the village, but he is now dead. I have tried to be priest, but it is hard when one has little knowledge of the Attiyq. I wish to learn from you. You can teach me, yes? I really want to learn!"

Émēr forced a grin. "Thank you, it is an honor."

You think you are now priest? What do you know of God?

He forced the thoughts away, thankful it was easier now than before. *Thank You, Attiyq!*

Passages from the Attiyq's sacred books bubbled into his mind, and a teaching blossomed. It grew in his mind as the passages drifted by him. Doubt struck at his heart but again, Émēr forced them down.

I trust in the Attiyq!

Conell repeated his question about the priest.

"It means nothing. It is only words," Émēr answered quietly buying time in order to sort it out himself first.

The warrior's village came into view. The small cabins were built onto the branches of towering trees and swaying rope bridges linked the lodges. The homes stretched deep into the forest. A few women who wore long, flowing dresses crossed the bridges. The tinging sound of the smithy drifted in the breeze.

Imogene gasped and pointed. "Oh wow! Look at that! It's like something out Tolkien's books!"

Aabon grinned. "You have never seen our villages?"

She shook her head. "No, never. It's amazing. How did you do it?"

"These have been here for generations. This is our warrior's village. Our homes are deep in the forests. We guard the borders."

"Guard the borders?" Conell asked.

"Yes, we guard against the Barbarians and the Brodénians."

"Brodénians?" Imogene asked.

"Those who follow King Brodén. Legends say he stole our king and tried to destroy our lands. He was greedy for wealth and slaves. So, we guard what is left of the Maúl Warriors."

Émēr's heart pounded in his chest. "What is left?"

"The castle is that of Anú, our Great King." Aabon said. "Anú ruled this land before Brodén stole him away from us. For centuries, we have had no king to protect us."

Imogene slowly turned to stare at Émēr. His lips pursed, and he kept his gaze on the trees. Now he was to be priest and ruler? Yet he had nothing and could give nothing. Ūmá slipped her hand into his and squeezed his fingers. He gave her a small smile.

"You would make a wonderful ruler, my husband," she whispered.

Aabon followed the stone path to a large cabin that sat below the trees. Women watched them from the bridges and pointed at them. The men gathered around. "My brothers and sisters, this man is a Maúl priest and is guarding Anú's castle. He has come to give us a lesson on the Attiyq."

A man with graying hair and beard grasped Émēr's face in his hands. "Your face tells the story of a child who survived his testing of the Maúl warriors. Why do you, a priest and warrior, have no other markings?"

Émēr shoved the shame down to his feet. "I will explain in the meeting hall."

The elder studied Émēr, then moved aside. "I look forward to hearing your message, Priest."

Aabon nodded as he passed the elder and escorted the villagers to a large meeting cabin. Attached to a pole that stood outside the house was the Maúl flag, which flew proudly in the wind. Émēr stopped and bowed before it then entered the room. Simple wooden candelabras stood around the room, giving off a soft glow. Carved elder chairs lined the walls. In the middle of the room were long benches and tables for the people, and a small platform was at the other end of the building. Off to the side was a large fireplace. The people gathered and took their places at the tables while the elders sat in their chairs. Aabon led Conell, Uma, Émēr, and Imogene to seats near the platform. Taking a deep breath, Émēr forced his feet to make his way to the assigned seating for guests. His party followed him and took their places. He sat beside them and waited for the senior elder to call him forward.

Imogene gave Émēr a thumbs up sign. "Remember how you taught me? You got this!"

He gave her a small nod.

Once the people had filled the room, the elder rose from his chair in the back and made his way up the aisle. He stood on the platform and raised his hands. The congregation raised their hands also.

"Blessed be the Attiyq, the Eternal One. Father of us all. The Redeemer of all mankind. The First and the Last. The most powerful of all gods. Bless us today!"

The crowd murmured their approval.

"Today, the Attiyq has brought us a priest to help us in our walk with Him. He is called Émēr." He stepped from the platform.

Émēr took a deep breath and made his way up onto the small stage. His chest tingled and tightened, and his breath came quickly. All eyes were on him. Imogene gave him another thumbs up sign. He assumed it was her approval.

"My fellow Maúl, I come to you from across the borders where my cousin and I were held in prison for five years. A cruel queen accused us of a crime we did not commit. But my cousin and I stood strong, relying on the Attiyq, and did not waver from Him. As you see on my face, I have a child's markings." Shame slammed into his chest. The words of the Attiyq countered them. "*You are the Attiyq's art, formed by His hands.*" Émēr continued.

"I have a child's markings because my father, my clan, and my elders died in honor while in battle with the Barbarians. I was only a child when my father ordered me to guard the young prince of Ézású from the Barbarians. All perished in the castle. I and the prince survived. Then I was thrown into prison and had no one to finish my training. Enduring in the Attiyq is like walking when blisters form on your feet, when food is limited, and the walls threaten to crush you. It is to sleep with bugs and rats. But it is also knowing that the Attiyq's hand is always upon you and that He prepares a path for you."

The words of Japik echoed in his mind. "We sometimes believe that these things are punishments. But could this also be a great path that He has chosen for us? A path that has already been laid with riches? Do you not believe that our Attiyq has answered our petitions and our prayers? He has made a covenant of Blood with us, to care for us and guard us. He will always remember his covenants to those who trust Him. The Attiyq has promised to destroy your enemies, Maúl. They will attack you from one direction, but He will cause them to scatter from you in seven directions. His Name is mighty to save. He is Fire who consumes the wicked. Listen to His still, small voice and He will give you all this land. Your faith in Him is real, and it destroys the demon. There is freedom on this path, freedom for all, and yet, some have called it punishment."

He paused. The eyes of everyone were riveted on him. Tears trickled down Ūmá's face, and she nodded.

Felim locked his young eyes on Émēr. He took a deep breath and plunged into more of his adventures and trusting in the Attiyq. Of how His hand guided them across the borders, away from harm. What seemed like a few minutes turned into an hour, and still the crowd listened intently.

Then the words stopped, and Émēr let out a deep breath. "Elder, I am finished. Please lead us in prayer."

The Elder rose and lifted his hands. "Great Attiyq, lead us by Your faithful Hand, put us onto the right paths as You have called us. Grant us wisdom, in Your name."

"Amen," echoed the congregation.

Felim quickly made his way through the crowd and grasped Émēr's hands. "Brother, that was wonderful! It helped me much!"

Émēr gave him a small grin and bowed. "You honor me. Thank you for your kind words."

"Please come to eat with me. I wish for you to meet my father."

An image accosted Émēr's mind. A bloody Felim lay at Argus's feet, a dagger planted in the young Maúl's back. The demon laughed and kicked Felim's body. A shudder raced down Émēr's spine, and he blinked away the vision. *Oh Attiyq, what do I do with this?* Émēr forced a smile on his face.

"I am so sorry," Conell said. "But we must be returning to the cave. We have others waiting for us."

"You will return, *Klao*?" Felim's eyes danced.

Émēr cringed inwardly at the sacred title of Maúl priest. "I will try."

Felim bowed.

"You must leave us so quickly?" Aabon asked. "The warriors were talking, and we would like to add more fighting lines to your face. Perhaps later?"

Shame rushed over Émēr's heart. "I apologize," Émēr said. "But as my cousin has said, we must leave."

"I wish to speak to you again, *Klao*." Aabon leaned into Émēr. "I fear the demon."

Émēr numbly nodded. "I understand. But now he is in Ézású. I do not think he will come this far south. Yet, it may be wise to move into the mountains until we can learn more."

Aabon pulled Émēr from the others. "That would be wise. How long has he been free?"

Émēr shrugged. "I think for maybe twenty years. He appeared during Queen Jezebel's reign."

"Jezebel? What of Brodén's heirs?"

"The entire royal family, except for one son, were killed in an attack from the barbarians."

"The whole royal family?" Aabon asked.

"Yes. Jezebel was Efuko's priestess, and once he and the family were dead, she stole the throne from the boy prince. He is safe now, away from Jezebel's eyes."

Aabon nodded. "That is good, I suppose. We have been at war for so long. Felim's father, Tuder often spoke of Efuko. He was a wise king at one time."

"One time?"

"Well, yes," Aabon said. "It was years later when Efuko spoke of war with the Southern Lands."

"Efuko never asked for war."

"Yes, he did, many times." A darkness covered Aabon's eyes. "We feared the worse and sent guards to the borders. That must have been when the family died. I pray the prince does not seek war."

Émēr shook his head. "No, last I heard, he wished for peace."

"Humph! What do the Brodénians know of peace?"

Émēr turned to see an older man with long gray hair and a grizzled beard standing behind them.

Aabon extended his hand. "This is Tuder, Felim's father."

Émēr bowed. "I am pleased to meet the father of young Felim. You have a fine lad."

Tuder narrowed his eyes. "Yes, he is fine lad." He crossed his arms. "My question is, though, how can one be a Brodénian Maúl and still worship the Living God?"

Émēr opened his mouth but quickly closed it.

Aabon escorted Émēr to a corner of the room. "Forgive him, *Klao*. He is a religious man."

He nodded. "I have encountered some of them in my traveling."

Conell motioned to Émēr, who held up his hand. "I wish to speak to you about this further, Aabon, but I must take my leave. Thank you for your kindness and hospitality. I will do all I can to defeat the demon."

Aabon stopped Émēr. "You are the *Klao*. You are the only priest in this village. What you spoke was from the Attiyq. It encouraged us."

Émēr's brow furrowed. All of this came too quickly. First Ūmá and marriage, then finding the cave and Anú's writings, and now he was Priest. "Thank you, but I must focus on the demon. Please for your own safety, do not come near the cave. Also, it might be best to go deeper into the mountains until we are able to contain him."

Aabon nodded. "Yes, *Klao.* But please allow me to meet with you again. Perhaps in a few days?"

Émēr took a step towards the door. He stopped and took a deep breath before turning to Aabon. "You are the priest here. Protect these people. Please leave now. Take your wives, children, and animals and go into the mountains. I fear the demon may have found us. In a vision I saw Felim lying dead at Argus's feet. As priest, I order you to leave this place. Hide in the hills, go as far south as you can with your little ones. Do not stay here, for death reigns."

Shock whipped across Aabon's face. His hands trembled. "Yes, *Klao*, we will leave today."

Émēr took Conell by the elbow. "Please, I wish to leave now!"

Conell herded the women to the door. Ūmá proudly slipped her hand under Émēr's arm and held her head high as they exited the door. After a long bidding of farewells, Émēr gladly hurried towards the cave. He let out a breath of relief once the village was out of sight. "I have never been so frightened in my life. I do not wish to do this again."

Conell laughed and slapped Émēr on the back. "Captain, I chose you as the leader of my guards because you are brave, and yet, speaking in front of others is what puts you into the grave?"

Émēr shrugged. "I am not afraid, I am just ... cautious."

Imogene giggled. "Cautious? I would say standing like a statue. But you did good. It was a good Sunday service. I mean, it reminded me of our church services back home. I haven't gone for a while; it was good to go back. You make a good preacher. I mean priest."

Émēr gave her a humble nod.

Conell led the others off the path and near some trees. "It is important that we say nothing to Māhōn regarding this village. I fear we may have to keep this from Frigg also. I fear what Māhōn will do if he finds out this information."

Émēr kicked at the ground then stared at the passing clouds. "I fear Māhōn will kill them all or try to recruit them. I was wrong to bring him along. I should have left him behind. Now he threatens my clan and my prince."

Imogene punched him in the arm. "It's okay. Don't worry. We'll get by."

Émēr studied her. "Imie, I saw something in my mind back in the meeting hall. Felim lay dying, and Argus stood over him. I told Aabon to take his people and leave. He said they will leave today."

Conell exchanged glances with Imogene, then focused on Émēr. "Would the demon come back to that which once held him? Surely he will dread this place."

Émēr shrugged. "I have heard whispers in the cave as if someone was there, yet the room appears empty. I fear we are not alone."

Imogene rubbed her forehead. "Oh great, another problem, like we don't have enough already."

"What do you mean, whispers?" Ūmá asked.

"I mean, something or someone is in there with us," Émēr said. He slipped his arm around Ūmá's waist. "I do not like to see you frightened."

"You heard whispers?" Imogene clarified. "Could it have been wind? Bats? Something?"

Émēr shook his head. "It was whispers. I have never heard the language. I fear Argus has found us."

Imogene gestured. "But where can we go? We're stuck here."

Conell nodded then slowly walked in the forest. "Áepoo, I need you."

Wind blew the leaves around them, and Áepoo trotted from the forest. "I am here, Prince Conell. What is your bidding?"

"What is in the caves with us?" Conell asked as Émēr and the others gathered.

A frown covered Áepoo's face. "It is the demon's children, his favorite of his demons, and General Bode. They now follow you."

Imogene shook her head. "How do we make them go away?"

Áepoo's eyes locked on Émēr. "Ask the priest," the angel said. Then he galloped into the sky.

Conell stared at Émēr. "You really are the priest? You said it was just words. This could have helped us in the past. This could have helped us find food for the villagers."

Émēr's face burned. "I was made the Áho by Cian before he passed from this earth. But I am not a priest. As I said, My Moji, it is just words."

Conell pointed to where Áepoo had been standing. "He did not act as if it were only words."

"Isn't this getting old?" Imogene asked. "You keep saying you aren't fully Maúl. Now you say you're not a priest. Get it together! Demons are everywhere! When are you going to become *something*?" She stomped to the road then turned. "I didn't ask for any of this and I'm handling it a lot better than you are!" She ran down the trail.

"I will get her," Conell said in her wake.

Émēr rubbed his eyes. "She is right, Ūmá."

Ūmá kissed his forehead and laid her head on his shoulder. "Do not fear, My Lord. You will find your way."

"I trust you are right. But when? The time is long past."

His bride held his elbow and leaned into him as they walked. It was enough for now.

Ruárc stepped from behind the tree and watched the group make their way down the road. He grinned. "So that is where you are hiding." After readjusting his pack, he quietly made his way among the trees. The group stopped at the opening of a cave and met a slender man with dark hair. He spoke to Conell who brushed past him. Émēr and the man exchanged words as Émēr and the woman entered the cave.

Then the dark-haired man caught Ruárc's gaze. Ruárc ducked behind a tree. When he peeked from behind it, the man was gone.

He let out a sigh of relief, then found a place a distance from the cave and laid out his bedding. It would be cold tonight as it was too risky to start a fire.

A twig snapped behind him and Ruárc raised his weapon. The dark-haired man stood behind him.

"For a Maúl, you are clumsy," Ruárc said.

The man smiled. "I am Māhōn of the New Maúl. And you are Ruárc, guard of Queen Jezebel. Am I correct?"

Ruárc cocked his head. "How would you know who I am?"

"Argus has told me much about you. For instance, how Conell murdered your brother."

He sucked in his breath. "You know the demon."

Māhōn smirked. "Yes, very well. You are also looking for the girl and the medallion for the Queen?"

Ruárc nodded.

"Then I have a proposition for you," the stranger said as a smile slinked across Māhōn's greasy lips.

And Ruárc listened.

Do not allow fear to tell you who you are.

-Anú

21

"It seems Māhōn has disappeared," Erák said as he sliced vegetables for dinner.

While Imogene and Ūmá set the table, Émēr brushed the greens into a large pot, and Conell and Frigg added chunks of meat before carrying it to the kitchen fireplace.

"Frigg, check the hall please," Conell said as he poked at the flames.

Frigg entered the hallway then ducked back into the kitchen. "Māhōn is not there. Do you wish for me to find him?"

"Yes, thank you, Frigg," Conell replied. He waited until Frigg trotted down the hall, then he closed the door and turned to Émēr. "What did Áepoo mean when he said, ask the priest?"

Erák glanced at Émēr from the corner of his eye. Émēr kept his eye on the vegetables.

"Émēr, I asked you a question. Please, what did Áepoo mean? And why did you say, it is only words?"

Émēr placed the knife on the cutting board and wiped his hands on his pants. "My Mojí, I have held secrets as you have held secrets." He eased onto a nearby chair, the weight of Mojí's question adding to the weariness creaking in his bones. The tension eased a bit when Ūmá placed her hand on his shoulder. He grasped her hand and kissed it.

"My Mojí, I was with Cian when he died. I held him in my arms as he passed. He placed his hand on my head and made me priest of the group. I am the priest now."

Conell leaned against the counter and crossed his arms over his chest. A look of concern lay on his strong face. Émēr stared at the floor. Conell was becoming the king.

Imogene placed the plates on the table. "Oh, you were with Cian? I'm so happy he didn't die alone." She paused. "What does it mean you are the priest?"

"It means," Conell said. "That Émēr has more influence that he has kept hidden. We could have used this information months ago."

"The angel that Ūmá saw in the mirror when she was in the castle has been teaching me the ways of the Attiyq," Émēr admitted.

Imogene's hand froze as she clinched a fork handle. "Wait, an *angel* has been teaching you? Why would you not tell us?"

Conell's jaw twitched. "I agree. Why did you not tell us?"

"I know why," Imogene declared as she slammed the forks on the table and stomped towards Émēr. "Because you've been feeling sorry for yourself because you see yourself as a child. But you aren't a child. Who saved me from a demon? Who saved Conell from murdering pirates?"

"Barbarians," Erák corrected.

"Barbarians, pirates. Whatever. Who rescued Ūmá and married her? Who brought us here so we would be safe? Not a child. What is childish is you constantly whining and complaining about being a child. So, stop it! Seriously, just stop it! Take your place, be the priest, do what you are supposed to do, and get over it!"

He opened his mouth then closed it.

Ūmá peered from behind him. "My Lord, she is correct. You rescued me, you saved all of us, you gave strength and courage to the villagers. You are the priest, and you are Maúl."

"But how do I put these feelings aside? I still do not know what my place is or what I am to do. I do not know the adult paths of the Maúl, and I do not know how to be a priest. Yet, I am to be both."

Imogene's face softened. "You're right and I'm sorry. Both of us are learning our places. I'm still not sure what a seer does, so I guess we're in the same boat."

"Boat?" he asked.

"Situation. Maybe instead of us working separately, maybe we need to work together. Help each other." She placed the food on the table. "We all worked to set this nice table and make this food. Maybe this is how we should work together. Each person doing their part." She held up her hands. "Like a body."

He nodded. "Yes, I would like that. And you are correct, I need to take my place as priest."

Ūmá finished setting the table and led Émēr to his chair. "We will eat first," she said, "then together we will study the scrolls."

Émēr grinned. "My heart is happy that I married you."

The door swung open, and Māhōn strolled into the room. Frigg followed like a puppy trailing his master.

"I hope you would not start without us," Māhōn said, plopping onto the nearest seat at the table.

As the others took their seat, Émēr held up his hand, forcing himself to ignore Frigg's choice to sit next to Māhōn. From his place at the table, Émēr caught Conell's expression. His Mojí was making no effort to hide his displeasure at the burgeoning "bromance" between the two, as Imie called it.

"Please let us give thanks before we eat," he began. All eyes locked his way and Émēr cleared his throat. "Attiyq, we give You thanks for what You have done for us, for this day and for this food. In Your name, amen."

Ūmá and Émēr strolled along the corridors to the library. She leaned her head on his arm, which sent tingles down to his toes. Her hair smelled like summer flowers. He slipped his arm around her waist and pulled her close. Upon entering the library, she lit the table candles and took her seat while he thumbed through the scrolls.

"Husband," she said, "I have a request."

"Yes," he said as he examined a scroll.

"I want to say Yes to a dress."

"That is fine – wait, what?" He turned to her.

"Imogene said that women in her world try on a thousand white gowns at a magical Place called Kleinfelds in her village of New York until they find one that makes them weep. Then a handsome man named Randy asks the question, do you say yes to the dress? And the bride says yes, and everyone cheers and cries. The couple invites everyone they know to what Imogene calls The Wedding in which they stand before a priest who has them say vows before all their friends, and then they are married. They have a large celebration with music and dancing. The bride throws flowers at the single women to see who will marry next. The bride is to say yes to dishes also. She must pick out a certain kind of dishes called China. She said it is a great feast. Then we go on a Honey Moon. I am not sure what one does on the Honey Moon. When I asked, she only raised her eyebrows and said, you do STUFF."

He stared at her. "I have never heard of the Land of Kleinfelds, but we will find this gown for you if it is what you wish." He laid the scroll on the table and pulled up a chair.

"What do you think we are supposed to do on this Honey Moon?" she asked as she leaned over his shoulder to inspect the scroll.

Her hair tickled his neck. Visions of her sprang up in his mind, visions that made him blush. He pushed aside the visions and their accompanying thoughts and adjusted his shirt. "It seems to be warm in here."

She sat beside him and studied the words. "Husband, what does this say?"

The candlelight bounced off her soft hair, giving her an ethereal shine. She was more beautiful than the angel in the woods. The fear that hung over the castle disappeared, and all that remained were the two of them. He lifted her chin and kissed her and she did not pull away.

Eagla and Amhras stood in Argus's chambers, waiting for their father to return. Amhras paced the floor. "Father will explode when he finds out that Anú's seed has found the forbidden cage."

Eagla fussed with her hair as she studied her reflection in the full-length mirror. "Father will be heartbroken, and that is why you, his favorite, must tell him. Brón certainly will not tell him and neither will the General. Will you tell him of the villagers, too?"

He flicked his hand. "They are simply rodents. It is the scrolls that we must fear."

Argus opened the door and raised his eyebrows. "I am surprised to see you."

Eagla rushed into his arms and kissed him. "Father, I have missed you."

"As I you, my child." His gaze shifted to Amhras. "You have news?"

"Father," Eagla said. "You must not be upset."

He shoved her away. "What is it?"

Amhras took a deep breath. "Father, Émēr has found scrolls and The Cage."

Argus sucked in his breath. "What else has he found?"

"He has not found Anú's secrets to holding you in the cage. But the Attiyq has led them there. Áepoo and his armies guard the place."

Argus's lip twitched. Eagla dove into the floor and disappeared.

Amhras swallowed hard and averted his eyes. "Father, there are still others who are on your side. Māhōn has lured Ruárc into his trap. Plus Brón, General Bode, and I are here."

"What have you heard from Émēr?"

Amhras paused as a bead of sweat dripped down his face. "My Father, please, you know the Attiyq's strength."

Argus slammed his fist into the stone wall. Pieces of rock fell to the floor. "What. Did. He. Say!"

"I do not know, Father. The Attiyq has hidden some things from us. As they walked down the road, Émēr spoke to Conell, but we could not hear the words. Sometimes the cursed angel stands before us, and the humans' words are silent to us. But I do know he is getting closer to the truth, My Father."

Argus wrapped his hand around Amhras' throat and slammed him against the wall. "If Émēr puts me in that cage, you will join me. Do you understand me, Favorite Son?"

Amhras choked. "Yes, Father."

Émēr stared at the ceiling as Ūmá snuggled against his chest, her warm body nestled under his arm. He kissed her head and stroked her hair. She was now truly his wife.

The blanket they lay on did little to soften the hard floor, but it mattered little to Émēr. He closed his eyes as gratitude to the Attiyq swelled in his heart. She would give birth to his daughters and sons. Mother would be pleased when she saw her family growing. "Mother, where are you?" he whispered.

Émēr opened his eyes when he heard the rustling of papers. At the library table, Augustine stood huddled over Anú's diary. Émēr blinked and rubbed his eyes.

Augustine looked his way. "There are things you need to see."

Émēr eased away from Ūmá and gently repositioned her onto the blanket. "Of course, my brother."

"Do not fear," Augustine said, "the Attiyq is on your side."

Ūmá stirred, and he glanced her way. When he turned back, Augustine had disappeared.

Émēr swallowed and stared at the book. "Brother, this is not your journal, but this is Anú's book. What do you want me to see?" Answering a nudge inside, he re-read Anú's poem.

Augustine and Dia
Augustine, the warrior, strong and brave,
Fought for his king and clan
And locked away the Darkness and his child.

Dia fought by his side
Power flowed through his arms,
And placed his enemies at the Attiyq's feet.

Both men fought
Back to back
Their ears closed to Darkness's ballad.

The enemy taunts
The swords slash
Against sinful words

Trapped forever Darkness remains.

Émēr shook his head. "I do not understand, Attiyq," he prayed in an undertone. Taking a seat on a chair, he read it again.

Ūmá opened her eyes and smiled at him. "My husband," she said and held out her arms.

Émēr brought her the book. "My wife, something has happened." He sat next to her, and she lay her head on his leg.

"Yes, something did happen."

He chuckled. "I saw Augustine sitting at the table. He said I was to read this poem and that the Attiyq is on my side. But what does it mean?"

"It is hard to care this moment. It is a miracle. You have erased Argus from my mind."

Émēr leaned down and kissed her. "That was my plan."

A scream erupted from the hallway and echoed off the walls. Émēr sprang to his feet, his eyes riveted to the door. Ūmá pulled her dress over her head handed him his clothes. Émēr pulled on his clothes and stuffed the book in his pocket. Once he grabbed *Cukdilok Dulk,* he slowly opened the door. What happened now was in Attiyq's hand.

Stand up to the enemy and he will never move you again.

-Anú

22

Émēr scolded himself. A warrior is always ready even in the arms of his wife. He held Ūmá back as he scanned the hallway.

Erák and Frigg rushed from their quarters. "Did you hear that?" Erák asked as he fumbled with his sword belt.

Émēr motioned for them to keep back as he crept down the hallway. The sobs were coming from Imogene's quarters.

Conell sat on Imogene's bed, holding her in his arms. He frowned at Émēr. "Where were you?"

Émēr's face flushed. "I am sorry, My Prince." He motioned to Ūmá. "We were, um."

"We were together." Ūmá drew Imogene into her arms. "It is all right, my sister."

Conell tugged Émēr into the hallway. "Émēr, what happened?"

Émēr stared at the stone floor. "Ūmá and I were together. We came together in the library."

His eyebrows rose. "Oh, my heart is glad for you, but still, I need you to be alert."

"Of course, My Mojí."

Conell placed his hand on Émēr's shoulder.

He nodded towards Imogene's quarters. "Is she al lright?"

"I am not sure." Conell shut the door behind him. "I heard her scream, and I found her sobbing."

Émēr slipped past him and returned to Imie's room. "My wife, what has frightened her?" he asked in his Maúl tongue.

"I think she had a nightmare, but I am not sure. Tell me what happened, Imie."

Imogene raised her wet face. "I dreamt I was back with Argus. There were rats all over me." She stifled a sob. "They were crawling all over me. And Conell and Émēr…" Her voice cracked, and she buried her face into Ūmá's shoulder.

Conell placed his hand on her shoulder. "*Chuōhá*, please tell me."

She pulled away from Ūmá. "Your heads . . . were on big sticks. Please don't tell me this is from Him. I can't do this anymore."

"That would be quite disappointing." Māhōn leaned against the doorframe. "Imagine, the great Maúl, dangling from a spear like a dead fish."

Émēr's blood turned cold. He turned. "Yes, that would be disappointing and how much more if my sword found its mark in your belly."

Erák slipped between the two men. "Cousin, this is not wise."

Émēr pushed Erák to the side. "I made a mistake in bringing you here, Māhōn. I should have left you behind. You have threatened my clan, and now you mock me. If you wish to see me dangling like a fish, then perhaps you should be the one to try. This is Anú's home. You are no longer welcome here."

Conell raised his eyebrows. Frigg and Erák exchanged worried glances.

Māhōn took long strides to face Émēr. "This is what it has come to? The great Maúl betraying his clan? We are of your clan, yet now you have taken the hands of others. Anú would be disgraced."

"It is not I who has betrayed Anú. You would use my sister as a shield to protect you from the enemy and my wife as a source of income. You have no interest in Anú's teachings, and yet, you say I am as a rusty bucket. If that is so, then fine, I will be a bucket at the feet of my God, but you will leave this place today." He spread his arms wide. "I have all I need here in these caves. You will leave tonight."

The edges of Māhōn's thin lips twisted slowly with mocking malice. "Yes, my brother, we will leave tonight, but you, your clan, and your men will come with us. We have things to discuss."

General Bode stepped beside Māhōn. The demon extended his dark sword and sneered. "Did you really think you could escape my king?"

Émēr held *Cukdilok Dulk* before Māhōn and guarded Ūmá and Imogene. Conell drew his sword and stood beside his captain. They exchanged a kindred look. Émēr nodded to his Prince.

Erák tugged the women to their feet.

Frigg licked his lips. "Master Māhōn, please, he is still my prince."

Māhōn's eyes grew thin. "Choose your allegiance, Frigg. Come with me and become a champion. Or, stay with them and die."

Frigg's fearful eyes flickered from his prince to his master.

Bode laughed. "Humans are so weak. Kill this one. He is useless."

Conell's face softened. "Frigg, stay with me. We are not dead yet. Do not dishonor your father." He held out his hand.

Frigg lowered his gaze. "I am sorry, my prince, but you have Émēr, I have no one." He stepped next to Māhōn and glared at Bode. "I am not weak."

"We will see, little one." Bode winked.

Conell's face dropped, and he pulled back his hand. "I have never said you were weak."

Émēr took a step towards him. "Frigg, I saved you in the castle because I see your worth not only to me but to the prince and the Attiyq. If you truly want to learn the ways of the Maúl, I told you I could teach you."

"I want it now, not ten years from now. Māhōn can teach me."

Māhōn slapped Frigg's back. "Now you are a warrior. No longer will the Maúl live in an underground cave. Instead, we will be the New Order of Maúl and live with the Queen. You, my young Frigg, will be my student."

Frigg grinned.

Émēr swallowed his vomit. As Māhōn fawned over his new student, Émēr slipped Anú's journal to Ūmá, who tucked it into her sleeve.

Māhōn gestured to the door. "Please come this way. I have something to show you. Something I think you will enjoy."

"You have me and the prince," Émēr said. "Leave the others alone. Let Erák take them into the mountains."

Māhōn chuckled. "Do you really think that will happen?" He motioned towards the door. "Please, my brother."

Émēr glanced at his Mojí, then he took Ūmá's hand while Conell wrapped his arm around Imogene's waist and led her to the door. Her face had turned white and she trembled.

"Do not be afraid. I will not let them hurt you," Conell said.

Erák followed behind them. Out of the corner of his eye, Émēr saw Erák slip a dagger under his sleeve.

Bode grabbed his hand and snatched the knife from him. "Māhōn, this little one wishes to fight you."

Māhōn cocked his head and studied the young man. "For one so young, you have much spunk."

"Māhōn, it is me you want, not Erák." Émēr's heartbeat thundered in his ears. "Let him be."

The demon wrapped his long gray fingers around Erák's neck and slammed him up against the wall.

Émēr leapt in front of the demon. "You will not do this!"

Bode's left eyelid twitched, and fire burned in his black orbs.

Māhōn shoved Erák and Émēr out of the room as he addressed

Bode. "Master Argus has not given us permission to kill them, General." He forced them past the statue of King Brodén, up the massive stairwell, and out into the sunlight.

Émēr glanced down the path to the village. He nudged his Mojí, who followed his gaze.

"Do you think they are safe," Émēr whispered.

Conell nodded.

Māhōn led them down a path opposite of the village. A stone table with trails of dry blood on its sides sat in the clearing. Imogene gasped. Ruárc was securely tied to the slab and Argus filtered into view.

"Prince Conell, help me!" the guard bellowed. "He said he would bargain with me!"

Argus placed a knife under Ruárc's throat. "I did make a bargain with you. Māhōn will sacrifice you to me. I need sacrifices." He leaned over Ruárc. "I like sacrifices. The way I liked your brother." His long tongue ran up Ruárc's cheek.

Ruárc pulled away "Leave me, Demon!" Argus only grinned. Ruárc's wild eyes turned to Conell. "My Prince, please help me!"

Conell turned to Frigg. "Is this what you want? To be a part of this human sacrifice? Does being a Maúl mean so much to you? Is this the tribe that you now desire?"

Frigg face turned white, and he shook his head. Māhōn shoved Frigg towards the altar.

Argus thrust the knife into Frigg's trembling hand. "Māhōn sacrificed a woman when he first joined me. I took her young daughter as my slave. Come, young Frigg, join me, and I will make you a conqueror of men!"

Imogene tried to turn to run, but the guards stopped her.

"Welcome, my young seer and my slave." Argus sneered at the women.

"Do not fear him," Conell whispered to Imogene and pulled her close. "Demon, you will not touch her!"

"She belongs to me," Argus replied.

Conell stepped in front of her. She clung to his shirt, her head against his back.

Émēr placed his arm in front of Ūmá. "You cannot have the women of my clan. They are under my protection." Ūmá grasped his arm and hid her face behind his shoulder.

A dark smile grew across Argus's face. "How sweet. The Last Maúl, the spawn of the worm Anú wishes to protect his whoring wife. Is she as good for you as she was for me?"

Battle rage flashed in Émēr's eyes. He lunged at Argus, but Conell held him back.

"You will not speak to my wife!" Émēr squirmed against Conell's grip. "Release me!"

The prince turned Émēr around to face him. "Think! He wants you to attack him so he can kill you. Do not give in to him!"

Émēr jerked from Conell's hands. "Demon, you stay away from my wife!"

Conell positioned himself between Argus and his people. "So, Argus, you and Māhōn have been working together? To do what, exactly? Murder, loot, and plunder like common criminals? Honestly, I would expect more from seasoned miscreants such as yourselves."

Māhōn stepped to his master's side. "Argus is my master."

Frigg dropped the knife and stumbled to Conell. "I am sorry, My Prince, I did not know."

Conell placed his hand on Frigg's shoulder and steered the young man behind him. "It is alright, Frigg. Stay with us."

"Go then, weakling. Not even I could turn someone so worthless into a real Maúl, not in a hundred years," Māhōn snarled. His expression softened as he offered the knife to Émēr. "Brother, we are rebuilding the New Maúl. Join us. I will allow you to keep your women. Argus will give us whatever we want. Bow down and worship him through this sacrifice."

Émēr shook his head. "As much as I dislike Ruárc, I do not wish to see him die in such a fashion. And I will not give my soul to the demon. I only bow down to the Attiyq."

Argus snarled.

Māhōn laid his head on Argus's shoulder and stroked his

feathers. "Master, you promised."

He brushed Māhōn's check with the back of his fingers. "Yes, I did. General Bode, take them."

The Maúl follows the path of Mercy.

-Anu.

23

Conell stepped beside his captain and gave a small nod. Émēr reached behind him and took Ūmá's hand as Conell whispered, "Áepoo."

The winged creatures circled the sky and landed quietly behind Argus, who kept his eyes locked on Conell and his small group.

Argus's men gasped and pulled swords from their sheaths. The female angel from the woods gently landed behind Argus. "Have you found your bottle yet?"

Argus screamed and whirled. Áepoo and his companions stood like a wall behind the angel. She laughed and wiggled her fingers at him. Māhōn shrieked, dropped his sword and his dagger, then raced down the path.

Argus's men glanced at one another as more angels arrived, dropping to the ground like lightening flashing across the sky.

Argus lifted his sword. "Japik, I will enjoy slicing you into pieces."

She laughed. "The Attiyq's power surrounds me."

He cringed.

Bode snarled. "Lovely Japik, you could have joined us. I would have given you a place in my army. You were special to me."

She cocked her blond head and gave him a puzzled look. "But why would I fight with those who have been defeated? You made your choice. I begged you not to rebel against my God, but you are filled with evil. I will not join you. And I was never special. The only one who is special to you is yourself."

He chuckled. "True."

Bode lunged but she shot into the air. He followed her and swung his weapon, but she countered his move. Angels swarmed around the General and he swung blindly as the heavenly host surged overhead.

Áepoo rushed to Conell's side. "Come Mojí, we must leave now. Japik and the others will keep them busy."

Ruárc squirmed against his bindings. "Prince Conell, please have mercy on me."

Émēr leaned into Conell. "Should we save him?"

He shrugged. "He did try to kill me..."

Before he completed his thought, Imogene picked up the knife Māhōn had dropped and zoomed to the stone slab.

"My Lady, please, I know I have harmed you, but I beg of you, help me!" Ruárc lifted his head and his wide eyes searched her face.

Imogene slid the knife under his throat. "How does this feel? Not fun, huh?" she yelped.

Ruárc's watering eyes held hers as his lips moved. "My children!" he whispered. "Have mnercy!"

Émēr rushed to her side and pulled her hand away. "Imie, revenge does not help and will only bind you."

Imogene yanked her hand from his grip and rested the tip of the knife under Ruárc's chin. "I swear, if you hurt me or Ūmá ever again, I'll have the guys hold you down and I'll slice your throat, drain your blood into bottles, and make you drink it. Understand?"

Ruárc eyes grew wide and he nodded.

Émēr leaned over him. "And I will enjoy holding you down."

"Right!" Imogene barked and used the knife to cut his bindings.

Ruárc tossed the ropes away and slowly rose only to bow before Émēr. "I am in debt, Lord Émēr."

"What are you doing?" Conell led Imogene to Áepoo.

"I'm supposed to do this." Imogene climbed onto Áepoo's back. She looked to the sky and pointed upwards. "He told me."

Émēr nodded. "Yes, I have heard the words also. He must come."

Émēr and Ūmá climbed on Etta's back as Frigg and Ruárc took Oota and Erik climbed upon Asechi. The beasts galloped then rose from the ground. Émēr glanced over his shoulder. Japik locked Argus in her duel as her forces fought the demons around her. Soon they drifted from sight.

The angels landed on a small island on the coast of Opize Territory. Émēr slid off Etta and scratched the angel's ears. "I have missed you, old friend. You have brought us to a safe place." He turned to the others. "This island will keep us safe until we decide our next move. No one has lived here for thousands of years. It is sacred to my people."

He helped Ūmá off the beast as the others took in the surroundings.

Ruárc leaned on his knees then stood and bowed before Émēr. "I owe you a life debt now. My family and I are in your service for life."

Still burning with revenge, Émēr pushed past him. "It is your death I want not your life."

"I know where your family is, and I will take you to them."

He turned. "What?"

"I took your mother and sister as prisoners. The others are with the slave runners. Mostly they are women and children; although, I am unsure how to rescue them."

"You have my family? Why have you come here?"

Ruárc looked away, then caught Émēr's puzzled gaze. "Because I have a wife and several children. The Queen has given me an order. Bring the seer and the medallion to her and kill everyone else or she will kill my little ones. I know you have no debt to me, but I am in debt to you. But I beg you, I cannot lose my family."

Imogene cocked her head. "Wait, you have kids? Seriously?"

He nodded. "Yes, four. And a beautiful, fat wife whom I adore."

"But you wanted to…hurt me."

Ruárc chuckled. "I am still a guard and a man."

She rolled her eyes and walked away. "Whatever, Freak."

"What do you want me to do?" Émēr crossed his arms over his chest. "You know I can let the Queen kill your family."

Ruárc shook his head. "No, you will not allow that to happen. You are Maúl, you are honor while I am not. You will not cross lines that I cross."

Ūmá squeezed his hand. "He is right, my husband."

Émēr touched her cheek then turned his purple gaze to his enemy. "Alright, Ruárc. Give me my family, and you and your family will be under my protection. But do not cross me."

Ruárc bowed. "Thank you, My Lord Émēr. I will not disappoint you."

Émēr shot a glare to his Mojí who remained silent.

"We need to fly to the Barbarians' lands. That is where your family is hidden," Ruárc said.

"Can you travel, Áepoo?" Conell asked.

The angel laughed. "Of course, my prince. Come, let us rescue the Maúl's clan."

An hour later, the beasts landed safely in Barbarian territory.

Ruárc slapped Émēr's back, making him stagger. "You will not see the Barbarians' weapons here. They are now also your clans as I am of their clans. Barbarian laws state that whoever is connected to them, so will all the clan be connected to them and that includes you, Captain Émēr. You are now a Maúl and a Barbarian, I mean Kalk. That is the name they prefer."

Imogene sputtered out a laugh. "Aren't you lucky!"

Émēr sent her a sour glance. "So, my enemy is now part of my clan?"

Ruárc laughed. "You are the one who has always said the Attiyq works in odd ways."

"Yes, I did."

Ūmá slipped her arm through his arm. "Come my husband, I wish to meet my new clans."

"Ha!" Imogene said.

Ruárc led the way down the path to his small clearing. The sound of feet beating on the path came towards them. Four small children burst from around the curve in the path. "Father!" The cries of small voices interrupted the singing birds.

Two young girls threw themselves into his arms, and he scooped them up as butterfly kisses covered his face. Two older boys who looked to be around ten years of age stood at attention as they struggled to keep smiles off their faces. Ruárc set his girls on the ground and stood tall before his boys. He placed his hand over his heart and gave a small bow. The boys followed his motions then rushed into his arms. "Father! We did as you commanded and kept the enemy of Oozeka way!"

He laughed and kissed them. "I know you did, my brave sons."

One of the girls, the one Ruárc called Chia, eyed Conell. He raised an eyebrow and returned her stare.

"Why is your hair like that?" she asked.

Imogene snickered. "Yeah, why is your hair like that?"

He gave Imogene a surprised look. "It is what my father commanded."

Chia took his hand and led him down the path. "You are now my prisoner, and you have to do what I say. But we really have to do what Mother says." She paused and gave him a very stern face. "She can get angry."

Conell nodded. "Of course."

"You are really cute with kids," Imogene said.

He gave her a nervous glance. "I am not used to being around them. Children." He pointed to Chia.

"Well, you are her prisoner now. I guess you'll have many tea parties to attend."

"What?"

Imogene laughed.

The boys raced down the path towards the village. "Father is coming, and he brings prisoners!"

Ruárc avoided Émēr's eyes. "I do not have the courage to tell my sons of my failure."

Émēr let out a sigh. "Perhaps we can say we fought together in battle and we won against a common enemy?"

Ruárc lifted his face. "You would do that for me?"

He grimaced. "Yes, I will."

Ūmá tightened her arm around Émēr's waist. "Thank you, my husband."

"It seems this pact is getting more uncomfortable for me," Émēr said.

As they entered the small clearing, a large woman with red curly hair met Ruárc and smacked a kiss on his lips.

"I have missed you, my wife. No one is as beautiful as you, my Chara."

"You lie so well," she said, kissing him again. She took in the small group. "You have brought me more prisoners to feed?"

Émēr bowed. "I am Captain of the King's army Émēr Muiris Amgets. Your husband and I fought a great battle with a common enemy, and we won."

Chara gave her husband a suspicious eye.

"It is true," Ruárc insisted. "We did fight a common enemy. Argus. He betrayed him and tried to kill me. The captain saved me and now we fight as one clan. I owe him a life debt."

The sharp look drifted from Chara's face, and she took Ruárc's hand and kissed it. "You have returned, and this is all that matters. And to you, Captain Amgets, thank you for helping my husband. I am sure he fought proudly and strong. You are here for your family?"

Émēr nodded. His heart beat his chest. "I accept the life debt. It can now be repaid, and I will release you and your family if you will return my family to me and allow us to leave unharmed."

Ruárc pursed his lips and placed his hand on Chara's shoulder. Chara bit her lip and gathered Chia in her arms.

"You do not accept this?" Émēr asked.

"The Queen has demanded that I return the seer and the medallion to her and to kill the others. If I do not do this, she will hunt us down. There is no place for my family to hide." He glanced at his wife. "Yes, we will accept it. You may go in peace."

Chara kissed her daughter's hair and stifled her tears. Ruárc slipped his arm around her waist and pulled his daughter to his side.

"Émēr," Imogene said. "As much as I don't like Ruárc, we can't just let Jezebel kill the kids."

"Ruárc, I cannot protect you. I do not have an army."

"And I am no longer the prince of my land," Conell said. "But as Imogene has said, we cannot allow the Queen to harm the children. Come with us, and we will protect you as well as we can. I cannot promise you and your family will be safe, but you will die if you stay here, and Argus will take your children as slaves."

Chara studied her husband. "We can go up to the mountains with the Barbarians. We will be safe."

Ruárc shook his head. "No, you go with the children, I will fight along with the prince. I should have done this a long time ago." He pulled out his sword, fell to his knees, and raised the weapon to Conell. "This is now yours, and I will fight alongside you, My Prince, My King."

Conell touched the steel. "I accept."

Aurc stomped over to his father and knelt before Conell. He lifted a stick. "I too will fight along with you."

Conell gave a lost look to Émēr who shrugged. Imogene gave him a sharp shake of her head.

He coughed. "Young one, I will need you to protect your clan. They will be alone. Will you do this great act for the King? Then I will accept your sword. You will be Lord Aurc, Protector of the Innocent."

Aurc rose and lifted his chin. "Yes, I will do this bidding!" He turned and ran down the path. "I get to protect the clan! And I am a Lord!"

"Mama, I want to be a lord," came a cry.

Chara bowed to Conell then disappeared into a hut. A moment later, she returned with two women.

Émēr's face lit into a smile and the women rushed into his arms. "Mother! Aine!" He kissed their heads. "I thought I had lost you!"

His mother patted his face and kissed him. "My boy! I knew you were alive."

Aine hugged him. "I knew you would find us."

He pulled away from his family and turned to his wife. "Mother, Aine, this is my wife, Ūmá. She is Maúl."

Laoise studied Ūmá. "I have not seen you in our village."

Ūmá shot a nervous look to Émēr.

"She is not of our village, Mother," Émēr said. "She was a prisoner of Argus. I married her to save her from a cruel man who wished to use her as a paid joiner. Since that time, I have fallen in love with her, Mother, and I wish for you to love her also."

Laoise straightened and exhaled. "A joiner?"

Ūmá's face turned red with shame. "It is not something that I wished. I was Argus's prisoner."

Aine touched her mother's arm. "Imogene spoke of such a girl in the castle. Are you the one of whom she spoke?"

Imogene grinned and placed her hand on Ūmá's shoulder. "Yes, she is. The girl who was left behind."

Sternness fled Laoise's face, and she hugged Ūmá. "Of course, welcome, child."

"Mother," Émēr said, "there is more. I fear you will not be pleased." He motioned to Ruárc. "I saved Ruárc, and now he has given me his life debt. He and his family are in danger, and the Prince has decided to give him and his family sanctuary. They are under our protection now."

Laoise stared at him. "You now help those who destroyed your village?"

"Laoise," Conell said. "I made the decision. I do not approve of the acts committed by Ruárc, but I cannot allow children to die."

Her lips tightened, but she gave a curt nod. "As you wish, my King."

Conell placed his hand on her shoulder. "I am tired of bloodshed, Laoise."

She placed her hand on his cheek. "As am I."

Ruárc licked his lips and shuffled his feet. "Forgive me, Lady Amgets, for the destruction of your clan. We are in your service as are my children and my children's children."

Émēr pulled Ruárc away. "Please feed my clan."

The guard nodded and motioned to his wife. She gave a small smile to Émēr and Laoise, then turned and herded her children into their hut.

Conell pushed himself away from Ruárc's family table and patted his stomach. "Your wife is an excellent cook."

Frigg wiped his face and folded his napkin. "It was very good."

Erák used his bread to sop up the remaining food on his plate and nodded.

Chara grinned at him. "Why do you think he married me?"

"Because you are beautiful." Ruárc kissed her cheek.

"You lie so well."

Laoise stacked the dirty plates in the center of the table. "I must admit, it was a good meal."

"I can teach you, if you wish," Chara said.

"Perhaps one day." Laoise refused to meet Chara's gaze. A look of anger crossed Laoise's face.

Aine glanced at her mother as she stacked the utensils on the plates. "Yes, we would love to learn."

Laoise gave her daughter a stern glare.

Aine returned the sharp look. "Mother, be kind."

Chia and Nika struggled through the front door with a bucketful of water for the dish washing. Imogene took it from the girls and dumped the water into the large pot that hung in the fireplace. She added more wood to the fire.

"What are you doing?" Aine asked.

"Boiling the water before we wash the dishes. It kills the germs."

"Germs?"

Ūmá giggled. "My sister has a fear of them."

"They'll kill ya faster than a knife to the throat."

Chara placed her hand over her chest and gave a laughing snort. "Child, what are these creatures?"

"I do not know," Ūmá said. "But she has a hatred of them."

"I must finish washing our evening dishes, it will take time to boil the water," Chara said.

"Trust me, they'll clean better if you boil the water," Imogene said. "Sit, relax, the dishes will be there."

Chara gave an exasperated sigh as she gathered the dirty plates and utensils.

Ruárc shook his head and chuckled. "So, Prince Conell, what are your plans for defeating Argus?"

Chara frowned at him. "Wait until I get the children into their room, then you can discuss." She herded her little ones up the stairs to their sleeping chambers.

Conell shrugged. "I have yet to come up with a plan. He is stronger than I anticipated."

"You have the medallion, do you not?"

Émēr gave him a sharp look and quick shake of his head.

"We have yet to discover its secrets," Conell replied.

Ruárc growled. "We should use it to destroy Argus and that witch."

Ūmá sat near the fire with Imogene and Aine, and joined them in working Chara's drop spindle. Ūmá placed her small fingers on the cotton, gently spun the spindle, then carefully manipulated the material until it made a long piece of yarn. Imogene studied Ūmá's skill with a sense of awe.

As he gazed at his wife, Émēr's heart swelled with pride. The moonlight bounced off her hair, turning her strands into auburn. Her skin was soft like goose down and a flowery scent lingered in her tresses. His wife was brilliant, handpicked by God.

She yawned and stretched.

Émēr rose and took her hand. "Come, My Sapphire, it is time we retired."

She took his hand.

Imogene gave her a sly grin. She whispered to Aine who giggled. Émēr resisted the urge to roll his eyes. Now he had two sisters who loved to tease him.

They said their goodnights to the others and retired from the room. The camp was dark with the only light coming from the full moon that hung over them. He slipped his arm around her waist. "There was a full moon on the night we left the compound and one when we came to the cave and now another one hangs over us." He nuzzled her neck. "I think it is a good sign from the Attiyq."

Her soft giggles made him smile. "Yes, I remember those nights. I also remember how patient you have been with me. I am forever grateful."

He kissed her. "It is my honor to be patient with you." He opened the door to their sleeping quarters and escorted her in.

Later that night, a gentle knocking at the door woke him. He shook his head and stared into the darkness. The knock repeated.

He rose, pulled on his clothes, and stumbled to the door.

Áepoo stood before him. "You must come with me, Captain. Come, climb upon my back."

"It is late, Áepoo. Is My Mojí in trouble?"

He shook his head. "No, but there is something you must see."

Émēr swung his legs over Áepoo's back, and the horse-man galloped and slowly ascended into the sky. A flock of geese flew past the moon. They looked like tiny insects against the white massive ball. He leaned forward and gripped Áepoo's mane as the birds' honking filled the air. If only Ūmá was here to enjoy it.

Áepoo began to descend until he landed in a small dark clearing. Émēr slid off and stretched his legs. The breeze rustled the leaves in the trees, making a soft, sighing sound. Crickets chirped out their songs.

"Áepoo, why have bought me here?"

As Áepoo stepped into the moonlight, his horse torso changed into a seven-foot man with long white hair that merged into a white silk robe. His clothes shone as sun-kissed metal. In Áepoo's hand was a double-bladed sword with strange letters embedded in the blades. Émēr stepped back and shielded his eyes. The white light filled the dark clearing, chasing all shadows away.

"Do not fear, Captain Émēr, we are servants of the Attiyq and take many forms. Come, there is much the Great One wishes for you to see."

Émēr stared at Áepoo's weapon.

The angel smiled. "Humans say that angels are simply mindless servants of God, but instead, we have joys and heartaches as do you." He lifted the blade. "This blade tells the story of when the Great One created me, of my battles won, and how He always gave me victory. Much like your face markings. But come, there is much to see."

He led Émēr down the fog-laden path until they came to a ridge overlooking a valley. The moon shone brighter and filled the land with a dim light. Émēr rubbed his arms against the chilly air. A broken road of white stone ran down the center of the valley. Crumbling white buildings lined the street. Weeds grew between the cracks in the stone lane. Two leather-winged men resembling Argus crouched as they raced across the road, the moonlight shing off their long black swords. Curses against the Attiyq spewed from their evil lips. A fire from a huge pit lit up the sky.

Émēr turned to Áepoo and asked, "What is this?"

"This is Argus's domain, created by the Attiyq for his punishment. His human followers drown in flames that never quench. The Attiyq's great heart is broken by Argus's deceit and grieves for the Lost People. You must save the people of Ézású. You must fight against Argus and take your place as high priest in the line of Anú. If you walk away from this battle, Argus will conquer the land and destroy all who stand in his way."

Émēr furrowed his brow. "I do not understand. Why does the Attiyq Himself not destroy Argus and his followers and bring peace to the land?"

"Because of His great mercy and love for His people, He wishes that not all should perish in the flames. That is why He now wishes to equip you, to protect His people. To draw them from Argus's destruction. If you refuse, the Attiyq will choose another."

Still Émēr hesitated.

Áepoo crossed his arms over his chest. "If you will not do it for yourself or your prince, do it for your son."

Émēr raised his eyebrows. "My son? But we were only together one night."

Áepoo smiled. "It only takes one night."

Émēr nodded with surprise and deep thankfulness.

Áepoo placed his hand on Émēr's shoulder, his serious expression returned. "Captain, if you do not take your place as High Priest, you and your prince will die. Erák will fulfill your wish and take Ūmá as his bride. He will take your clan into the mountains and hide them from Argus's eyes. But Ūmá will die in childbirth because Erák must keep them moving. Erák and your clan will try to raise the boy, but he will wish to avenge his family and will die in the process.

Argus will capture the seer, Imogene, but she will refuse to follow Argus, and will jump from the castle window to her death. All will be lost. Argus will create what is before you, destroying what is left of the Maúl and your clan and destroying all Ézású. Will you take your place, Maúl?"

"Of course, Áepoo, I will do whatever I can to protect my family."

Áepoo smiled. A Man stepped beside him. A sense of pure love rushed over Émēr and filled every crevasse of his body. It drove away the hate and anger and made him feel whole. Émēr dropped to his knees. "Attiyq!"

The Attiyq smiled and raised Émēr's chin with His hand that was bent as if it had been broken. "Hello, Émēr, my son."

"Attiyq, please forgive my doubt and my anger."

"Of course, I forgive you. I have made you whole so that you can stand before Me. You are Mine. I bought you many years ago, when Argus and I fought. He thought he had won. But I am the victor."

Cian stepped beside the Attiyq. Émēr fell into the old man's arms. "Forgive me, Cian, for refusing to listen to your words. I was a fool."

Cian smiled and placed his hands on his shoulders. "Son of Anú, you will now wear my mantle and will be the High Priest for all of Ézású. All the people will look to you for protection and to lead them in the ways of the Attiyq."

Émēr cocked his head. "Why do you say, 'son'?"

Cian grinned. "You have not deciphered this mystery? You are Anú's descendant. You are the King of the Maúl."

Émēr gawked at Cian, dumbfounded.

Cian placed his robe over Émēr's shoulders. Then he uncorked a flask and poured sweet-smelling oils over Émēr's head. It flowed over his hair and down onto the robe. The Attiyq's hand lay upon Émēr, forcing him to the ground. Power surged through him and took his breath away. He lay there for a long time as the Attiyq's glory flooded his soul. A loud, evil scream, echoed from the woods and spread across the whole land. Argus's vision land wavered, then disappeared. The hills and mountains of Ézású returned.

The Great Power lifted from Émēr as the sun began to rise. Áepoo, now in the form of the horse-man, stood patiently at his side. Émēr climbed to his feet and took deep breaths. He glanced at the angel. "That was amazing!"

Áepoo laughed. "Yes, standing in the presence of the Almighty is a wonderful place to be. But come, we must return to the others."

"You know about the medallion."

The angel nodded. "Yes, I have known for some time, but was prohibited from telling you. It was something you had to discover."

"What do I do now?"

"You have your answer in the scrolls."

Émēr climbed onto Áepoo's back. "What if Argus destroys them?"

Áepoo galloped then rose into the sky. "He will not enter the cave. It frightens him. Besides, I fear he has other plans."

"Áepoo, Augustine told me to study Anú's diary. Do you know what that means?"

He shrugged as his massive wings kept in perfect rhythm. "If he told you to do it, then you should."

"It seems every time I solve one mystery, several more arise to take its place."

Áepoo laughed. "God is a mystery also."

He landed near Ruárc's small village, and Émēr slid off his back. He turned to thank him, but the angel disappeared.

Émēr made his way down the path and into the small compound.

Ūmá rushed into his arms. "Where have you been, husband? I have worried over you!"

He held her tightly. "I am sorry, my wife. Áepoo had something to show me." He placed his hand on her stomach. "My wife, life is getting better."

She gave him a confused look.

"Áepoo told me you are with child."

Her eyes blinked several times. "What?"

"You carry my son."

She shook her head, struggling to find words. "Praise Attiyq!"

"Our first child." Émēr's face broke into a sloppy grin, and he hugged her tightly. "Indeed. Attiyq has blessed us."

She buried her face in his shoulder. Conell stood behind her and crossed his arms. A scowl covered his face, the scowl of a king.

Émēr released Ūmá with a kiss on her cheek. "I must speak to my Prince." He turned his eyes to Conell. "I have much to tell you."

"I am not pleased when my captain suddenly disappears into the night," Conell grumbled. "We sent out a search party earlier this morning but found nothing. Imogene was the one who said we must return to the village."

Excitement, horror, fear, and love for Ūmá swelled in Émēr's heart. "My Mojí, Áepoo took me to see something from the Attiyq. I saw Him. I touched Him!"

The anger evaporated from Conell's green eyes. "*Him*?"

"The Attiyq!" Émēr took a step towards Conell. "We must talk, now."

Conell led the way to an empty hut. "Should I sit down for this?"

Émēr grinned. "Ūmá bears my son!"

"He told you that?"

"Yes. And other things."

Conell dropped into a chair. "Tell. Other things?"

Émēr paced the floor. "I had a vision or something. I saw Argus's kingdom and that which he longs to do. It was frightening." He stared out the window and saw past the forest. "He wants to destroy all of Ézású." He faced Conell. "All of it, the Southern Lands, Eastern Lands, every land." He turned back to the pane. "My people, the Maúl. My wife, my son."

Conell took a deep breath. "What did the Attiyq say to do?"

Émēr took in the branches of the trees and the mountains that rose on the horizon. To explore such beauty once more. "I am to become High Priest over all of Ézású." He turned to Conell. "I do not know where to begin."

Conell waited a long while before he answered as only rulers do. "You know the Attiyq better than me or any other person in Ézású. I am no longer angry at Him, but my faith is weak. I know He exists for I have seen His angel. But your question, I have no answers."

Émēr nodded. "I saw Cian. He gave me his mantle and poured oil over my head. He said I am now the High Priest. He said I am King Anú's descendent. The Maúl throne is mine, if I wish to take it."

His eyes softened. "A king. I always thought you would make a good king. I am sure Imogene will be pleased to hear of Cian."

"Mojí, there is something I must ask of you. It is quite delicate, but as head of my clan, I must. I have seen your eyes on Imogene. Do you think she could make a good queen?"

His mouth dropped open, then snapped shut. "I did, I mean, I did not …"

Émēr laughed. "Now you are in the net, My Mojí!" He erased the smile from his face. "She is only sixteen. In our lands, she is ready for marriage, but in hers? I question. She is like a child at times and an adult at others. If you wish to pursue, then I will give my blessings. But please, do not break my adopted sister's heart. Be pure with her."

Conell closed his eyes. "Yes, my heart has turned to her, but as you said, she is as a child." He pulled a necklace from his pant pocket. "I keep this with me, so I do not lose it. I kept it hidden all these years in a hidden place in the dungeon. When we saved Imogene, I pulled it from a hiding place in the wall." He dangled a chain with a locket engraved with wildflowers.

"That was your mother's. The flowers were from the Sea of Blood, am I correct? Her favorite place?"

He nodded. "Yes, Father made it for her years before I was born. She gave it to me months before she died." He wrinkled his brow.

"It was odd. She always wore it, then suddenly, she gave it to me, saying I was to give it to the woman I would marry." He slipped it back into his pocket. "It just seemed odd to me that she would give it to me at such an early age. I hid it in the dungeon for fear pirates would steal it."

"Will you give it to Imogene?"

"I do not know. I do not know if she will accept it."

"Love was forced into my arms, but you must step carefully as you are royal blood."

"Being King is easy; finding a woman to wear my mother's locket is hard."

Émēr chuckled. "Finding the next queen is even harder. Now who is fearful? As head of her clan, I give permission. But I think telling her that would be harmful to both of us."

Conell nodded. "Agreed."

"But you will make a promise. You will not be improper with her, and you will give her the rights due to her as a member of my clan."

"I promise," Conell said. "I will be a gentleman; I will not touch her improperly, and I will give her the *TTisho* rights. I will make sure one of your clan is with us to protect her honor, I will give my sword to protect her from the enemy, and if we survive, I will present her to the Courts at the castle as a *TTisho* Lady of the King's Courts."

Émēr nodded. "I will watch as head of her clan that her honor is always intact and that she is presented with the greatest of respect to the King's courts. As all women should be presented." He paused. "Speaking of Imogene, the Attiyq told me that if I did not take the place of High Priest, Argus would kill us, meaning you and me. Erák would take Ūmá into the mountains, but Argus would take Imogene. She…" Émēr swallowed. "Immie would take her life by jumping out of the castle window."

Conell's eyes grew wide.

"Yes, and there's more. If I do not accept, after Ūmá dies in childbirth, my clan tries to raise my son, but he seeks revenge and

Argus kills him. I must take my place if I am to protect my family, you, and Ézású."

"Attiyq help us," Conell whispered.

"Áepoo said I will find the answers in the scrolls. I must study Anú's journal. Before Argus's attack, I saw Augustine studying Anú's journal. Then he told me I needed to study it." Émēr rubbed his jaw. "The elders in the village said they would draw more Warrior lines on my face. I feel it is time."

"We return to where we began. Chara has said that she wishes to give us a celebration. I want to go to this to see what information Ruárc can give us. Do you believe we can trust him?"

"A life-debt is like a *cuqumon*," Émēr said.

Conell raised his eyebrows. "A *cuqumon?* Father often said the covenant agreement was deeper than the blood of one's kin."

Émēr nodded. "The two once opposing clans become one clan by mixing the blood of two warriors. He will never betray us."

Everyone has a past.

-Imogene

24

Chara set the platter of meat in the center of the table and smacked Aurc's hands as the boy reached for a bite.

The boy cradled his stinging fingers and scowled. "I helped hunt it."

"And we will all eat soon." Char ruffled his hair. "Bring me the plates, and no arguing."

The boy returned with the plates, followed by Nika who delicately placed a plate of potatoes next to the main course. Muarc and Chia placed the drinking mugs and utensils on the table and scurried back in the kitchen area.

As Nika set the cutlery and mugs uniformly next to the plates, her mother let out a sigh. "You always take so long setting the table."

Nika focused on straightening a knife. "It must be perfect."

Ruárc led his new family members to the table and spread his arms wide. "My family is to serve your family. This will be our Bringing Together celebration. You and I are now family."

Imogene gave Ūmá a sour look, and Ūmá bit her lip to hide her giggle.

"We are most pleased that you have done this great thing for our clan," Émēr said. "We receive with great honor."

He pulled out the seat for his mother as she sat to his right, stating that she was second in command of the family. He took his seat at the head of the table, signifying he was the leader of his clan. Aine sat left of him, then Imogene, Erák, and Frigg. Ūmá sat next to Laoise.

Ruárc sat at the other end of the table which stated his home was used for the feast, with his wife to his left, then their children, eldest to youngest. Conell sat on his right, the place reserved for royalty. Conell gave a nod to Ruárc, who bowed.

The peace that comes of gratitude settled over Émēr. It was only a year ago when Ruárc and Conell met with their swords. Now the men bowed in the union of family. *Attiyq, you do have a sense of humor.*

The warm scent of meat and vegetables filled the air. Chara returned to the kitchen and brought out the fresh cooked bread and a bowl of butter and took her seat next to her husband.

Émēr stood and lifted his hands. Ruárc opened his mouth, but his wife quickly hushed him.

"Attiyq, thank you for this great feast you have created. Thank you for guiding us to this place and giving us shelter. Thank you for your goodness to us," Émēr said.

The others muttered, "So be it."

Ruárc scowled and stabbed at the meat, bringing it to his plate. "My clan does not serve the Attiyq. We serve Oozeka, god of the heavens."

Émēr shrugged. "I am now a High Priest of Attiyq. I apologize if we offended you, but He is my God and I only follow Him."

"When did you become this High Priest and who made you into one?"

"Cian. Before he died, he placed his hand on my head and announced that I am to be High Priest. I never followed it because of my concern for my prince and my family. But now, I take that place."

Ruárc piled potatoes and green vegetables onto his plate. "Well, I still choose Oozeka. As do my clan."

Émēr nodded. "Accepted."

Chara rose and served the meat to each person as they complimented her culinary skills. Her face broke into large smiles, and she feigned humility. Even Laoise had to admit the meat was tender, spicy, and juicy, the potatoes soft, and the green vegetables were crisp, not soggy.

Imogene slathered butter over her bread. "This is like the holidays back home, only people aren't fighting."

Émēr glanced around the table. He was at one time alone, one Maúl with childlike markings. Then came Conell, Frigg, Imogene, Ūmá, his unborn son, Erák, Aine, Mother, and finally Ruárc's family. His clan had grown into a tribe that he now led for his Prince who would become King soon. Like Brodén and Anú. All had come full circle.

Once the others had finished eating, Ruárc grabbed a flask from a shelf and opened the top.

Chia gave him a scowl. "Do not bring out the barbarian's wine. You do not have the stomach for it."

He scoffed. "Do not speak to me like one of the children, woman." He guzzled the wine and wiped his mouth.

Chia shooed the children outside to play. "I will not have you drunk before our children." She returned with her daughters and gathered the dishes in a wooden crate then went to the kitchen to wash them.

Ruárc laughed. "She is like an old hen." He waved Émēr over to his end of the table.

Laoise and Aine exchanged glances then stood from the table. Ūmá tapped Imogene's hand as she followed the other women. Imogene pushed back her chair, cringing as it scraped against the floor. "Sorry," she mouthed to Laoise.

"I think it is time for us to retire as well," Laoise said as she bowed. "Thank you so much for your hospitality. This Coming Together Celebration will be celebrated each year. It has been wonderful." Then she led the women to their sleeping quarters.

Émēr let out a breath of relief and joined the men at the end of the table. Erák gave his seat to Émēr and sat on the other side of Ruárc.

Ruárc raised the flask. "Woman! Bring mugs for the men!"

Chia stomped into the room and slammed the tray of mugs before him then returned to her dishes.

Conell and Émēr traded exasperated looks. Frigg passed the mugs out.

The Mojí put his hand over Frigg's mug. "I am sorry, Frigg, but you are much too young to drink barbarian wine."

Frigg's face fell.

Erák slapped Frigg's back. "As I am too young to drink it. Come, Frigg, you and I will retire to our sleeping quarters and drink warm milk." He lifted Frigg to his feet and escorted the young man out of the room. Frigg gave one last longing glance at the wine and the men surrounding the table before Erák pulled him from the room.

Ruárc laughed. "Now the men can be men." He poured the rich blood-red liquid into their mugs. "Drink!"

Émēr sipped the wine, forced the cough away and lifted his mug. "It is very good." His voice cracked.

Conell chuckled.

"My father made a pact with the Barbarians; now, you must befriend them as well. You will need their help," Ruárc said. He swallowed more of the liquor and weaved on his chair. "The old woman says I get drunk when I drink this. She knows little."

Émēr stared at the wine in his mug, and his stomach rolled. He pushed the mug away. "I will not take the hands of the ones who murdered my father."

Ruárc laughed. "Killed your father? Oh, you are one who walks in darkness. The Barbarians did not kill your father, High Priest!"

Émēr took a deep breath and pushed his chair away from the table. But Conell caught his arm.

"Hear him out."

Ruárc pointed his cup at Émēr. "It was that feathered big bird Argus who slaughtered your Pa. His men flew into the castle and killed them all. I saw it from that cold room in that cursed guard tower that you, Prince Conell, put me and my poor brother in to die. But we survived by being quiet like mice." He placed his finger against his lips. "Shhh! Toál said. Be still."

He poured more wine into his mug and handed the flask to Émēr and Conell.

"No, but go on," Conell said.

Ruárc leaned forward. "It was a secret that Mee Queen had all along. To kill them all. Take your throne for herself. She found that demon from hell somewhere. I do not know where, but he was somewhere. She was the demon's joiner." He stared at the red liquid. "I heard them screaming. Women. Children. Begging. Toál held onto me. We prayed hard to Oozeka. So many screams." He gulped the wine and refilled the mug. "And then they were quiet. That was the worst part. The quiet."

Émēr looked down at his lap. "It never occurred to me that you were a victim in all of this madness."

He sneered. "My brother was never a victim. We survived."

"Of course," Émēr said. "Forgive me. Please continue."

"There is nothing else to continue. All died. I saw you, High Priest, leading the young ones out of the castle in the morning. You are blessed by your God that the villagers found you instead of that foul Jezebel. She would have killed all of you, then the throne would be hers. But instead, I am sure she was celebrating with her demon.

She was surprised to see you all alive. But she could not slay you, not with the villagers looking."

"Which is why she pretended to take care of us," Conell said. He leaned back in this chair and crossed his arms.

"Why did she tell us it was the Barbarians?" Émēr asked.

Ruárc chuckled and slammed his hand on the table. "You are still a babe! You would have sought revenge against her demon-lover."

"Where did Argus come from?" Conell asked.

Ruárc raised his arms in an exaggerated shrug. "I do not know where demons come from. Hell, I assume."

Conell leaned forward. "Do you remember him in the castle before the attack?"

He squinted as he dredged up the old memories. "I saw the Chee female and the demon in the woods at times, but no, not in the castle. Your father, the King, would have killed him. She kept him hidden well, like a key to something she didn't want anyone else to get their hands on." He twisted his hand as if he twisted the key. "Argus follows that Chee-female like a pet, yet it is Argus who rules the throne, not her. But she thinks she does." He pointed to his head. "It is like she is in a trance at times."

Émēr glanced at Conell. "Like how he had Imogene in a trance."

"Do you think Jezebel is under his spell?" Conell asked.

"We are all under his spell. Demons in hell do that; they get inside your mind and turn you into the walking dead. When that she-wolf came to your father, she was only fifteen years old. Marrying age. My Chara married me when I was just fifteen and she was twelve." He lifted his chin. "She adored me."

"HA!" Came Chara's snort from the kitchen.

Ruárc wobbled on his chair. "She could not keep her hands off of me." He winked.

"Yes, I am sure, but please about Jezebel," Conell said.

He waved his hand. "Who cares about that witch?"

Conell poured more wine into Ruárc's cup.

The guard chuckled. "You bribe me now! She came to your father, Conell, when she was a fifteen-year-old girl. She was shy, would only talk if talked to, but that Thing kept her in line. Argus swept her away to a temple and trained her. Then she reappeared as your father's priestess five years later." He leaned over the table to Conell. "Your father despised her. Hated her from the start and often tried to send her away. But the temple elders always talked him into taking her back." He burped. "Then something happened. He changed."

Conell caught Émēr's eye. "What do you mean, changed? My father?"

Ruárc nodded. "Yes, changed." His eyes grew large. "She oversaw the castle's temple. The King insisted that he oversee the temple, so he started staying out there longer. The Queen…" He grew quiet.

Chara leaned against the kitchen doorframe as she wiped a plate. "She cried a lot, is that not what you said?"

"Yes," Ruárc said. "She cried. I never liked the King, but I liked your mother. She treated me with kindness. Even Amgets hated that witch. He tried many times to send her away, but the King insisted. The Queen often wept on Amgets' shoulder."

"Father never spoke of it," Émēr said. "If I had known, I would have told you, Mojí."

"When did Argus arrive?" Conell asked.

Ruárc's glassy eyes sought him out. "After," he whispered. He swallowed the wine and filled his mug, sloshing it onto the table. "So much happened after. Argus … hurt people. Toál and I tried to stay away from him. We were only children. Toál always watched out for me." He swirled his drink. "I was the eldest. I was to watch out for him. But Toál was always older."

Chara returned to the kitchen.

"Argus seemed to like Toál, but he was only eight years of age and was afraid of Argus. I made him leave and I stayed in his place. Argus liked the boys." He guzzled the wine and let it flow down his chin. He stared at the empty cup and whispered, "He really liked me."

Émēr's heart squeezed with compassion that he had never believed he could have towards a man like Ruárc. "Ruárc, I did not know. I am sorry, for what Argus did to you," Émēr said low.

Ruárc slammed his mug onto the table. "Do not pity me or my brother! We survived!" He rose from the table and pointed to his chest. "I survived!"

Émēr held up his hands. "You are right. You are a great warrior. You endured your enemy, and you will defeat him."

Ruárc plopped into the chair and snorted. "I will hang that bird from my son's ceiling." He clutched Émēr's forearm. "Please, my little ones, protect them. I am not fearful for me or my wife, only my children. Argus, what he did to me, he will do to my children."

Émēr nodded. "I give you my word as High Priest of the Attiyq, I will protect your children."

Ruárc released his forearm. "I owe you much."

"You owe me nothing," Émēr said. "You kept my family safe."

"How was it that we never saw Argus?" Conell asked.

"That Mee female kept her pet locked away." Ruárc dumped the last of the wine into his mug. "Woman! More wine!"

Chara ignored him.

"Useless woman!" Ruárc grabbed Émēr's mug and drained the liquid. "You never knew he existed. The Mee Queen kept him away from you and Amgets. While you were learning the courts, Argus…" He ran his hand through his hair. "Toál and I found peace in the tower. Argus hated the chill of the room." He chuckled. "The cold that we hated protected us from the demon. Surprising that the thing you hate becomes your paradise."

Émēr nodded. "Go on. Where did she keep him?"

Ruárc grinned and raised Émēr's mug to Conell. "God save the Queen. In your mother's room."

Conell's eyes grew wide, and his neck and face flushed a deep red.

Émēr placed his hand on his friend's arm. "Do not allow your anger to overcome you."

"She spoiled you." Ruárc's eyes grew hard. "She kept you occupied."

Conell looked away. "That was why she gave me all that I wanted."

Ruárc turned his mug over and shook his empty cup. "She had to keep you out of the way. You asked questions." He put the mug to his mouth and tapped on the bottom of the cup. After draining it, he slammed it on the table. "When you were nicely locked away, Argus simply stepped out and took his place."

"Where did Jezebel come from? Which temple?" Émēr asked.

Ruárc shrugged. "I have no idea. She never mentioned it. In fact, she never mentioned it to Amgets. Now, he was another one that asked too many questions. Him and the King were at one time almost brothers, as you and the captain are now. But that she-mee came between them. She told the King that the Maúl would one day betray him. She used words of the Attiyq against them. Finally, he listened. He listened and then all were dead. Including him. Maybe he listened too well?"

Conell tapped his fingers together and pursed his lips. "Émēr, remember when I told you about the curtains moving and a Maúl Elder saying it was the angels' hands reaching for my father? He was very upset over something, and fear sat in his eyes. I question now did this have something to do with him? With her? Could the witch have betrayed him as she did me?"

Émēr shrugged. "Tell me more of Jezebel. Where did she study? Who was her mentor?"

"Cian told me that she appeared one day out of nowhere," Conell said.

Ruárc reeled on his seat. "That she did, my boy. She appeared, but with a priest like Cian. Only he was not as kind as old Cian. And not as powerful, but still a priest." He leaned back in his chair and belched. "Toál often played tricks on him. Not Cian." He let out a loud laugh. "He would often hide snakes in that old priest's bed. It was such fun watching the old man run from his bed, wearing a nightgown, and screaming down the halls of the castle." He paused.

"Amgets hated him too. He hated just about all of them. The old man handed Jezebel over like she was his newborn babe. Proud as any father. But no one knows where she came from. She just appeared." He chuckled. "But Argus. Now, he is a strange one. No one had ever seen a winged man. Legends have it that winged men once covered the lands, before man walked Ézású, and that Argus is the last of them. Maybe true, maybe children's stories."

Aurc ran into the room and stood next to his father. "Father, you know how we love stories."

Conell leaned back in his chair and crossed his arms over his chest. "Tell me this children's story."

With a snorting laugh, Ruárc hugged his son. "You are starting to look and sound like that long-haired king. Alright, Your Majesty, I will tell you my tale."

Ruárc rose from his chair and stumbled against the wall. "Years ago, before Oozeka rose to his throne in the sky, winged men walked the earth. They ruled each continent with an iron hand. Oozeka placed the winged men to rule over the animals, and then Oozeka made man to worship him high in his skies." Ruárc swept his flabby arms up and over his head. He fell against the table.

Nika and Muarc ran into the room and surrounded their father.

"Oozeka gave the winged men power as none had ever seen. Power to raise up the mountains."

"How high, father?" Aurc asked.

Ruárc stood on his toes and tried to touch the ceiling. He toppled but caught himself. "Higher than the goddess moon herself."

Muarc stood on his chair and reached his hands over his head. "This high!"

Ruárc laughed. "Yes, my son, that high. But the winged men became jealous of Oozeka, for Oozeka ruled the skies and the stars and the moon, while they only ruled the ground. They could fly, but only so high. Oozeka cursed their wings, not allowing them to reach him."

But one day, the king of the winged men rose up in rebellion. He fought against Oozeka and rose into the sky and swung his sword at the great god. But Oozeka cursed the winged men, and he plummeted to the ground. Since then, the winged creatures could only go so far, before dying in the air. A curse on all who follow."

The children gasped. Nika hid under the table and Muarc slashed the air.

"A curse!" Muarc raced around the table.

"Bed! Now!" Chara stood in the doorway with her hands on her large hips.

The children raced up the stairs and slammed their doors.

Ruárc bowed. "I hope I entertained you, Your Majesty."

Conell raised his hands. "A fine performance."

Émēr patted the seat. "Please sit. You are drunk, and you shame my clan as well as your wife."

Ruárc grunted and plopped onto the seat. "You see, Argus is of the cursed ones. He cannot fly as high as the sun, but still he flies. He and his men are all that is left. Cursed forever."

Chara placed her hands on her husband's shoulders. "I think it is time for you to sleep before you shame all of us. Do you need us, Master?"

Émēr shook his head. "No, Chara, take him to bed."

She gently led him up the stairs to their sleeping quarters as Ruárc sung in a language Émēr had never heard.

"Father told me a similar story," Émēr said. "But it was not the sun god who pronounced a curse, but the Attiyq. But we do not know who he cursed. He was one that the Attiyq assigned to watch over Ézású, but he misused his powers. The Attiyq cursed him and forced him to walk the land, serving those who were to serve him. What if the winged men were the ones the Attiyq cursed?" He paused. "I read a passage from Anú's journals that talked about this very thing. That He cursed someone who tried to rise above the heavens."

"Émēr," Conell said. "I want you to do something difficult." He paused. "I want you to look into befriending the Barbarians as Ruárc has asked. I am of royalty, and if I remember protocol correctly, I am ineligible of breaking the mark."

His eyebrows rose. "A covenant? With the Barbarians? My Mojí!"

"I know this is difficult, but I believe we will need their help, as Ruárc has said. It is time for this war to end. If they did not kill our people, then we must bring peace before Jezebel or Argus can attack. I could order you to do it, but I am asking you to do it."

Émēr scratched his head. "What you ask is difficult. Can I give you an answer in the morning?"

Conell gripped Émēr's shoulder. "Of course."

The corner of Émēr's mouth twitched. "You act more and more like a king with each passing day."

Laoise tapped on the door and slowly opened it. "Is he gone?"

Émēr smiled and nodded. "Come, Mother, I have questions for you."

She eased onto one of the chairs and placed her hands in her lap. "This place smells of that disgusting alcohol. Your sister is telling me not to judge, but I do not like them."

"I know, Mother," Émēr said. "But I have promised to protect them." He returned his attention to Conell. "What if Argus is the one spoken of in Anú's journals, the fallen one cursed by the Attiyq?"

"Then that would mean Argus is thousands of years old," Conell said. He wiped the table with his napkin. "How could that be?"

Émēr shrugged. "I think I need to return to Anú's castle. I believe our answers lie in the journals."

Conell nodded and tossed the rag into a nearby bucket. "What did he mean, Father and Jezebel became allies?"

"Mother," Émēr said, turning to her. "Ruárc said Father and the King were no longer friends after Jezebel became his priestess. What do you know of this?"

She shrugged. "I only know Jezebel came between your father and the King. She seemed to weave a spell over him. I often talked to your mother, Naomh, and she was at times very upset. But still she trusted her husband. Often, she saw Jezebel and the King walking in the fields after the prayer times. He said she was giving him teachings, but I think the Queen thought there might be more. I do not wish to upset you, Mojí."

Conell released a long breath. "You think Father joined with Jezebel?"

"I do not know, Mojí, but I do not think that he would destroy his marriage and his nation for one night with that horrible woman."

He stared at her. "But what if he did?"

At times, one must take the enemy's hand in order to destroy a common opponent.

-Anú

25

Émēr climbed out of his bed, careful not to disturb Ūmá. Even in slumber, her smooth face and long brown hair captured him like a bird in a net. He left the warmth of the cabin and breathed in the chilly, fresh morning air. The first sun rays peaked over the horizon, turning the sky into the color of honey. He sat on the ground as the sun slowly rose above the mountains, sending fiery red fingers over the land. "Attiyq, Your sunrises always take my breath away."

Chara opened the door to her hut and herded her sleepy-eyed children to an open field, where they chanted in a strange language, then bowed in the direction of the sun.

Émēr looked away. "The Attiyq is the only God."

Having completed the ritual, Chara led her children back into the hut and shut the door.

"Attiyq, thank You for what You have done for me," Émēr said. "You have led me to my family, given me back my titles, and strengthened my hands. You will forever be the one True God."

Émēr finally made his way to the creek where after a quick bath, he gathered berries for breakfast. Out of boredom, he picked up an axe and chopped the wood left by the side of the house. With each chop, more questions seeped into his mind.

Why am I here? What do I do next? What of the cage? Argus? Who is he? A covenant with the enemy!

Émēr stopped and wiped his brow. "Attiyq, I only ask that You guide me. I am unsure of my ways. Your paths are pure and whole, and I need Your promised Right Hand. What am I to do now? If the Barbarians had nothing to do with the attack, then maybe it is time to make peace with them? A covenant? To bring our tribes together?" He shook his head. "No, my father would never have agreed to it." The thought rang like a bell in his head. "I cannot make a covenant with them."

"Who can you not make a covenant with?" came a voice behind him.

He turned.

Ruárc leaned against the doorway. His heavy hand shielded his bloodshot eyes, and his black greasy hair hung around his face. "You are too loud when you chop wood. Chop quieter."

Émēr chuckled. "That is why I stay away from Barbarian wine."

Ruárc grunted and scratched the back of his head. "It would be wise for you to cut the mark with them. You and they have a common enemy as do I: Argus and the Queen."

He studied Ruárc's face. "It would be nice to rid the country of that flying demon," Émēr said. "My King will need an army. Would they fight next to him?"

"Probably, if you cut the mark with them. Your wars will be their wars." Ruárc stretched and wandered towards the woods, calling out over his shoulder as he went, "But do not go to meet them without me. I must do my morning business."

Émēr tossed the axe into the stump and made his way to the Mojí's quarters.

Imogene exited her hut and stretched her arms. "The bed was kind of nice. Way better than the cold ground. Is there a river nearby where I can wash?"

He pointed through the woods. "Once Ūmá rises, I will take you both to the river. I do not want you alone. Ruárc is … he has business in the woods."

She nodded. "What's for breakfast?"

Émēr tapped on his Mojí's door.

"Enter!"

He entered the hut and closed the door behind him. "I have decided. I will cut the mark with the Barbarians."

Conell grinned and crossed his arms over his chest. "I am glad. You bring honor back to your family."

"My father's ghost will rise from the grave once I take the mark, but I think you are right, I need to do this. I will allow him to haunt you."

Conell laughed and pulled his shirt over his head. "I will take it. We will need to leave right away."

He patted the bag that was slung over his shoulder. "I will give Anú's book of poems to the leader as a gift to honor the Covenant. Ruárc has offered to take us there."

"Are you sure you wish to give Anú's treasure?"

"Yes. It will show that I am willing to stay bound to him."

Conell nodded. "The women will stay behind, along with Frigg and Erák. If we do not return, then they are to take the women across the sea."

"Yes, Mojí."

Conell led Émēr to the main eating hut and found Chara feeding her little ones. Ruárc sat at the head of the table, Laoise, Aine, Ūmá ,and Imogene sat across from Chara's family. Frigg and Erák followed them and took empty seats at the table.

Once all were seated and eating the berries and eggs Chara had made, Conell cleared his throat.

"Émēr has an announcement to make."

Émēr stood and gave a small cough. Ūmá gave him a puzzled glance.

"Mojí and I were talking, and we decided it is best to make a covenant with Barbarians."

Ūmá's eyes grew wide, and Frigg dropped his fork.

"Mojí, no!" Erák shook his head. "That is foolishness."

"No," Conell said. "It is not foolishness. It is wisdom. Émēr, Ruárc, and I will meet with them, the rest of you will stay here. If we do not return, then Erák, you and Frigg will take Émēr's family, Imogene and Chia and her family to the seacoast where you will go as far from Ézású as you can."

Chara scowled. "I will not leave my home."

Ruárc kissed her hand. "You are my bride and although I may drink too much, I still love you. Please go. The Witch Queen will not stop hunting you or our little ones."

She touched his cheek and kissed him. "When will you leave?"

"Today, after breakfast." He gave her a wink then plowed into the eggs.

Ūmá shook her head. "No! I will not have you go!"

Émēr reached for her hand, but she pulled it away.

"I do not wish to speak to you here," she whispered. She dropped her napkin on the table and hurried from the room.

Émēr gave his Mojí a surprised look then followed her.

She leaned against a tree with her arms wrapped around her.

He placed his hands on her shoulders. "Ūmá, talk to me."

"It has taken me months to trust you, and now you will leave me to others." She moved away from him.

"Ūmá, no! That is not why I go. I go for us, for our child." He hesitated. "I met with the Attiyq last night, face to face."

She turned. "Did He tell you to do this?"

He shook his head. "No, but He told me things that might happen if I run, if we run. Things I think you do not want to hear. All I can tell you is that we must stay." He took her hands into his and kissed her fingertips. "You are my greatest gift. I almost threw you away, but I will not do that again. I must go."

"And if you do not return? I will take Erák to be my husband and father of my child?" Her blue eyes drilled into him.

He winced. "Ūmá, I cannot have you in the hands of Jezebel or Argus." He paused. "Ruárc said Argus enjoys children besides women. I fear for our son. I do not do this because I throw my life away, but I do this to protect you, our child, and our clan."

"I wish you had spoken to me first."

He nodded. "I know, I should have. But you were sleeping so peacefully, and I did not wish to wake you. But yes, you are correct, I should have asked, and I ask for your forgiveness."

"Alright, I forgive," Disapproval sat in her eyes. "But I expect you to come back to us. And next time, ask me first."

He kissed her. "I promise, I will always speak to you first. I will return. It seems the Barbarians hate Argus and the Queen more than I do. They will join us."

"And if they refuse?"

"Then we will trust the Attiyq to help us."

He slipped his arm around her waist and led her to the dining hall.

Chara hurried to her hut then returned with a backpack. She slipped it onto her husband's shoulders. "Return to me, husband."

He touched her cheek, then swooped up his daughters in his arms. "You will help your mother?"

The girls nodded and wrapped their small arms around his neck.

His sons stood tall before him. "Father, let us go too!"

"And who will guard the camp?"

The two young warriors nodded. "We will guard against our enemies."

"Take their heads from them if they approach our home," Ruárc said, winking at his wife.

The boys' faces turned stern, and they gave stiff nods.

He lowered his girls to the ground and ruffled his sons' hair.

Émēr kissed Ūmá and pressed his forehead against hers. "Remember what I said. You must keep safe."

"Safe as you," she said, smiling as she wrapped his sword belt around his waist.

He lifted his arms and gave her smile. "You remember *Cukdilok Dulk.*"

"You will need it to prove you now lead the Maúl tribe," she said, tightening the strap.

Conell glanced at Imogene, who gave him a shy smile.

"Watch yourselves," she said.

He nodded. "As you. Frigg, Erák, if we do not return, take the women and go, understand?" He stared at Imogene and placed his hand on her shoulder. "You will be safe with Erák and Frigg."

She smiled at him. "I thought you were some big bully when I first met you in the castle."

He chuckled. "And I thought you were annoying. But I was suffering, and I was wrong to have been so cruel."

She placed her hand on his hand. "It's okay. Thanks for coming for me, I mean, in the dungeon."

Conell squeezed her fingers. "It was my honor."

Émēr's voice broke the spell, and he gave Conell a stern look, "It is time we go."

The three men made their way down the pathway. "It will take us a day to get to the village. You must always be behind me. There are scouts along the way. They will see us and alert the village. I enter, then bring a boy with me when I return to you. If the boy does not return, the leader will kill you, understand?"

Émēr glanced at Conell.

"Yes, I understand." Conell pulled the binding off his arm.

"Are you sure you want to expose the sign of the King?" Émēr asked.

"Yes, I do. They must know I am the prince of Ézású, or shall I say, the King."

Émēr smiled. "So will Imogene be your queen?"

He grunted. "Now is not the time to discuss that."

Émēr laughed. "I wonder if the Barbarians can give us any information on Anú's castle?"

Ruárc looked over his shoulder. "Yes, they know much about it as Anú has been their sworn enemy."

"The more information we get, the better," Conell said.

The men walked deeper into the woods. The branches became a canopy that rose high in the sky.

"Mojí," Émēr said as he scanned the trees. "I have never seen trees so high. We are truly in Barbarian country."

The small troop made their way down the narrow, worn path. The trees around them were thin but tall. The trunks twisted around each other, locked in a silent dance. Some bent at the root before jutting into the sky. Others grew at odd angles, resembling sticks children planted in the ground.

Émēr stooped and examined the path. "It seems these people rarely leave a trail. I see the footsteps of young ones, but I can barely see the steps of adults. They are well trained."

Ruárc grinned. "Watch them, and do not trust them until you have cut the mark. After you have made the covenant, then you can walk with them in peace."

The twisted tree limbs entwined high above them and blocked out the sun as if to hold them in a prison. A chill sat in the air. Émēr rubbed his arms as strange creatures chattered around him. "This is what Imogene means when she says creeps."

Ruárc laughed. "Has the great Maúl become frightened of woods? Nute's ancestors chose this area because the people claimed the woods are guarded by ghosts who live in the trees. That is why they are bent. Legends say that if one enters this forest and they are evil, then the trees will become evil and do that evil deed."

Émēr scratched the back of his neck as he glanced at Conell.

The group walked silently down the trail, Émēr often looking over this shoulder. Chills spread over his back and his hand rested on Father's *Abtoo*. They rounded a curve in the road and on the side, was a skull planted on the top of a spear.

Émēr stopped his Mojí and pointed. "Look. They are headhunters. We must move with care."

Ruárc nodded. "Yes, they often display the heads of their enemies. They also display the bodies in the woods as a way of boasting to anyone who would trespass on their lands. They are a sickening group. If Father had not made a treaty, I would have nothing to do with them."

It was early afternoon when Ruárc motioned for them to halt. Émēr scanned the trees. The sound of the branches cracking drifted to him. "They are watching us from the trees," he whispered.

Ruárc nodded. "Yes, they are. I will go ahead of you and will return with a boy. Do not speak to the boy. If he senses no ill intent, then he will return to the village to summon the leader. If he does not return, then the tribe will hunt you down."

He soon returned with a boy who looked to be around twelve years of age. Blue strips were smeared down the sides of his face. He wore trousers made of animal skin, and he carried a small spear. The boy eyed the two men and slowly approached them, his sharp eyes roaming over Conell and Émēr.

Ruárc spoke the strange language to the boy, who nodded.

"I want you to learn their language," Conell whispered to Émēr.

"Yes."

The boy looked past Ruárc and motioned for the two men to follow him. As they continued down the path, men stood on branches and looked down on them.

The path opened to a small village of circled huts with cone-shaped thatched roofs. Women scurried away from them and pulled their children to their sides. The old men who had gathered to share exaggerated stories rose from their seats and studied the small group. The men were bare chested and wore animal skinned trousers. Blue tattoos covered their chests, arms, face, and legs. Some of the men had a metal ring around their necks while others had nothing.

Émēr touched his face. "They have markings such as I do. Surely we are not related?"

Conell shrugged.

The women wore long dresses made of dark cloth. Some looked at him with hatred in their eyes, others out of curiosity.

Ruárc strolled to a large man with several neck rings who sat on a large wooden chair. The king of the Barbarians curved his dirty fingers over the armrest. Ruárc bowed before the man.

"Highest Leader Nute, these are men from the North. They have come in peace. They are enemies of the one you fight, Queen Jezebel," Ruárc said.

Nute's eyebrow rose in a mocking look. "You were the one who wished to have war with the Brodénians, and now you wish to make peace?"

Ruárc took a deep breath. "Yes, King Nute. I did seek war with the Brodénians, but I did so because the Queen's sword was on my neck."

"To die is honor."

"Yes, but my children would grow up without me."

Nute laughed. "Lessrama, you are still the same. Come, tell me of your 'friends'."

A sour look crossed Ruárc's face, but he plunged on. "They are fleeing from the Queen and wish to make peace with the Barbarians."

King Nute's eyes shifted from Ruárc to Conell. Émēr straightened, and his hand drifted to his sword.

Nute's gaze jumped to Émēr, and his eyes narrowed. "You are Maúl." He rose from his throne.

Émēr gripped his sword, but Conell stopped him.

"Let him speak," the Mojí said.

King Nute approached them and ran his fingers over Conell's sacred king's mark. Conell met his stare with equal strength and ferocity.

"It is improper to touch the Sacred markings, is it not, King of the North?" Nute smirked.

"I overlook such things. I am looking to destroy Jezebel."

"And what will you do after you have destroyed the witch? Kill my people?"

Conell shook his head. "No, I will keep my word. Your people will remain free. All I ask is that you do not harm my people."

Nute chuckled and turned to Émēr. "The last Maúl. You have children's markings on your face. Are you a child?"

Anger reared up in his chest, but he pulled his hand from his sword. "I am no longer a child. My people were murdered by Argus, the Queen's demon. The last order of my father was to protect the prince, which I have done to this day. I may have the markings of a child, but I am no child today." He pulled *Cukdilok Dulk* from its scabbard. "I carry the sword of Anú, *Cukdilok Dulk,* to prove I am of the Maúl."

Nute took a step back and nodded. "You are correct; you are no longer a child."

"I am also a priest of my people."

Nute's eyebrow rose. "As am I." He cocked his head. "I destroyed your village, Maúl. I killed your people and sold the women and children to Slavers. Do you still wish to make peace with me?"

"I can rescue my people. And yes, I wish to make peace. The Witch is destroying all people with her magic. She will come for you and your children. You will be next."

Nute stared at him, then grunted. "I know of the Slaver's camp. It is not far from here. There are few guards. Your women and children are there. I do not agree with taking Brodénians' hands in friendship, but I also know that your words ring true. They will come for us." He turned his attention to Conell. "Tell me, King of the Brodénians, why do you wish to make peace with me."

"The Queen killed my mother and father along with all in the castle. She imprisoned me to steal my throne, and now she hunts me along with my captain and some other survivors. I cannot allow her to rule over my people any longer."

"Do you wish for revenge?"

Conell shook his head. "No, revenge is not what I wish, but I do wish to protect my friends and those who follow me. I am of the blood of Brodén. It is something I must do."

"The crown weighs heavy on the King's head."

Conell chuckled. "Its weight indeed sits hard upon me."

"As mine and my fathers before me." Nute stared at Conell. "Are you willing to walk this path that lies before you?"

"Yes," Conell said.

Nute turned to his fellow warrior who stood by the side of his throne and spoke the strange language. The man nodded and pointed at Conell and Émēr.

Émēr studied the two men. The warrior often referred to Nute as *Lisivil*, which must be Leader. The other words fluttered past him. Women spoke near the huts and their language was more casual and more fluid. Different words for different classes of people. This would take time.

Nute caught Émēr's eye and grinned. "You are Maúl. You do not disappoint me. I would be insulted if you did not learn my tongue."

Émēr chuckled and focused on Nute's face. "I would hate to insult my enemy when I wish to make a covenant with him."

Nute cocked his head. "What will you give me in return for the covenant? I will give you your children, the Maúl."

Émēr took a deep breath and handed Nute Anú's book. "It is what is left of Anú. His poems. It is worth much money and speaks of Anú's heart."

Nute eyebrows rose. "I did not know Anú wrote such things."

"Neither did I. Will you accept it?"

"Is it your most prized possession?"

Émēr paused. "Well, no. My father's weapon is my most prized possession. You wish to have my father's weapon?" *Forgive me, Father!* He pulled the hammer from his belt and handed it to Nute.

His gaze dropped to the weapon and back to Émēr. His eyes softened. "You do wish for peace."

"I wish for peace from Jezebel," Émēr said. "She has a demon that she controls. He has followed us and tried to kill us. He will find you and destroy your village. He cares nothing for anyone but himself."

"Argus. Yes, we know of him. *Lessrama* fears him." Nute nodded to Ruárc. "Many fear the demon."

A young woman with long brown hair pushed her way through the crowd and stood before Nute. She held a baby close to her chest and spoke the strange words to him. He kissed her forehead and gestured with his hands. She shook her head and pointed at the two strangers.

"You are Maúl. You kill children," the woman said to Émēr.

Émēr stepped back in shock. "I do not kill children."

"Each mark on your face is a child you murdered."

He shook his head. "I am not one who kills innocent children. That is not the meaning of the marks."

Nute slipped his arm around her waist. "This is my wife, Alaka, and my son, Pute."

"She is not your slave?"

"She was a slave to the traders, but I bought her and married her. She is a good wife and mother to our five children. We only take slaves of our enemies. But if I am to be your ally, then we must return your people to you. That is, if we make this agreement." Nute kissed Alaka on the top of her head and turned her away from the group. "She fears any outsiders."

"Why do you not return her to her home?"

Darkness covered Nute's eyes. "Because she belonged to Argus at one time. She managed to escape but was caught by the traders. Before she could be returned, I bought her and rescued her."

"Then Argus will kill you, her, and your children. You are marked by his wrath. Perhaps making a covenant is not worth the death of your family. If he finds out she is here, he will come for her." He reached for his hammer. "Please, I withdraw my offer."

Nute studied the weapon. "Why did you give me this and not the sword at your side?"

"Because I wish to destroy Argus and Jezebel. I have seen what the demon is capable of doing. I have seen who he really is, and you will not survive him. I will not have the death of your wife and little ones on my head. Please, I do not wish to have a covenant with you."

"Why did you not give me the sword at your side? *Cukdilok Dulk*? You have found Anú's underground home."

Émēr lowered his hand. "Yes, we have found it but how did you know?"

"Your sword means, 'War is a force to rule the stars,' does it not? The Maúl are not as wise as they seem. My people have known of Anú's cave for centuries. At times, I send scouts to inspect the cave. It has remained empty until now. We knew there was a way into it, but we could never understand its secrets."

"I know many of its secrets and some are nightmares. There is a large cage in the bottom level of the cave that I believe held Argus at one time. Please, do not make a covenant with me. I cannot have your blood on my hands."

Nute stared at Émēr. "You are saying that you wish to protect us? Your enemy?"

"You are no longer my enemy, but a victim of the demon. He will find you. He will find *her*. Please, let me take my people. Take your clans and hide in the mountains until the demon is destroyed."

Nute lifted his hand and snapped his fingers. Young men appeared to place cups and bread at Nute's feet.

Émēr groaned. "Please, do not do this."

"You are wishing to risk your life to protect your enemy. That is reason enough to break the mark. You will keep your father's hammer and *Cukdilok Dulk*. You need Anú's sword to prove you are the leader of the Maúl."

An older man with a graying beard and hair that spread thinly across his narrow shoulders placed a long knife in Nute's hand. He extended his arm to Émēr. "To deny this of me is to insult my clan."

"I cannot promise you will survive the demon's wrath."

Nute smiled. "We are Kalk. We will survive."

"Kalk?" Émēr asked.

He chuckled. "We do not like to be called Barbarian. We are called The Kalk, which means Bird. We believe our dead return to us in the birds."

"Forgive me. I was rude to call you Barbarians. Do you not wish to discuss the rules of the covenant?" Émēr asked.

He shrugged. "What rules? I will not kill your clan; you do not kill mine. If you betray me, then my god who lives in the souls of the birds will find you and destroy you. The birds will pluck out your eyes and eat your grains. For my god is mighty. If you keep this covenant, then my people will fight alongside the Maúl until the sun falls from the sky. We will live and die in great honor."

Émēr bowed. "And if you betray me then my God the Attiyq will fight for me. He will curse your lands, your children, and your people. He is the strong God of the air, the land, the sea, and beyond. If you keep this covenant, then He will bless your lands, your fields, your children, and your children's children to a hundred generations. I will fight alongside you and will come to you if the enemy is pursuing you. I will give my life for yours."

Nute grunted. "Your God sounds powerful."

Émēr stared at him. "I have seen the power of my God. He is strong, and He fights for those who trust Him. Do you still wish to join me?"

He grabbed Émēr's elbow and bound their forearms together with leather binding. He drew the knife across both their forearms and allowed the blood to pool between their arms. The elder rubbed dirt into the cuts, then unwrapped the leather and wrapped a cloth around their wounds.

"Come," Nute said. "Eat with us."

Émēr shrugged at Conell. "That was easy."

Conell gave him a cautioned look.

"I will be careful, and yes, I know what I am doing," Émēr said. "Imie will tell us to clean the wounds because of her enemy the germs."

Conell snorted. "Yes, she will."

Nute led them into the meeting hall and sat at the far end of a long wooden table. Émēr, Conell, and Ruárc sat next to him. Older men and women filed in and sat opposite of them. A boy around twelve years of age placed mugs of wine and plates of bread and fruit before them.

Émēr and Conell watched the others before eating. Ruárc kept his hands in his lap, so Émēr dropped his into his lap. Conell kept his on the table. Émēr suppressed a smile. Conell had remembered his teachings in their Hospitality classes despite hating the reading and all the lectures.

Nute nodded approval to Conell who returned the gesture. The Kalk king sipped from his wine mug and broke the bread. Then he handed his cup and plate around the table. Each man took a sip of wine and ate a bite of the bread. Again, the teachings of the Covenant at the Table stayed with them. Émēr offered a silent thanks to the Attiyq for making them stay in the lectures when they longed to play in the fields. He smiled. The Attiyq made such a covenant centuries ago with man.

Once the cup came back to Nute, Émēr followed. He sipped from his mug and broke a piece of bread then handed his plate around the table.

Nute clapped his hands and laughed. "Now, we are one clan!"

Sometimes all you have to do
is just listen.

-Imogene Katherine Reazley

26

Émēr wiped his hands on his cloth napkin and dropped it onto the floor. The boy snatched it up with a grin that took up most of his face. Émēr nodded to the boy who suppressed a giggle. The elders also dropped their napkins as did Conell, Émēr, and Ruárc. The boy quickly snatched them up and hurried out the door. The sounds of children's laughter drifted into the room as the little ones ogled over each warriors' napkins, keepsakes for when they grew up to become warriors.

Nute let out a loud belch and scratched his stomach. "My people know how to cook, do they not, King Conell?"

Conell nodded with exaggerated gusto. "Aye, they do, King Nute. A fabulous meal!"

Émēr swallowed his grimace. The meal was among the blandest he had ever tasted: boiled meat with soggy, overcooked vegetables. He forced the food down his throat and longed for Chara's flavorful meals. "I agree, it was a wonderful meal. We thank you for your generosity to my prince and to us."

Nute nodded. "You honor my people."

The elders also grunted their approval.

"I wish to see Anú's book," Nute said. He took a swig of his wine. The liquid dripped from his lips and down his chest.

When Émēr handed it to him, Nute opened the book and read the words out loud. The Elders grew quiet.

"I want you to look at this one," Émēr said as he flipped to the page.

Augustine and Dia

Augustine, the warrior, strong and brave,
Fought for his king and clan
And locked away the Darkness and his child.
Dia fought by his side
Power flowed through his arms,
And placed his enemies at the Attiyq's feet.
Both men fought
Back to back
Their ears closed to Darkness's ballad.
The enemy taunts
The swords slash
Against sinful words
Trapped forever Darkness remains.

Nute grunted and furrowed his brow. "It is an odd poem."

"I am drawn to it by many spirits."

He leaned forward. "Spirits?"

"Augustine." Émēr rubbed his forehead. "I have seen unnatural things in the castle. Ghosts but not ghosts, as if many are speaking to me."

"Anú speaks to you from the grave?"

Émēr rested against the back of his chair. "I am not sure if it is my God or the ghosts, but someone or something leads me to this poem. I have seen shadows and heard evil whispers in the castle. I feel we are not alone. Even now."

Amhras hovered over the Covenant Table and frowned. Father would not be pleased with this intrusion. He swallowed hard and wished the General was here but Argus had other plans for him. He glanced at the tall, narrow death-black creature who stood beside him. His lips stretched across his thin face and protruded up to his high, spiny ears. Long, jagged teeth lined his large mouth. His tongue flicked up to his forehead.

"Nephew, why have you brought the son of Anú to my realm?" the demon asked.

"Forgive me, Uncle Philas. It was not I who brought him here. Father will not be pleased."

"Neither am I." A sharp, claw-like fingernail brushed under Amhras' chin, making him shiver.

Amhras licked his cold lips. "Uncle, he has an angel who follows him."

Philas's hand gripped Amhras' throat and brought his face close to his. Amhras struggled against the death stench rising from Philas's throat. "Do not ever mention those cursed creatures to me! They stole my throne!"

Amhras tore at his uncle's grip. "Forgive me!"

"You should have stopped him!" He threw Amhras against the wall. "Your Father will bind you in his fire for such mistakes!"

Amhras struggled to regain his balance. "There is still time! You have control over your slave. He and his clan worship you! Surely there is something you can do!"

Philas's head slowly turned, and his red eyes pierced him, making him shrink against the wall. His three long steps covered the precious distance between them. He knelt before the younger demon and grabbed Amhras' chin. "He and the son of Anú bound themselves in a Covenant. I cannot touch him due to the Attiyq's power surrounding the son of Anú and the one bound to him." His hand slipped behind Amhras' neck and forced his face into the Light that surrounded the two men. A burning stench rose as the Attiyq's glory burned his soft flesh.

Amhras screamed, and Philas threw him against the wall. "Your father should have left you to die when he and I raised the Rebellion!"

Amhras cowered on the floor and pointed his finger. "Anú's book!"

Philas turned. Émēr revealed the dreaded book of the first Maúl. The beast who almost destroyed them all. He paced before the last Maúl. A bright light filled the room making Philas shield his eyes and Amhras hide his face.

Japik stepped behind Philas's servant, Nute, and whispered words in his ear. Her long white hair floated around her face, and her gown moved like waves around her body. Nute, the one who loved Philas and prayed to him, slowly opened the dreaded book. Philas roared as Nute read the poem aloud. The words swirled around the room like a mace. Amhras darted towards the ceiling and hovered above the humans. The utterances sizzled against Philas's black, molded skin. He screamed and tried to swat them away. But they grew hooks and dug into him. He pulled out his knife and cut them from his skin. Black blood dripped onto the floor. He narrowed his eyes and dove at Émēr.

Japik wrapped her long white wings around him.

Philas jerked to a stop. "Japik! The slave of a weak God. Have you come to experience more pain?"

She laughed. "I will not be the one who begs for mercy on His Judgement Day!"

Philas gritted his teeth and swung his large sword. She raised her blade and deflected his blow. He rose above her. "Come, Coward, and fight me here, if you dare!"

She tightened her wings around her charge.

He slashed at her exposed back, making her arch and wince.

"You are still weak, Angel, like your God. Fight me!" He dropped behind her and slashed at her knees. She kicked him away.

He circled around her. "Such loyalty to a foul creature. Come, join us, Japik, you will be worshiped as a god!"

She shook her head. "I serve one God."

His eyes fell on Conell. "You have lost, Japik!" He bore down on the young prince.

Japik gasped and shielded Conell with her sword. His blade cut into her arm. She screamed but kept her arm over Conell.

Áepoo plunged into the room and rammed Philas against the wall. The demon paced and glared at Áepoo who dared to stand between him and the humans.

Áepoo glanced over his shoulder. "Lady Japik, are you wounded?"

She shook her head. "I can continue."

He raised his sword to Philas. "This one is marked by the Attiyq. He is not yours!"

"His hatred for the Attiyq drives him. I can smell it on him. He is mine, you know this. Give him to me!"

"You are covered in filth and lies. The Attiyq rebuke you!"

Philas flew back and crumpled to the wall. "Amhras, get down here and help me!"

Amhras shook his head and dashed from the building.

Áepoo lifted his sword. "You should follow him."

Philas cursed him then hurried from the hut.

Japik huddled over Émēr and stretched her wing over Conell.

Áepoo placed his hand on her shoulder. "It is over, you have done well. Now, let us reveal Anú's secrets to our charges."

Brothers walk together even if the path leads to Death.

-Nute

27

"Not alone? Your words make no sense, my brother," Nute said.

Émēr shrugged. "I can only say what I have seen and heard. Argus's demons followed us to Brodén's Cave. I have seen visions of dead men and spirits in the castle. Never have I seen such things. And now this."

Nute thumbed through the book. "Where did you find this?"

"My sister found it in Anú's library."

He grunted. "A wise selection. A sister you say?" Nute studied the words, but gave Émēr a sideways look. "Perhaps your sister is looking for a good husband to keep her in her ways?"

Émēr and Conell exchanged amused glances.

"I appreciate your offer, King Nute, but she is betrothed to another in my village," Émēr said.

"Pity." Nute's finger followed the words in Anú's book. "It is interesting how Anú wrote such words. Why are they made in such a pattern?"

Émēr shrugged. "I thought it was a form of art, like a picture."

He shook his head. "I do not think so, my brother. The poem is not what it seems:

Augustine, the warrior, strong and brave, Dia fought by his side. Both men fought, the enemy taunts, fought for his king and clan. Power flowed through his arms, back-to-back, the swords slash and locked away Darkness and his child and placed his enemies at the Attiyq's feet. Their ears closed to Darkness' ballad against sinful words. Trapped forever darkness remains." Nute sat back and grinned like a boy who passed the test.

Émēr's mouth dropped open. "What? I never saw it!" He pulled the book from Nute and followed the words. "Anú was very wise! The first lines of each section are a poem, then the second lines, then the third lines. But why?"

Conell studied the sonnet. "Perhaps he was hiding it from someone or something?"

Émēr's eyebrows rose. "Like demon enemies?"

"Like Argus?" Conell asked. "Their ears closed to Darkness' ballad against sinful words. Trapped forever darkness remains."

Émēr nodded. "That explains Augustine and Dia's bodies outside the cell and why Imogene and I saw a vision of Argus. They put him in the cell. But how? Why?"

Nute cocked his head. "Others locked the demon away? That makes no sense!"

"Yes, I agree, it makes no sense. How did they lock him away and why? For how long? Augustine and Dia were killed by the beast centuries ago. If they died trying to keep Argus in the prison, then how will we get the beast in the cage. If we should put him in the cage."

The Kalk king opened his mouth as if he was about to speak but chose instead to drink more wine. "Too many questions."

"What do you know of him?" Conell asked. "Of Argus?"

"Argus? *Eger Aro*, Evil One, not much. He chased our people into the forest years ago during the time of Brodén, or that is what the elders say. Those stories are ones their mothers told them. Where he came from, only he can tell you. Mothers tell their little ones stories of a demon who eats the disobedient child's flesh. Elders speak of the demon, but in hushed tones. Fear runs through their veins." He stared at the dark liquid in his cup. "Sometimes I feel the fear in my dear wife. Her dreams haunt her. She tells me of shadows that moved around the castle when no one was there. Of voices that came from paintings."

Conell licked his lips. "Yes, a woman who was captured by Argus told me the same stories, that my father scolded her from his picture. She could not comprehend why he would do such a thing."

Nute nodded. "What else did she tell you?"

"That his eyes blazed like fire, that he kept touching her. I too have seen things. Red eyes that blaze in the demon's face. The air growing cold at his arrival. My own breath being ripped from my lungs. You said that he chased your people here during Brodén's time. Did Brodén fight him?"

He shrugged. "I told you they were stories told by mothers to their disobedient children. I do not have answers. Have you seen the trees in our forest? It is said that the demon cursed the trees to come to life and eat my people in the night. I have traveled those woods alone and none of the trees came to life. Yet, they twist around each other as if following me, and I wonder …"

Émēr pushed the cold boiled meat around his plate with his fork. "I have to go back to Anú's castle. There I will find answers among Anú's manuscripts. I have read some of them, and they speak of a demon. Also," he paused. "I saw Augustine's spirit, and he told me the answers are in this book. Nute, you are my brother now, but I cannot take you there. Your wife and little ones are now in danger because of me. You must take your clan and go into the mountains for safety."

Nute shook his head. "No. I will fight along with you. Your enemies are now my enemies. We will explore Anú's castle together. *Eger Aro's* eyes see past his walls, and he walks in unknown lands that do not belong to him, yet he lusts after them."

"What unknown lands?" Conell asked.

Nute lifted a shoulder. "You are like your father. You ask too many questions."

"Please, Nute."

"*Eger Aro* walks where others have not walked. He travels to lands that are foreign, more foreign than the lands of the South or North. He speaks to the dead and can summon others such as himself. He is the king of the *imdarvurrd.*"

Conell cocked his head.

"*Imdarvurrd.* The place of the dead."

Émēr and Conell exchanged glances. Ruárc quickly swallowed more wine.

"You did not know this about him?" Nute asked.

Émēr shook his head. "No, we only thought he was demon."

"He is a demon, but he is the ruler of all demons. You know of the New Maúl?"

"Yes," Émēr said. "I have encountered Argus's follower Māhōn."

"The old Maúl always warred against us yet had great honor. The new Maúl slaughter our women and children. I am pleased we have made this Covenant. Now my little ones are safe."

"And you will not harm mine."

"It is so. You believe we killed your family, do you not, Maúl?"

"I did, but Ruárc tells me it was the winged men."

Nute scoffed. "You are a foolish Maúl. Barbarians do not kill but take slaves and women for our mates. Do you think we would destroy so many that would bring us so much? Yet the new Maúl are dangerous to us. Māhōn is evil."

Émēr gave Nute a long look. "It seems that you and I have the same opinion. I too do not trust Māhōn. He is the demon's slave."

Nute nodded. "I have seen Māhōn's lust for the demon. The *Eger Aro* controls his flesh and his mind. The *Eger Aro* is the leader of the new Maúl and does not *hururad*, honor, the Kalk as did Anú and his followers."

Émēr chuckled. "I do not understand the *hururad* of the Kalk."

Nute grunted. "Anú understood *hururad* as did his followers, but it has died within you. To die in battle means one lives forever in his father's home created by the first of the clan. If you were to kill me, I would live in my father's home beyond the stars. We would feast together at his table and rejoice. Yet Māhōn takes that from us. He does not kill in battle but kills in secret. His men are not trained as Maúl but as slaves."

Émēr shrugged. "Forgive me, Nute, but my father did not teach me such things."

Nute pointed his dagger at him. "And that is what separates you from Anú. He understood a man's heart and what his hands grasped at the time of his death, but you do not. You think a man should walk the same path, but not all do. Anú understood this and gave great *hururad* to those who did not walk his paths. He ordered his men to give the same *hururad* to those whose feet took them along another trail. Yes, Anú did tell us of the Attiyq and how He saves His people, how He became the bridge to lead all to Him. Yes, we have heard these words, and some have followed Him. But even Anú gave homage to those who did not and grieved for them. Māhōn only kills those who do not follow his words. He is *prorekkaa.*" Nute sought for the right word. "He became the judge of others, but not judging himself."

Émēr slowly nodded. "If I were to kill you now within your home, with your nursing child and his mother outside, that would be dishonorable in the sight of your god. What would happen to you?"

"It would not be *hururad* and my clan and my father who now waits for me would turn their faces from me. I do not wish to lose their love for me."

Émēr gave his new brother a smile. "Then I too wish to walk in Anú's footsteps. I give my *hururad* along with the Covenant that I will not harm you or your little ones, but I pray you die in battle. A glorious death."

The Barbarian gave him a smile. "Now you sound as Anú."

"Nute, I am the last of the Maúl. An angel of the Attiyq showed me *Eger Aro's* kingdom last night. It is a place of foulness and death. The roads are paved with broken stones and whitewashed tombs. Demons race across the roads, and fire burns constantly in the background. I am to fight this demon, but I need your help. I believe the Attiyq brought us here together for this purpose. Will you help me find a way into Anú's castle?"

Nute looked away from Émēr for a time but when he returned his gaze, it was with resolve. "You and I are now of the same blood. Your enemies are my enemies. Yes, I will help you. My wife and children will go into the mountains with my tribe."

"I will need to first see to my family," Émēr said. "Then I will return here, and we will make our way to Anú's castle."

Conell nodded. "I have a seer who will be traveling with us. She hears from the Attiyq and can help guide us. We will meet you here tomorrow morning. Is that agreeable?"

Nute gave Conell a long, stern glare. "You wish to bring a female on our quest? She will curse us. No, she will not come.'

"Forgive me, Nute. I too do not wish for her to join us," Émēr said. "She is my sister, and I fear for her life. But as My Mojí has said, she is a seer and will help lead us. I ask that you allow her to come with us. I will keep her far from you."

Nute scowled. "I cannot and will not ensure her safety. If she dies by the demon's hand, then I will not weep for her nor raise my hand to help her."

"Agreed," Émēr said. "We will meet you tomorrow morning."

Émēr breathed a sigh of relief when Ruárc's home came into view. His children raced down the path and jumped into Ruárc's arms. They squealed with delight as he scooped them up, two of them draped over his shoulders, the other two dangling from his arms.

His eyes caught Émēr.

"You will see them again," Émēr said, giving him a reassuring pat on the shoulder before the children tugged their father into the small encampment.

Ūmá's smile made the darkness flee as she jogged down the path and into Émēr's arms. She looked up at him and grinned. "Hi. I missed you."

He laughed. "As I missed you."

Imogene made her way down the path, her mischievous grin firmly in place. "Behold! The soldiers come back from the big meeting. How did it go?"

"The Barbarians, or Kalk as they call themselves, are now our allies," Conell said.

"Is that good or bad?" she asked as she walked beside him.

"I think it will be good. The leader's wife was a prisoner of Argus."

"Oh boy," she said. "More to join the Argusa club."

He grunted. "I have asked that you come with us. We will need to return to the cave for Émēr to search through the documents. I need your seer's gifts."

She nodded. "Okay."

He raised his eyebrows. "Simply okay?"

She shrugged. "I'm getting really good at being a Ghost Buster. I ain't afraid of no ghosts!" She laughed at what she evidently meant as a joke.

Conell looked back at Émēr who raised his hands in surrender. Fortunately, Imogene never seemed to get upset when they did not get her jokes. Rather, she had come to expect their confusion and usually explained herself before they even asked.

"Well, that is good. I am glad for your confidence as a…ghost buster," Conell said. "But you will need to follow the rules of the Kalk, which means Nute will not speak to you unless he must. And…" Conell gulped, narrowing his eyes at Émēr's smirk. "You will need to walk behind us."

"Excuse me?" She stopped and rammed her fists onto her hips. "What kind of rules are these?"

"I understand, my sister," Émēr intervened, taking pity on Conell. "But please, do this for us. I must keep Nute alive. He insists upon coming with us. I tried to persuade him to go into the mountains with his clan, but he refused."

"Fine, whatever! I'll take yet another hit for the team!"

Émēr kept his eyes on the path and sought for words. Now it was his turn to tell his woman things she would not want to hear. "My bride, you carry our son within you. I must keep you safe. Please go with Ruárc's clan who will meet with the Kalk. They will keep you safe. I must know you are far from the demon's reach."

She let out a deep sigh that almost came out as a huff. "As Imogene has said, I too will take a hit for the team."

He kissed her hand and laughed. "Now you are sounding like her."

Evening came quickly as Chara packed her children's belongings and loaded them into a cart. Ruárc stayed close to her and fussed over the bindings, then checked the harness on the ox again.

"You have tightened those a dozen times," Chara said, leaning against the ox.

"I will tighten them again if I must. I do not wish to leave your side."

She slipped her arms around his waist and laid her head on his chest. "I love you despite drinking Barbarian wine. I am glad that you came back to me instead of those women."

He raised his eyebrows. "You know?"

"I know. And I love you anyway."

He cradled her head against him. "I am sorry. I was wrong to do so many things. I have made bad decisions that have hurt so many people. Decisions that have killed my brother and put you in danger. I am so sorry."

Her smiling cheeks pressed against him. "I know. You always come home to me."

He held her face in his hands. "You are the only one for me. No more will I pursues others; I will only pursue you." He kissed her.

"If you break your promise, I might have to beat you," Chara said with a grin and kissed is nose.

He laughed. "Like you did before?"

"Yes, like I did before I married you."

His smile lingered a moment before he pointed to the path. "Stay on this path, and follow it up into the mountains. The Kalk will meet you there. They are expecting you."

She clung to his fingers. "We will look for them and stay on the path. I said a prayer to Oozeka and to the Attiyq. One of them will listen, yes?"

"Yes."

He helped her into the cart and handed her the reins. The children climbed up, afflicting their father with their sorrowful eyes.

Laoise straightened Émēr's shirt and brushed invisible dust from his shoulders. She fussed with his hair. Her eyes still saw a small boy looking up at him, not the leader of the Maúl. He grinned. "Mother, I am head and elder of this clan."

She blinked back her tears. "You are my son, my baby boy, and you always will be. Please be careful."

He kissed the top of her head. "I always am."

Aine laid her head on his shoulder. "Look after them, my brother. I love my sister very much."

"I will take care of her." He kissed her hair, then helped the two women into the cart.

Ūmá lingered by his side.

He stroked her cheek and wrapped his fingers in her hair. "I remember when I first saw you in the slave camp. You were beautiful."

She wrapped her arms around his neck. "And I remember when I saw you outside the castle. I knew one day you would save me. And you did. Please return to me. To us."

He pressed his forehead to her brow. "Yes, always." He kissed her, then helped her into the cart.

Erák and Frigg climbed up beside Ūmá. Erák laid his sword over his lap. "I give you my word, Cousin, I will protect your clan. If you die, I will take Ūmá as my wife and protect your sister and mother."

Émēr held back his tears. "I know you will. Attiyq's blessings on you, my cousin."

Chara slapped the reins, and the ox lurched forward, slowly tugging the cart down the lonely road. Ūmá's sapphire eyes remained locked with her husband's until the cart turned the corner.

Émēr took a deep breath and steadied his nerves as his Maúl ears strained to hear the distant squeaking of the wheels until that too faded.

Conell placed his hand on his captain's shoulder. "Frigg and Erák will guard the women. They will be fine."

"I know. What are your plans, My Mojí? It will take a day to reach Nute's village."

"Um, I don't think it will take us a day," Imogene said. "Is that him on the path?"

Both men turned to see Nute standing on the trail that led to the village. He stood tall and held his spear upright in his hand. His naked chest was covered with blue war paint as was his face. His dark hair was molded upright. His only clothes were a loin cloth made of animal skin.

Imogene glanced at Conell. "I know, keep quiet. And I'm okay with it."

Conell, Émēr, and Ruárc made their way down the path. True to her word, Imogene followed behind. Without a word.

Nute held up his hand. "Stop, brother. We cannot go to war just yet." He knelt on the ground and opened a small case. He took out a carved stick and dipped it into blue paint. "I had said you had the markings of a child. But you have proven you have the heart of a man. Give me honor, my brother."

Émēr bowed. "You bring great honor to my clan. Yes, please." He knelt before Nute.

"Um, is that sanitized?" Imogene asked, cranking her head to see over Conell's shoulder.

The four men stared at her.

She rolled her eyes and lifted her hands. "Oh, I forgot, I'm taking one for the team. Well, if you get an infection on that pretty face of yours, then it's your problem, not mine. And yes, I am being quiet."

Nute slowly turned his head to Conell. "She sounds like my seer. Disobedient, strong willed, and one who often rebels."

"You have spoken true words," Conell said. "Please proceed."

Imogene clicked her tongue. "Whatever," she whispered.

Nute carefully carved swirls and vines of the blue ink into the right side of Émēr's face. Émēr forced his muscles to be still as the needle dug into his skin.

"I will leave the other side for your warriors to finish." He stood back and admired his work.

Imogene leaned over him and inspected the swirls. "That is awesome. You did a great job, Nute. I had a friend who made tattoos, and yours look as good as his did. Now if I remember correctly, you'll have to keep the tattoos washed at least twice a day to prevent infection."

Nute stared at her. "Infection?"

"Come," Conell said, pulling Imogene away, "We must be on our way."

Nute nodded, then proceeded down the path. "We must leave now if we are to reach the castle of Anú. It will take us a season to reach it."

Conell's eyes met Émēr's. "We can trust him, Mojí," Émēr said. "Nute, it will not take a season. We have special transportation from my God."

Nute's eyebrows rose. "Transportation?"

"Áepoo!" Conell shouted.

Sometimes the harder path
is the correct path.

-Anu

28

A gust of wind blew the branches of the trees, and the dust swirled around them. The four-winged beasts appeared before the small group. Oota had once again joined them. Émēr swallowed the lump in his throat. Imogene gently approached the Bull and stroked his muzzle. "How's my friend, Cian? Have you seen him?" Oota licked her hand and she laid her face on his head. "I guess that means he is well."

Áepoo stomped his feet. "You have summoned me, Prince Conell?"

Nute stepped back, and his mouth dropped open. Then he fell on his knees and worshipped the beasts.

Áepoo reared back on his back legs. "Do not insult me by worshiping me. I am not to be praised! Only the great Attiyq is to be honored. Rise, foolish human!"

Nute stumbled to his feet and stared at the angel. "You are of the Attiyq?"

"I am a servant of the Great One! I am in and out of His Presence daily."

Imogene walked past Nute with her nose in the air. "Not bad, huh? Hi Áepoo, it's good to see you *again*."

The angel bowed his head. "As it is to see you again, Lady Imogene."

She looked back at Nute, gave a "hmph," and climbed on Áepoo's back.

Émēr rolled his eyes as he mounted. "Humility brings happiness, My Lady."

Conell laughed and climbed behind her. "Do not show your face to the thief, My Lady, or he will steal it from you."

"What does that mean?" she asked.

"Do not be arrogant, but let humility clothe you as a gown," Émēr said as he settled onto Etta and patted the lion's neck. "I have missed you, my friend."

"Which one should I take?" Ruárc asked. He stepped gingerly to Oota, the bull, who turned his large head towards Ruárc. He lifted his hands and stepped back. "I mean you no harm."

Áepoo spoke to Oota in his language and the bull snorted and ambled to Ruárc. "As I said, I mean you no harm." He gingerly moved Oota's large horns away from him and jumped onto his back. The bull looked at him as if to see if he was settled then snorted.

Nute's gaze jumped from the animals to the men. "Am I to ride the Eagle beast?"

"His name is Asechi," Imogene said. "As-she."

Nute swung onto the back of the eagle-horse. Asechi squawked and shook his head. Nute grabbed the feathers and leaned forward. "What will they do now?"

"Hold on tight!" Imogene said.

The animals galloped, spread their wings, and rose into the sky.

Nute lay on Asechi's neck and wrapped his arms around the beast's neck, gritting his teeth and keeping his eyes tightly shut.

Imogene giggled.

"Do not let him see you laugh, *Chuōhá*, or you will insult him. He deserves honor," Conell said.

She muffled her laugh. "Of course, I'm sorry."

The angels soared over the forests and green pastures of Ézású. Nute opened his eyes and marveled at the beauty below him. "Never have I seen such lands! Our lands are barren, but this is lush and green!"

"You are my brother, now," Émēr said. "I will help your people explore my lands."

The great mountains of the Southern lands sprang up before them. Nute led them to the north side of Brodén's Cave, where they landed.

"My village spies have watched this cave for centuries. There is another passage through which we may enter," Nute said. "But that was before I was born. The entrance may no longer exist."

The small group made their way through the forest to a small grove. Nute walked around the perimeter and peeked into the bushes.

"My brother," Émēr said. "What is it that you seek?"

"My elders said to find the place of ghosts where no trees grow. It is said such places are cursed. There you will find the door to Anú's home."

Imogene glanced around the trees. "What does it look like?"

Nute glanced at her. "For a female, you speak freely."

She suppressed a giggle. "Yeah, they let me do that sometimes."

He chuckled. "You are like my seer. We are looking for a patch of land that has no trees." He explored a moment more before he pointed toward a clearing. "I think this might be it." He walked around the clearing and found a hole dug in the ground. The opening had collapsed years ago. His face fell. "It is caved in. We cannot go in this way."

"What of the glass windows? Perhaps we could crawl through one of them?" Émēr asked.

They picked their way around the back side of the cave to the rocks piled in the ravine. Émēr motioned the others back while he and Nute scurried around to the front of the cave.

Émēr parted the branches of a bush and pointed. "Look, my brother, there is a winged demon guarding the entrance."

A chill sat in the air like a dead man's touch and chased away the sun's warmth. A six-foot being stood before the cave entrance. His skeleton face was framed by long, greasy burnt-orange hair. His thin leather wings spread out from his shoulders, and horns grew out of his forearms. His boney hands held a flaming sword. A tall, formless shadow stood beside him.

A hand reached out from the shaded blob and stroked the demon's face. A smile spread across his decaying lips showing rows of fangs. He nodded. The blob hovered around him as if in a ghostly dance.

Émēr pulled Nute away and returned to the others. "A demon guards the entrance to the castle. I do not know if they have entered. I think Nute and I should go in first. You two can follow us. I do not think any of us are safe outside."

Nute nodded, his face ashen. "I do not know what I saw."

"Death has come to Anú's castle," Émēr said, wiping the sweat from his brow. "Mojí, I have never seen such a horror."

"Oh boy," Imogene said. "Back to Creepy Cave."

"Oh Oozeka, protect me!" Ruárc said.

"Come, my brother," Émēr said. "We have the strength of my God behind us."

He helped Imogene over the stones and boulders as Nute, Ruárc, and Conell picked their way to the windows. They quietly rolled the large stones away, revealing a broken stained-glass window. Long, withered stalks of dried flowers hung from the window frames. Émēr tore down a handful. "I know this weed," he whispered. "It is called Angel's Wings. They once believed it could ward off evil. The Maúl covered the windows with the weeds, then piled the boulders." He lowered his head. "After Argus killed Augustine and Dia, the Maúl must have tried to trap him in the castle with Angel's Wings."

"I do not think it worked," Nute said. He yanked the weeds, slipped between the shards of glass, and dropped down onto the floor.

Émēr helped Imogene into the room, then assisted Conell and Ruárc. Except for the light streaming in from the broken window, darkness devoured the chamber. It was no longer a place of awe and respect. It was now a place where evil reigned.

"I fear Argus is in the castle," Émēr whispered to Conell.

Imogene rubbed her arms. "It seems colder in here."

"We need to find our way to the records room and gather all we can," Émēr said. He held back his hand and made his way to the door. He waved the others over. "No one is in the hallway. We will take all the scrolls and then leave quickly."

Imogene pointed to the alcove off the side of the throne room. "Nute, that's where the cage is at, down the stairs. It's super creepy."

"I need to see it, Brother," Nute said as he crept towards the dark alcove.

Émēr lit a torch and followed him. "We must hurry. I do not want to be trapped in this castle."

He led the way down the spiral staircase to the cage. The small group stopped at the bottom of the stairwell. The enclosure's door had been ripped from its hinges and now lay on the floor. "Argus was somehow captured and put in the cage." He turned and herded the others up the stairs. His heart pounded and fog suffocated his brain. *Get out! Get out!* "We must not linger."

He peeked into the hallway that led to the stairwell.

"How will we find our way down there?" Imogene asked. "It's pitch black."

"We go slow," Émēr whispered. He forced his feet to take one step at a time. Nute's hot breath tingled his back. He glanced over his shoulder. Ruárc's eyes were wide with fear. His Mojí took the rear. Émēr lit another torch and handed it to him. "Use this, My Mojí."

The group slowly found their way to the side stairwell that led to the upper floor. The smell of smoke slammed into Émēr's nose. His heart plunged. "The scrolls!" He raced to the library. All Anú's scrolls lay in a burnt pile on the floor. He dropped to his knees and tried to salvage some of the sacred words. A few scrolls survived. He shoved them into his shirt. Nute pulled others off the shelves and put them in a bag.

"We must get to the weapons, My Mojí," Émēr said.

Nute nodded to the door. "You go, your prince, Ruárc, and I will salvage the scrolls. Meet us here."

Émēr rushed to the armory. "We must leave quickly!"

Imogene hurried after him and pulled the swords off the wall. "Do you think Argus is still here?"

"I do not know. I only know that we must leave now."

"Ah, but you just arrived, my brother."

Émēr dropped the bundle of weapons in his arms and drew his sword. Imogene squealed and dropped a shield. It hit the ground with a large clatter. He placed himself between Māhōn and her.

Māhōn leaned against the doorway. "I have missed our talks, brother."

"Māhōn," Émēr said, "please, come with us. I can keep you safe from Argus."

Māhōn's eyes grew wide. "Safe? Safe from my master? Great Maúl leader, Émēr. So much you do not know." He pushed himself from the doorframe and paced in front of him. "You are so mistaken about the Maúl. You seem so high and mighty with your 'heritage'. My father had heritage also, and your father betrayed him!"

Émēr stepped back. "My father never had a chance to betray anyone!"

"Oh, you are so wrong." Māhōn's face turned red. "My father was a great man among the Maúl until Amgets betrayed him. My father had questions about the Attiyq, and he came to the elders to ask their advice. Instead of teaching him, your father encouraged the tribe to turn from him and exclude him from the clan." He balled his fists. "They threw my father from the Circle of Elders for having simple questions. He, my mother, and I were cast aside. My father had to take a job as a stable hand, spending his days shoveling horse manure! He grew angry and bitter. My mother left us and returned to her father. I was alone with him." Māhōn let out a deep breath. "He began to lose his mind. I begged the Tribe to help us. I told them what had happened to him, and your father…" He pointed at Émēr. "Turned away from my father, saying he betrayed the Attiyq, for simply asking questions! My father taught me what he could of the Maúl. He made the scrolls that you studied. You put your filthy hands on my father's scrolls."

Émēr blinked several times as the cruel words beat against his skull. No, his father was a good man! "I am sorry for the destruction of your family."

Māhōn stared at him. "You are sorry?"

"This is not what I wanted; I am sorry for the sins of my father. He never told me such a thing."

"There was a lot your father never told you, Émēr! Argus took me in years ago after my father died. He gave me a home, a place, and honor. While you gave me nothing. You let me rot."

"I did not let you rot; I was in prison with my Prince."

"Argus gave me a name, what did you give me?"

"I do not know what my father did to you, but I apologize for it. Argus does not have your best interests at heart."

"Oh, and you know this how? Your *God* told you? Your pretend person who lives in the sky?" Māhōn's face twisted. Darkness covered his face, and rage sat in his murky eyes.

Émēr shivered. Argus had that same look. "What do you want?"

He pointed to Imogene. "Her. Give me her, and all will be forgiven."

Imogene whimpered.

Émēr raised his sword. "No, she is not for sale."

"You have no choice."

"My God has given me the choice, Māhōn. This is between you and me. Let the others go."

Māhōn laughed. "Your God is an insect compared to my Argus. Give me the woman and the medallion."

Émēr opened his mouth, only to shut it quickly. *Māhōn must not find out the medallion has no powers!* "No. If you want the medallion, then it is yours. But the girl stays with me. She is now my sister, and she is under my protection."

"You know that only a seer can use the medallion. It is worthless to us without her."

Nute peeked into the room, then ducked back into the hallway. He crept behind Māhōn and quickly placed his knife against Māhōn's throat. "You will do as my brother says."

Conell snatched the sword out of Māhōn's hand. "Tie him up. We take what we can."

Ruárc eyed the weapons as he held Māhōn to the wall.

Māhōn laughed. "My master is here; you will not leave this place alive."

"I am sure we will be fine," Émēr said.

He tossed Conell a rope who tied Māhōn's feet and hands.

"This is not over!" Māhōn tugged at his ropes. "My Master will destroy you. You saw the cage in the dungeon. He will not be caged again, nor will you and your pathetic God stop him. He will take over this world and the worlds beyond. Your head will be mounted—"

Émēr stuffed the gag in his mouth. "We must make our way back to the throne room. It is our only way out." He tugged Imogene from the room as the others followed them.

The sound of stomping feet came from the entrance of the cave. Émēr leaned over the balcony and saw the demons making their way into the castle. "They have found us!"

Leather-winged men stood at the bottom of the staircase. Red eyes glowed in the darkness. Émēr shoved the others back. Imogene screamed. Nute lifted his bow. Émēr pulled him away from the stairwell.

"We can't get out!" Imogene stumbled back.

Ruárc stood in front of her and held his sword in his trembling hands.

"Áepoo!" came Conell's strong voice.

Áepoo appeared as a man above the staircase. His long black hair flowed behind him as if he stood in water. His large white wings beat the air. A deep blue breastplate covered his chest. Metal boots covered his feet, and he held a long double-edged sword. He was no longer a beast, but an angel of the Most High.

The demons sneered at him. Áepoo laughed.

General Bode stepped between the hissing creatures. "We meet again, Defeated One."

Áepoo glared at him. "These beings are under God's protection. You cannot hurt them."

Bode laughed as his red eyes locked on Émēr. "The Maúl has given us permission to be here. Hate is deep in his heart. It fuels us, gives us the strength we need to overcome him." He laughed. "Do not think this will end here! My Master is smarter and faster than all of you. Even now, he is taking over Ézású and the lands beyond. You will die, Áepoo. You should have joined us."

Áepoo's eyes narrowed.

Émēr swallowed. A nudge inside of him told him the demon spoke truth. He lowered his head. "He is right. I have given them permission to enter Anú's castle." He placed his raised hands together and bowed to Conell. "I forgive you, My Mojí. I forgive those who harmed my family. I forgive!" Émēr lifted his head and stepped down the stairs. Nute tried to pull him back, but Émēr brushed away his hand. He pointed at the demons. "Leave my house now! You are no longer invited!"

An invisible hand grabbed Bode by his waist and yank him back. His feet and arms rose in the air. He screamed and tried to break free, but the force rammed him through the wall and he disappeared. The demons stared at the empty spot, then turned to Émēr. They shrieked and scattered into the walls and floor.

Émēr breathed deeply as he stared at the dark room. "What just happened?"

Áepoo smiled. "The Attiyq has given His authority to those who follow Him, to those who will take it. Today, you have taken it. Use this force that the Great One has given you. Now you are the Priest." He disappeared.

You do not have because
you forget to ask.
-Anú

29

Émēr sat on the stairs and rubbed his face. *Ūmá! I need you!*

Imogene sat beside him and rubbed his back. “Are you okay?”

He clasped his hands. “I am not sure what happened. Something strong and holy rose up within me, then the pain and the anger fell away. It left. When I forgave, it left. The words just came out. I am not sure what to do now.”

“Well,” she said. “I think leaving this place should be first on the list. Māhōn is still back there, and Argus won’t be happy that his boys are gone. It’s not safe here.”

Ruárc sat beside him. “What did you do?”

He shrugged. “I only said what the Attiyq told me to say.”

Ruárc leaned his elbows on his knees and gripped his hands. "I have prayed to Oozeka for years, and he has never done anything for me. Your God is powerful. It is much to think of."

Émēr nodded and rose.

Worry covered Conell's firm face. "Can you go on?"

"Yes. We have all the surviving scrolls. I still need to examine them. But not here."

Nute laid his hand on Émēr's shoulder. "Come to my village, my brother. Your wife will be there."

He loosed a sigh of relief. "Ūmá. It will be nice to see her again. She can help me with the scrolls."

Once outside, Conell called for Áepoo, who appeared as a man-horse along with his companions. They flew the small band to Nute's village. Émēr grinned as he saw Frigg, Erák, and Chara in the middle of the village waving at them. Ūmá's small figure stood out from them. She shielded her eyes and lifted her hand to him. He waved back.

The beasts landed and Émēr jumped from Etta and into her arms. "Oh Ūmá, it was frightening but amazing. We have scrolls that we must examine."

"Let me get you something to eat first." She led him to their tent and placed a plate of bland food before him. "It is not as good as Chara's meals, but it will nourish you."

He quickly gobbled it down, then met Nute and the others in the community hut. Nute cleared the tables and Ruárc and Conell laid out the scrolls. Émēr frowned. Out of almost fifty scrolls, only thirty remained.

Émēr selected one and unrolled it. "Please, Great One, lead me!"

The first scroll told of Maúl fighting techniques which were new to him. His fingers moved across the stiff yellow paper. "My wife, we will keep this one for us. Once we are done, we will need to return to Maúl lands to teach the others."

She grinned at him and kissed his cheek. "It is my honor."

He quickly scanned the other scrolls. He placed the historical documents in one pile, the Maúl training scrolls into another, and the religious teachings into a third. "Well, that is all, Ūmá." He tapped the three sections. "Māhōn must have looked at each one and destroyed anything that spoke of Argus." He rubbed his forehead. "I was a fool to bring him with us."

Ūmá kissed his hand. "You were being kind and loyal. Those are good traits. What is done is done. God will lead us."

Nute led a woman with long gray hair and wrinkled face to the table. Her long brown dress hung loosely on her thin frame.

She touched the markings on Émēr's face. "I am called Fashta, the Seer, and I heard the Maúl and the Kalk became one tribe. Anú's child and Niko's child have merged the two tribes into one. Those that fought now eat at the same table. Those who hated, now respect. Peace now reigns." She made a sign and bowed.

Émēr bowed his head to her.

She opened a scroll and examined it. "Anú was wise. He tried to preserve that which belonged to his tribe. I hear you have lost many scrolls."

Émēr nodded. "Yes, Māhōn burned the ones that spoke of Argus. He also destroyed the cage that held him."

Imogene sat down beside them. "I'm apparently a seer too, so welcome to our little club, Fashta. Émēr, what did that demon mean when he said Argus is taking over other worlds?"

Fashta turned to Nute. "Did he say such a thing?"

He nodded. "Yes, he did. He will take over this world and the world beyond. But what is beyond this world?"

She shrugged. "That veil is closed to me, My Lord." She opened a leather book and laid it before Émēr. "This belonged to my ancestors. It does not go back to Anú, but it does go back several generations." She pointed to a page. "My great-great grandmother had a vision of the Evil One attacking a land in which the people spoke the Queen's word and wore strange clothes. They lived in towers in the clouds. She saw the Evil One destroying that world and Ézású. She feared for her children, so she wrote down her visions."

Émēr looked over the strange writings. "I cannot read this. Can you read this for me?"

"It is an ancient language." Fashta said. "But I have translated most of it." She turned the pages. "Ah, here it is. My great-great grandmother wrote:

> Many times, my ancestors have visited my sleep. Many times, they stood by my side and wept for the loss of the Kalk. I have tried to hear their words. Sometimes they come to me in the day; other times as I am tending to my children. But today, my ancestor sat beside me and told me of the Evil One. The One the hated Maúl was to guard. But they failed. They were weak and as children. They fled from the Evil One. The One their God gave to them to guard. And yet, their hands dripped with blood of innocence."

Émēr glanced at Ūmá, and she patted his hand.

> "The once wise became foolish and they left their prisoner behind. Foolish warriors! Ones who retained no honor."

Fashta turned her light green eyes to Émēr. "Forgive my grandmother. She was filled with hate for your people."

Émēr gave her a sad smile. "All is forgiven." Then he continued.

> "It is said the Evil One wishes to find other lands to conquer. He once roamed this land as a guardian watches over his children. But the Evil One became greedy. He longed for the riches under the ground and for slaves to worship him. The Attiyq gave The Evil One to His servants to guard. But they failed. The Evil One's eyes looked to lands unknown to me. My ancestor said The Evil One's heart was full of hate and lust. He longed for Towers in the Clouds. For people unknown to us. I fear for my life. I fear for my children. He walks between the realms of worlds."

"What is meant by Towers in the Clouds and realms of worlds?" Imogene asked.

Fashta shrugged.

Imogene bit her thumbnail. "Argus often said things like using the medallion to find my mother. You don't think he meant *my* world, do you?"

Fashta studied Imogene, then glided her fingertips over Imogene's check. "You are not from here are you, child?"

Imogene caught Conell's eyes.

He placed his hand on her head for a moment then took the lead. He pulled the medallion from around his neck. "Imogene claims this necklace brought her to our world. I believe she comes from the land of Towers in the Clouds."

Fashta studied the medallion. "Yes, this is of the Maúl. Anú's writings. I too heard it had powers."

Conell let out a deep sigh. "I do not want to keep this from you, *Chuōhá*. Émēr found a scroll that said the medallion has no powers. It is just a sign of the seer."

Imogene's face fell. "Are you serious? Nothing at all? We've been on this crazy Hot Topic ride for how long? Months? Looking for something that doesn't exist? No!" She stood and rubbed her temples. "He tried to rape me, imprison me, and he beat me up for a toy? How did I get here if this thing didn't bring me here? I can't do this!"

Conell reached for her, but she slapped his hand away.

"Don't touch me!" She stormed out the door.

Émēr groaned and rose from his seat.

Ūmá pushed him back. "She is my sister. You stay and study the scrolls. I will help her." She squeezed his shoulder as she followed Imogene out of the hut.

Conell caught Émēr's gaze. "What did I do wrong?"

Fashta shook her head. "You did nothing wrong. The child is lost, alone, and frightened. You told the truth, and the truth frightens her."

"But I told her I would not allow anyone to harm her," Conell said. "What more can I do?"

"Tell her. Show her." Fashta winked.

"How?" Conell asked.

She nodded to Nute. "My King Nute found a beautiful slave woman. She was frightened, lonely, and in danger. My King rescued her and now keeps her safe from harm. The child needs to feel safe."

Émēr met Conell's gaze. "Walk carefully, My Mojí."

"Prince Conell, you said the medallion has no powers?" Fashta asked.

Conell nodded. "Yes, Émēr discovered it in one of the scrolls. It was meant only to be a sign of the seer."

Fashta cocked her head. "Is that so? Many rumors surrounded it. Legends were made claiming the medallion had powers greater than the gods. Whomever owned it could rule the worlds."

Émēr shrugged. "According to Anú, it was simply a gift to the seers."

"Have you tried its powers?" Fashta asked.

"Well, no. We would have no idea how it works. But the girl claims it brought her to our world. She is from distant lands. I agree with my prince that she is from the Towers in the Clouds," Émēr said. "But as she said, if it did not bring her, then how did she come here?"

"Tell me more," Fashta said.

"When Ruárc brought her to our cell in the Ézású prison, she said the medallion grabbed her and pulled her into our world. What if it does have powers that no one understands?"

Ūmá led Imogene back into the room and poured her a cup of water.

"I promise, my sister," Ūmá said, "these things will not come upon you."

She nodded and sipped the liquid. "I know, but still."

Conell leaned over the table and lowered her cup. "Imogene, I have kept you safe all these months. I have guarded you and rescued you from Argus. I will not stop now. I made you a vow, and I will keep it."

She gave him a soft smile. "Okay. But how did I get here?"

Fashta studied her. "What do you remember?"

Imogene wrapped her hands around the cup. "I remember finding it, and I reached for it, then the chain wrapped around my hand. I fell into like a pit and then I landed here. And well, the rest is history."

Fashta pulled three sticks from her pocket. "We will ask my ancestors for the answers."

An uneasy feeling came over Émēr as if danger lay ahead of his trail. He laid his hand over the sticks. "Please allow me. My God will give me the answers."

She raised an eyebrow and frowned but stepped back. "I have heard of the great Attiyq but have never seen His works. Perform for me."

Émēr let out a deep breath. *Attiyq, please help me! I am turning to You for answers. Lead me, please. Do not fail me.*

He stilled his mind and focused on the words of the Great One. A single word soared into his mind. *Áepoo.*

Émēr glanced at his Moji with a serious nod. "Áepoo brought Imogene here."

With a surprised humph, Conell rose from his chair. "I would be interested in what he has to say." He abruptly exited the hall with the others following him. Once outdoors, he said in a low voice, "Áepoo, please, we must talk."

The angel appeared before him as a man with large wings that sparkled like sunlight. His long black hair flowed behind him as if touched by the wind. His pure white skin shone like glistening snow in the morning. "Yes, King Conell, what is your bidding?"

Conell smiled. "I am not King yet."

"In the eyes of my God, yes, you are."

"Émēr said that you brought Imogene to our world. Yet all she remembers is the chain wrapping around her wrist and pulling her down."

Áepoo grinned. "Yes, it was I. I brought the girl here."

Fashta crouched before Áepoo. "The great one! Tell me what offering I must bring to you!"

Áepoo's smile turned to frown. "I am not to be worshipped! I am a servant of the Most High. Rise, do not insult me!" He crossed his arms over his chest and looked away. "Humans!"

She climbed to her feet and studied him. "I am confused. May I touch your wings?"

He gave an exasperated sigh. "If you must." He extended a wing to her. "Why do humans insist on touching my wings?"

Her fingers brushed the soft feathers. "You are like the birds of the air!"

"No, I am not like birds of the air. I am a servant. I go in and out of the Presence of the Ancient of Days. I do His bidding; I live in His anointing."

Conell nudged Fashta away. "Áepoo, please tell me what happened."

"The Most High asked that I bring her here. The medallion has waited for her for hundreds of years. My fellow angels have guarded it until now. She picked it up, and I brought her here."

"Well, that explains that," Imogene said. "Why didn't you just tell me before?"

Áepoo blinked his bright blue eyes. "Because you never asked. You have nothing because you ask for nothing. Seek your answers, and you will find them."

She opened her mouth, then closed it. "But why? Why me?"

"I do not know. The Attiyq chose you. You are the seer."

Imogene sighed. "No, I'm not a seer. Who says I'm a seer?"

He cocked his head and his forehead wrinkled.

"I know, I know." She pointed up. "He did."

He smiled and nodded.

She pulled the medallion that lay around Conell's neck. He stumbled after her.

"This medallion, does it have powers?" she asked.

Áepoo shrugged. "I do not know."

"How could you not know?"

"The Attiyq has all the answers, not I."

She let out a deep sigh. "Are you saying it does or does not have powers?"

"I am saying I do not know if it has powers."

Conell unwrapped her fingers from the necklace. "Argus thinks it has powers and that is dangerous to us all. I do not believe it has powers. If he should find out it is just a trinket, then there is no reason to keep Imogene alive." He glanced at her. "You will die here."

Her face turned white. She lifted her arm, showing Argus's wooden bracelet. "I still belong to him. I can't escape him."

Áepoo gave her a confused look and touched the bracelet. It fell from her arm. "You never belonged to him. You now belong to the Attiyq. Your faith has made it so."

Her mouth dropped open, and she rubbed her wrist. "It's that easy?"

"Áepoo," Émēr said. "Legend has it that there are weapons to defeat Argus. What are they?"

Áepoo gave him a quizzical look. "What do you mean *what* are they? Perhaps you should say, *who* are they?" He presented his hand in front of them. "The King, the Priest and the Seer who use the Attiyq's great powers. Those are the weapons you seek."

Imogene pointed to herself, Conell, and Émēr. "You mean, us?"

With a smile coupled with a regal tip of his chin, the angel disappeared.

To protect the sick, innocent, and defenseless even if it is your enemy.

-The Maúl Creed.

30

Argus grabbed Bode around his throat and slammed him against the wall. His red narrow eyes bore into the general.

Bode squirmed. "Please, My Lord! I could not stop them!"

"You mean you did not try."

Bode shook his head. "No, My Lord, the Maúl has found his voice. We cannot stop him!"

The winged guards threw Māhōn at Argus's feet. Māhōn scooted to the wall and brought his knees to his chest. "Lord Argus, forgive me."

Argus kept Bode locked in his strong grip. "You are my strongest general, and yet you allowed the Maúl to cast you through a wall."

"It was not the Maúl, but the Attiyq!" Bode pointed to Māhōn. "Your human disciple has failed you too!"

"I am not finished dealing with you. Perhaps releasing you on the humans was far too difficult for you."

Bode shook his head. "No, My Lord, give me another chance."

"Amhras!"

The young demon floated up from the floor and stroked his father's wings. He held Bode in his mocking eyes. "Yes, Father."

"Tell me, what should we do with Bode?"

Amhras laughed. "Send him to the pits to harvest the human souls."

Bode's eyes grew wide. "No, My Lord, I am your servant!"

"You are my fool!" Argus released Bode and nodded to Amhras. "Take him."

Bode screamed as Amhras dragged the demon through the floor.

"Ah. I'll let him stay there for a few years, then call him back." He walked past Māhōn, who cringed against the wall.

A guard pointed to the young man. "My Lord Argus, what of the human?"

Argus paused and his red eyes turned to the leader of the New Maúl. "I had one quest for you, Little One, stop Anú's child. And I find you tied up in the weapon's room. There is no room for failure in my house."

Māhōn swallowed and nodded. "I understand, but there were too many of them."

Argus gave him a sad look. "Too many? For a Maúl? You could not stop two men and a woman? My woman? I could have the medallion and the seer, if not for your mistakes."

Māhōn's breathing became shallow. "I have never failed you before."

Argus laughed. "Brón!"

The female demon walked through the wall. She adjusted her skull barrette and pushed her tangled hair from her gray face. "Yes, My Father?"

Argus moved aside. "Take him."

Brón giggled. "Father, you have few human allies. Perhaps you should keep this one alive?" Her long fingernail stroked Māhōn's cheek.

Argus cocked his head and listened. "My Queen! My spells are fading from her." He knelt before Māhōn. "One more time, fail me, and you will die."

Māhōn nodded eagerly. Argus grabbed his hand, and they disappeared.

Jezebel sat at her dressing table, staring at the tiny wrinkles around her eyes. The haze that once hung in her mind like wet curtains were drawn before a sunlit window. She placed her fingers on her temple and pushed the skin apart. "I am old now. How did I end up here?" She rose from the table and mindlessly thumbed through the dresses hanging in the closet. Red, blue, pink, orange gowns hung on the racks. "I used to love these, now I feel like a child playing dress-up."

Her hand stopped on a hanger and she pulled the blue pants from the closet. A smile lingered on her lips as she held the trousers before her.

"My old blue jeans." She weaved against the armoire. Visions flooded her mind.

Mother was working late again at Phil's Bar-B-Que in the small town of Dryer, Indiana. Jezebel's boredom led her to her cousin's Ouija board stuffed in the hall closet. Mother hated this game. She said it was of the devil. She grinned. Mother wasn't here. She spread the board on the living room floor and gently placed her small hands on the pointer. The pointer moved to the letters across the game as if guided by some invisible force.

ARGUS.

"Is your name Argus?" the fourteen-year-old Jezebel asked.

The pointer moved to YES.

She pushed her long black hair out of her face. "Argus, did you die here?"

NO.

HELP.

Her young heart beat faster. "Are you in danger?"

YES.

"Tell me what to do, Argus?"

BRING ME THROUGH THE MIRROR.

"What mirror?"

BRING ME THROUGH THE MIRROR.

She sat back and mentally went through the rooms to find a large mirror. She grinned and gathered the board and pointer and jogged up the stairs to Mother's room. A large mirror in a round wooden frame leaned against the wall. She sat on the floor, opened the board, and placed the pointer on it. "I'm here in front of the mirror, Argus, what do I do?"

LOOK UP.

A handsome man with long black hair and large white wings stood in the looking glass. She scooted back against the bed. He smiled and placed his hand on the mirror. She cocked her head, then rose and placed her small hand against his.

"How can I help you, Argus," Jezebel asked.

His mouth moved, but she couldn't hear his words. She sat on the floor and placed her hands on the pointer.

PULL ME THROUGH.

She rose and pressed her hands on the mirror. "I don't know how." She settled her fingers on the pointer.

PRESS YOUR FINGERS AGAINST THE MIRROR.

Jezebel dug her fingers into the mirror. Argus's hands grasped hers and she pulled him through like Alice in Wonderland.

She stood back and studied him. "Are you an angel?"

He grinned. "Yes, I am. I am Argus and I was trapped by a demon who locked me in a cage. I come from the land of Ézású. You rescued me. Tell me, Fair Princess. What can I do for you?"

Jezebel felt her young cheeks burn. "I wish I could get away from my nagging mom. All she does is work all the time and I never get to go anywhere. I want to hang out with my friends, but instead, she makes me stay here and clean the house, do the dishes, make the meals while she's off working."

Argus's eyes turned into pools of sadness. "What a horrible life."

The sound of the front door opening and closing drifted up the stairs. Keys dropped onto the table followed by the high pitch of a woman calling "Jezzy!"

"And here she is," Jezebel said. "I need to hide you."

He brushed past her and took the stairs to the main level.

Jezebel hurried after him. "My mom won't understand. I have to hide you!"

An older woman wearing a blue, waitress dress stood in the hallway as she hung her coat in the closet. "Jezzy, I hope you have dinner cocked. I'm so tired. I have to go back to the restaurant tomorrow morning, a double shift. Everyone is sick." She turned to find Argus standing at the bottom of the stairs. "Who are you? Jezzy!"

Argus sneered at her, then raised his hand. She grabbed her chest as her face turned white. She gripped the hall table, then dropped to the ground.

"Mom!" Jezebel rushed past Argus and knelt next to her mother. "Mom! Talk to me! What did you do to my mom?"

Argus held his hand out to her. "Come. Jezebel. I will make you into a queen. There is nothing here for you."

The wet curtain closed her mind and she saw her hand rise into his large palm. His strong fingers gripped hers and he led her back to Mother's room. They passed through the mirror.

Jezebel pulled her dress top tight over her chest. His hands touching her, groping, making her do things only adults do. She pounded her fists on the table. "Oh God, how did I get here? Mama, I'm so sorry, I didn't know! I should have made him stop!"

The door to her chambers slowly opened. Argus's large frame filled the doorway. "I heard a sound. Are you all right, My Queen?"

She glared at him and gritted her teeth. "YOU KILLED MY MOTHER!"

He cocked his head and grinned. "Yes, I did, and I made you a queen with great powers. You freed me from my cage and I freed you from yours and brought you here. I have given you power, beauty, conquest. What more do you wish from me?"

She hunched her shoulders and sobbed. "You didn't have to kill my mother."

"Yes, I did. You would never have come with me if I had left her alive."

Hate poured from her eyes. "You tricked me!"

Argus smirked and whispered, "Yes, I did." His strong footsteps echoed off the wooden floors as he entered the room. The door closed by itself behind him. "I needed a queen that I could control. You see, the Attiyq has rules that even I must follow. I am not allowed to rule in this world. So, when you contacted the world of the dead, I answered." Argus glanced over his shoulder. "Māhōn, come!"

Māhōn slowly opened the door and entered the room but stood at a distance. "Yes, Master, what is your bidding?"

"The Queen seems to be confused. She will be taking leave in order to heal. You will be the new Regent King of this land."

Māhōn bowed. "Thank you, Master! I will not fail you!"

Argus stared at him. "No, you will not fail me again. Fail again, and Brón will drag you into my domain."

Māhōn swallowed and nodded. "Yes, Master!"

Jezebel jumped to her feet and charged at Argus. He grabbed her hands as her nails sought his face. He threw her to the ground. "You are so pathetic. So weak, so easy. I gave you my bed, dresses, fine food, a castle, and a witch's power, and you became putty in my hands. And now the seer is close and so is her medallion. With it, I will rule all worlds."

She lay on the floor and stared at him. "I don't understand, why her? I gave you so much."

"Because, Imogene is the seer and with her medallion, I can destroy God and rule. But I need to push her to come to me and once I have her family she will do as I please."

"I hate you. Get out! I'm still Queen, and I still have power."

He laughed. "Power? That I gave you?" He lifted her wet face. "No, My Lady, you have nothing."

"I'll find Conell, I tell him everything. He stopped you once, he'll stop you again!"

His eyes narrowed. "No, you won't."

He yanked her to her feet.

"Guards!" she screamed. "Help me!"

The door swung open and two sentries stood in the doorway.

Argus held up his hand and the guards slammed against the wall. He dragged her to the mirror and pulled her through. The guards rose and searched the room. But their queen was gone.

End of the second passge of

The Chronicles of the King

Volume 15 in the year 1055 as told by King Bran fifteenth king of Ezasu to his scribe.

Book Three

is underway! Please "Follow" the author on Amazon to be alerted as soon as it hits the shelves. Thank you & God bless you and yours. ~ the Publisher

About the Author

Illinois native Kim Kouski has been writing since she was a teen, and as an adult, ventured into the YA speculative Christian Fantasy realm. Her desire is that every writer finds his or her way to publication, and fulfills all that God has for them.

Also from Little Roni Publishers

Award-Wining Christian Fantasy Fiction

Check out our *Christian YA Historical (American Civil War) Fiction!*

Little Roni Publishers
109 Friendship Circle | Clanton, AL 35045

Send correspondence to:

Little Roni Publishers

submissionsLRP@gmail.com

www.LittleRoniPublishers.com